Postcards from the Canyon

Lisa Gitlin

Bywater
BOOKS

Ann Arbor
2017

Bywater Books

Copyright © 2017 Lisa Gitlin

Print ISBN: 978-1-61294-111-0

Bywater Books First Edition: December 2017

Printed in the United States of America on acid-free paper.

Cover designer: Ann McMan, TreeHouse Studio

Bywater Books
PO Box 3671
Ann Arbor MI 48106-3671
www.bywaterbooks.com

Dedicated to Susan Abramson
Dear, generous, wonderful friend
1951–2014

Introduction

It's a hot summer afternoon and I'm sitting at McElroy's on Fourth Avenue in Brooklyn, which is underneath one of those little Mexican kitchens where you can get a meal for about three bucks. McElroy's is my neighborhood bar. It's clean and cozy and old, a cross between a dive bar and a respectable saloon, and it's run by an old Irish dude who right now is pouring me another shot of Jack and feeling sorry for me because I'm old and drunk and female, which spells "pathetic" when you're out drinking by yourself.

I do feel pretty pathetic because my mom died three weeks ago and it was *awful*—just *awful*—the way it happened. She was ninety, and people think well that's okay then, but barely more than a month ago she was one of those healthy and stylish ninety-year-olds, getting her hair done every week and driving her Chevy Caprice around her suburban Cleveland neighborhood and going to her Yiddish club and to lectures and concerts and lunches with her girlfriends who were still alive. And then she had some trouble urinating and was admitted to the hospital with a kidney infection, and I drove to Cleveland as fast as I could (she has four kids but I'm the oldest and the one she depends on), and I spent a week frantically monitoring haphazard medical interventions by random people, and then they performed this invasive procedure on her to "stabilize" her kidney function, and the next day she was moaning in pain but they

3

insisted on discharging her anyway. I begged them to let her stay at least another day but they said they couldn't justify it to the bastard HMO that made all the decisions about her medical care (instead of her doctors), so I drove to the rehab facility to wait for her, and when they brought her there on a stretcher she was unconscious and an hour later she was dead. Apparently the "cap" they used to keep the stuff from spilling out from the procedure broke and all these toxins got into her system. I was in shock through the funeral and the *shiva* and I'm still in shock, and I don't even know why I'm writing about this because it just happened and it's not such a good idea to write about the death of your mother when it just happened; you have no distance from it, you're just ejaculating words, except I'm a writer and I think I have to write write write. But at least I'm in this nice bar and I can drink, which makes me feel a little more in control of my life, which doesn't make any sense under ordinary circumstances but your mom dying is not ordinary, it happens only once, and it changes everything. You're like someone who's been struck by lightning and will never totally recover.

My best friend Molly just left the bar after getting drunk with me but she had the good sense to leave while she could still walk, and she tried to get me to go with her but I don't feel like going back to my apartment at the moment even though I love where I live, which is in a cruddy old tenement on Third Avenue underneath the monstrous Gowanus expressway. If you went there you wouldn't even know what century you were in. It's down-and-dirty Brooklyn, frozen in time. I've been living in my apartment for twenty years and I never want to leave. But right now I'm kind of leery of going home, because at any moment FBI agents could show up at my door, demanding to know why I haven't gotten a psychiatric evaluation.

Do you think I'm kidding? Well, I'm not. After a lifelong dedication to various forms of misbehavior, I have finally gotten the attention of the FBI. Two agents showed up at my apartment last week after I did something rash and impulsive. To tell you the truth, the whole situation just seems absurd right now. I actually started laughing about it while Molly and I were drinking and she just stared at me with that look she gets. But when your mother dies and you're wallowing in a morass of grief, everything else that happens loses its immediacy. Even the FBI telling you to see a shrink. You know what? They probably won't do shit to me anyway. If they really thought I was a threat to society they would have arrested me instead of just sitting in my apartment giving me a hard time. It's not as though I went out into the streets and *did* anything—I just made a very pissed-off phone call to the Mike Stevens show that got everyone's underwear all in a bunch.

I probably shouldn't have turned on the TV in the middle of the day. I hate daytime TV with all these sprightly cackling people tossing around their opinions of serious issues like beanbags. But since my mom died I'm not following my normal routine, so I turned on the TV at 1 p.m. and there was Mike Stevens interviewing that reactionary right-wing lunatic Sandy Shrewsbury, who has the nerve to be running for U.S. Senate with her two-figure I.Q. I should have changed the channel to avoid getting aggravated, but being aggravated is a special talent of mine so I just sat there and watched Shrewsbury blither on and on about how people who are receiving "government hand-outs" (which I took to include Medicare) should not expect to have the same quality of medical care as people earning enough money to pay for the best doctors and hospitals. She said something like, "If these people expect to have the red carpet rolled out for them as soon as they get sick and enter a hospital, they should move to some communist country where they believe that people on the dole should have the same privileges as the industrious worker bees."

Ordinarily I would have just reacted to Shrewsbury's bab-blings by yelling profanities at the TV. But I was still wigging out over the profiteering health care system that killed my mom, so I kind of went crazy. I snatched up my phone and called the show and screamed at Mike Stevens that his guest was an "imbecile" and that someone should "plant a bomb under her ass

5

and blow her to the moon because she and her reactionary idiot friends are trying to ruin this country." Of course Mike Stevens hung up on me (I got bleeped before the viewers could hear what I said but everyone on the show heard it including Sandy Shrewsbury) and I was so furious that I *actually called back and demanded to speak to him again* and of course the screening guy hung up on me. After I calmed down I was kind of freaked out that I did that but I thought well, so what, but the next morning there was a knock on my door and I opened it to find a beefy, crew-cutted man and a sexy dykey woman standing there, flashing their badges. I've never been a big fan of the FBI and I wasn't very cooperative but they could see that I was just this irritable old Jewish lady and not some frothing lunatic making bombs in my house, so they just ordered me to get a psychiatric evaluation and have the shrink send them a report stating I'm not crazy or violent.

For some reason I haven't done what they told me to do. Instead I just call all my friends and obsess about the situation, and now I'm sitting here in this bar getting drunk. Molly told me today while we were sitting here drinking that the only reason I don't want to cooperate with the FBI is to indulge my "juvenile fantasy" of going to a "nice little ladies prison." Well, so what? What would be so bad about going to one of those prisons like the one where they sent Martha Stewart and someone crocheted her a poncho? I'm really tired of taking care of myself while I'm all fucked up and disoriented, and it would be kind of nice to be told what to do all day. Maybe I would even find a girlfriend in prison. I've only been in love once in my life and that has worked out about as well as the Bay of Pigs invasion, but if I got locked up maybe I could meet some tough but warm-hearted old dyke who would make me forget about this witch I'm still in love with who doesn't want me anymore. (I'm way past my prime but I'm still what people might call "attractive"—I'm petite with thick wavy hair and nice Jewish features, and I have a couple of tattoos which might give me some street cred among the prisoners.)

6

When I tried to articulate all of this to Molly she threw a pail of cold water on all my assertions. She said I would hate prison, that there would be all these "fascist guards" ordering me around and they would make me get up at 7 a.m. and that my dormitory would be full of "loud street people blasting Kanye West on their radios." That totally bummed me out, because what if she's right? I figured that one good thing about going to prison would be that I would have plenty of time to write my new book. I can't have Kanye West blaring in my ears while I'm trying to write. That would drive me nuts and I would end up screaming at everyone and maybe getting beat up, which would be very humiliating, especially since I pride myself on my self-possession around tough street people.

It's important that I write my book with a minimum of distractions. It's going to be an autobiographical account of my growing up with a group of friends and I have high expectations for it, even though Molly calls it "the book that's going to make me look like an idiot." I can understand her concern, since she was my best friend then as she is now and her "character" will figure significantly in the book. But it's going to be "creative nonfiction" (or whatever the hell they're calling it these days) and not an actual memoir, so it's not even going to be all true. Anyway, I'll show the book to her before it's published to make sure there's nothing in it that will make her hate me for the rest of our lives. I might even consider showing parts of it to her while it's being written, since I do trust her judgment. Molly is kind of my alter ego rather than totally separate from me so I'm hoping she'll facilitate my process and not derail it.

One thing is for sure. If I don't get another book written and published pretty soon, my literary reputation will fade into oblivion. Since I make no distinction between my literary self and my actual self, what this means is that *I* will fade into oblivion. Yessiree. I'll dry up and blow away like pollen! That will be so sad. I was a freelance writer for many years and have had hundreds of articles published, but once you write a novel you become an "author" and you have to keep writing books because that's what people expect. I wrote a humorous novel about gay life in New York City that was a big smash, but that was twenty years ago, and then I wrote a second book, a 9/11 novel that was accepted for publication a few months ago, but the contract negotiations were taking place during a merger with a larger house, and the new asshole marketing director decided my book was "outside the parameters" of their product line and they tossed it back to me like a dirty Frisbee. Can you imagine how devastated I was? It took me eight years to write that book, and I was so relieved to have it accepted and I was picturing my nice big advance and rave reviews and finally being interviewed on *Fresh Air* and I end up with *bupkes*. So now my agent is back to shopping it around, but I can't just sit around and wait for her to call. I need to start a new project to keep from going insane. Two days before my mom died she said, "You need to write your new book and I'll read it from wherever I am." Now I'm crying again. This is so fucked up.

My book is going to be about growing up in the sixties. Did I really just write that? It sounded kind of dumb, didn't it? Like, "what I did on my summer vacation." My journalist father once told me that there are no boring subjects, there are only boring writers, and he was right. I hope I'm not being boring right now because that's the worst thing you can be. It's better to be an asshole than to be boring. Norman Mailer was an asshole and he's a modern legend. No boring writers are modern legends. Well, I can think of one but a lot of people don't think he was boring even though he wrote this one thousand-page book that was insufferable to me but I won't mention his name because it wouldn't be nice. Anyway he's dead so he won't do it again.

As long as I'm writing everything that's floating around in my head I'll tell you one great thing about growing up in the sixties. Back in those days, the kids and the adults lived separate lives. We kids had our own society that the grown-ups knew nothing about. They didn't care what we did as long as we didn't get in their way or embarrass them. It wasn't like today when parents insert themselves into their kids' lives in order to be cool. Our parents didn't give a crap about our opinions and attitudes. If we criticized or made fun of them they waved us off like flies. And that's what I miss. Not being a kid, but living in a society in which the adults left the kids alone. There was an unpredictable wildness to our lives back then. You never knew when someone was going to get hurt. But if you were a kid who liked excitement and adventure, why would you want to grow up in today's world, with grown-ups twitting around you, trying to protect you from every little scratch? Everyone says kids today have it worse than we did, with all the drugs and internet bullying and school pressures and whatever else everyone is warbling about, but kids today don't ride in cars without seat belts or play in cement playgrounds or breathe in cigarette smoke wherever they go. They don't have to walk to and from school in snowstorms four times a day, which is the story old fogeys tell their grandkids, but it was still true. Even though we grew up in economic boom times, we weren't spoiled. That's just a myth perpetrated by people who resent our generation. Most of us lived in little houses with one bathroom and one car and one black and white TV, and there were usually a bunch of kids and the houses were crowded and noisy. When we were bad we got spanked. There was none of this "time out" stuff. We weren't spoiled at all. We were tough little customers.

Now that my wheels are turning I should go home already and start writing, but Tommy just put a free shot on the table and patted me on the shoulder and said, "Sorry to hear about your mum, darlin'," and now I'm going to down the shot and sit here for awhile. At least I'm writing. I'm writing in a notebook, with a pen. Old school! But instead of writing about my life in the sixties I'm writing about what's happening now. I suppose I can make this part of my book. Then I can become part of the "Look at me and my ugly warts" movement that's all the rage these days. It will be more fun for you, the reader, because when you can no longer stomach reading about the frolicking children of the sixties, you can return to the present day and remind yourself that we're now old and deflated and that our "garden" is now a toxic wasteland. Unless you are a child of the sixties, and never get tired of remembering those fantabulous days. Although you know what they say: *If you remember the sixties, you weren't there!* Which is so ridiculous. Like nobody remembers seeing the Beatles on Ed Sullivan. Or the first time they dropped acid and looked in the mirror and saw this creepy distorted version of themselves. Or thinking that listening to music was more important than eating. Which was true! Like, if you were crazy about the Stones, listening to "Sympathy for the Devil" through your headphones gave you more nourishment than eating a scrambled egg! Except if you had the munchies. Then a scrambled egg would be good with jelly or ketchup or anything. You could eat a scrambled egg with some prune yogurt.

I just read what I wrote and I may have had a little too much to drink. It's probably time to go home. Maybe the walk will clear out my head. Then I can have a cup of coffee and start writing about my "fizzy little life," as Molly calls it. Except it will be a highly subjective account, so don't assume it's all true. Which you will but there's nothing I can do about that. Especially since I'm using my own name in my story. But it won't be me. It will be some version of me, someone who lived a life similar to mine. There's no way I can remember everything that happened a half century ago when I can't even remember what I had for breakfast this morning. I know I had *something* besides coffee. Even though I have no appetite, I'm trying to eat breakfast for my mom. She always said breakfast was the most important meal of the day.

Part One

Childhood

1954–1960

You meet your lifetime best friend, Molly Katz, when you're both three years old, on a summer afternoon, shortly after Molly has moved onto your street of brick ranch "starter homes." Her mom, Shirley, has used her Jewish radar to learn that people named Jacobs live in the corner house across the street, and one afternoon she shows up with a homemade Hungarian strudel and her younger daughter in tow. "And this is our daughter Joanna," your mother says. She loves your name—Joanna Lee Jacobs—and never resorts to diminutives like "Joey" or "Jo" favored by your dad and other relatives. Before you even speak to each other you and Molly are already well acquainted, like all three-year-olds when they first meet. You know your common history involving potty training and Farina and mashed carrots, the confinement of a crib and the freedom of a "real bed," and the admonishments to stay away from the street. But after the mothers go into the kitchen and leave the two of you to play in the living room, you discover some important differences between yourself and your new friend. Molly tells you she has an older sister, Sarah, who is seven, a parakeet named Matey, and no father. "He died of a heart attack," Molly says, and you feel a little shock when you hear her say that. "Heart attack" sounds scary, like the word "German" or "hit," and the fact that Molly knows what a "heart attack" is gives you the sense that your new friend is smarter than you, that she has things to teach you.

By the age of four you and Molly are best friends, and you make a cute picture running around together, you with your shiny dark hair and saucer-brown eyes and Molly with her blond braids and freckles, who could be mistaken for a Norwegian milk maiden. You eat and sleep at each other's houses, search for four-leaf clovers, color in your coloring books, play Ring around the Rosie with your baby brother, and dance to records like "Doggie in the Window" and "Tubby the Tuba." You feel safe and secure at Molly's house where it's quiet and calm and "no" means "no," and Molly loves being at your house where your mother lets you do whatever you want while she chases the baby around and yells at your grandmother who comes over to help her. Molly is more of a parent to you than your own parents are. She teaches you that the smell in the basement is from diapers that haven't been washed (your mother says there is no smell), that Peapod and Gumduck are "imaginary friends" (your father tells you they are real), and that when you twirl around and around the world isn't really spinning, it just looks like it is because you are "off balance."

After school starts, the differences between you and Molly become even more apparent. At school you're supposed to learn how to function in the outside world, which Molly has no trouble doing, whereas you have very little concept of what constitutes appropriate behavior for a child of your age and are a constant annoyance to your teachers. In kindergarten you walk around with your shoelaces untied, color a purple mess over the face of the beautiful princess, and walk in on the teacher while she's on the toilet and are terribly hurt when, instead of answering your question about the alphabet song, she yells at you to "shut the darn door!" In the first grade you shout out answers instead of raising your hand, clap the erasers on the wood sides (thinking you're supposed to make a "clapping" sound), and bring six raw eggs to class for Easter egg painting instead of the required hard-boiled ones and drop them on the floor, making a big yellow mess. In the second grade your efforts to win the affection of pretty, popular Miss Getty, which include addressing her as "Miss

Spaghetti" and asking goofy questions like, can you jump off a building and not die, don't go over at all.

Everything changes when you enter the third grade. You are now the oldest of four kids and have gained some "big sister maturity" over the summer, and when school starts you realize you are actually smart in some things. The teacher places you in the top reading group, along with Molly, and during spelling bees you're usually the last one standing. Miss Schultz, a tall, blond woman with a close-mouthed smile, isn't as sweet as Miss Getty, but she is pleasant, and she treats everyone fairly. As someone who has never been in a teacher's favor, you beam with joy over every small praise she bestows on you. Molly also loves the teacher, but for her this is just the normal response of an eight-year-old to being showered with A's and gold stars. Your love is more of a hysterical love, like the love of a cult member for a charismatic leader.

And then, one snowy day in December, a new girl shows up in class. She has curly brown hair and an upturned nose covered by a spray of freckles, and she looks like a normal kid except for her odd, jaunty smile as she marches into the room holding a note from the principal. Something about the girl's odd smile gives you a strange unpleasant sensation and you stiffen as she walks by your desk and gives the teacher the note. The only person who has ever made you stiffen with alarm is your father when he loses his temper. But this is a different kind of fear. Your father's rages scare the hell out of everyone, including your mother. Susie Moscowitz is like a scary person coming after you in a dream, someone who terrifies you while everyone else just goes about their business.

"Class, this is our new pupil, Susie Moscowitz," Miss Schultz announces after she looks at the note, and instead of looking around at her new classmates, like most kids would have done, Susie just keeps beaming at Miss Schultz as though she's just laid eyes on her fairy godmother. And then, as soon as she's shown to her seat, she starts trying to take over the class. After every question the teacher asks about multiplication tables, Susie waves her hand in the air and bounces up and down on her little tush, yelling, "Oh! Oh! I know the answer to that one!" You look at Molly and wrinkle your nose, and she wrinkles her nose back.

During recess, while you and your classmates frolic in the snow, the new girl stands next to the teacher observing all of you with a superior smile, as though to say, "Aren't they all so silly?" Molly comes up to you and says, "Did you know that the new girl lives on our block? She moved into the house they just finished building."

This is very bad news. You say to Molly that she doesn't seem very nice.

"Well, maybe it's just because she's new," Molly says.

For the next several weeks you never see Susie out in your neighborhood, since her mother drives her to school and she doesn't ever play outside, but she continues to act as obnoxious in class as she did on the first day. Not only is she snooty and patronizing to her classmates but she's the first teacher's pet you have ever known, always offering to pass out papers or clap the erasers, and she does this infuriating thing of bouncing up and down and frantically waving her hand to get the teacher to call on her. Most of the kids tolerate Susie—eight-year-olds are pretty *laissez faire*—which makes it hard for you to understand why this girl's presence upsets you so much. Whenever you see Susie give the teacher her "special smile" or do some favor for her, you want to run up and kick her. What makes it worse is that the new girl really is smart, and soon is earning as many gold stars as you and Molly, which you feel like ripping off her forehead.

After Susie shows up, you start to wonder if Miss Schultz really likes you. It starts to bother you that the teacher is just as pleasant to snooty Susie, and even to the class misfit, Randy Bishowsky, who can't even read and makes crazy faces all day, as she is to someone like yourself, who not only gets all A's but is also nice and considerate of her classmates. As the days and weeks go by, you become more and more anxious about getting back the special relationship with Miss Schultz that you thought you had before. One day you stay after school, hoping to have a little one-on-one talk with the teacher, but unfortunately Susie has the same idea, and you have to stand there listening to her jabber about how her other classroom had a pet rabbit that ate bananas. Finally, just when your irritation is escalating into panic, Miss Schultz looks up and says, "Yes, Joanna?" and you tell her you were wondering if cannibals can walk across the "strip" between South and North America and eat people.

Susie laughs her tinkly laugh. "That's ridiculous," she says. "Of course cannibals couldn't walk here. We live thousands of miles away from South America." And she looks at the teacher and smiles.

"That is correct, Susie," Miss Schultz says. Then she shows her disapproval of you by opening her mouth a little and showing her teeth, which she almost never does, and she says, "Joanna, time to go home," and you slink out of the room while Susie keeps talking to the teacher. As you walk home alone, you feel like a green, watery booger.

You spend the next couple of months working hard and trying to act perfect in class to restore your reputation with the teacher as a pupil beyond reproach. And then, one day in March, Miss Schultz invites all her A students to her house for Saturday lunch. Immediately you see this as an opportunity to completely redeem yourself. To someone who recently turned nine years old, being invited to a teacher's home is pleasantly shocking, like being invited into the cage of a large animal at the zoo. You're thrilled that Molly will be going to the luncheon, and even though you wish that Susie wasn't going, it's better than the luncheon not happening at all.

The evening before the luncheon, your parents, Sam and Isabel, go with Molly's mom to a PTA meeting at the school, and you and Molly spend the evening in the bedroom telling "witchy" stories to five-year-old Rosie. After a while Rosie drifts off to sleep, and you and Molly curl up on your bed and talk about what you're going to wear to the luncheon, and what Miss Schultz's house might look like, and what kind of food she

17

might serve. Pretty soon you hear the parents come home and say good-bye to *Bobie*, your grandmother, who lives on the next street. A cupboard opens and shuts which means coffee is being served, so you go back to your chatter. Suddenly you hear your dad's voice, and it sounds angry. You strain to listen, and then you motion to Molly and the two of you sneak into the living room to hear the conversation.

"Joanna seems to like her very much," your mom says.

"Isabel, I don't *care* that Joanna likes her!" your dad says. He only calls your mom "Isabel" when he's mad. Usually he calls her "Donut" or "Baas" which is short for "Lebasi," her name spelled backward. "Joanna is a nine-year-old child!" your dad says. "The fact that she likes her doesn't negate the plain fact that the woman is a German bitch." You and Molly clutch hands and stare at each other. You know that your father hates Germans after fighting them in the war, but he hasn't gone into one of his tirades about them for a long time. He hardly ever gets angry, but when he does, it's like Hiroshima. "Did you notice the frozen smile?" your father yells, with his voice rising in the womanly way it does when he's losing his marbles. "Did you notice how she almost *winced* when we introduced ourselves and she heard our name? Isabel, don't be naïve! The woman hates Jews!"

"Just because she pronounced our name *Joh-cobs* it doesn't mean she hates Jews," your mom says. "I agree she's not such a big personality girl. It doesn't mean she's a Nazi."

"I tend to agree with Sam," Shirley says. "I have never been impressed with that woman. I wouldn't say a word to my Molly, but she seems cold as ice to me. I think she's from German stock even if she was born here. She has some of that German inflection in her voice." We hear the *phoom!* of the flame in Shirley's lighter, and a loud exhale of smoke.

"The girls are going to her house for lunch tomorrow," your mom says. "Please, Sam. I don't want there to be any crazy business about Miss Schultz. Please!" Your mom hates it when your father gets mad because it's scary mad, not just hysterical mad the way she gets.

"I thought I heard something," Shirley says. "Girls! Are you out there?"

You and Molly tippy-toe into the hallway.

"I thought I heard something too," your mom says. "Joanna!" she calls. "It's time to get ready for bed!"

You lie awake for a long time, not knowing how to deal with what you just heard. Your father's words have wiped out your nice feelings about your teacher. You try to get them back, but nothing works. You picture Miss Schultz putting a gold star on your forehead, but you see the scary pink fingers of a German. You picture her smiling, but all you can see is the scary smile, the one with her lips pulled up exposing her teeth, which she displayed when she told you to go home after you asked her the cannibal question. Finally you drift off to sleep, but then you have a dream that Miss Schultz is sitting on a chair talking to you but she has no face, just wisps of blond hair around a blank doll's head, and then her face comes into focus and she smiles but her teeth are piano keys, and you wake up in a panic.

The next day, you and Molly walk to Miss Schultz's house in your party dresses and spring coats, and although you're trying to be happy, you're feeling confused and nervous. Do you think Miss Schultz was a Nazi? you ask Molly.

"She wasn't in Germany during the war," Molly says. You say how do you know, and she says, "My mom told me. She said her parents might have been there but that she was probably born here."

Do you think she doesn't like Jews? you ask. Does she like Susie Moscowitz?

"Nobody likes Susie Moscowitz," Molly says, and you smile.

Miss Schultz answers the door in a red dress. "Come in, girls, come in," she says, stepping aside to allow you into the living room. Four of your classmates are standing awkwardly in the room—Barbara Cook with her leg braces, Darlene Michaels in her pretty plaid jumper, Joey Peroni with his cowlick plastered down, and serious little Alfred Cohen. The living room is neat and spotless, with a snowy white carpet, a flowered sofa, two

19

identical orange chairs, a rectangular whitish coffee table with a big ashtray that looks like it was made of green and blue jelly beans, and paintings on the walls of people dressed in fancy clothes. It looks just like how you imagine a German house to look, orderly and well organized to a fault, like the Nazi parades you've seen in newsreels at the movies.

Susie Moscowitz arrives, wearing an old-fashioned yellow skirt and a wool coat even though it's a warm spring day. "Bye, Mommy!" she trills as she walks in, and then she says, "Well hello there, Miss Schultz! My mother walked me all the way here because we can't drive on *Shabbos!*" You and Molly roll your eyes at each other.

Miss Schultz ushers Susie into the living room, and then she says, "You children make yourselves comfortable while I prepare the lunch." For the first time, you think you detect a German accent in the teacher's speech. It sounds as though she said *cahmfortable*. After the teacher goes into the kitchen, you spot a display of German-looking dolls on two shelves on the wall. There's a boy doll with blond hair standing straight with his arms at his sides and a girl, either his girlfriend or sister, with blond hair and a little green jumper, and her arm is out like she's giving a Nazi salute. There's a man doll in shorts, like the brown shorts that the Nazis wore in the summer. All the other dolls in the collection look German as well, with their blond hair and costumes that look as though they're ready to march through the streets.

You nudge Molly and whisper, look at the Nazi dolls.

"Ssh!" Molly says, as though the teacher can hear you all the way from the kitchen. Molly has always insisted that Alfred Cohen was standing right there and heard you make the comment about the Nazi dolls, but so what, he probably wouldn't have noticed or cared since Alfred lived in his own little genius world.

In a couple of minutes Miss Schultz calls everyone to the table. The dining room looks suspiciously German to you as well. There's a huge painting over the bureau of two naked blond women with big puffy German-looking feet, and a photograph on the bureau of a group of adults dressed in old-fashioned clothes, smiling meanly, as though they have just killed a bunch of Jews. The table is set formally, with a red tablecloth, white plates, sparkling silverware and glasses, and place cards indicating where each child is to sit. You think of the formal German dining room in the movie *Heidi*, where Heidi and her poor crippled cousin have to sit stiffly and not talk or laugh. You sit down at your assigned seat, and are relieved to see that Molly has been seated next to you. When Susie sits down next to Molly, Molly makes her "mad bunny" face at you and you snicker.

The table contains bowls of mashed potatoes and green beans mixed with slippery things Miss Schultz calls "spaetzle," and a pitcher of gravy and hot rolls piled up in a basket. Miss Schultz walks around the table serving everyone from a platter of roast beef. Then she sets the platter down, sits at the head of the table, and looks down at her lap, and you wonder if she's noticed a spot on her dress. After a moment the teacher looks back up, smiling in an odd way, and instructs everyone to start passing the side dishes around the table.

Miss Schultz, who are those people in the picture? you ask, pointing. You're distracted by the Nazi-looking people staring at you and you're hoping the teacher will dispel your bad impression of them so that you can enjoy your lunch.

"Those are my parents and their cousins in Germany," Miss Schultz says.

But your parents weren't Nazis, were they? you ask.

"*That* is a really rude question!" Susie says with a snooty smile.

All you want is for the teacher to say, "No, of course not, no one in my family was a Nazi, God forbid!" so you can get back the warm and fuzzy feeling you had for her before you heard your father's angry words. But instead, she says, "Yes, Susie, it is a very rude question." Then, while you sit there wanting to sink into the floor, Miss Schultz launches into a lecture about the magnificence of the German people, how hardly any of them knew anything about the Nazi crimes, that they were victims just like everyone

21

else, that they were a good and high-minded people who had nothing to do with the terrible things that happened. After ranting about the high-mindedness of the German people, she plunges into a whole new speech about the Germans' cultural superiority. "Germany is known for its cultural contributions to the world!" she proclaims. "Many of the very best musicians, composers, artists, and philosophers come from Germany. Most Americans know next to nothing about the history or culture of Germany and they should keep their mouths shut until they better inform themselves! Associating the majority of wonderful German people with those few people who committed crimes is stupid. Just stupid." She shakes her head in disbelief at your stupidity, and then she starts cutting her roast beef.

You are swimming in shame. You stare into space, not eating, your appetite gone, while Susie, refusing to be subdued by the teacher's agitated outburst, starts chattering like a magpie. "Miss Schultz, you should see what a klutz I am in the kitchen when my mother tries to teach me to cook!" she chirps. And, "Guess what? After practicing my head off I think I finally have my multiplication tables memorized!" And, "My father didn't want me to come because we keep kosher but my mother said it was okay as long as I didn't have any milk or butter with my meat!" Each time Susie says something, the kids at the table just stare at her but the teacher answers with a big smile. "Well, it takes a long time to learn to cook properly!" "Congratulations on having your tables memorized!" "Well, it's a good thing I'm serving lemonade and not milk!" While Susie babbles on and on Molly grimaces and leans away from her to keep Susie from chirping in her ear.

But you're not paying attention to Susie. You feel terrible about offending the teacher. The luncheon is on the verge of being ruined, and along with it your whole life. You're desperate to let Miss Schultz know that you had no ill intentions when you asked the Nazi question, that you meant no harm. So as soon as you can insert yourself into Susie's jabbering, you say, Miss Schultz, what are those dolls up on the wall in your living room?

You intend to say something nice about them, like, their clothes are very interesting.

But Miss Schultz doesn't give you a chance to be polite about the Nazi dolls. She glances at you, curls her lip up to expose her teeth, and says, "They're obviously just a collection of dolls. I don't know what you want to know about them."

At this point you're so hurt and embarrassed that you blank out to keep from crying. Your mind drifts away in a soap bubble and everything looks gray and watery. Your body is still at the table, and you're still eating, but you don't feel yourself stabbing the food with your fork or putting it in your mouth or tasting it. Suddenly Molly pokes you in the side, and the bubble bursts and everything comes back into focus. You look at Molly. Quick as lightning, your friend reaches over and pokes her finger in Susie's mashed potatoes. You explode with laughter, and Molly starts laughing as well. You're both laughing so hard your faces are practically in your food.

The two of you know that you're misbehaving, but nothing prepares you for what happens next. Miss Schultz yells, "All right, that's enough!" You and Molly look at her, not sure who she's talking to. Then the teacher stands up and points to the dining-room door. "I want you girls to leave!" she announces. It sounds to you like, "I vant you girls to liff!" Briefly you picture a swastika armband around the teacher's raised arm. You're getting everything confused. But Molly has heard the teacher clear as day.

"We're sorry, Miss Schultz," Molly says.

"Sorry is not good enough!" the teacher yells, looming over the table in her red dress. "I invited you here to enjoy a nice lunch and you mess it all up with your ugly words and actions! I want you both to leave before this occasion is totally ruined for everyone. I'm serious! Go! *Go!*" (Recalling the incident as adults, the two of you will jokingly add, "Schnell! *Schnell!*" to the teacher's command.)

Molly gets up from the table and pulls you up by the arm. You're too stunned to mobilize on your own. The teacher marches after you, and once you're in the living room she yanks your coats from the closet and hurls them at you like footballs. You catch your coats and put them on. You walk out of the house and into the spring sunshine, and the teacher slams the door behind you.

Both of you lie your heads off about the luncheon. You tell your parents you had a very nice time, what the teacher served, and who was present. You don't think the teacher will tell your parents what happened, because she would be embarrassed. Even if she did, it's possible that your father would take your side, but you can't predict how parents will react in situations like this. It's best not to have them mucking around in your school life.

Back at school, Miss Schultz doesn't say a word about the luncheon, but she's no longer very nice to you or Molly. She seldom calls on either of you, and she hands you your gold stars instead of sticking them on your foreheads. Molly no longer bothers to act enthusiastic in class, and in fact is listless and sullen. She has already absorbed the lesson of the luncheon, but it takes you longer to process it, which is typical. But about a week after the incident, Miss Schultz hands you a gold star and you feel relieved because you don't want this woman touching your forehead. And at that moment you understand that the teacher's animosity toward you and Molly has something to do with your being Jewish. You also know that she's just faking being nice to the other Jewish kids in the class. It's not something you can even say or talk about; it's more like breathing in something nasty. You never mention this to Molly, and you don't talk about it until many years later. You just stop talking about the teacher outside of school, and instead discuss whatever is happening at the moment, such as how to smear peanut butter on Wonder bread or whether to watch *Howdy Doody* or *Rin Tin Tin* or why your dad takes so long in the bathroom on Sundays after breakfast.

The last day of school, as you and Molly walk home on that spongy layer of air kids feel beneath them when they're looking forward to three months of freedom, Molly says, "You know the teacher we're getting for fourth grade? That Miss Amos? She's supposed to be a real grouch."

You've heard this too. You say, Yeah, I heard that she just stands in front of the room and complains.

"I'm going to get her goat," Molly says.

You look curiously at your friend. A clean, joyful feeling fizzes up in you and you start bouncing along on the balls of your feet. If Molly is going to be bad, then you won't have to be bad alone. Furthermore, since Molly is always right, then it must be *good* to be bad. For the first time in your life, you feel separate from adults in a good way. You actually feel superior to them. Nine is the age when you sense the similarities between adults and yourself, when you see that they are not perfect, that they are often wrong, that they can be as mean and crazy as children, and you step over the line. Nine is the dangerous age.

Warm September Day

Molly just left after reading what I wrote so far and I'm not sure it's such a good idea to show her my book because I will end up in a nuthouse. She said "the writing is very good," but before I had a chance to be happy she started in with a litany of complaints. She was annoyed that I referred to her in my introduction as my "alter ego" when she is a totally separate person from me, and she said that this was typical of my "boundary issues." Then she said that when we were kids she had as many problems as I did and I make it sound as though I had all the problems. *Then* she declared that she didn't stick her finger in *Susie's* mashed potatoes, she stuck her finger in *my* mashed potatoes, which is untrue. Why would I have laughed that hard if she had stuck her finger in *my* mashed potatoes? The whole point of what she did was that it was a *subversive action*! She's rewriting history for some reason I cannot fathom. I probably shouldn't even be showing my book to her. She's my best friend and flew to Cleveland for the funeral and has been calling or coming over every day, and I can't imagine what I would do without her, but she's also very critical of me. She thinks I'm this big narcissist and that everything is "all about me," which isn't true. Compared to her, everyone is a drama queen, because she acts as though being knee-deep in shit is just part of life and you're supposed to just accept it. Her baby daddy is a heroin addict and she insists on treating him like a normal family man, like one of those hale and hearty husbands on a TV sitcom. I may be dramatic but at least I don't pretend my life is normal when it's not.

For example I know it's not normal to have the FBI show up at your home and order you to see a psychiatrist. But now I don't even know what to do about it. After I made that incendiary phone call to the Mike Stevens show I can't say that I was all that shocked when the two agents knocked on my door the next morning. In fact I almost laughed when I saw one of them, Agent Charles Buford, who looked like the stereotypical FBI man with his husky frame and buzz cut and dour expression. But I wasn't at all prepared for the other one, Agent Deborah Neufeld, who looked and talked like a Jewish lesbian in her 60s from New York City. What kind of Jewish lesbian from New York joins the FBI? I didn't know how to process it at all. I have always had a negative attitude about the FBI and when I saw them standing there I had to restrain myself from acting rude. After the routine flashing of badges, Agent Neufeld asked me if I was the one who made that "provocative" phone call to the Mike Stevens show, and I said "Who wants to know?" which maybe was a little rude, and she said "Do you mind if we come in?" and I hesitated, and she said, "Or we can come back with a warrant" so I said "Whatever" and let them in.

After that I proceeded to make a rather bad impression. They planted themselves on my couch, and I plopped down on my green chair with my arms folded, and Agent Neufeld said, "The reason we don't have a warrant to search your apartment is that we wanted to assess your situation first. Your record consists of a couple of marijuana busts and one for public intoxication but those took place some years ago and there's no record of violence. Can you tell us why you felt compelled to telephone the Mike Stevens show during the call-in portion of the Sandy Shrewsbury interview and state that—"she looked down at her notes—"someone should plant a bomb under her behind and blow her to the moon."

"I think I said someone should plant a bomb under her *ass* and blow her to the moon," I said.

"Listen, Joanna," Agent Neufeld said. "You need to take this seriously. You used incendiary language over public airwaves. Given the current atmosphere in the country, I'm sure you understand why this behavior would come to the attention of the FBI. We learned a little about you, and we understand that you just lost your mother. But as upsetting as that may be, it's no excuse for terrorizing an innocent talk show guest. You could end up in prison; are you aware of that?"

She was being reasonable, but since my mom died I have absolutely no self-control, so instead of biting my tongue the way I should have, I jumped up and started screaming at her and waving my arms around. "*Oh, really!*" I said. "I could end up in prison just for calling a TV show and making an angry comment? I'm not going to blow up Sandy Shrewsbury! I'm a harmless senior citizen who is grieving her mother! Why don't you send *her* to jail for being a danger to society? She's running for the United States Senate! God knows what kind of damage she and her demented cronies in Congress will inflict on the people of this country!" I was actually furious that the FBI was hassling me when I was in the worst state of grief I'd ever experienced in my life. I know that wasn't rational but I am not a rational person.

After my outburst at Agent Neufeld I plopped back down on the chair and folded my arms and glared. And then the cranky partner, Agent Buford, started getting all feisty with me. "Look, ma'am!" he yelled, using the most irritating form of address imaginable (although I did refer to myself as a "senior citizen," but I only use that term as verbal ammunition against bureaucracies that are trying to fuck with me). "You issued what can be interpreted as a serious threat over public airwaves!" Buford barked. "You think you're going to get away with doing something like that? You'd better shake the rocks out of our head and start cooperating with us, or we'll be in your business so fast you won't know what hit you."

"Oh, come on," I said. "Why are you even wasting your resources?

Go out and hunt down real killers and terrorists. I'm just this exhausted woman who got upset and did this impulsive thing. What are you going to do to me for making a damn phone call? Send me to jail for the rest of my life? I think that would be rather ridiculous."

"We're obviously wasting our time here," Buford said. "This lady has no intention of cooperating."

Then Agent Neufeld said, "Are you seeing a psychiatrist, Joanna?"

"*Excuse* me?" I said. I wasn't insulted that she asked me that. I just wasn't about to say yes right away.

"I'll repeat my question," Agent Neufeld said. "Are you seeing a psychiatrist?"

"Sometimes," I said. "So what? Everyone has a shrink in New York City." I almost added, "You probably have one too," but I had the good sense to choke it back.

"All right, now we're getting somewhere," Agent Neufeld said. "Look, I agree with Agent Buford that we're wasting our time here, but in spite of your lack of cooperation with us I'm going to cut you a break because I don't really think you're going to act on the feelings you expressed in that phone call to the Mike Stevens show. What I need from you is a letter from your psychiatrist stating that you made that phone call during a period of emotional duress but that you do not pose a threat to Sandy Shrewsbury or any other citizen. If we are satisfied with the report, we will consider not pursuing this matter any further. And let me add that I'm taking a risk letting you off the hook here."

I became alarmed because I honestly didn't know how I was going to accomplish this. "But my psychiatrist won't do that!" I said. "He doesn't even know me. He just sees me every few months and talks to me for five minutes and prescribes my Ritalin and sends me away!" A lot of my friends say I'm too self-revealing, but I'm a writer, so what do they expect. Writers are always spewing chunks of their lives all over the place like projectile vomit.

Then Buford resumed his role of bad cop. "Now look!" he barked. "That's the deal and you can take it or leave it. I suggest that you take it, although I doubt that any psychiatrist would be willing to vouch for your sanity. I think we're dealing with something a little more serious than just a little lady grieving her mom. I think you're mentally unstable and potentially dangerous and if it were up to me I'd search every inch of this place because I don't trust you as far as I could throw you."

Instead of just mumbling some sullen response like a person in her right mind, I leapt back out of my chair and started screaming at him like a lunatic. "You have some nerve, Mister!" I shieked. "You have some nerve accusing me of being untrustworthy when your agency has a whole history of sinister behavior! They use vulnerable street people to entrap innocent Muslims into confessing to crimes they didn't commit. They persecuted John Lennon and Martin Luther King! They brought Nazi war criminals over here to help fight the big bad communists! Did you know that? Did you know that your esteemed agency aided and abetted Nazis while destroying the lives of decent American citizens during their anti-communist hysteria? They tried to prevent my father from getting a job after he served his country for four years! His best friend died in his arms after a sniper shot him in the head! Fuck your agency and that fucking moron Senator Joe McCarthy who is probably your hero!" Then I shifted my glare to Agent Neufeld. "And what the hell are *you* doing in the FBI?" I said, pointing at her. "You look like someone who grew up on the Upper West Side and made a wrong turn somewhere! What are you, some kind of *traitor*?"

"SIT DOWN, JOANNA!" Agent Neufeld commanded, and I did. I sat down and folded my hands back in my lap. "All right, just stop it," she said. And this is when I really noticed her eyes. She had these beautiful sapphire eyes with long lashes that you usually only see on boys. "You need to start exercising some self-control or you're going to be in a lot of hot water," Neufeld said. "As I said, I don't believe that you're intending to blow anyone up in spite of your allusions to a bomb during that phone call. However, I do agree with Agent Buford that we need to keep an eye on you. Right now we're making this very simple for you. Have your psychiatrist send us a report assuring us that your action was triggered by an emotional crisis and that you are in no way potentially dangerous or violent. If we do not receive this assurance we will come back and pick your life apart like spiders picking apart a fly. Do I make myself clear?"

"Well, that idiot Sandy Shrewsbury should not have gone on TV in the first place, spouting her reactionary views and provoking me," I said. "She should be at home in Montana riding her dirt bike instead of campaigning for the U.S. Senate." Then I said, "God! I miss my mom! What are you guys even *doing* here?" I was screaming again. "I need to write my book! I have no time for this! I can't *deal* with you people right now!"

"Then you shouldn't be making threatening phone calls to public figures," Buford said.

"Why did you have to bring him here?" I said to Neufeld, and I swear, I think I saw a flicker of a smile. But then she stood up and picked up her briefcase. "I don't think there's anything more we can accomplish here," she said. "We will expect to have that report in our office by the end of next week. Here's all the information about what needs to be included and where to send it." I snatched the paper out of her hand and flung it on the end table. As Agent Neufeld walked out the door trailed by Agent Buford, she turned and pointed a finger at me and said, "You will learn soon enough, my dear, that you don't fuck with the FBI." When she said that I got all turned on, and pictured her issuing orders to me in a more intimate setting. I am a very sick individual.

This all happened more than a week ago, and I still haven't gone to my shrink because I know he won't write that report. He's already lost his license once for his casual attitude toward writing prescriptions. (I always pay him in cash.) It was obvious that Agent Neufeld was the dominant one of the two agents, and I got the feeling that she didn't want to waste her time with some irritable Jewish woman that anyone with half a brain could tell wasn't going to run out and kill someone. But still, they'll probably show up here again at some point demanding to know why they haven't received the report from my shrink. The funny thing is, I'm not scared of them sending me to jail. I'm afraid that they'll disrupt my life. They'll screw up my schedule, or they'll come in here with a warrant and mess up my house. I keep my home very orderly. I wouldn't think of not making my bed every day. There's so much chaos inside my head that I have to keep my environment orderly to stay in control of my life. If the FBI came in here and started tearing my place apart it would drive me crazy.

But right now I feel kind of peaceful. I'm here in my apartment, writing on my sofa, and it's nice and quiet with the phone turned off and rain pattering against the window. I love my apartment. I love that my neighborhood, Sunset Park, has more Asians and Mexicans than white people. I love that my building, a narrow railroad tenement facing the elevated expressway, reminds me of the Lower East Side tenements where all the Jews lived during the great migration. I even like being the only one living in my building at the moment, although I miss my friend, Irma Hernandez, who lived upstairs in the third-floor apartment and died in her sleep a couple of months ago. The only other tenant is the chop shop downstairs that's full of rough Mexicans who would come to my rescue if anyone tried to mess with me. Even though my building looks like shit, my actual apartment is a gorgeous one-bedroom with high ceilings and great big windows, and I have it fixed up beautifully. It's every bit as "well appointed" as my friends' apartments in Park Slope and Carroll Gardens, or even in Manhattan. In fact my apartment makes some of my friends' places in Manhattan look like dumpy little closets.

The nice thing about this moment is that I feel as though my mom is here, watching over me. She would be furious with the FBI for coming over here and threatening me. She used to call Sandy Shrewsbury "that reactionary idiot." If she found out that I called the Mike Stevens show and told him that someone should plant a bomb under her ass, Mom's only objection would have been that I said "ass" on TV. She would have said, "A writer should be able to get her point across without using profanity." Other than that, she would have liked what I did.

31

Summer of 1960

Whenever you see Susie Moscowitz perched on a tablecloth in her front yard, having her solitary picnics, you want to go over there and beat her up. You know your antipathy is kind of crazy, since she's just minding her own business, but you're terribly offended by the way she sets herself apart from the other kids, even more than she did during the school year. At least in class she dressed like the other girls, but now, instead of wearing pedal pushers or shorts and sneakers like the other girls, she prances out of her house wearing ridiculous, old-fashioned clothes, long skirts and clunky shoes that remind you of photographs of your grandmother in the old country. While you and the other kids tear through the neighborhood, playing ball, riding bikes, roller-skating, jumping rope, hula-hooping, and playing red rover and hide-and-seek, Susie sits on her flowered tablecloth in her weird clothes, doing odd things like reading cookbooks and eating tuna fish sandwiches cut into little squares. Sometimes you even see her *knitting*. Even the mothers in the neighborhood don't knit. They're interested in being modern, and buy their socks and sweaters and scarves at downtown stores like Halle's and the May Company. (Bucking the trends, Susie's mother wears shlumpy clothes that look like she brought them over from Poland, probably in obedience to her husband, who wears yarmulkes and baggy long-sleeved shirts and trousers, but this doesn't give Susie an excuse for acting weird, since other kids with foreign parents act perfectly normal.)

What's most infuriating to you is the way Susie snubs her peers while sucking up to all the adults. If a kid yells, "Hi, Susie!" she responds with a dismissive wave, but a minute later she'll call out to the mailman, "Hello, Mr. Williams, do you have a lot of mail to deliver today?" Or she chirps, "Hello, Mrs. Rasmussen, I see you're out on your daily walk!" to the crone who lives around the corner. Once you even see her jumping up and down and waving to a policeman cruising down the block, the same cop who threatened to take five-year-old Danny Jordan to jail for throwing a snowball at a car.

Molly will later claim that you got some kind of thrill from hating Susie, which isn't true. Not only do you not fully understand your antagonism toward Susie, but you're distressed by it. You can be tyrannical with your little brothers and sister, but with kids your age you're usually pliant and cooperative and want to get along with everyone. Before "the incident" that cements your hatred and puts a crack in your soul, you make a valiant effort to fix Susie, to get her to see the error of her ways. When you see her reading a book called *Recipes from the Borscht Belt*, you yell to her, Hey! Why are you reading that dumb thing instead of something normal, like a Beverly Cleary book? and you're horrified when Susie replies that she finds the queen of kid authors "boring." When you catch sight of Susie knitting, her yellow ball of yarn tucked next to her butt, you demand to know why she's sitting there knitting "like an old lady," and Susie doesn't even dignify this with an answer, but instead waves her little yellow patch of knitting at you like an obnoxious puppet.

Just when you've pretty much given up on trying to reform Susie, you're forced into further contact with her, and it's Molly's fault. It happens that Susie lives next door to Bonnie "Bagel" Green, a kind, easygoing girl with mousy brown hair and glasses who moved into the neighborhood at the beginning of the summer, and you and Molly became instant friends with her. You love going over to Bagel's house, hanging around in her playroom that's stocked with games and sampling the intriguing foods she gets to eat because of her allergies. One day, after completing a game of Sorry and gorging on Mrs. Green's freshly baked "banana" cake made without bananas, the three of you charge out of Bagel's house and see Susie on her tablecloth next door, wearing a long polka-dot skirt and reading her stupid cookbook. "Let's go over and make friends with her," Molly suggests. Scowling, you drag over to Susie's encampment with your friends, and you sit on the grass in quiet agony while Susie talks about all the things her mother cooks for Shabbos dinner, how she chops her own horseradish instead of serving it in a jar and that she puts a secret ingredient in her matzoh balls to make them fluffy. Finally you leave, but now that the three of you have already started socializing with Susie you can't just go back to ignoring her so you continue to go over there every day and talk about things that are even more boring than Mrs. Moscowitz's horseradish, such as whether Molly's socks are "sunshine yellow" or "lemon yellow." You interject that pee can be different colors of yellow as well, and Molly shoots you down, telling you to stop being "immature," although you know that if Susie wasn't there Molly would get right into the spirit of talking about pee. The next day you start a game of seeing animals in the clouds, but then Susie starts correcting everyone, saying a cloud doesn't have the proper number of legs or eyes to be a grasshopper or a gorilla, and it's no longer fun.

The visits with twerpy Susie come to an abrupt end a few days after they began, when you and your friends trot over to visit with her and see that she's wearing a big, round "Nixon" button.

That's wrong, you say, standing on the lawn pointing. You're supposed to have a Kennedy button.

"No it's not wrong, Joanna," Susie says. "My parents and I are for Nixon."

You can't believe this. Your parents have told you that almost all the Jews are for Kennedy. Anyway, even if Susie's parents are for Nixon, which is possible since they're so strange, you're not supposed to be for someone because of your parents. You're supposed to make up your own mind.

Nixon is a big fat creep! you yell. You glare at her, outraged that she would advertise this appalling preference after you've bent over backwards to be nice to her.

"He's the best man for the job," Susie says, obviously parroting her father, a thin, humorless man who, like his wife, speaks with a Polish accent.

Nixon looks like a bulldog with his face hanging down like this, you say, pulling your cheeks down.

"Why don't you shut up, Joanna!" Susie says. "I can be for whoever I want!"

Then Molly, bless her heart, comes to the rescue. "That doesn't mean it's right," she says. "Nixon tried to put Joanna's father in jail." Nixon was on a committee with a horrible senator named Joseph McCarthy that got your father blacklisted so that he had trouble finding a job. Your parents hate Nixon almost as much as they hated Hitler. Even though he had not actually tried to put your father in jail, you're delighted with Molly's defense and don't bother to correct your friend's misrepresentation of the facts.

"Well, you Kennedy-lovers can just get out of my yard," Susie says, standing up to indicate the party is over. "I don't want to play with you anymore. Bagel can stay."

Just then the front door opens and Susie's mother sticks her head out and yells at Susie to come inside and do her Hebrew school homework. You and your friends get up and leave, Bagel giving a tiny wave, and Susie goes in the house to do her home-work. At that moment you actually feel a little sorry for Susie that she has such mean parents who make her go to Hebrew school, even during the summer. You go to a Sunday school where you call the teachers by their first names and sing songs about brotherhood and unions and putting an end to war. But then you figure that Susie likes that her parents are that way, and you go back to hating her without reservation.

For the whole next week you and your friends ignore Susie on her tablecloth, just walk right past her without speaking,

although Bagel gives her fleeting smiles. And then, one afternoon, the three of you are walking Punky, Mr. Harrison's dog,
and that's the day the whole summer blows up in your face. Mr.
Harrison, who lives four houses down from you, loves animals,
and a couple years ago he went to the pound and fell in love with
Punky, who had been burned in a fire. Punky has a huge, hairy
head, floppy ears, and a tail that Mr. Harrison said reminds him
of a cricket bat. One sightless eye sticks out like a yellow grape,
he's bald on the lower three-quarters of his body, and his lower
teeth stick out. When you ask Mr. Harrison what kind of dog
Punky is, he replies, "A monster dog." But Punky's sweetness and
enthusiasm make him the love of the neighborhood.

As you approach Susie's house, you see Susie on her tablecloth
with her blob of yellow knitting. You're holding the leash, and
you let Punky pull you across the lawn so he can sniff Susie.But
before he gets within ten feet of her Susie jumps up and screams,
"Get that horrible ugly dog away from me!"

Aw, go on and pet him! You're hurting his feelings! You want
Susie to be nice to your dog friend who was burned in a fire.

But Susie obviously has no concern about Punky's traumatic
history. "I said get that thing away from me, Joanna!" she yells,
pointing at Punky, who looks at her quizzically.

You walk over to Susie with Punky and say, Look! He just
wants to be friends! Punky walks onto the tablecloth and leaps
on Susie, trying to lick her through his pointy, sticking-out teeth.

"STOP IT!" Susie screams. "GO AWAY!" But Punky keeps
leaping on her and Susie gives him a shove and falls on her butt.
You crack up laughing as Punky sticks his big hairy head in her
face and starts licking her ecstatically. Susie looks in horror at his
bulbous blind eye and tries to push him off, screaming bloody
murder, but Punky continues to lick her face as though it's an ice
cream cone. "Get this hairy monster off of me!" Susie screams.

He's just trying to make friends with you, stupid! you say.
Come on, Punky. You tug at his leash and he leaps off of Susie.
Still in a playful mood, he snatches up the ball of yarn that's
attached to her patch of knitting and drops it at your feet.

You wanna play ball? Let's play ball! You pull the yarn ball from his mouth and unravel some of the yarn and toss the yarn ball into the air, and Punky catches it in his slobbery jaws. Good catch! you say.

Susie gets up and stands on the tablecloth with her eyes bugging out. "Give me my project and get that ugly dog out of my yard," she screams.

Your *what*? You start laughing. Why do you call it a project? Look at that thing! You point at the sad patch of knitting attached to the yarn ball in Punky's mouth and say, That's just a square! You pull the yarn ball from Punky's mouth and yell, Here, Punky, have a project! and toss it to him again. As he lunges for the yarn ball the leash flies out of your hand, and Punky snatches the yarn ball from the grass and starts dashing around the yard with it, dragging Susie's "project" behind him.

Whoops! you say, and Susie screams, "I'm going to kill you!"

Molly is getting annoyed at Susie's hysteria. "Susie, you're just getting him more excited with your screaming," she says. "Stop being such a baby."

"You should try to make friends with him," Bagel says. She goes over to Punky, who's still flying around the yard with the yarn ball, and pets him while he jumps all over her. "See Susie? He's so friendly! You don't have to be scared of him!"

Susie runs up her front steps and stands there. "I'm commanding you to give me my knitting and take that animal and get out of my yard!" she yells.

"You're commanding us?" Molly says. "What are you, a ship captain?"

I command you to stand on your head! you yell at her, pointing into the air.

Bagel trots to Punky, gets the ball of yarn from him, scoops up the patch of knitting from the grass, and gives the whole sorry mess to Susie. Susie takes the remains of her "project," runs into the house, and slams the door.

Boy, is she mental, you say and make a "crazy" face at the slammed door.

37

"She definitely has some problems," Molly agrees.

"Maybe she was scared of Punky's eye," Bagel says.

You say that you think Punky's eye is cute. The three of you walk around the block with Punky and drop him off back at home.

That should have been the end of it. But that evening, after supper, while you're playing "running bases" with the Jordan boys in their backyard, you hear your father's voice calling you. "Joanna!" he yells. You're alarmed, because your father never calls you. It's always your mother who does the calling. And besides, he called you by your full name rather than "Jo" or one of his nicknames. You walk around the Jordans' house and see your father standing on the porch. "Come inside," he orders, in a not-nice voice. You cross the street and go into the house, and find Molly and her mom, Shirley, sitting on the gray couch, and your own mother is sitting on the gray chair, as though they've been summoned to a solemn meeting. "Sit down," your father orders.

What? you say defiantly, but really you're terrified. Your father is obviously angry about something, and you can't understand why Molly and Shirley are sitting there, looking all formal. You plop on the couch next to Molly.

"Shirley and your mother and I got calls today from Susie Moscowitz's father," your father says, looming over you like a giant. "He said Susie told him you allowed Mr. Harrison's dog to attack her."

The hard lump of fear inside of you explodes like a bomb. Now you're boiling. To you, tattling is a crime worse than murder. You don't even let your little brother Danny tattle, and he's only four. He didn't attack her! you yell. He's friendly! He was just licking her!

"Some people are frightened of dogs," Shirley Katz says. "Especially that dog. You should have known better, Molly. Both of you girls should have known better."

"The dog didn't hurt her, Mother," Molly says. Lately she's been calling Shirley "Mother."

"I don't care," Shirley says. "That dog is very enthusiastic and he looks strange. Not everyone takes to him the way you girls have."

Oh, she's just a big sissy! you snarl. She would be afraid of a mouse!

"Never mind, Joanna," says your mom, who is terrified of mice. "Susie's father said the dog was completely out of control."

"You're not permitted to let the dog off the leash!" your father yells. "Did you let him off the leash?"

"She didn't let him off the leash," Molly says. "He got away from Jo and ran around the yard while he was still on the leash."

"Mr. Moscowitz says the dog pushed Susie down and went for her face," your father scolds.

You can't believe this absurd interpretation of the events. What do you mean, 'went for her face'? you yell. It's called licking, Daddy! He was just licking her! Punky is *friendly*!

"Do you know what would have happened if that dog had bitten her?" your father continues, as though he hasn't even heard you. "She would have had to have a series of very painful rabies shots!" (It doesn't occur to you until years later that Punky would have had all his rabies shots. Mr. Harrison is a very responsible dog owner. But your father tends to exaggerate when he wants to make a point.)

What a big baby, you say. Scared of a nice little dog.

"Did you know that Susie's parents were threatened by wild dogs in Poland?" your father yells.

Well who cares about *Poland*! you yell back. Punky isn't a wild dog in Poland! He's a friendly dog in America! We're not in *Poland*, Daddy!

Your mother jumps back in. "And what about Susie's knitting project, Joanna?" she says. "The dog did something to it?" She turns to Shirley for confirmation.

"Apparently he totally ruined it," Shirley says.

Oh, who cares about that stupid thing! you scoff. It wasn't even in any shape! It was just a square! What nine-year-old person knits anyway? That's something old ladies do. When you say this

Molly starts to laugh but her mother gives her a look and she stops.

"It is not something old ladies do," your mother says. "Aunt Jean knitted you a lovely scarf for Hanukkah."

So what, you say. Susie Moscowitz is not Aunt Jean. I hate her guts. I'm going to beat her up! You jump off the couch and storm toward your bedroom.

"You're not going to beat her up," your father roars. "You're to stay away from her for the rest of the summer, is that clear? Joanna!" But you just go into your room and slam the door, and your father doesn't pursue you, probably because he himself is annoyed with the whole foolish business. (Once he called Mr. Moscowitz a "putz.") You lie on your bed and seethe, and after a couple of minutes you hear Molly and her mother leave. You want to kill Susie. What especially enrages you is that the fathers were involved. It was Susie's *father* who called to complain, and your *father* who delivered the lecture. That built up the whole incident to a high crime, instead of it just being considered mis-behavior, the way it would have if only the mothers had been involved. Furthermore, you had good intentions. You were trying to get Susie to make friends with Punky, to teach her how to be a normal kid instead of an annoying little twerp.

Because Molly is forbidden to have anything to do with Susie, and Shirley would kill her if she disobeyed, you have to depend on your brothers to help you get revenge. You get seven-year-old Michael to sneak into her yard and trample all over her table-cloth. Michael also joins you in calling Susie names, and once when Susie is walking down the street with her mother Michael runs up behind her and smacks her on the tush, and while you watch him running away you're as proud of him as if he had fallen on a live grenade during the war. You also get four-year-old Danny into the act, and he performs with relish, throwing mud and stones at Susie and calling her a "stinker!" and a "B.M. face." In spite of these assaults on her, Susie still sings out, "Hello, Mr. and Mrs. Jacobs!" when you and your parents walk down the street on your way to visit Aunt Tillie and Uncle Joe (who aren't a real aunt and uncle, just family friends) and you have to restrain yourself from running across the street and kicking her in the face.

When you're not plotting revenge against Susie, you hang around at Molly's, watching her color in her "teen queen" coloring book or talking in a funny voice to Matey, the green parakeet. Sometimes you go over to Bagel's and lie on the floor of the playroom twirling pinwheels. Or else you play catch with Michael or one of the neighborhood boys.

But as much as you try to distract yourself, you can't get Susie's treachery out of your mind. You walk around with it day and night. Susie's tattling has aroused in you a murderous fury that you know isn't normal. You don't know at the time that sometimes when you're enraged at someone, when you want to tear her apart with your bare hands, it's because that person is acting like some part of you that you have rejected, a part of you that you split off from because it's repulsive to you. You can't stand seeing Susie suck up to adults because way down deep you hate adults for turning you into a fake version of yourself, a cooperative little girl who never throws tantrums but instead dries the dishes and practices the piano and sings songs and recites poems during the stupid weekly "shows" your parents host in the living room. You resent your parents and the other adults in your life for not loving the real you, the bad child, and you hate yourself for being fake around them so they won't reject you. When you see Susie smiling and chirping at adults it's like watching a loathsome caricature of yourself performing a spiteful song and dance act.

Late September 5:30 PM

I need to pull myself together. This is not good. Writing about "little Susie" has upset me terribly. I'm furious at her all over again for ratting on us about that dog, which is ridiculous because it happened more than fifty years ago but I'm also furious with "little Susie" about this other situation that I'm not going into now, especially because I can hardly concentrate on writing with a horde of Chinese people swarming through my building and marching around upstairs right over my head. Yesterday I saw about six of them coming up the stairs as I was going down, and they looked at me as though I was someone from ICE even though I look nothing like an immigration authority, especially with my new jeans that have two holes in them. I was thinking, *who the hell are they*, and then I heard them walking around upstairs in Irma's apartment. Then in the evening when I went out to get a bite to eat two more of them, a man and a woman, were coming up the stairs and when they saw me their eyes froze, as though they had just encountered Death, and they just kept walking past me up the stairs, trying to ignore me. And now they're all clomping around right over my head. Apparently my crazy Russian landlord has decided to turn my building into a safe house for undocumented immigrants, and I am having the most politically incorrect feelings about the whole situation.

Molly came over about an hour ago and she is no help to me at all. When I told her about the Chinese people taking over my building, she said maybe I need to learn Mandarin so I can talk to them. I said that wasn't funny. Then I asked her if she wanted to see the latest chapter of my book and that was a mistake. She sat there reading it with that look on her face she gets when she's listening to a speech by the president of her board, which I recognized because I've been to two of her board meetings. So I didn't have much hope that she would be very complimentary about my chapter. Which she wasn't. All she had to say about it was that I "exaggerated" Susie's obnoxiousness on the tablecloth, the way I always do when I recall the events of that summer, and that she, Molly, never wore yellow socks. "I've always hated the color yellow," she said. For God's sake. Why would she make an issue about the color of her socks? I happen to distinctly remember those yellow socks but yellow socks, green socks, blue socks, who cares? Obviously she can't concentrate on my book because she's preoccupied with her own insane life. Right now she's sitting here texting her daughter Zoey, and I'm sure they're discussing their favorite subject, of how to get Billy to be a more responsible father and contribute more to their "household," when they know perfectly well that Billy lives in a "household" of white powder. Molly is so stubborn, the way she keeps haranguing Billy when she knows perfectly well you can yell at a drug addict until you're blue in the face and it won't do any good. You would think that a person who runs an influential tenants' rights organization and who even has a personal relationship with the *mayor* would conduct her personal life as though she had a modicum of sense.

Oh dear, oh dear, this is not a good day. This morning Myra, my agent, called and told me that two more publishers have rejected my second novel, which would already be in circulation if that jerky marketing guy hadn't decided it was unfit for publication. It was weird enough that he even read my book, especially after it had already been accepted for publication, and then he decided to take offense at one of my best characters, a psychotic CIA agent who had foreknowledge of 9/11 and allowed it to happen. This marketing schmuck, John Morton, is from somewhere in that remote part of Staten Island that isn't even part of New York City, psychologically speaking, which kind of explains it. Most normal New Yorkers would have no trouble envisioning a rogue CIA agent who had foreknowledge of 9/11. Anyway, whatever happened to *editors* having the final word about what gets published? My editor just acted like a big weenie, not returning my phone calls after he told me he would try to fight for my book. I hate him now as much as I hate that idiot John Morton.

I can't deal with my book not being published and I can't deal with writing about "little Susie" (for a whole number of reasons) and especially I can't deal with my mom being dead. This grief has hit me like an avalanche. I used to talk to my mom a few times a day. I would be at Rite Aid and call her and ask her what color of Dove soap I should buy, or walk around the supermarket talking to her. Sometimes we talked for hours, analyzing my siblings or gossiping about her friends. I drove to Cleveland three or four times a year and helped her with all aspects of her life. I got together with her and her friends. I took her to her doctor's appointments. I helped her with her finances. I shopped for her. I helped her around the house. I became kind of her partner after my dad died eight years ago, which is what eldest children often do (especially unmarried daughters), and I never really minded because she loved me and would have walked in front of a bus for me. And now that she's gone I feel so disoriented. After I got back to New York I thought I would start feeling more normal but I didn't because that lunatic Sandy Shrewsbury had to upset me with her asinine comments about the American health care system. And I have no idea when the FBI agents are going to come back here and castigate me for not getting a report from a shrink stating that I am sane. Which I am not sure that I am. Especially now that these Chinese people have taken over my building and are making me feel like an interloper when I'm the one who's been living here for twenty years. I feel like the person in that painting *The Scream*. Not only because the person is screaming but because everything around her is all wavy and weird. I feel wavy and weird, and everything around me is wavy and weird. I can't even feel any solid comfort from my best friend sitting right here next to me on the couch. In fact she's making me kind of paranoid because I think she hates my book.

I should just go to work already, which I will do as soon as Molly stops texting and gets out of here. I'm driving people around town for a new company called Voom. I haven't taken on any writing assignments in almost a year because I got burned out of writing articles. Anyway it's hard to write articles when you're working on a book. But I don't feel ashamed working for Voom because everyone's got some kind of hustle these days. Even older "professional" people like me are waiting tables and working for Uber and Voom and turning their apartments into B&Bs and selling their goofy jewelry that they make out of scrap metal they scavenge out of junkyards. Everyone's trying to keep one step ahead of the beast nipping at their heels. I used to teach writing at the New School but at some point I stopped doing it. I don't even think I got fired or anything. One day I just wasn't doing it anymore. Does that sound crazy? It's because I'm in that painting. My sense of time and space are shot to hell. I can't believe my mom is, like, dead. I have a friend who calls dying "transitioning" but when I told another one of my friends my mom "transitioned" she said in this annoying gentle voice, "Joanna, can't you just say your mom died?" So now I have to say my mom died. I mean she's right. I don't even like the word "transitioning" because transitioning is something I have a lot of trouble with. I hyperfocus on whatever I'm doing and then it's excruciating to tear myself away to do something else. Even getting up and going to the bathroom can produce intense anxiety. Can you imagine how much I'll freak out when I have to die? That will be a lot more disorienting than going to the bathroom. Why am I even talking about this? This is depressing.

Molly wants to borrow my computer to write something. She'll probably write something mean about me.

The writer of this book has a tenuous hold on reality.

I'll leave that in just to humor her.

1960–1961

The first day of school is always magical. When you walk in the classroom with Molly and Bagel, wearing your new plaid jumper, shiny new saddle shoes, and a new clasp in your hair, your embattled summer seems like a long time ago and your whole life is ahead of you. The classroom looks bright and clean. The blackboard is black and shiny, the tiled floors are free of scuff marks, and even the old wood desks gleam with polish. The windows are all ajar, letting a breeze in. The bulletin board has "Welcome, Fourth Grade!" posted in big yellow letters. Everyone wonders where the teacher is. Miss Amos has a reputation for being mean, but you're not concerned about this. Sometimes a mean teacher is nice on the inside, just as a nice teacher can be mean on the inside, as you and Molly learned with Miss Schultz.

Susie walks into the room. She has the same old superior smile on her face, but instead of wearing the bizarre old lady clothes she wore during the summer she's wearing a normal plaid skirt, a white blouse, and a pair of brown tie shoes. Your stomach clenches. Molly told you that Susie might be going to an all-girls' Hebrew school and, being a natural optimist, you assumed this was true. And now here she is, with her typical snooty look. Hey, creepy! you yell. Susie looks over a row of heads, gives you a spiteful smile, and sits down in the front center seat. She wants to kiss the teacher's feet, you say to Molly. You actually have to restrain yourself from jumping out of your chair and shoving your nemesis onto the shiny tiled floor.

The bell rings, and as if on cue Miss Amos enters the classroom. She wears a dark skirt, flat shoes, and a tan blouse with a bow at the neck, which makes her look more rather than less severe. She has thick, short black hair, a yellowish complexion, and several dark beauty marks on her face. Unlike the other lady teachers, she wears no makeup. You've always thought the fourth-grade teacher looks like a lady outlaw on *Gunsmoke* or *Bonanza* who lives out on the range and shoots rattlesnakes with a six-gun. Now she strides to the center of the room and claps several times. "All right, all right, everyone be quiet!" she yells, and her pupils fall silent.

"I am Miss Amos," the teacher announces, which everyone already knows. She scrawls her name on the board in big, sweeping strokes, then returns to the center of the room, clapping chalk off her hands. "I'll tell you this right off the bat," she continues. "I am probably the least warm and cuddly teacher at Judson Elementary. I have no patience for shenanigans. If you do your job, which is to do your assignments faithfully, you'll be rewarded with good grades. If you slack off, you flunk. It's as simple as that. Every Friday you'll have a quiz on any subject, so you need to be prepared in all your subjects. If you fool around and don't pay attention, you may find yourself left back and you'll have to repeat fourth grade—with me." She smiles meanly. You and Molly look at each other, and Molly makes her crazy scared bunny face, wrinkling her nose and showing her top teeth, and you laugh.

"I told you she was the meanest teacher in school," Molly says during the walk home. "She made Sarah cry once." Molly's older sister Sarah is a perfect child and you feel a stab of anger toward the teacher for making her cry.

"Maybe she'll get better," Bagel says.

Yeah, if she dies, you say.

"That's terrible," says Bagel. "You're not supposed to say that."

"Well she is going to die," Molly says. "We're all going to die."

Which kind of closes the subject.

47

Miss Amos' reputation for being mean has to do with her sarcasm. She gives what your father calls "back-handed compliments" such as "Denise! You actually do have a brain tucked inside all that fluff!" or, "Gregory! You have discovered that wondrous thing called arithmetic!" Her sarcasm even extends to the people she's teaching about, such as Nikita Khrushchev, the Russian leader, who she says is "a total idiot" for threatening to build a wall to keep the East Germans, who are controlled by the communists, from moving to West Germany, where people are free because they're controlled by the Americans.

One nice thing about the teacher is that she has allowed the class to arrange their desks into clusters of four, "so you can learn from one another rather than sitting and staring at me like a bunch of sheep." You and your cluster mates, who include Molly, Bagel, and cute little Frankie Lobo, spend most of your time goofing around, and very little engaging in the interactive learning that's the purpose of the teacher's seating arrangement. You shoot rubber bands across the room, paint your arms with Elmer's glue, and laugh practically until your eyes pop out of your heads. True to her promise in the spring to "get the teacher's goat," Molly laughs and giggles during lessons, answers the teacher's questions tersely, as though she couldn't care less, and pays more attention to her new outfits than to her grades, which slip to B's and C's. At first Bagel tries to behave, but you and Molly work on her, sticking a homemade paper hat on her head and painting her arm with Elmer's glue, and after a day or two she starts joining in the fun. (One thing that makes you like the teacher a little teeny bit is that she calls your friend by her pet name of "Bagel" rather than by her formal name of "Bonnie.")

The only thing interfering with your fun in class is the irksome presence of Susie. Much to your annoyance, Susie has chosen as her cluster mates the two most unlikeable girls in the room, Candice Baker, a thin, plain-looking, painfully shy C student, and Darlene Panelli, another quiet girl who gets excellent grades but because she's so aloof and unsociable nobody notices or cares. But you have nothing against Candice or Darlene. It's Susie whose existence you can't tolerate, and you pester her every chance you get. You toss spitballs at her, hit her in the back on the way out the door, and call her "Susie Ratcake," after Molly tells you that a tattletale is called a "rat" by gangsters in the movies. You get no pleasure from badgering Susie. You just want her to atone for her crimes so that you can forgive her. The first day of school during recess you say to her, You know, all you have to do is apologize for finking on me and Molly, but Susie says, "But I didn't do anything wrong; you allowed a dog to attack me," and you say, you stink, and walk away.

One sunny October day, something happens to take your mind off Susie completely. As you file out with the class for recess you walk past Miss Amos and the teacher smiles and gives you a little wink. It gives you a strange feeling, like a fuzzy worm crawling out of your belly button and slithering up your stomach. When you return to class, Miss Amos has changed. It's as though you're looking at a completely different teacher. Her black hair shines like the hide of a racehorse, her dark beauty marks look pretty, and her sarcastic smile seems warm and playful. You sit at your desk and stare at Miss Amos until Molly hits you on the shoulder and says, "Hey. What are you lookin' at?" and you say nothing, and drag your eyes off the teacher.

Suddenly you're aware of Miss Amos every second. Before, you acted up carelessly, even defiantly, but now you start misbehaving to get the teacher to notice you. You laugh loudly, slam your desk shut, and pop in and out of your seat like a jack-in-the-box. Whenever Miss Amos makes one of her sarcastic comments to you, such as, "Joanna, remind me to bring some marbles to class tomorrow to replace the ones you lost," you feel a pleasant nausea, as though your stomach is making more room for the teacher to fit in. Once Miss Amos says to you, "Joanna, you're acting obnoxious again; please desist," and during recess you run around with your friends yelling, please desist, please desist!

You start watching Miss Amos all day long and pointing out things that she does to Molly, Bagel, Frankie, and anyone else who happens to be listening. You say, look at the way she holds her pencil, or, her bowtie is untied! You speculate about what she does outside of class. Maybe she goes on dates with bank robbers. Maybe she eats strange sandwiches like peanut butter and ketchup. You propose what-ifs: What would she do if the Russians dropped a bomb on the school? What would she do if Randy Bishowsky brought a bug into the class and ate it right in front of her? Better yet, what if Alfred Cohen, the class genius, did it? But one day Molly turns to you and says, "Who cares what Miss Amos would do? You don't have to talk about her every second," and you want to sink into a crack in the floor.

You continue to make fun of Miss Amos with your friends and write mean things about her in your little red diary. Your feelings about the teacher feel creepy, like wanting to eat your boogers. You have never heard of someone having a "crush" on a teacher, and having these gooey feelings would be bad enough if Miss Amos was pretty and popular, but she's mean and ugly and nobody even likes her. Whenever you sneak smells of the teacher's sweater in the cloakroom, or "accidentally" bump into her on the way out the door, you space out, as though it's someone else that's doing these things. At night your confusion about Miss Amos comes out in disturbing dreams. In one dream Miss Amos yanks your hair right out of your scalp in two pieces like a torn hat, and in another dream, you're in a cage littered with chicken bones, and a lady is walking around the room that doesn't look like Miss Amos but you know it's her, and she's fattening you up to eat you. When you wake up, you long to be back in the cage, and in order to not feel crazy you grab your diary and write, *Last night I dreamed that Miss Amos was a witch, which we already knew anyway ha ha.*

All the kids are excited to learn that Miss Amos will be giving out candy on Halloween. A teacher giving out candy on Halloween is always special, no matter who she is. But your excitement is way beyond what's normal. You hope that going to the teacher's house, even just for Halloween candy, will give you access to Miss Amos' personal life. You even imagine that it's your own special qualities that have motivated the teacher to participate in Halloween.

On Halloween night you storm onto the street with your brother Michael in his headdress and war paint, Bagel in her hobo tatters, and Molly, whose talented mom has turned her into a very realistic carrot. You have insisted on dressing up as "Hansel" even though your mom told you it was weird to be "Hansel" without "Gretel." As you make your way up 176th Street, filling your paper bags with treats, all you can think about is getting to Miss Amos's house. You finally arrive at the teacher's white bungalow on Miner Drive. It needs a coat of paint, and the grass isn't freshly cut, but the outside light is on, and a jack-o'-lantern is grinning on the porch. When Miss Amos answers the door wearing a pair of slacks, you feel happier than you've ever felt in your life. The opened door seems like an entrance to a magic kingdom.

Are those pants your costume, Miss Amos? you ask.

"Yeah, Jo, they're my everyday costume," Miss Amos says. "They're much more comfortable than dresses."

You're thrilled that the teacher favors pants over stupid dresses. I wish I could wear pants every day! you say.

"Indeed," Miss Amos says, her eyes floating to your companions. "Speaking of costumes, what do we have here? Let's see—Bagel is a hobo, Molly is a carrot—very original costume, Molly—and who is this scary character with the feathers and war paint?"

This is my brother, Michael, you say proudly.

"I'm a wild Indian!" Michael says.

"You look pretty wild," says Miss Amos. "I'll bet you've had some wild Indian lessons from your big sister." You glow. "And who are you supposed to be, Miss Joanna?" the teacher asks. You tell her and she says, "Very creative. Where, pray tell, is your sister Gretel?"

She's probably in a cage in your kitchen, you say, trying to peer into her house. I'm gonna have to rescue her before you eat her for dinner.

Miss Amos laughs and says, "Well, I give you my word I won't eat your sister. I'll just keep her as my slave." She says this in a scary witch voice, and everyone laughs.

What about me? you ask, hoping for the right answer.

"You!" Miss Amos says. "You're going right in there with her! You're gonna be my main slave." You feel a strange, gooey heat slide up through your body as Miss Amos grins and goes back in the house. She returns with four candy apples.

Candy apples! you yell. Wowee zowee!

"Thank you, Miss Amos," Molly says, smiling, and you know that your friend is genuinely pleased with the treat. Usually she sounds a little sarcastic when she speaks to Miss Amos.

"This is great, Miss Amos," Bagel says. "Thanks."

That night you're so excited you can't sleep. You keep hearing Miss Amos' voice saying, "You're gonna be my *main* slave." Of course the teacher didn't mean it literally, but you hope that she was implying that she wanted you to come to her house and help her with various chores. You picture yourself in Miss Amos' yard, chopping wood, while the teacher stands behind you with her arms folded, complimenting you on your strength. (You've never chopped wood in your life, and Miss Amos probably doesn't even have a fireplace—most people with small houses don't have them—but this is the chore that you first imagine doing for Miss Amos.)

The next day, there's a new, festive feeling in class. When you walk into the room, Miss Amos is joking around with Alfred Cohen, telling him that he looked more like Clark Kent than Superman in his costume. Later, when the teacher is lecturing about current events, Denise Robinson calls out, "Miss Amos, you should be a newscaster on TV like Walter Cronkite!" and the teacher says, "Why, pray tell?" and Denise says "Because you have the voice of authority!" During recess, Susie Moscowitz prances into the playground with a candy apple that Miss Amos has saved for her, since her parents wouldn't let her go trick or treating. "I didn't even have to walk all the way to Miss Amos' house to get *my* treat!" Susie says, and you yell, Oh, be quiet! Later that day, you see Miss Amos guiding Randy Bishowsky's hand to help him write more legibly. A few weeks before, she told Randy that his handwriting "would put a caveman to shame."

Instead of making you feel good, the teacher's new popularity throws you into a panic. In order to compete with your class-mates for the teacher's attention, you start acting like a crazy little maniac. You swing back and forth in your seat until Miss Amos orders you to stop. You laugh hysterically, even at things that aren't that funny. Once, when Mike Montello makes a stupid joke to the class, you laugh until you fall off your chair, and you lie on the floor, still laughing, until the teacher comes over and gives you a little kick and barks, "Up-up-up! Try acting like you have some sense!" Another time you saunter in from recess ten minutes late, and are overjoyed when Miss Amos follows you to the cloakroom, waits for you to hang up your jacket, and then marches you by the arm to your seat and sits you in your chair as though you're a four-year-old child.

It doesn't take long for Miss Amos to get tired of your antics. On voting day, the gym is set up with mock voting booths, and after voting for Senator John F. Kennedy you march around bouncing a basketball and the teacher pretends not to see you. The next week you crawl onto the radiator, open a window, and stick your tongue out to capture the snowflakes pouring down. You wait for the teacher to ask you what in God's name you are doing, but Miss Amos just lets you act the fool. You would have preferred staying after school and writing *I am a stupid moron* a million times to being ignored. The final indignity occurs when you check out a library book about anthropology, which the teacher is studying at Western Reserve University, and read it during study period to impress her, but instead of saying, "Oh, I see you're interested in my favorite subject!" she says to you, "Joanna, library books are to be read at home, not in class." You feel like crying.

You're so preoccupied with Miss Amos that you're not paying any attention to what's going on with your classmates. One day you're wandering around the playground at recess in your brown winter jacket and white boots and you see Denise Robinson and Pamela Gray standing next to the swings in their plaid coats, and they're looking at you. Then Denise whispers something in Pamela's ear and they both laugh. Although you feel upset and uncomfortable for the rest of the afternoon, you try to push the playground incident out of your mind. You have no way to interpret it, since you've never experienced other kids making fun of you, except in a friendly, teasing way. By the end of the day your mind is back on Miss Amos and how you've failed to charm her with your delightful antics.

During Christmas vacation you do the usual things, lighting Hanukkah candles with your family, watching Mr. Jingeling, the elf who broadcasts his Christmas show every year from Halle's department store, and messing around with your siblings, but you have no enthusiasm for anything. Now that Miss Amos doesn't like you anymore you don't feel like going back to school. You don't feel like being with your friends, and just lie around on your bed reading childish books like *Peter Pan* and *The Five Little Peppers*. One Saturday afternoon you get restless and put on your jacket and walk to Lawson's to buy some licorice sticks for yourself and your family. As you walk out of the store with your bag of candy you see a bunch of girls spilling out of Denise Robinson's house. Streaming down the front walk are Pamela Gray, Donna Miller, Janey Donleavy, and Barbara Golden, and behind them are Molly, Bagel, Susie Moscowitz, and a couple of other girls. Feeling suddenly embarrassed, you hurry around the corner and hide behind a tree until you see Molly, Susie, Bagel and Pamela turn the corner, and then you step onto the sidewalk and stand there until they catch up with you.

"Hey," Molly says.

Hey, you answer. What are you guys doing?

"We were at a par-ty!" Susie sings out.

"Denise invited us to her pigtail party," Molly said.

You stare at them and say, What's a pigtail party?

"Oh, it's just something she made up. It was really just an afternoon party, where we discussed, um, things," Molly says, and everyone giggles.

What 'things'? you demand, clutching your bag of licorice sticks.

"Just 'things'", Pamela says, and everyone giggles again.

LIKE WHAT? you yell helplessly. You try to get control of yourself. What 'things' are you talking about? you ask, more softly.

"Like things with WIENERS!" Pamela sings out.

"Don't listen to them, Jo," Bagel says. "She's just talking about hot dog wieners like you make from pigs. That's why she called it a 'pigtail party.'"

You walk with them in furious silence, grunting when Pamela says good-bye at her house, and not speaking a word to Molly, Susie, and Bagel, who chat about the party. Bagel tries to include you in the conversation but you ignore her, and when you get to your house you storm inside, toss the bag of licorice sticks on the coffee table, go into your room, and lie on your bed trying not to cry.

The next day Molly and Bagel come over to apologize about the Pigtail Party. "I thought Denise had invited you, I swear," Bagel says.

You glare at Molly. Did you know that I wasn't invited? you ask her.

"Well, kinda," Molly says. "I was gonna tell Denise to invite you but my mom said maybe she had her reasons."

But she invited Susie Ratcake! you yell, suddenly angry at Shirley for suggesting that Denise would have "reasons" for not inviting you to her party. Why would Denise invite stupid idiot Susie and not invite me? you yell.

"Susie's not so bad now," Molly says, and Bagel nudges her but it's too late.

She's not so bad! you scream. You're on *her* side now?

"Of course she's not on her side," Bagel says. "Anyway, Denise didn't invite her two buddies, Darlene and Candice, either."

Oh, great! So the only girls that weren't invited were Darlene and stupid Candice and me? you say. You've never felt so insulted in your life.

"All right already!" Molly says. "It wasn't our party! Don't blame us!"

You fake your way through the rest of the winter. You pretend to have fun fooling around with Molly, Bagel and Frankie in class, and you pretend not to be bothered that Molly suddenly seems to like Frankie and his cute little pompadour more than she likes you. You no longer act nutty to get the teacher's attention but instead start behaving yourself, even folding your hands and listening quietly during lessons, but the teacher continues to ignore you while suddenly acting all buddy-buddy with Molly, who's been snippy to her all year. "Your hair looks nice without braids!" she chirps to Molly one day, and another time she sings out, "Good job, girlie!" as she returns Molly's "B" paper (and then hands you your "A" paper without a word). You wake up every morning with a stomachache. You're sick of winter, sick of going to school every day in your puffy brown jacket and shiny white boots and leggings under your stupid dresses while the boys saunter along in their corduroy pants and leather hats with ear flaps and neat black boots with buckles. In February you turn ten years old and you pretend to enjoy your party, laughing and clapping at the magician's tricks and exclaiming Neat! and Wow! at your presents, but secretly you hate being ten and suspect that your friends came to your party just because their parents made them.

One Saturday morning in late March, you wake up and see that green grass has broken through the snow, and you go outside and a warm wind hits your face. Spring fever flies into you like a bug. Suddenly you feel like doing stuff. That day you go down in the basement and build a wagon out of a cardboard box and roller skates, and you put Danny in it and pull him down the street. The following week you send away for a multibladed Boy Scout knife with a Frosted Flakes box top. Baseball season has started, and you listen to some games, and root for the Tribe, and you talk Andy Jordan into giving you Rocky Colavito, the Indians' popular outfielder who was traded last year, which caused the whole city to have a conniption fit. (Andy has given up baseball cards for a stamp collection.) You fill out the form to join the *Plain Dealer* "Cookie Club," and a couple of weeks later you're delighted to see yourself featured as a new member, with your photo and a whole paragraph about yourself that mentions your school and your siblings and your hobbies, which are accurately listed as "sports, reading, and eating hot fudge sundaes."

On a warm day in May, you're lying on the couch, twirling your hair and staring into space. It's quiet in the house, for a change. Bobie is hanging up laundry in the backyard and your parents have taken Danny to the art museum to pick up Mike and Rosie after their Saturday art lessons. The front screen door opens and Molly walks into the living room, clutching her Barbie doll.

What are you doing with that? you ask. Molly hasn't played "Barbie" in over a year.

"I thought I would give her to Rosie. If she wants her I can go home and get all the clothes and stuff."

Rosie won't want it, you say. She's still playing with her Tiny Tears.

"Oh," Molly says. "Well I guess my mom can give her to the Salvation Army."

You reach over and grab the doll from Molly.

"Stop it!" Molly says. "Give it back."

You hold Barbie at arm's length and look at her, and then a strange smile floats over your face. Let's roast her and eat her, you say.

Molly smiles and says, "We can't. She's a doll, not a cow."

You jump off the couch and head into the kitchen. "What are you doing?" Molly says, following you. You set Barbie on the counter, pull off her clothes, and toss them in the garbage. "Naked Barbie," Molly observes. You open the cupboard and pull out an old frying pan. "Are you really going to eat her?" Molly asks. "Do you think you're a cannibal?"

Yum yum eat 'em up! you chant, quoting the wild man from Borneo in the famous *Little Rascals* episode, who chased the kids around the house making them think he was a cannibal when he only wanted candy. You stick the frying pan on the stove, put naked Barbie in the pan face-up, and turn on the fire.

"Do you think she'll melt?" Molly asks.

Look! you say, pointing at Barbie, who has already started losing her shape.

"BOOM boom boom boom, BOOM boom boom boom!" Molly chants, imitating the drums in the Tarzan movies that used to terrify you. After a few seconds Molly peeks into the pan and says, "She's all gone." Sure enough, all that's left of Barbie is a lump of plastic and her hair.

"We can't eat her," Molly says. "We'll get sick."

We can pretend to eat her, you say, and get a knife and try to scrape off the doll's remains, but the plastic is stuck to the frying pan. Uh-oh, you say.

You and Molly go outside with the ruined frying pan, hurry past Bobie who's still hanging clothes on the line, get your dad's shovel from the garage, and dig a hole behind the garage. When Bobie, who has gotten suspicious, comes back there and sees you shoveling dirt onto Barbie and the frying pan, she promises not to tell and is true to her word. She tells your mom that she took the pan to her own house to fry some onions, but your mom doesn't believe her and will continue to badger her about the pan her whole life. More than thirty years later, your mom will find out the truth during a gab session with you and Molly, and she will smile and say, "Shame on you girls" but she will really be kind of pissed at her mother for lying to her. But you can't yell at a dead woman.

Early October, 1 PM

I'm not showing Molly any of my book anymore. I showed her this chapter yesterday after she came bopping over here before a meeting and everything she said about it was churlish and derisive. She's not reading it with a critical eye; she's just taking it all personally. First she said that she was SHOCKED! SHOCKED! that I had a crush on our crabby fourth-grade teacher who everyone hated, then she said that she couldn't believe that I hadn't gotten over not being invited to "that silly little party" already, and her final helpful comment was that, during the cooking of the Barbie doll, *she* never danced around chanting "Boom boom boom boom," that *I* was the one who did this, and that she actually had very little enthusiasm for the project and only went along with it to indulge my infantile whims. The whole time Molly was reacting to my chapter I was feeling personally attacked by her, like excuse me for being me when I was nine or ten years old. I don't know why she even bothered to be my friend if I was such a nerd. It was a big mistake to think she could be a partner in the process of writing this book. I don't know how people can be in these writing classes and have twenty people yammering their opinions about every word they write. That would drive me crazy. But of course I felt compelled to defend myself against Molly's derisive comments, so I said that I wasn't about to let anyone know I had a crush on that stupid teacher because I was embarrassed about it myself, that just because I wrote about not getting invited to that bitch's party doesn't mean I haven't gotten over it, and that I have a distinct memory of Molly smiling serenely while watching Barbie melt in the pan, so even if she didn't dance around chanting she still enjoyed cooking the doll. I was feeling like the whole discussion was this big put-down of me, so after we stopped talking about my book I got back at her by telling her that the FBI paid me a visit yesterday when I was drunk. I kind of giggled when I saw the look on her face that I know so well, and she said it won't be so funny when you're trying to write your "little book" with Kanye West blasting in your ear in the dormitory, and I laughed even harder because I've become mentally deranged.

I don't know why I should feel guilty about being drunk when Agent Deborah Neufeld and her attack dog, Agent Buford, showed up here yesterday. I do have a right to get drunk in my own home, after all. If they had given me any warning about paying me a visit I might have postponed breaking into my new bottle of Hudson Valley brandy. But when they came a-knocking I had just consumed my third glass and was in that euphoric stage of drunkenness in which you have no sense of danger and everyone is your friend. I opened the door and there stood this sharp-looking woman with her stylish haircut and navy trousers and crisp white blouse and luminous blue eyes, and even though Buford was standing next to her looking like the same old grouch, in my drunken state I even felt a burst of affection toward him. "Well look who's here!" I yelped. "What a pleasant surprise! Come on in!"

They walked in, giving me funny looks, and planted themselves on the sofa, and I proceeded to annoy the shit out of them because I had no sense of the gravity of the situation. It's amazing how alcohol can remove all the sharp edges from your world and make you feel warm and cozy and safe. I plopped down on the chair, stuck my hands behind my head, and said, "So what's up, dudes?"

"What's up is that we have not yet received the evaluation from your psychiatrist," Deborah said. "Have you been to see your psychiatrist since we last spoke?"

"Yeah," I said. "But I didn't ask him to do it."

She looked at Buford, who gave her an "I told you so" look. Then she turned back to me and said, "Why didn't you ask your psychiatrist to send us the report?" She looked harder at me. "Were you afraid of what he would write in it?"

"No," I said. "I *told* you this! He wouldn't have done it! He's not, like, a therapist for God's sake. He just prescribes my drugs! What is wrong with you? Don't you know how shrinks work these days? They talk to you for five minutes to make sure you like your drugs and then they write out a new prescription and that's the whole visit. Haven't you guys ever been to a psychiatrist? Oh yeah you probably have, to make sure you're fit for your dumb job. I'll bet they gave you psychological tests. Did you get an ink blot test?" I pointed at Agent Buford and said, "I'll bet he tried to give normal responses when actually he was seeing really weird, sick things!" Then I laughed.

"She's drunk," Buford said.

"I'm drunk," I affirmed, and laughed some more. Then I picked up the bottle of brandy on the floor and took a swig, right from the bottle. "Want some?" I said. I held the bottle out to them.

Buford looked disgusted and Deborah just waved the bottle away and said, "Tell me, Joanna. How much of that brandy have you drunk today?"

"Who cares how much brandy I've drunk today?" I yelled. I was actually pissed at her for refusing to take a sip. She was acting like a goody-two-shoes, the way Susie used to act, except Susie had an excuse because she was just a child. Of course it wasn't at all reasonable to expect Agent Deborah to drink brandy with me, but my reactions were all out of whack, not only because I was drunk but because underneath the drunkenness was this nagging grief. People die, you go to a million funerals, but nothing prepares you for losing your mother. I have shock waves going through me all day long. "I really think you should try some of this delicious brandy," I said to Deborah, holding out the bottle to her again. "It's made with New York state cherries."

"You clearly are drunk," Deborah said. "Are you an alcoholic, Joanna?"

This is so typical of this uptight society we live in now. If you're drunk you must be an alcoholic. "God!" I yelled at her. "What is *wrong* with you! My mom just died and I'm having a few glasses of brandy! That is *normal*! That is not a sign of alcoholism!" I should have stopped right there, but instead I went on one of my rants. "This whole society has a stick up its ass!" I screamed. "It's all because of that fucking nine-eleven! Nine-eleven ruined all our fun! Everyone's afraid to do *anything*! Don't tell me the two of you weren't knocking 'em back like sailors back in the old days, when we were all young, before everyone had a stick up their butt. Am I right? Come on, people, don't lie," I cautioned, goofily waving my finger at them. "Remember, lying is a sin!"

"This is a waste of time," Buford said.

Deborah gestured quickly at him, and then she said, "Are you done with your little speech?" I stopped ranting, suddenly hypnotized by her sapphire eyes. "Now you need to settle down and listen to me," Deborah said. "Going through a personal crisis in no way excuses you for making that terribly irresponsible call to the Mike Stevens show. I strongly advise you to get that evaluation from a legitimate psychiatrist as soon as possible. So far you've managed to avoid more serious consequences for your behavior, because I've been protecting you. There are people in my department that think you should be arrested and detained for issuing an incendiary threat over public airwaves."

That got me started all over again. "Well they can all fuck off," I said. "What did they think, that I was going to hop a plane to Montana and blow up Sandy Shrewsbury? If you want to investigate real criminals, there are a whole bunch of Chinese people that just moved into the apartment upstairs, and you know they have been made into slaves by the criminals that smuggled them into this country in crates where they probably almost suffocated. And now they have to give the gangsters every last dime they make working like dogs in restaurants and nail parlors eighteen hours a day." Right away I realized I might be getting my neighbors in trouble and I felt bad about shooting off my drunken mouth, although with all the flap about illegal immigration the authorities pretty much leave the Chinese people alone, I suppose because they think Chinese people never do anything bad. "Never mind," I said. "Forget it." I took another swig of brandy.

"We are not here to investigate illegal immigration activities," Agent Neufeld said. "We've been assigned to make sure you're not a danger to society, and you're not taking this seriously enough. If you want to go to prison for ten or twenty years, keep screwing around with us and you'll see where it lands you."

"Ha!" I said. "Go ahead and send some harmless little lady to prison for the rest of her life because she called a TV talk show and said something not very nice. You're the one who should be sent to prison, for being a big boob. Speaking of boobs, you are really hot. I'm not kidding. You look *good*. How old are you anyway? Sixty-seven? Sixty-eight? I'll bet you work out. You got any tats?" I was really having a wonderful time.

Deborah stood up, obviously disappointed that her surprise visit failed to provide her with any assurance of my sanity and self-control. "We're going to keep an eye on you, Joanna," she said. She walked to the door with her attack dog following her. As she passed me she said, "You'd better watch your drinking."

"You'd better watch your . . . your . . . whatever." I started laughing like a lunatic. "Did you hear that?" I said. "I couldn't think what to say so I said 'whatever.'" Deborah stopped and gave me this look, and it was the first time that I liked her. In fact, when I saw her face soften like that I kind of loved her. After the two of them left I had another glass of brandy and I felt all keyed up and excited to be in this kerfuffle with the FBI and I even thought I could get Agent Deborah to have sex with me. I started calling all my friends and telling them the whole story and when they expressed concern I just laughed and said fuck them, let them send me to prison for making a stupid phone call. I was really high. One funny thing about this kind of grief is that you have all this adrenaline, and mixed with a lot of really good alcohol it can send you bouncing over the moon.

Of course this morning when I woke up I felt like the biggest idiot in the world and wanted to kill myself. What made it worse was listening to the Chinese immigrants clomping around upstairs. They still refuse to greet me or even acknowledge me. They're making me feel marginalized in my own building. This has been *my* building for the last twenty years. I've had dinner parties and book club and political meetings here and my friends and I hang out on my fire escape in the summer and people are always visiting from out of town. My sister often visits, and when Irma was alive she used to come down here with a plate of homemade tamales, and the two of them would sit at my little kitchen table drinking Mexican beer and jabbering in Spanish and interpreting their jokes for me. And now Irma is showing Mom around heaven and her apartment has been taken over by these depressing people who treat me like a noxious odor they're trying to get away from. When I see them trudging up the stairs with their dour looks, instead of feeling compassion for them I want to take a hose and spray them out the door. I know that sounds awful.

Molly keeps telling me to make an appointment with my shrink or any shrink to get that report done and get the FBI off my back and also to get some different drugs to calm me down. She's very drug-oriented, which is why she continues to put up with her baby daddy who is a heroin addict. She herself takes some kind of SSRI (in addition to pot and tranquilizers when she needs to chill out) but I refuse to take one of those boring antidepressants that she and all my friends are on. They make me feel emotionally and sexually dead. Molly doesn't believe that I have ADHD and thinks that I just take Ritalin for fun, which is not true. But even if I could benefit from some different drugs, Molly should know as well as I do that no shrink wants to get involved with the FBI. They've got enough aggravation with the DEA waiting to snatch away their licenses if they prescribe too many "bad" drugs. Anyway, if the FBI really thought I was some dangerous nutcase they would have hauled me in by now. I think that's what that jerky Buford wants to do, but Agent Deborah is calling the shots and she secretly likes me. That's what I told Molly and I won't bother to tell you her response.

1961–1962

It's a beautiful Saturday afternoon in the fall, and you and Molly are walking home from Lawson's candy store on 176th Street. In between bites of your red licorice stick you're singing the "Jets" song. 'When you're a Jet you're a Jet all the way from your first cigarette to your last dying day!' You've been fascinated with juvenile delinquency ever since the beginning of the summer when you read a magazine article about street gangs in New York City. Last week Molly's mom took you and Molly to see a new movie called *West Side Story* and since then you've been bouncing around your neighborhood singing songs from the movie, picturing yourself as a street kid, wandering among tenements and fire escapes. The other day Molly asked you if you want to be "Anybodys," the geeky girl wanting to get into the Jets, and you were so hurt that you didn't talk to her for hours. Over the summer you grew four inches and sprouted a couple of pimples, and you feel more disgustingly similar to the gruesome Anybodys than to the boy delinquents that you envy, who sport Elvis-style hair and look like the cute pop singers in Molly's fan magazines.

'When you're a Jet let 'em do what they can! You got brothers around, you're a family man!' You bounce along on your sneakers as you sing, imagining that you and Molly are on your way to a rumble with switchblades and homemade "zip guns."

"Shut up!" Molly says, poking you with her elbow. "Look. Your dad is talking to Dr. Simon." You look down the street to where Molly is pointing. Your father is standing on the sidewalk talking to the Negro man who recently moved onto 176th Street, which forms a "T" with Forest Drive. The Simons were the first Negro family to move into the neighborhood, and when your father watched through the window as the movers unloaded the van he said, "Well, all hell's gonna break loose now." You didn't know what he meant but you're always ready for a little excitement. Since then, two other Negro families have moved nearby, and "for sale" signs have begun popping up in front yards. You saw one in Susie's yard and you feel strangely sad at the thought of your old enemy moving away.

Maybe my dad is talking to Dr. Simon about getting his teeth fixed, you say to Molly.

You've been avoiding your father ever since a few months ago, when the Cleveland *News* folded and he lost his job as a newspaper reporter. A few weeks ago he threw Michael's friend Jimmy Rigatoni out of the house for no reason and then screamed at Michael that this dopey, inoffensive kid was "a little piece of shit that you kick around in the street." Last week in the car he flew into a rage at Danny for losing his shoe and started smacking him over and over at a red light and didn't stop even when a man in the next car yelled "Hey you! Stop hitting that kid!" A few days ago he dragged all four kids out of bed for making too much noise and lined you all up in the hallway with your noses touching the wall, and he commanded you all to say "Yes, sir" when asked if you were ready to go back to bed, and when Rosie said "Yes, sir, dumb daddy" he swatted her on the behind (which was the first and last time he ever laid a hand on her). During these events your father's face turns red like a tomato and his eyes get shiny and unfocused, and when he changes back into the jolly, affectionate daddy, minutes or hours later, you're supposed to act as though nothing has happened.

Your father's unpredictable rages are one more reason you envy the street kids who sleep on rooftops and in rail yards and never have to go home. But as you and Molly approach the two men chatting on the sidewalk, your father looks so out of place standing under the bright blue sky in his trousers and sport coat that you suddenly feel protective of him. He looks like a duck out of water. You walk up to him holding out your bag of candy and say, Hi, Daddy! Want a licorice stick?

"No thanks, honey," your father says. "Hi there, Molly Magee." He ruffles Molly's hair, and Molly smiles. Your father has been like a father to her ever since she met him at the age of three. She's never seen him turn into a monster.

"Well, thanks for the advice, Sam," Dr. Simon says. Like your father, he wears trousers and a sport coat and no tie. He doesn't greet you or Molly, but instead looks somewhere over your heads.

"Sure thing, Dave," your dad says. "Remember, these people are idiots. They don't represent the feelings of the rest of your neighbors."

"I know, I know." For some reason, Dr. Simon looks embarrassed. "Thanks again," he says and walks back to his house.

The three of you walk across the street and you say, What happened, Daddy? Who are the one or two idiots?

"Some very sick people put a paper bag full of something that stunk in the Simons' mailbox."

What was it? you ask.

"Probably poop," Molly says, and your father says, "You got it."

Did he call the police? you ask. Your father shakes his head. You ask him why not and he doesn't answer. He doesn't seem to want to answer your questions. "Did the poop get on the rest of the mail?" you ask, but your dad just waves a hand at you and walks up the walk toward your house, and you and Molly continue walking around the neighborhood.

During recess on Monday, you and Molly tell Bagel about the poop put in the Simons' mailbox, and Bagel says that wasn't very nice. But then she adds: "But maybe they shouldn't have moved there in the first place."

Why not? you ask her.

"Yeah, why not?" Molly says. "The Simons are nice people." The day after the Simons moved in, your mom and *bobie* went over with a Jell-o mold to welcome them to the neighborhood, and the next day Molly's mother went over with a Hungarian strudel.

"Well, they have their own neighborhoods to live in," Bagel says. You tell her that Negro and white people should all live together. "That's not true, Joanna," Bagel says. "A lot of them are dangerous. Do you want people walking down our street carrying knives?"

What are you talking about? you say. You're terribly disappointed to realize that your friend is one of those prejudiced people, like the bigots down South who use the word *nigger*, which is the worst word in the English language, and hang Negroes from trees and burn crosses on their lawns. In an instant your whole opinion of Bagel has changed. I don't know where you heard that baloney, you say to her.

"From my father."

You say, well I think your father is wrong. The bell rings and you return to class, where you are enjoying the fifth grade. The teacher, Mrs. Weiss, is a popular livewire who is amused by your passion for *West Side Story* and even allowed you to recite "Cool" in front of the class. ("Boy, boy, crazy boy, be cool boy!") Another nice thing about fifth grade is that Susie is no longer acting snooty, but instead has become strangely quiet and withdrawn in class, which you assume is because she feels guilty about how obnoxious she's been since moving to your neighborhood and coming to Judson Elementary.

The following Saturday, you and Molly walk down to the Shaker Lee Theater to see *The Ladies Man* with Jerry Lewis, and afterward the two of you decide to see what's going on at your house and you find your parents and Shirley, Molly's mom, setting up folding chairs in your living room.

You ask your parents what they're doing, and where all the chairs came from.

"From the JCC," your father says, meaning the Jewish Community Center. "We're having a little meeting here tomorrow evening, after you get back from Sunday school."

"Your parents have invited some of the neighbors over to talk about the Negro families moving in," says Shirley, who looks nice in her blue A-line dress which she wore today at her job at Higbee's department store. Shirley is nice to look at, with her curly auburn hair, high cheekbones, spray of freckles over her nose, and blue eyes that miss nothing. Molly is always fighting with her mom, but you love her. You always know where you stand with Shirley, unlike with your own parents, who are either hysterically mad or wildly affectionate.

What are you gonna talk about at the meeting? you ask.

"Shirley and your mother and I prefer living in an integrated community," your father tells you, as he opens one of the folding chairs. "That's what the meeting is about."

You mean to try to get more Negroes to move in? you say. Your father looks slightly annoyed, so you don't pursue it and instead you ask if you and Molly can come to the meeting.

"You may come and Molly can come if it's okay with Shirley," says your father.

The next day, more than twenty people crowd into your living room. Your mom has sent Michael, Rosie, and Danny to spend the evening with Bobie and Zadie, who live on the next street even though they spend most of their time at your house. You and Molly sit on the couch, nicely dressed in slacks and sweaters. Shirley sits next to Molly, wearing a sharp-looking green pants suit. You're proud to see that you and Molly are the only kids in the room. Bagel's parents, Joey and Donna Green, are sitting in one of the back rows, and you wonder what they've told Bagel about the meeting. You're pleasantly surprised to see Mr. Harrison sitting next to Bagel's dad, since he's a bachelor who doesn't interact much with his neighbors except for the kids who come over to play with Punky the dog. Your mom is all dressed up in one of her stylish skirts and blouses, serving coffee, in plastic party cups, that she's made in a big percolator. She's smiling and chatting, but you can tell that she's a nervous wreck without Bobie there to help her. You love your mother when she's with other people, acting all nervous and girlish.

The bell rings and your mom scurries to the door and lets in Mr. and Mrs. Moscowitz. "Hello, how nice to see you," your mom says. "Have a seat and make yourselves comfortable. Can I take your coats?"

"No, tenk you," Mr. Moscowtiz said. He and his wife walk past your mom to the back of the room, behind the other guests, and just stand there in their coats, and the smile drains from your mother's face. You want to strangle Susie's parents for being rude to your mother.

"Can I have your attention please," your father says. He's standing in front of the guests, wearing his trousers and sport jacket. You wish he would occasionally dress like Bagel's dad, in jeans and flannel shirts, but he doesn't work in a factory like Joey Green and always has to look perfect. Your mom offers your dad a cup of coffee and he says "No thanks, honey," and your mom puts the coffee on a bookcase and sits down in the front row.

You suddenly feel scared for your father. You're afraid he'll say something that people will think is stupid, even though your mother told you he had the second highest I.Q. in his division in the Army and everyone usually shuts up whenever he starts to talk. But lately your father isn't very normal-acting, although he seemed happy that he finally landed a job with a public relations company last week and is due to start work tomorrow.

"First of all I want to thank you all for coming this evening," your father says to the people gathered in the living room. "To tell you the truth, it was probably completely unnecessary for me and my wife to invite you over here tonight, because I know that my neighbors are all intelligent enough to see the utter stupidity of stuffing the pockets of real estate agents who feed on irrational fear."

"Mr. Jacobs, get to the point," says a bald man that you've seen hosing his bushes when you and your friends stray from your block. You want to tell the man to shut up and listen, but you're afraid that maybe your father didn't say the right thing to start the meeting. Maybe people are already getting bored, before the meeting has even started.

"My point, John, is that blockbusters work very hard to con- vince people that a single Negro family will cause their property values to sink lower than the Dead Sea," says your dad. "And even though I've seen for-sale signs pop up here and there, I have every confidence that most of my neighbors understand the value of living with respectable Negro neighbors who want the same things for their families as they do."

"Like what for instance?" calls out a thin, pointy-nosed woman. "Like shooting birds and squirrels in back alleys and cooking them?"

"What are you talking about, Gertie?" a man says, and you are wondering the same thing.

"That's what they did when they started moving onto my block on Kinsman," says the pointy-nosed woman. "They act like they're still living in shacks down in Alabama!" You're wondering if this woman should have been invited to the meeting. Maybe she got in by accident.

"Now that they've taken over Kinsman, why can't they just stay there?" says a huge woman in a floppy hat. "But no-o-o! They have to come over here and run our neighborhood into the ground!" She waves her hands around at the imaginary invasive Negroes.

"What's your name?" your father asks the large woman.

"Sally Butz," the woman says. "I live around the corner, on 175th Street, and I've been very happy there until now."

"So, Sally," says your dad, "you're trying to tell us that Dr. Simon, the dentist across the street from my house, and his schoolteacher wife are going to run the neighborhood to the ground? Come on, you know better than that. If anyone is going to run the neighborhood to the ground, it's the idiots who stuck a bag of crap in the Simons' mailbox yesterday."

"It serves them right for coming where they're not wanted!" says the pointy-nosed woman.

"Now now," says a tall, older man. "Let's get hold of ourselves. We can just make a pact to not sell to 'em. If we just stay put we can keep things as they are. It's not gonna do any good to panic."

"What are you talking about?" says the big woman in the floppy hat. "We represent maybe one percent of the people in this neighborhood. How are we gonna stop 'em from selling to the first colored family that makes them an offer and hightailing it outa here? Those people back there already put out their for sale sign. I don't even know why they showed up here." She's talking about Mr. and Mrs. Moscowitz, who are still standing in the back of the room with their coats on.

"I showed up to be polite to Mr. Jacobs," Mr. Moscowitz says. "He came personally to my house to invite me." You and Molly look at each other in shock. Your father actually went to Susie's house to invite her parents to the meeting? You wonder how many other houses he went to while you weren't looking.

"So take off your for sale sign and stick around," says the bald man to Mr. and Mrs. Moscowitz. "Stick around until more of 'em come and pretty soon they're all over the place, eatin' their fried chicken and watermelon in their yards and tossin' chicken bones in the street." The man laughs an ugly laugh that reminds you of the laugh of the devil in one of the *Twilight Zone* episodes.

"Now listen," Shirley Katz says. She leans forward on the couch so she can address the bald man. "I don't like that kind of talk. The people who have moved into our neighborhood are no different from us. They're hardworking people who want to raise their families in a good neighborhood and live decent lives. Dr. Simon across the street is a dentist and his wife is a school-teacher, and their daughter is in the gifted program at school. I had a Negro art teacher, Sarah Pendleton, who was as classy a gal as you'd ever want to meet. I don't buy this nonsense about chicken bones thrown all over the yard." You notice that Molly is sitting up straight and tall, instead of slouching like she usually does around her mother.

"Thank you, Shirley," says your father. "It's about time some-one here spoke something other than utter nonsense. As I was saying, there are a lot of greedy blockbusters out there who are profiting handsomely from the . . . the *ludicrous* misconception that Negroes are any different from anyone else."

"They are different, Sam," says Joey Green, Bagel's father. He stands up and puts his hands on his hips, the way he does when he's joking around, but now he's not joking. "You need to face reality, my friend," he says to your father. "I've lived among colored people. I grew up with them. I don't need to be educated by the likes of you or anyone else about colored people. There are a lot of decent ones, and I certainly don't excuse anybody putting a bag of whatever in the mailbox of Mr. Simon over there—"

"*Dr.* Simon," sneers the large woman in the floppy hat.

"Dr. Simon or whatever," Joey says. "But like I was saying, by and large, my experiences with colored people have been negative, and I don't need to go through all that again in the neighborhood where I have chosen to raise my family!" Some people clap, and Joey sits down and nods at his wife.

"Joey, you don't know what you're talking about," says your dad.

"Yes, Mister, he does!" yells a woman with puffy hair and caked-on makeup. "He knows exactly what he's talking about! You invite us all over here and then stand up there and act like you know better than everyone. You might not know what these nigras can do to a neighborhood, but you don't have to pretend that it's perfectly fine to live with a bunch of 'em all around you. Like those people standing up back there, I just came to your little meeting to be polite, but I'm beginning to see that it's a waste of my time. The reality is, like that gentleman just said, they ruin every neighborhood they live in because they don't know how to behave. They're not clean and they engage in criminal behavior. These are proven facts. So don't be preaching to people who know better than you. I don't care if you are some kind of professional whatever-you-are."

You can't believe what you're hearing. The color has drained out of your mother's face, and your father just looks confused. You want to run up to them and throw a blanket around them, like men on TV do to their horses when a storm is coming.

"Well, the Jews don't mind living with the colored," the large woman says. "Our grocer down on Kinsman, Mr. Stein, even hired a couple of 'em to sweep up the store and things like that."

"They'll rob him blind," says the pointy-nosed woman. She clutches her purse to her chest and nods self-importantly.

"What about those Jewish folks back there?" says the bald man, looking back at Mr. and Mrs. Moscowitz. "They're getting the hell out of here as fast as they can. They probably already sold to a colored family."

"I didn't sell to nobody!" Mr. Moscowitz sputters, pointing a quivering finger at the bald man. "I came to this country to live wherever I wanted to live! I come from Poland! You know what it was there, in Poland? It wasn't so nice there! I come here to live among nice people! I don't need nobody telling me who to live with, who to sell my home to, nothing! I am a free man!"

"Nobody said you weren't," says Mr. Harrison. "This is the land of the free." You hope that Mr. Harrison isn't being sarcastic, since he's always been nice to you, letting you walk Punky and calling you "Red" because you wear Red Ball Jets sneakers.

"If I want to go to a different part of the city, I will do it!" Mr. Moscowitz fumes. "If I want to live on a good block with good decent people, this does not make me some kind of bad guy! All right, so the guy over there, the doctor, is okay. That doesn't mean I want to live with a whole bunch of *schvartzes* all around my house!"

"What you could say, Moscowitz," says your father, "is that you want to live among people who are good neighbors, regardless of what color they are. But clearly you don't have the good sense to understand what decency is all about, since you are very quick to use the most indecent language when referring to Negroes."

"What's he talking about?" the puffy-haired lady says loudly.

"*Schvartze*," Joey Green says. "All it means is black in Jewish. He's blowing his top over a simple word that means black."

"It's an offensive word," Shirley says. "It's simply not nice to use that word to refer to a person of a different color."

"Oh, come on, come on," Mr. Harrison says. He stands up and puts his meaty hands on his hips. "Try opening your eyes there, Jacobs," he says. "Joey is right. The colored people are different. Are you gonna be best buddies with some colored family that moves next door to you? You expect the Moscowitzes back there to stay put while those people that moved in down the street let those two boys of theirs do whatever they want with their daughter? I've been your neighbor for a long time and I never had no problems with you or your kids, but I've often thought you were a little highfalutin for my taste, and this damn meeting proves it. You're livin' in another world. Everyone knows those people carry diseases, they let their kids run wild, they steal and rob in the middle of the night. They're dangerous, and if you want your daughters around their sons, that's your business. That guy back there has the right idea. Get the hell out. Sonny boy, you're living on a different planet from the rest of us, and that's all there is to it."

Who's sonny boy? you whisper to Molly.

"Your dad," Molly whispers back.

You feel sick. Mr. Harrison, who's always been so nice to you, who adopted an ugly scorched dog that nobody wanted, has turned into the devil before your eyes. Nobody has ever called your father "sonny boy" before, and nobody ever will again. Your father is standing there, looking upset, and you wonder if he's going to blow up and kill everyone in the room. But then you see your mother shake her head briefly at him, and he just waves at the room in disgust. "Well, I guess this meeting was a waste of time," he says.

"Darn right it was a waste of time," Mr. Harrison says. "I'm goin' home to watch *Perry Mason*." He grabs his jacket from the back of the chair and starts walking to the door.

"Hold on, Pete," Joey says. "We're comin' with you." Joey gets up and starts putting on his jacket, and your mom hurries into the bedroom and returns with his wife's coat. Bagel's mom takes the coat without even saying thank you, and they follow Mr. Harrison out the door. After that the room is a flurry of jackets and coats being returned and put on and people leaving. You sit on the couch, frozen. You feel like dying. Your mother is trying to smile at people and you know she feels awful, and your dad is just standing in the front of the room looking dazed.

Most of the people leaving after the meeting have not a word to say to your dad, and maybe a cursory "thanks for having us" to your mom. But at one point during the mass exit a man with a stubbly face and gray hair goes up to your dad and says, "It's okay, buddy, you had the right idea. These people just don't understand tryin' to make the world a better place. You just keep on doin' what you're doin'." Your dad nods at him, and the man pats him on the shoulder and walks to the door. "Thanks for the coffee, sweetie," he says to your mom, who smiles at him and lets him out.

Mr. Moscowitz walks out the door without a word, but Mrs. Moscowitz goes up to your mom, who is clearing away cups, and says, "Tenk you for inviting us, Isabel. You're a good lady." "Thank you for coming, Ida," your mom says, and Mrs. Moscowitz says to your dad, "Good-bye, Sam," and walks out the door after her husband. You decide that you don't hate Susie's mother anymore, only her father. Maybe Mr. Moscowitz is keeping both his wife and daughter enslaved in that awful house, making them serve him Polish tea and stale bread.

For the next several weeks you feel bad about the meeting. You wanted your parents to be the heroes of the neighborhood. Even though you prefer to keep your distance from them lately, you're proud of them. They're attractive and charming and stylish, and seem to be the center of the adult universe. Their friends and relatives enjoy gathering at your house, listening to your father lecture about politics, and vying for your mom's attention, sharing all their personal business with her. You've never seen any adults act hostile with your parents, the way your neighbors did at the meeting, and you're shocked and repelled by their nastiness and bigotry.

A few weeks after the meeting, Susie and her parents move away. You and Molly stand in front of Susie's house, watching the movers load the van with furniture. Susie comes out of the house not looking at all like herself. Her curly brown hair is uncombed and she's wearing blue jeans, of all things.

What are you doing in jeans? you say to Susie.

"I made my mother buy them for me," Susie says. "I'm going to wear them every day, even at school!"

You can't wear them to school, you say, giving her a strange look. You ask her where she's moving.

"We're moving far, far away!" Susie turns and waves her arm somewhere into the distance, as though signaling a plane. "To a wonderful place called Cleveland Heights!"

You ask her where it is. You've never heard of Cleveland "Heights."

"I don't know, it's somewhere," Susie says, still smiling, but you can tell that she's sad, although you're not sure why. Susie's never acted as though she likes Forest Drive.

Susie's parents walk out of the house and lock the door. Well, bye, Susie Ratty, you say, softening the less friendly "Susie Ratface."

"Good luck," Molly says.

The three of them get in their old green Studebaker, and Mr. Moscowitz backs down the driveway and follows the moving van down the street. You make a comment to Molly about how weird Susie was acting, but watching the car disappear down the street you feel an ache in your gut, which you don't understand. You don't even like Susie, and yet watching the car leave you feel almost as sad as if it had been Molly disappearing down the street.

Winter settles over Cleveland and your neighborhood quiets down. During Christmas vacation you go with your family to a family camp called Circle Oaks, where the kids sleep in cabins and the adults sleep in a lodge with a big fireplace, and in the evenings everyone gathers in the lodge and sings songs like "This Land is Your Land," "If I Had a Hammer," and "I'm Stickin' with the Union." A famous musician named Pete Seeger visits the camp and gets everyone singing along with him to "Michael Row Your Boat Ashore" and "Joe Hill," which is about a dead union hero. ("I dreamed I saw Joe Hill last night alive as you and me . . .") You're having a wonderful time at camp until one evening when your father gets into an argument with a man who brags that he was a conscientious objector during the war. Your dad calls the man a "despicable coward," and you're confused because your parents have always said that peace is a lot better than war, and you feel bad that once again your father is making himself an outsider in a crowd. What makes it worse is that these are your parents' people, the people who believe in peace and brotherhood and unions. It doesn't seem right that your father should be an outsider in his own tribe, and drag your mom along with him. Your mom always wants to be part of things and to get along with everyone.

After the winter thaw the blockbusters start doing their work, just as your dad predicted. They don't go to your house, most likely having been warned about the crazy Jewish man, but they go everywhere else, warning people to get out while they can, and the color of the neighborhood changes rapidly. Bagel's parents sell their house to a Negro man who works at Joey's plant, and they move with their daughters to the west side of Cleveland. Your dad says it's a strange neighborhood for Jews to move to. "I guess Joey figured it was better to be the only Jews than the only whites," he says. You and Molly go over to say good-bye to Bagel, promising to visit her on the West Side, but you know it will never happen.

After the school year, Shirley Katz, who is tired of being harassed by the blockbusters, moves with her daughters to an eastern suburb called Greenvale, where a lot of Jews are moving. You go over to say good-bye to Molly, and are surprised that you don't feel very sad. Maybe it's because, unlike with Bagel, you know that this friendship isn't over, although you would feel somewhat better if your friend was moving downtown, which is the only other part of the city you're familiar with. You love going to baseball and football games at Cleveland Stadium with your dad, and you also love going downtown on the yellow "rapid transit" with your mom, where the two of you go shopping and then enjoy a special "ladies' lunch" at Higbee's. When you picture the "suburbs," you envision rows of rectangular houses with nothing around them but empty air.

Your parents have decided they need a bigger house, especially because they want your grandparents to move in with them, and they've started looking in Ludlow, Cleveland's only "integrated" neighborhood. Just when they're about to give up finding a four-bedroom house in Ludlow, your dad gets a call from his best friend, Harold Eisner, who lives in Greenvale, where Molly has moved with her mom and sister. Harold tells your dad about a good deal on a four-bedroom colonial there, and a month later you and your family move into the house, on a winding street of stately homes about a mile from where Molly now lives. There are no Negroes in Greenvale, but there are plenty of Jews, which suits your parents fine. They like living among Jews even more than they like living among Negroes.

A year after the meeting at your house, the only whites left on your half of Forest Drive are Dora and Frank Szabo, the Hungarian couple who bought the Moscowitzes' house. But the Szabos, who both have numbers on their arms, don't much care about being the only whites in the area. With all the trouble they've had in their lives, none of it has been with Negroes.

Nice October Day 1 PM

I finished the above chapter yesterday morning, and it made me very sad, which I hadn't anticipated would happen. I thought it would lift my spirits to recall the way certain adults, like my parents and Molly's mom, rose above the bigotry and intolerance of the time. Our parents may have been clueless about how to raise their kids, but they had good "values," which meant they respected their fellow adults, no matter what color they were. (In those days, *respect* didn't usually extend to children, who were considered possessions rather than separate people. Parents loved their children, but respect for them was as foreign a concept as respect for your dog.) But that meeting came back to me so clearly, and it was even worse than in my story. Not only did Mr. Harrison (his real name) really call my father "sonny boy," but this horrible man named Horace Hickman spit in my father's face before he walked out the door. And my dad just took out his handkerchief and wiped his face, like Gregory Peck in *To Kill a Mockingbird*, except that Gregory Peck was dignified about it and my father was just kind of stricken. Whenever I recall the looks on my parents' faces after that meeting it breaks my heart. They were so bewildered, like those abused animals in the commercials that I can't bear to watch.

After I finished writing yesterday, the whole day went to hell. I decided to do what my mother and grandmother used to do, which was to introduce themselves to new neighbors by bringing over a homemade dish. I made a lovely raspberry Jell-o mold and took it upstairs and knocked on the Chinese people's door. The mold looked all nice and rosy on the plate, jiggling like a plump lady's thighs, and I waited for someone to open the door and smile at my offering, but instead people kept looking through the peephole and walking away. I kept knocking and finally a haunted-looking man in his thirties opened the door and I smiled at him and presented my gift, and he looked at it with fear, as though there were bugs crawling on it, and then he said "sorry, sorry" and shut the door. I went back down and stuck the Jell-o mold in the fridge. What a stupid idea. The man probably never saw a Jell-o mold in his life. He may not even have known it was food.

I lay on my couch, trying to relax before I had to meet my friends at a wine bar in Williamsburg. At some point I heard people running up the stairs and a few moments later I could hear loud male voices upstairs, which sounded to me like people yelling at my Chinese neighbors. It wasn't the first time that I had heard these voices, but I've just been trying to ignore them. But then a few minutes later I heard footsteps on the stairs, and then banging on my door. "What the fuck?" I said, and I got up and opened the door and there were four little punks about sixteen years old standing there. And then it occurred to me that the loud voices had belonged to them, and that they were probably enforcers sent to collect money from those poor people up there, who probably owe every cent they earn to whoever smuggled them out of China.

The kid standing in the front, a good-looking Asian kid with tattoos all around his neck and a strange bowl haircut, said to me, "We need to get in here."

80

"Excuse me?" I said. "What do you mean, you need to get in here? This is my apartment."

A tall, skinny kid behind him, who had tattoos all up and down his arms, said, "Our phones don't work upstairs. They ain't got no connection up there."

"Well go to a Starbucks!" I said. "I don't know you! I don't even know how you got in this building! I'm not letting some strange kids into my apartment. You think I'm crazy?"

"You're crazier than a bedbug with no head and no legs." I looked at the kid who said this and I realized that he wasn't even Asian, like the other three. He was *Jewish*. He was dressed in baggy jeans and a baggy tee shirt like the others, but he was wearing a *yarmulke* and even without the skullcap he had Brooklyn Hasid written all over him. I opened the door wider and stared at him and said, "What the hell are *you* doing here?"

"I'm working," the kid said with the slightly Yiddish accent they all have. "You got a problem with that?"

"I have a problem with a bunch of kids I don't know running around in my building and demanding to enter my apartment," I said.

And he says to me, "Go fry in hell, mama."

My mouth dropped open. "*What did you say to me?*" I said. "*I'll give you such a ZETZ your eyes will fly out of your head!*"

And damn if this little punk didn't try to push through his friends to get at me! But the first punk pushed him away toward the stairs, saying, "Come on, we ain't got time for this bitch now anyway." They started down the stairs, and then the kid bringing up the rear, a chubby Asian kid, turned and grinned at me and made a circle with his thumb and forefinger and jabbed his finger through it a few times.

"That is so rude!" I yelled. I stood there until I heard them leave the building. And then I heard someone coming up the stairs, and I recognized Molly's footsteps. She often stops by lately after meeting with this recalcitrant developer whose office is right down the street from my building. We walked inside, and she asked me who those kids were that she saw leaving the building and I told her what happened.

"Well, what are you going to do?" she asked.

"What the hell am I supposed to do?"

"Report them to the management office?" she asked me with this "duh" look on her face.

"Oh, that's a wonderful idea," I said. Molly knows perfectly well that the "management office" of my building is in the back of a Second Avenue warehouse where two Russian girls who look like pole dancers sit and file their nails. I've never even seen the owner, a Brooklyn "businessman" named Alexi Yurkovich who apparently runs the building as a money-laundering operation. "I'm sure the pole dancers over on Second Avenue will take immediate action as soon as I tell them that four schmendricks are running loose in my building and demanding entrance into my apartment," I said.

"Well you can't just ignore it," Molly said.

"Maybe they won't come back."

"What if they do come back?" I didn't know what to say. "I suppose you think you're going to make them into your little friends," she said.

I almost laughed. Molly knows better than anyone that I tend to over-identify with behaviorally disordered children. "I have no intention of befriending little punks who try to shove their way into my home and tell me to fry in hell," I said.

Since she was done working for the day, I talked her into going with me to meet some of our friends in Williamsburg. On the train she dropped the subject of my altercation with the punks and complained that Billy left a stain on her new sofa, and I tried to be sympathetic although I have no idea how to help her with her junkie baby daddy. When we got to the wine bar our friends were already there, sitting at a big round table. We ordered drinks and then Molly had to go and tell everyone about the rude little thugs, and I had to listen to more ridiculous suggestions.

"You should call the police and report them," Lin said. "You have no idea what they're capable of doing."

"I'm not calling the police, Lin," I said. "First of all I don't want to risk getting my neighbors in trouble. They drive me crazy, but I don't want to be responsible for getting them deported."

"Well they're not supposed to be crowded into a one-bedroom apartment in the first place," Lin said irritably. "It's a health hazard. They might burn the whole building down with you in it." Lin has a terrible attitude about recent immigrants. Her Cantonese family came to New York a million years ago, and they're now ensconced in some McMansion enclave in New Jersey as far away as possible from what Lin calls the "seedy new Chinatowns."

"Those boys are probably packing guns, Joanna," said Marjorie, ominously.

"Oh, for God's sake, they're not going to shoot me," I said. "Just because someone is packing a gun it doesn't mean they're going to shoot you."

"They could kill your neighbors," Julie said. "Did you ever think of that?"

"They're not going to kill my neighbors!" I yelled. "They're just collecting money from them! Anyway I'm not calling the cops on any kid! I don't care if they're carrying M16s!"

"Honey, nobody carries M16s anymore," Louis said. "That's from the Vietnam War." And he looked at his husband, Damien, and they both snickered.

"Like you both know so much about Vietnam," I said.

"Have you ever considered moving out of there?" Julie said. "I know you're fond of that building, but isn't it kind of falling apart?"

"No it's not falling apart, Julie," I said. "Older buildings are made of sturdier materials than a lot of the newer ones. And anyway, where am I going to find another one-bedroom apartment with high ceilings and nice big windows in New York City for a thousand dollars a month? *I mean please! You know what? You're all starting to get on my nerves!*"

"Like she never gets on our nerves," Molly said, and everyone laughed, including me because I'm such a wonderful sport.

Anyway, after I woke up today I wasn't mad at my friends anymore because they mean well. Instead of getting all upset with them I should have just let their "suggestions" roll right off me, since they're all crazier than I am. Lin and Marjorie have been married for two years but when you're with them they don't sit together or talk to each other or even act as though they know each other, which I find extremely bizarre. Louis and Damien are doing some kind of purge where they throw up every two hours, and Julie is fucking a three-hundred-pound dominatrix up in the Bronx that she's fallen in love with. Meanwhile Molly spends her whole life yelling and screaming at her baby daddy for not helping with Zoey's college tuition when he can barely afford his heroin.

I don't know why I have to have crazy friends. Most of them are gay and gay people do tend to be crazy, especially older ones who suffered so much oppression during their youth. But a lot of gay people have managed to deal with their shit and find the perfect partner and maybe even get a kid or two and lead well-adjusted lives. I even know some of those people, but they're not my close friends. Most of my close friends are these tormented, unstable crazy people. Except I do have one group of friends, my dinner group of straight Jewish women, who are mostly happy and contented and successful, but actually they irritate me as much as my crazy friends, with their bubbly chatter about their adorable husbands and their Alaskan cruises and the latest farm-to-table restaurant. Junie, my former therapist who is now my friend, would say, "Why do you think you can't stand your friends lately?" And I would have to say, "Because I can't stand myself." Actually we did have this conversation, on the phone the other day.

Oh God. I just got a text from my buddy Robbie. He saw an FBI-looking sedan drive past him on Fourth Avenue and turn onto Forty-Fifth Street. I'll bet they're coming here with a warrant. They'll tear my whole place apart. They'll find my pot. I should get out of here RIGHT NOW! If I go out the back door they won't see me. My car is parked on the side street and I can get an early start on my Voom shift. Oh-oh. Robbie was right. There's the unmarked car, parking under the expressway. There's something really wrong with me. I'm high as a kite that Deborah Neufeld is coming here. Maybe it's not her. Yes, it is. Deborah is getting out of the car. She's crossing the street carrying her briefcase, and guess what? That dickhead, Agent Buford, is not with her. Maybe she wants to have sex with me. I think instead of trying to escape I'll stay here and see what she wants. Or else I could tell her I'm busy and refuse to open the door. That would be almost as entertaining as the last time she came over here, when I was drunk on my ass.

1962–1963

Greenvale is a soulless lily-white suburb when you move there with your family in the summer of 1962 (although in recent years your mother was surrounded by black neighbors who adored her and came to her funeral). But when you arrive in Greenvale at the age of eleven, you're not conscious of the neighborhood at first; you're just excited to be living in a big new house. You and your siblings romp through the empty rooms, watching them gradually fill up with beautiful furniture and paintings, and your parents take you and Rosie to pick out carpeting, curtains, and bedspreads for your rooms. (Before you turned it into a den for yourself many decades later, the green-and-purple room with its shag carpeting was absurdly frozen in time.) It's nice to see your *bobie* hurrying through the kitchen, making her delicious foods like stuffed cabbage and chopped liver, and *Zadie* sitting at the table hunched over his herring and his Yiddish newspaper.

But after about a month of being enchanted by the house, you want to get away from your family and go outside, the way you've always done, and you realize that you're trapped. The only people you ever see outside are the mailman, a lady walking a big white dog every evening, and the man across the street who obsessively prunes his bushes. The street is eerily quiet. No chorus of kids' shrieks and yells and laughter. No balls slapping into gloves, roller skates roaring over pavements, little girls breathlessly chanting "A—my name is Alice and my brother's name is

Brian!," mothers calling out their doors, "Time for dinner!" No after-dark games of hide-and-seek and Ollie ollie in-free or catching fireflies in jars, or flash gatherings around the ice cream truck. (Strangely, your siblings seem contented to play inside the house all day, but they're too young to understand that they've been transported to a kind of prison.)

Molly has been living in Greenvale since the beginning of the summer, and you think about her all the time and wonder what her neighborhood is like. You know that she lives near Steven Eisner, whose dad is your dad's best friend, and you've been to Steven's house many times with your parents but you've usually played inside. All you know about the neighborhood is that it's called "Little Jerusalem" because it's so full of Jews. You've talked to Molly a couple of times on the phone, and your friend has told you about some of the kids she's met on her block, and you realize that you're going to have to compete with them for Molly's attention. It makes you tired just thinking about it.

On a hot August day, a few weeks after moving to Landover Lane, you can no longer contain your curiosity about Molly's new life and you get on your bike and ride to Little Jerusalem. You're surprised to feel nervous as you cross Belmont Boulevard and turn toward Wren Drive. You peddle up Wren and cross Terrace Road and enter Little Jerusalem, and suddenly you see where all the action is in Greenvale. Kids on this side of Terrace Road are swarming all over the place, running in and out of the box houses, darting through sprinklers, riding bikes, walking down the street in shorts over bathing suits, towels slung over their shoulders, on the way to Beemis Park pool. It reminds you of your dad's home movies, when the people and houses are frozen and he hits a button and everything starts moving again, everything comes back alive.

You turn down a side street and find Doris Drive, and ride halfway up the block, where you find Molly standing on the sidewalk talking to a girl and two boys, one of whom is Steven Eisner. You've known Steven your whole life. Since you were four years old one of your favorite activities has been to make "ickle bickle," a disgusting concoction of any liquids you can find in Steven's sticky, messy kitchen or your own spotless one, and daring each other (unsuccessfully) to drink it. You're pleased to see Molly and Steven together. You always like your friends to get to know one another.

"Hi, Joanna!" Steven says as you brake next to the group of kids and straddle your bike. His bright smile reveals new braces. Since you last saw him, many months ago, he's grown a couple of inches, but he's still skinny, with the same old cowlick sticking up. He wears a striped tee shirt and brown shorts, and his bright brown eyes look as though they want to pull you into them and give you a warm bath. Steven loves being around people.

"Hi," Molly says to you, not looking exactly ecstatic to see you. But you understand that Molly is getting to know new kids and that you're distracting her. Molly wears a fashionable outfit of red shorts, a yellow and red polka-dot top, and sandals, and her blond hair is in two neat braids.

So where's your house? you ask Molly.

"Right here." Molly nods toward the house you're standing in front of, which looks like all the bungalows on the block, except the shutters are painted different colors. Molly's shutters are painted a light green.

Oh, you say. It's nice.

"They were telling me about our sixth-grade teacher," Molly says.

"He wears a bow tie and yellow socks, if you can believe it," says the girl. She has frizzy red hair and braces, and she wears white shorts, a sloppy-looking orange blouse, and old-looking blue sneakers. Because she looks smart, you get the impression that she dresses like this deliberately, rather than because she doesn't know any better.

"My sister had him," says the other boy, a stocky, nice-looking kid with a crewcut who bounces up and down on the balls of his feet. His eyes dart around and his mouth twitches with amusement. He gives the impression of being what your mom would call a "livewire." "She said he brings his pet rats to school."

"You'll probably let them out of their cages," Steven says, and the boy and the girl laugh.

"I heard he's really hard," the girl says. "Doesn't he assign, like, ten-page book reports?"

"Well, we are in the gifted class," Steven says. "The work is supposed to be hard."

Are we all getting him? you ask.

"I don't think you're getting him," Steven says. "I'm pretty sure you're going to be in Miss Finkle's class."

What do you mean? you say. What about Molly?

"They're putting me in the gifted class," Molly said, wrinkling her nose and showing her teeth, but her "mad bunny" face doesn't make you laugh the way it usually does.

And I'm not in it? You turn to Steven, hoping you heard wrong.

"For some reason they put you in the other class." After seeing your reaction, Steven looks as upset as you are. "My mom said you really belong in the gifted class," he says. "She said you're very bright and the only reason they didn't put you in our class is that you don't test well." You remember taking "standardized tests" at school but never paid much attention to them. But you assume that Steven knows what he's talking about. Joan Eisner volunteers a couple times a week at Borland Elementary and knows everything that goes on there.

"Your teacher is kind of a crazy lady," the crew-cutted boy says.

"Ricky Klein, that's not nice," says the red-headed girl.

"Well, she kind of is," Steven says. He doesn't like to lie.

"Well, that's true," says the red-headed girl. "She wears these short-short skirts and these little white boots, like one of those tarty ladies in magazines. Last year she told one of the boys in her class not to throw the dodge ball at girls' bosoms because they're *sensitive*." Everyone laughs except you. "My mom said if I had been in that class she would have called the school and complained," the girl says. "She said she shouldn't even be teaching at Borland."

You try to pay attention to the rest of the conversation, but you barely hear the kids chattering about their teacher, Mr. Toledo, having lived in Copenhagen, Steven's nine-year-old brother Charley (a friend of your brother Michael) falling off his bike into a thornbush, the mean new lifeguard at Beemis Pool, and a neighborhood delicatessen called "Saul's" that serves a wonderful drink called a "chocolate phosphate."

"Why don't we all go to my house?" Steven says.

But you say you have to go home because your father is grilling out. You're both relieved to be leaving the other kids and heartbroken to be separated from them, from their future lives in the gifted class with Mr. Toledo. You ride your bike home blinking back tears. You hate yourself more than you have ever hated anyone in the world. You hate being so conceited that you thought you were smart, and now it turns out that you're really dumb. You hate being too tall and having pimples and an ugly bite plate and creepy, curly hairs that have sprung up on places on your body where you don't even like to look. You hate wanting to be a juvenile delinquent instead of a ballet dancer or a nurse or Princess Grace like some normal girl your age. As you ride home, you wish you were anyone other than yourself. You wish you were your cousin Mark.

You say nothing to your parents about not being in the gifted class. You're too ashamed about being considered "dumb" by the school authorities in spite of your excellent grades to even want to talk about it. For the rest of the summer you occasionally talk to Molly on the phone but don't go back to visit her or Steven. You spend all your time hanging around the house because there's nothing else to do. You feel like sleeping your days away, but you force yourself to act normal so that your parents won't bug you. You watch the Indians' games with your brothers and laugh with them, making fun of old Aunt Frieda who makes horrible lumpy casseroles and Uncle Harry whose shoes squeak when he walks. But the big house doesn't have the cozy, crowded feeling of the old house on Forest Drive. Strangely, it provides even less protection from your parents than the old house did, because you don't always know where they are, and at any moment one or both of them might walk into the room and start talking to you in their loud voices, bursting into your private space like a hand popping a paper bag. One day you discover a book on your parents' shelf in the den called *The Rise and Fall of the Third Reich*, and you find a chapter on horrible medical experiments conducted on Jewish prisoners at the Auschwitz concentration camp, and you pore over descriptions of the terrible things done to the starving, squirming, howling Jews by a monstrous man named Dr. Mengele. You return to the book every day after that, devouring the same nauseating passages, like someone gorging on hundreds of marshmallows burnt to a crisp and getting sicker and sicker but not being able to stop.

You're actually relieved to start school and end the dreary summer, and the first day you even feel a little frisky in your new orange and green skirt, matching socks, and new loafers. You walk to Borland Elementary with your three siblings (Danny is just starting kindergarten!), then part ways with them and find your way to your sixth-grade classroom. The teacher, who is standing in front of the room, looks like a witch. She has long black hair, pale skin, red lipstick and a mysterious smile, as though she knows which tree she has hidden the children in. She wears a very short black skirt and white ankle boots which later are to be called "go-go boots." The teacher smiles at you when you walk in, but fortunately you don't have to talk to her because she's put name cards on all the desks. The girls have pink name cards and the boys have purple ones. A glance around the room shows mature-looking twelve-year-old girls in pretty skirts and blouses, and dorky-looking boys of all shapes and sizes. You find your seat near the windows, next to a girl whose name card reads "Robin," and whom you instinctively know is popular since she is petite and blond and is smiling as though she likes herself. (It's an unspoken rule that if you're petite and blond you're automatically popular, even if you have zits, which Robin does not, except for a small one on her chin.)

The teacher waits until all the kids have arrived and the bell rings. Then she starts to talk. "Hello, dear boys and girls!" she says. "I'm Geri Finkle, your new teacher." You see one of the girls up front smirk at the girl sitting next to her, and the second girl rolls her eyes. "We're gonna have all kinds of fun in this class!" Miss Finkle says. "I don't go for this learning should be hard stuff. Learning should be fun! I'm not saying you won't work hard. But also I expect you to be EN-GAGED!" She writes the word "ENGAGED" in big white letters on the blackboard. "Engaged means intensely interested! And when we're interested in something, it's easier to learn about it. Am I right? Am I right, Alan?" She points at a big dumpy boy with frizzy hair who looks as though he's on the verge of falling asleep. The boy nods stupidly. "Okay, so." The teacher claps the chalk from her hands and continues talking. "This is a very confusing time of life for all of you. You are on the verge of adolescence. You are no longer children. Although you boys are still closer to childhood than you girls. You girls are maturing more quickly than the boys. That's why I want to see you act like YOUNG LADIES"—she wildly scrawls "YOUNG LADIES" on the board while continuing to look at the class—"and not silly little girls. For example. I see Robin over there chewing gum. That is not a womanly activity. In this class I will teach you social skills as well as academic skills. One thing you will learn is that chewing gum makes you look unattractive. I want my class to have class!" she says as she walks up to Robin, who looks a little scared. The teacher holds her hand under Robin's mouth, and Robin spits the gum into Miss Finkle's hand. As Miss Finkle tosses the mangled piece of Juicy Fruit underhanded into the wastebasket, Robin whispers to you, "She's crazy," and you nod enthusiastically, pleased to be chosen as a confidante and in total agreement with Robin. It's obvious that this teacher is off her rocker, and you wonder if the school authorities saw any evidence of it when they hired her.

Just as you've expected, the school year starts out very badly. Most of your classmates have known one another since kindergarten, and instead of being known as the funny, fun girl, as you were at Judson Elementary, you're known as the gawky, geeky new girl. The teacher seems to care about you even less than the kids do. She treats the more mature, popular girls like her girlfriends, whispering and giggling with them, and she flirts with the boys even though they still act like ten-year-olds, but she pays little attention to you, who are neither popular nor a boy. What makes everything worse is that this school has homework, which you've never had before, and although you trudge home with your books every day you can't concentrate on anything you read. Several times Miss Finkle puts you at a long table in the back of the room to work on your lessons while everyone else takes breaks and listens to the teacher tell amusing stories like about the time she went "skinny-dipping" with some friends and when she screamed the first time she got her period and her mother called it her "red scare." (The teacher will be fired at the end of the year.)

You refuse to accept being the dorky new girl and work hard to get your classmates to like you, but it's like trudging up a steep hill with rocks tumbling down towards you. You laugh loudly at a popular girl's fresh remark at the teacher, and another popular girl turns and gives you an annoyed look. You walk up to a group of girls chattering in the playground during recess but they're talking about their third-grade teacher so you have nothing to contribute and just stand there like a dork and finally walk away. One day, after making an excellent comment about a chapter in *Tom Sawyer*, you see the teacher glance over at you and pass a note to pretty, dark-haired Laura Davis, who is president of the sixth-grade book club, and Laura comes up to you during recess and says, "Joanna, I have to talk to you," and you expect her to ask you to join the book club but instead she says, "Miss Finkle asked me to help you do something with your hair." Although you're highly insulted, the next morning you brush your hair until it shines, and when neither Laura nor Miss Finkle comment on it you're almost as offended as you were the day before when your hair was made a subject of discussion.

You don't feel like visiting Molly or even talking to her because you're still ashamed of being in the "dumb class," and whenever you see her at recess, usually talking to one or more confident-looking girls, you're too shy to go over. Finally you can't take it anymore and call Molly one evening and ask her to come over and see your new house. Molly comes over on a Saturday and talks to your mom in the kitchen about how gorgeous the house is until you drag her upstairs where she tells you a horrible story about how babies are made, which makes you feel terrible about the whole human race. (Your parents read you a book a couple years ago called *The Wonderful Story of How You Were Born* but all you remembered from it was a picture of a dot in a frying pan which was "you" before you sprouted arms and legs.) After shocking you with her disgusting report, Molly chatters about her new friends, who include the two most popular girls in your class, Robin Solomon and Laura Davis, the girl who had offered to help you "do something" with your hair. You can't understand why Molly seems to have no trouble making friends and, with the exception of your old friend Steven, who often wanders up and talks to you during recess, everyone treats you as though you have cooties.

The week before winter vacation, Miss Finkle instructs your class to write a five-page book report on any book you choose. "You'll have plenty of time during your break to complete this assignment," she says while everyone groans. But you love to read and don't mind the assignment. You decide to write about *The Diary of Anne Frank*, which you've already read twice. Using the writing techniques taught to you by your journalist father you compose a masterful book report in your neatest left-handed scrawl.

A few days after school starts back up, Miss Finkle faces the class with the stack of book reports. "Your teacher has finished reading your book reports and she is far from pleased," she announces, amusing nobody but herself with her strange choice of pronoun. "We need to work on our writing skills, people!" she shouts, slapping the reports with one hand. "Most of these reports are written at fifth-grade level or below. BUT!" The teacher smiles and lowers her voice. "There are a few exceptions, and one in particular." As you were hoping she would, the teacher looks at you and smiles. "The report by Joanna Jacobs is extraordinary," she says. She walks over to you and places your A-plus report on your desk and then walks back to the front of the room. "Not only did your classmate choose a difficult subject, which is the persecution and extermination of the Jews in Nazi Germany," the teacher continues, "but she wrote this report with great passion, maturity, and skill. Reading this excellent report truly made my day. Joanna, would you please come up here and read your report to the class?"

You read your report, the kids all clap, and your glow lasts for the rest of the day, the whole evening during which your parents praise you for your excellent work, and the following morning, when you come to school feeling light and happy. The next day two kids approach you at recess and ask you to recommend books to read, and Laura Davis invites you to join the book club. That week Elise Scott, a sweet, well-liked girl, invites you home for lunch to sample her mom's famous melted tuna and cheddar cheese sandwiches, and David Roth invites you to his birthday party. (You're pleased to hear that not everyone in class has been invited to David's party, even though the only kids not invited are Alan Durst, who has tantrums during which he lies on the floor and kicks his feet, and Kenny Parisi, who once called David a "Sheeny Jew.")

Becoming the star writer in class is all you need to break out of your funk. You start to have fun again. During recess you have snowball fights with the boys and chat with the girls who like you, such as Elise. Sometimes you wander over to where the "gifted" class is gathered and talk to Molly and Steven and their friends, pretending to be interested in their funny stories about Mr. Toledo. One Sunday afternoon you and Steven go sledding with Ricky Klein, who sticks snow down your back as a gesture of friendship. Another time you invite Molly and Steven out to Kon Tiki with your family, and you all gorge on rich tropical food, and during the ride home Steven calls out, "Can we go out for ice cream?" and everyone cracks up laughing.

On your twelfth birthday the world caves in. You got your first period a few months ago, and you have cramps and aren't in the mood for any party, especially since no kids your age are going to be there. Your favorite cousin Mark is being punished, Steven and Molly both have the flu, along with half their class, and you don't know the kids in your class well enough to invite any of them. It's depressing that the only kids at your party are little kids, and you're especially displeased to see Cousin Leah and her obnoxious eight-year-old son, Barry, walk into the house. Cousin Leah is a dour, unpleasant woman whose husband left her for another woman, and your mom only invites her to all the parties because she feels sorry for her. Cousin Leah says to her son, "Say happy birthday to Joanna" and Barry just walks right past you into the kitchen, where your mom is preparing food, and you hear him yell, "I hate white icing on cake!" Your mom says, "Well, that's Joanna's favorite and she's the birthday girl," and Barry says, "I was the birthday boy last week," and you want to run in there and choke him. Barry wanders out of the kitchen and you go in there and say to your mother, Why does that little twerp have to be here?

"Joanna, please!" your mother says. "Help me with these cups!" She's a nervous wreck since Bobie is with Zadie in Florida and isn't around to help her. "I don't have time for this."

I don't know why you always have to invite them to everything, you say scowling.

"His mother is divorced from his father," your mother says. "Have you ever thought of that?"

That's no excuse for him to act like a little jerk, you say.

Your father comes in and says, "All right, Joanna, that's enough." You're not going to mess around with your father, so you try your best to smile when everyone sings "happy birthday" and when you open your presents, which are mostly clothes, which you care nothing about since even the most glamorous clothes can't make you look pretty.

After everyone leaves, your mom is drinking a cup of Sanka, and you're sitting across from her, talking once again about Barry. God, mom, you don't notice anything! you tell her. You were right there in the room when he said, 'na na na na na' to Michael when he won at paddle ball!

Suddenly your father walks into the kitchen, and you can see from his red, weird face that he's turned into the guy your mother calls "Mr. Hyde" from the book *Dr. Jekyll and Mr. Hyde* about the man who periodically turns into a monster.

"Joanna, I have one word to describe you," Mr. Hyde says, standing at the edge of the room, glaring at you. With his red face and glittering eyes, he's become inhuman, like a "thing" in human form that's propelled by electrical wires instead of blood running through its body. "Do you know what that word is?" Mr. Hyde says. "Very simply, it's '*rotten*'!"

You stare at this guy that you haven't seen in over a year. The guy is like death. When you're a kid, death doesn't visit you very often, if at all. But for all the Jacobs kids Mr. Hyde is something like death, visiting you without warning, wreaking havoc and devastation, and then vanishing, leaving you changed forever.

"While listening to you go on and on about this poor kid, a kid from a broken home, it occurred to me that your mother and I conceived three good kids and one rotten one," Mr. Hyde rages in a quivering, horrible voice. You start to retreat into your fog as Mr. Hyde starts in about the war. "Do you know what rotten is?" he says. "*Do you? Rotten* is the piece of human garbage who sat in my sergeant's tent after being captured by my unit and *smiled and laughed* as he described how he and his fellow Nazis raided a Jewish orphanage, herded a couple dozen kids into the back of a truck, and *gassed them!*"

"All right, Sam, please!" your mother says, standing up. "Please! That's enough!"

Mr. Hyde waves an impatient hand at your mother, as though she's the senseless one. "Can you imagine?" he says, his voice rising to a womanly shriek. "This piece of Nazi scum told my sergeant that he and his friends herded these poor helpless kids into the back of the truck, filled it with lethal gas, and *suffocated* them to death! He sat in the tent and *bragged about it!* He was *proud* of what he had done!"

"All right, Sam!" your mother says. "Please! I can't take this!"

But Mr. Hyde is on a tear. "The Nazis had nothing but hatred and contempt for vulnerable children!" he rages. "And now I learn that my own daughter has no more compassion for a weak and vulnerable child than . . . than a vicious Nazi!"

"Sam, I'm begging you!" your mother shrieks. "I'm begging you! Please! We had such a nice party. *Please.*"

"Obviously your daughter, who was the guest of honor at this party, who was the recipient of some wonderful gifts and a beautiful cake and a lot of well wishes, doesn't share your fond feelings about her birthday party," the monster says. He walks to the counter next to your grandparents' phone and snatches up your book report on *The Diary of Anne Frank* that he was so ecstatic about when you brought it home. "You see this paper?" he snarls, waving the report in your face. "You know how much value this has when the person who wrote it clearly didn't understand what she was writing about? This is how much value this paper has." He walks stiffly into the hall and your mother runs after him, yelling, "Sam! Sam! What are you doing?" Then you hear a commotion in the bathroom. "Sam, no!" your mother yells. "Don't! Please!"

You go into the bathroom and see your father stuffing your book report into the toilet. You feel sick. Then your mother pulls it out and you hate your mother even more than you hate your father. It wasn't right of your mother to pull your book report out of the toilet. It was humiliating. You pull the dripping report out of your mother's hand and throw it back into the toilet. Then you run upstairs into your bedroom and shut the door. You lie on your bed frozen with terror, not only because your father has turned into a murderous monster, but because you know that what he said about you is right, that you are rotten to the core. You are mean and snarly to your perfect parents, and you are greasy and ugly, and you read about Nazi tortures over and over like someone licking a lollipop. Your father is right. You are a Nazi at heart.

You hear the basement door open downstairs. (You later find your book report drying absurdly on a towel in the basement sink, rescued by your mother, the ink all stained and the edges sticking up). Then you hear your mother coming up the stairs. You hope she'll leave you alone but instead she flies into your room and shrieks, "Joanna please!," as though you were the one that threw a fit. "Please, Joanna!" your mom yells. "He didn't mean it! He didn't mean it!"

Shut up! you scream, hating yourself for losing control. Now it's obvious that you're rotten to the core. You screamed at the wrong person. It wasn't your mother who said horrible things and stuffed your report down the toilet. Your whole disguise as a good daughter is crumbling. Now it's obvious that you hate your mother and you hate your father and you have the heart and soul of a Nazi who would not have hesitated to gas children in the back of a truck. You don't even deserve to live. The next day, which is Sunday, your father insists on taking you out for lunch. Sitting there with him at the Brown Derby is as bad as listening to him spew hatred at you the day before. While your father eats his steak, acting all formal, asking you about school, you force down your surf and turf as though it's medicine and try to answer his questions, but you can hardly hear your own voice as you speak to him. Then he orders you a hot fudge sundae and you choke that down too, and when you get home you go quietly upstairs and throw up the whole meal, and of course your mother, who always knows everything that's happening in her house, comes up and bangs on the door, yelling, "Joanna! Are you all right?" and once again you want to kill your mother as much as you want to kill your father.

You return to school the next day and never say a word to your friends about what happened over the weekend. The whole world worships your parents, and you try to maintain an image of them as charming, attractive, and fun. You use them the way people use a sharp set of clothes to hide creepy imperfections. You might be too tall and too zitty and wear a bite plate and have to throw your bloody underpants down the sewer to hide them from your mother, you might have the soul of a Nazi who would shove orphans into a truck and turn on the gas, but when you have good-looking, popular parents, you can only sink so low.

Oh God. I can't believe I actually wrote about that hideous experience with my father. It was so horrible and demeaning that I've never talked to anyone about it, not even my therapist who I had for years. The funny thing is that I've forgiven him. But it's really sad, the way he destroyed his relationship with his kids who he adored and wanted to be close to. When you're a child and your jolly, affectionate daddy turns into a monster, you assume that the monster is the real guy and the jolly, affectionate guy is fake. It didn't occur to me until I was well into adulthood that the jolly, affectionate daddy was real and the monster wasn't. It was a disease (probably PTSD but they didn't call it that in those days) taking over his body, like alcohol poisoning or insulin shock, and I don't think he had any actual memory of these events after he returned to his senses, which is why he never apologized, which made everything so much worse. (My siblings have varying viewpoints on this matter—my sister sees it my way but my brothers, who had more physical encounters with the monster than I did, are not as forgiving.) Anyway, it was too bad he was so cruel at those times, because he was basically made of very good stuff. He was funny and brilliant and sensitive and compassionate, and he stood up against oppression. He taught me everything I know about writing. He was a good, boots-on-the-ground journalist with a hunger for knowledge about everything around him.

I wonder what my dad would think about my uncooperative behavior with an FBI agent. He would probably think I was acting like a blooming idiot. It's obvious that I'm not reacting in a normal way to Agent Deborah's intrusion in my life. The other day when Robbie texted me that he saw an "FBI-looking vehicle" headed toward my block, and I looked out the window and saw Deborah walking toward my building, I went into a panic, but now I realize it was more because I *wanted* to see her than I *didn't* want to see her. I opened the door and there she was, stylin', in a pair of trim black pants with pockets and a striped shirt with a *V* neck and expensive-looking sensible shoes, and I greeted her in the most inappropriate manner, the way I always do. I said "Hey girlfriend, what's up?" Then I felt kind of stupid that I had addressed her like that.

"What's up?" Deborah said. "Maybe you can tell me." She walked in and sat down on the green chair and put her briefcase on the floor, and I flopped back down on the couch and put my feet on the ottoman. I should have experienced her visit as one more stressor in my life after losing my mom and the Chinese people taking over my building and the little gangsters accosting me in the hall and getting rejections from publishers. Instead I was imagining that Deborah could rescue me, "take me away from all this," which of course was ludicrous. The only place she would take me was to some interrogation room. "So where's what's-his-name?" I asked.

"Agent Buford had other business to attend to," Deborah said. "But both he and I are concerned that we still haven't received the evaluation from your psychiatrist."

"Well, I'm still working on that," I said. I didn't mean that I had actually made an appointment to get the evaluation. I meant that I was still trying to figure out how to get them to stop bugging me about it. "Come on, Deborah," I said. "You know damn well that I'm not going to blow anyone up. Can't you all just chill out? I promise I won't make any more calls to the Mike Stevens show."

"You don't understand," Deborah said. "That's not how it works. We need to bring this case to closure. There are certain steps we need to take. It doesn't matter whether I feel in my bones that you're not going to go out there and blow anyone up. We have certain protocols that we have to follow when suspicious behavior is brought to our attention."

"Well, why can't *you* do the evaluation?" I said. "I'm sure you have extensive training in assessing people's emotional stability. Can't you give me a personality test on the computer or something? I'll bet you have a personality test programmed right there on your computer."

"Joanna, I'm not qualified to conduct a psychiatric evaluation," Deborah said.

"Why not?" I yelled. "You already know me better than my shrink! Just do some kind of assessment on the damn computer, and then tell your bosses you're confident that I'm not going to kill Sandy Shrewsbury or anyone else and that will be the end of it." I was actually getting off on the thought of Agent Deborah giving me a personality test. It would be like her seeing right through my clothes to my naked self.

"Look, Joanna, I can't spend a lot of my time arguing with you," Deborah said. "I asked you to do something very simple in order to get us out of your hair, and it's obvious that you don't want to do it, and I'm wondering why. I really think you're afraid to be evaluated by a psychiatrist." She sat back, spread her arms on the chair, and crossed her legs, dangling one foot as she studied me with a faint smile. "You know, you put on this big blustering act, but underneath it all you're just this scared little girl," she said.

This kind of tore at my heart. "Listen, the truth is that there's no way my shrink would do it," I said. "He's had a little trouble with the licensing board in the past. And where am I going to find another shrink to do this kind of thing? They won't touch it with a ten-foot pole."

"As I said, I think you're freaked out at the thought of getting a psychiatric evaluation," Deborah said. "You just lost your mom, you're not in the most stable state of mind, and you're afraid you'll flunk the evaluation and you'll never get rid of us."

I was kind of impressed. "See that?" I said. "You are qualified to evaluate me. I don't know what you're doing working for this nefarious agency. You should have gone into some other line of work. What's your story, anyway? I changed my mind about your being from the Upper West Side. Underneath your polish is some of that sexy roughness that suggests either Brooklyn or the Bronx."

"I didn't come here to chitchat, Joanna," Deborah said.

"Well just tell me. Are you from Brooklyn or the Bronx? Come on, Deborah. I'm not asking you your body measurements."

"I grew up in Brooklyn. It's not exactly classified information."

I got all excited. "Brooklyn!" I yelled. "Right here in Brooklyn. See? I knew it! Where in Brooklyn did you grow up? Come on, just *tell me*!"

"Coney Island, Joanna. Now can we get back to the business at hand?"

But she was giving me all the wrong answers if she wanted me to focus on the business at hand. "Oh my God!" I yelled. "I love Coney Island! Coney Island is my favorite place in the world! Did you like riding the Cyclone?"

"I didn't have time for running around in an amusement park," she said.

I stared at her as though she had told me she didn't have time for her morning coffee. "What are you talking about?" I said. "I'm saying when you were a kid!"

"I had a lot of summer reading, and I also had summer jobs. I had more productive things to do besides running around in Coney Island."

"That doesn't make any sense!" I yelled. "You could have gone there *after* you did your summer reading and your job. You could have gone there at *night*! The most famous amusement park in the world was *right next door*! You grew up in Coney Island and you didn't even *go* there? You stayed home and did your summer reading? I can't believe you were at home *studying* when you were a kid instead of running around Coney Island, riding the Cyclone and the Wonder Wheel and swimming at the beach. What kind of a *person* are you?" I realized I was furious with her. I wanted some kind of explanation as to why she didn't take advantage of growing up in the greatest city on earth. She should have been stuck in the soul-sucking suburbs like I was, and I should have grown up in Coney Island. "Didn't you ever get into any trouble when you were a kid?" I said. "What were you, some kind of goody-two-shoes?"

Agent Neufeld stood up. "Joanna, you seem determined to get my goat and I'm not playing along," she said. "If you don't want to get the evaluation, fine. You passed up your chance to get us to close the file on this incident. So we're going to have to keep an eye on you. But I've pretty much had it with you. Don't go to a shrink, don't get the evaluation, don't do anything. Just keep going along the way you've been doing, and I'm afraid you're going to come to a very sad end."

"What are you talking about?" I said. "That's a terrible thing to say!" She was standing up and clicking her briefcase shut, and for some reason I was in a panic. "Why would you say that? That's like putting a whammy on me!"

"I'm not putting a whammy on you. You're doing it to yourself." She walked to the door and waited for me to open it. I opened it and she said, "Have a good day," and left.

I shut the door and flopped back onto the couch. I felt awful. She had told me to go fuck myself, do what I wanted, don't bother to see a shrink. Obviously the FBI did have bigger fish to fry. But instead of feeling triumphant I wanted to die. I sat on the couch and cried and cried and cried for my mom.

I've been so demoralized since Deborah's visit that I haven't called back Steven, who my mom made the executor of her estate since he's an attorney. He wants to know when the other kids and I are going to start cleaning out our mother's house with its fifty years worth of stuff in it, but we don't know anything about cleaning out a house. My divorced brother Michael is using his sabbatical to "study" psychedelic herbs in the Amazon jungle, my sister is involved with some kind of naturopathic health initiative in Bolivia, and my brother Danny, the only sibling remaining in Cleveland, seems to have forgotten that Mom's house exists and spends all his free time watching cartoons and eating Cocoa Puffs, and even his own kids treat him like a little brother although he's a successful sports writer. But it seems to me that *somebody else* should be dealing with the damn house after I broke my neck trying to save our mother, chasing after doctors and nurses at the hospital to keep them from killing her in there and then having her turn up in that rehab place with the life draining out of her. After the funeral all our friends and family swarmed through the house treating me like a powerless child instead of the new matriarch, which is what I thought I was, and they closed the windows and turned on the air conditioner, and I had to vacate my room for my married cousins and sleep in my childhood bedroom with my older sister (who my father kept secret until we were all adults), and I had to listen to her chastise me for not being grateful that I had this wonderful mom instead of her witch of a biological mother who never wanted her.

People treat me like a child even though I'm practically an old woman. I have written books and articles for national magazines and been a devoted daughter and sister and friend, and I have attended countless funerals and cared for my parents in their old age and honored them in their deaths and seen a young country grow old, but I still feel like a young person in an old person's body. You're supposed to have *gravitas* when you're this old, like Maya Angelou or Toni Morrison or Eleanor Roosevelt had when they were in their sixties. I do not have it. But now that I think about it, who the hell has *gravitas* anymore? My friends don't have it, my siblings don't have it, and I don't think Agent Neufeld has it either. Maybe some old black ladies in Harlem have it. And that would be it. So I'm not going to feel too bad about it, because I'm not about to compete with some old black ladies in Harlem.

PART 2

ADOLESCENCE

1963–1964

You're sauntering down the hall of Greenvale Junior High, swinging your books down at your waist rather than cradling them in your arms like most of the girls. You're wearing a plaid skirt at mid-knee, a white blouse, knee socks, and square-toed brown tie shoes. You've just read your essay over the P.A. system to the whole school, about the country's love for President Kennedy. You're happy to be getting some attention for a change, since for the past three weeks President Kennedy has gotten all the attention. (Whenever the kids act bratty the adults say, "Don't you know what just happened?" But to you and your classmates it didn't "just happen." Three weeks is a long time to a seventh grader.)

The bell rings and kids pour into the halls. Steven rushes up to you wearing a big smile and a nice new outfit, gray slacks and a matching checkered shirt, purchased during a weekend shopping trip with his dad. (Steven couldn't care less about fashion, but it doesn't affect his popularity.) "Jo, that was great!" he says to you.

Well, if it wasn't for you I wouldn't have been able to read my essay, you say. Nobody but you and my parents would have seen it. You wrote the essay over the weekend, basically to please your parents because you feel guilty never wanting to talk to them or even to be near them, and they both told you how brilliant it was, and then you went over to Steven's and showed it to him, and he asked you if he could take it with him to school. You gave it to him, and on Monday he marched into the office and showed it to the principal and suggested that you be allowed to read it to the whole school. In his quiet way, Steven is a powerhouse.

Molly wanders up to you and Steven, cradling her books. She looks pretty in her pink and blue plaid skirt. She wears a blond flip and her zits are almost gone and you can barely notice her freckles anymore. "We listened to it in math," Molly says without bothering to announce the subject at hand. "Old lady Reese said it was one of the best essays she had ever heard, period, and the fact that it was written by a twelve-year-old was simply astonishing."

Really? you say, grinning. That's what she said? Simply astonishing?

"Uh-huh," Molly says. "She used those exact words."

"And you know old lady Reese," says Steven. "She doesn't give out compliments easily."

Your friend Renee Siegel charges up. She's tall and buxom and has pretty blond hair that hangs down to her shoulders. "Brilliant, JoJo!" she says. "Positively brilliant!"

Thanks, Rennie! you say. You call several of your friends by nicknames, just as you did as a little kid. Since you started Greenvale Junior High, your life revolves around school. Even when you're at home you socialize with your friends, over the phone, rather than with your family, and after the regular school day you often wander the halls instead of going right home. Most of your new friends are "different" in some way, although not unpopular. Tessie "Tootie" Bauman and Sarah Sachs, with whom you eat lunch and hang out sometimes on weekends, are sweet, smart kids who don't quite blend in because their parents are immigrants. Good-natured Renee Siegel is a fringe member of the popular crowd, but brashly defies the rule about sticking with your own kind. Another buddy, skinny, freckled Hilda Greenberg, is a gum-chewing kid with an attitude who takes delight in your wackiness. You enjoy being with these new friends, who admire you for your daring and crazy sense of humor and don't know your insecurities yet, the way Steven and Molly do.

"Did you guys hear about that girl that's here who was kicked out of Fairview ?" Renee says.

"I know," Steven says. "I saw her in the hall talking to some ninth-graders. She looks pretty nutso."

"I heard she was out of control at Fairview, and finally they gave up on her and kicked her out, and now she's living with her cousin, over on Franklin."

Who got kicked out of Fairview? you ask, suddenly more interested in this than in listening to compliments on your essay.

"Steven will tell you! I gotta get to math. If you're late old lady Thompson pitches a fit! Toodles!" Renee trots off down the hall.

Who got kicked out of Fairview? you ask Steven.

"This girl from Cleveland Heights. She was in Fairview and she kept running away, and now she's living with her cousin Rhonda, a couple streets away from me on Franklin. Her cousin's pretty wild too."

"She's in our grade?" Molly asks.

"Yeah, she's our age. I saw her walking around. She looks like a little Jewish rack."

Really! you gasp. It's unheard of for a seventh-grader to be a "rack," and very unusual for a Jewish kid to be one. The racks are eighth- and ninth-graders and most of them are Italian. The Jewish kids run the school, but the Italians command the world of teased-up hair, dark eye shadow, pointy shoes, and cocky indifference to grades and schoolwork. You're agitated to hear about a kid your age, a Jewish kid like yourself, who is so bad that she's been kicked out of Fairview, the residential center for emotionally disturbed children, which is in a neighboring suburb and has fascinated you ever since you heard about it. You're hoping that the kid is a weirdo, like Beryl Kaufman who walks down the hall mumbling to herself.

"Joanna's jealous," Molly says.

You say oh be quiet, but you know Molly is right. You're dying to know who this little Jewish rack is that has captured every-one's interest. You look around and say where is this kid? I want to see her.

111

"Well, you're about to get your wish," Steven says with a little smile. "There she is." He points down the hall at a girl your age talking to two older rack girls, who are looking at her with interest and amusement. Although the younger girl's hair is teased up, she doesn't look like a rack. She looks as though she belongs to her own club. She wears a flowered skirt, a black tee shirt, and weird green lipstick. You and Molly stare at the girl, then stare at each other with your mouths hanging open, as though you've just seen dogs rain down from heaven. The girl entertaining the racks with her animated talk is Susie Moscowitz.

Oh my GOD! you gasp. You and Molly run around the corner and both of you stand there with your hands on your cheeks and your mouths wide open.

Steven follows you around the corner and says, "What's going on?"

That's—that's—that's Susie Moscowitz, you squeal at Steven. "You know her?"

She's—she's—she's—. You can't complete your sentence.

"She lived in our old neighborhood," Molly says. "She used to be a goody-goody girl."

"Really? Well, I can't imagine that girl being a goody-goody."

She was! I swear! you insist to Steven. Then you say to Molly, Maybe it's not her.

"It's her, Jo," Molly says.

What should we do? you say, spastically waving your hands around.

"What do you *mean*, what should we *do*? That makes no sense." Molly says "tsk" and looks up at the ceiling.

The bell rings, signaling the start of the next class, and the halls are empty. "Obviously, what we should do is go to our next class," Steven says.

"I have gym so I can be late," Molly says, but she starts walking away.

No, Mu-mu! you yell at her. Don't go! I'm having a fit!

"I HAVE TO GO," Molly says, and walks off down the hall. You just stand there, frozen. "Don't you have English now?"

Steven asks. He's late for his algebra class, but unlike Molly, he won't abandon a friend in distress.

Uh huh, you answer him vaguely.

Steven grabs hold of your shoulders and points you in the direction of your English class. "Well, go!" he says. "You have the whole rest of the year to deal with Susie Moscowitz." When you start moving down the hall like a zombie he heads down the opposite hall toward his math class.

When you enter your English class everyone claps for you. The teacher, Miss Horne, compliments you on your essay, and you say thank you, but you don't hear a word of what the teacher is saying. You're so upset about seeing Susie that you feel crazy. You can't concentrate at all on the discussion of the assigned short story in the textbook. After English, you walk blindly to gym class, trying to smile at kids congratulating you on your essay. But you're so preoccupied with Susie that you don't even get excited when the big, bald assistant principal who has never even spoken to you or noticed you before calls out, "Excellent essay, Joanna!" as he passes you.

You walk into the locker room to change into your gym suit, and there is Susie, changing her clothes. You notice that she's wearing blue shorts and an orange blouse instead of the white gym suits with names embroidered on them, like the other girls. You look at this new version of Susie, with the teased-up hair and weird green lipstick and a whole different shine in her eyes, different from the shine that used to gaily greet adults walking down the street. This isn't the Susie Moscowitz that you knew back on Forest Drive. But you summon up your courage and walk up to her and stand there while your old nemesis buttons her blouse.

"Well hi, famous essay writer," Susie says.

What are you doing here? you ask her, annoyed to feel your heart thumping.

"I'm living with my cousin now."

Were you really in Fairview? you say.

"None of your fucking business," Susie says to you.

You've never heard anyone say the word *fucking* in your life. But the word shoots into you like a pointy bullet that blossoms into a wild, thorny bouquet of flowers once it's inside. You're enthralled with this new version of Susie. You're dying to know everything about her, but you just say okey-dokey and walk away.

But once you're in gym class, you can't help trying to get Susie's attention. The teacher has you practicing basketball, and when she's not looking you throw the ball at Susie's rump, but she just turns and looks at you in mild annoyance and doesn't speak to you for the rest of the period. Back in the locker room you watch Susie changing back into her school clothes. You want to talk to her but you don't know what to say. You regret having been so mean to her when you were kids. You were always pretty good at sizing up other kids, and you wonder if you had stupidly missed something, if this version of Susie was inside of her even when she was sitting on her tablecloth acting like miss prissy pants.

After gym, you see Molly walking down the hall and run up to her, looking disheveled, as though you've just come off the Scrambler at Euclid Beach. I just saw her in gym, you announce.

"I saw her in the library. We're going to Cedar after school." "Cedar" is Cedar Center, the shopping strip that's a magnet for all the kids.

You stare at Molly. You and Susie are going to Cedar?

"Yeah."

Can I come? you ask.

"You hate her."

No I don't! you scream, and Molly says "sssh!" and looks around, embarrassed. I don't hate her, you say, more quietly. I want to go.

"I'll call you after school," Molly says and walks away.

True to her word, Molly calls you after school. "You can come with us," she says.

What happened to her? you ask. Why was she sent away? Why is she at our school?

"She said she ran away from her parents' house. I'm not sure how she ended up at Fairview. But now for some reason she lives with her cousin Rhonda on Franklin Drive. My mom said she was probably abused by someone in her house, which is usually why a kid is sent to live with a relative."

You mean she was beaten? You can picture mean old Mr. Moscowitz beating Susie.

"No, Jo, that's not what I'm talking about," Molly said.

You don't really care what happened to Susie in her dumb old house. You're much more interested in what happened to her at Fairview, which you imagine to be a riotous year-round camp for misunderstood kids.

A half-hour later you walk over to Molly's in a light-falling snow. You're wearing jeans, your old loafers, a long-sleeved madras shirt, and a puffy pink jacket. It's four o'clock, and you tell your mom that you'll be back by six thirty. As you walk, you feel all mixed up inside. You're afraid that Susie will be mean to you, and you're furious at yourself for suddenly being afraid of dopey Susie Moscowitz. You wonder if Susie even approved of your coming on this excursion. But Molly, who understands you like nobody else, made sure that it happened. It's one thing to say no to you when you want a lick of her ice cream cone. It's another thing to deny you access to Susie Moscowitz after some kind of terrible magic has been worked on her.

The girls are waiting for you on the corner of Molly's street. Molly is wearing slacks, loafers, and a nice plaid peacoat, and Susie wears jeans and black boys' boots that somehow look good on her and a black nylon jacket. Her hair is teased and she's wearing blue eye shadow and lipstick. You feel kind of frumpy compared to them.

You go to Mawby's for hamburgers and fries, and then shopping at Woolworth's. Susie talks mostly to Molly, and when she talks to you it's in a condescending tone, as though she's talking to a four-year-old child. You feel hurt, but you can't blame Susie for her attitude. You're dying to ask her about Fairview, but you're afraid to bring it up. A couple of times Susie does mention it,

115

once when she talks about the terrible hamburgers they served there on Wednesdays, and another time to talk about a boy who was sent there after his father killed his older brother. "His father went crazy after losing his job," Susie says. "He shot Tommy in the chest, and Greg escaped out the door and ran to a neighbor's house." You feel sick to think of a father shooting and killing his own child. But when you ask her if his mother was home, Susie ignores you and turns to Molly and says, "I really like your hair that way."

When you're walking home, Susie says to you, "So now I guess you're a big famous writer at Greenvale." She says it snippily, but you're still pleased.

Not really, you say, smiling.

"I write poetry," she says. "If you're good maybe I'll let you come over sometime and read some of my poems."

Okay, you say amiably.

The next day, Susie treats you with the same condescension in gym class. Throughout the day you see her traipsing around the halls, always in the center of a group of kids, either older rack girls or kids from Brush Elementary, where she briefly attended sixth grade after running away from her parents' house and living with her cousin Rhonda in the older section of Greenvale, before Rhonda moved to Franklin Drive in Little Jerusalem. It occurs to you that Susie looks pretty much like a taller version of her nine-year-old self, with the same curly brown hair, pale complexion, straight teeth, big blue eyes, and wiry frame. She even still wears odd clothes. But now, instead of looking old lady-ish, she looks like a little rebel. You realize it's her walk. Her walk and the glittery, challenging look in her eyes. The thing that bothers you the most is Susie's instant fame. The moment she walked into Greenvale everyone seemed to know who she was, even kids who didn't know her personally. You love and crave attention, and it drives you nuts that your former enemy is strutting around your school all of a sudden like a little TV star.

You realize that you won't be able to eat, sleep, or concentrate until you make Susie Moscowitz your friend. Not only will being friends with Susie help you not be jealous of her, but you *like* this new Susie. It occurs to you that Susie has been changing ever since the fifth grade, when she seemed unhappy and preoccupied at school, and then the day she moved she was acting so strange and jumpy, talking to you and Molly with her crazy bright smile. And now she's reappeared in a whole new form, like a docile brown chick that disappears from the flock and returns to the barnyard one day with a cocky strut and a new coat of iridescent feathers. You need this new Susie in your life or else your own life will feel dull in comparison.

Without making it obvious, you try to let Susie know that you are her ally. When Miss Bushnell says to her, "I expect you to show up to class next week with the standard white gym suit that everyone else has to wear," you say why does she have to wear a uniform and the teacher says it's because it's the rule and you say, oh pish-posh. When the teacher orders Susie to do ten extra push-ups because she's lying on the floor instead of doing exercises, you yell what if she has a heart attack. You make a point of passing balls to Susie during scrimmages and games, and you back her up during conversations. When Susie tells Sandy Weiner that Mrs. Wannaker dyed her hair, and Sandy says she thought the teacher's red hair was natural, you say that her hair looks dyed to you, even though you don't really know what dyed hair looks like. In spite of your efforts, Susie keeps acting indifferent to you. She doesn't acknowledge you in the halls, except once, when she flashes a big smile in your direction as she's strutting along with Marlene Santini, and you smile back, but then you notice Marlene whispering something to Susie and you worry for the rest of the day that they were making fun of you.

All during winter vacation, you can't get Susie out of your mind, especially because she was in Fairview, where you picture kids running amok and driving the counselors crazy and doing whatever they please. When you're doing stuff with your friends you picture Susie doing those same things at Fairview. When you eat with Sarah and Tessie at the Hot Shoppe cafeteria, you picture Susie having a food fight in the Fairview cafeteria. When Renee takes you to her Sunday school class and the two of you fool around instead of listening to Bible stories, you picture Susie defying the teachers at Fairview school. When you and Hilda Greenberg are reprimanded by an usher for making noise during *It's a Mad, Mad, Mad, Mad World*, you picture Susie raising hell with her friends during movie night at Fairview. (You assume that Fairview has a movie night.) When you see Molly during winter break you're afraid to bring up Susie because you don't want Molly to figure out that you're obsessed with her.

It's easier for you to shake Susie out of your head when school starts again, because there's so much going on. Hilda Greenberg has supposedly shown her "bush" to Ronnie Carr; Robbie Henchel is in the hospital with a broken shoulder after his father pushed him off the porch; Mr. Polsky, the popular, wisecracking geography teacher, might be dating Miss Lansy, the popular, raven-haired English teacher. And then, the week of your thirteenth birthday, the Beatles appear on Ed Sullivan, and the next day the whole school is electrified, and the girls engage in lengthy debates about which one is the cutest, which is more important than the actual songs. (At first you're a little insulted when your friends tell you that you look like Ringo with your big lips and mop of hair, but finally you decide it's better than looking like no Beatle.) After the Ed Sullivan show, the Beatles replace Susie as the talk of the school, which is a big relief to you, since your jealousy has been eating you alive. You no longer think about Susie all day long, although you remain friendly to her in gym and greet her in the halls. (Sometimes Susie smiles and waves back at you and other times she snottily ignores you, apparently punishing you for the sins of yesteryear.)

One March day you go over to Molly's after school for dinner. Shirley has made her famous Hungarian stuffed cabbage in your honor, and you thoroughly enjoy yourself, as you usually do while eating Shirley's delicious food and hearing the same old arguments between Molly and her mother, that they've been having since kindergarten, about clothes and bedtime and eating everything on the plate before you get dessert. After dinner you and Molly retreat into Molly's room and the phone rings. "Molly! Phone!" her mom yells.

A few minutes later Molly comes back into the room and you ask who was on the phone. "It was Susie," Molly says. "She told me she just got the Beatles' album, *Please Please Me*. It's got some great songs on it." She sees the look on your face. "I've been to her house a couple of times," she says. "I would have invited you but you don't like to dance."

So what, you say. You're lying on the floor, looking blankly at the ceiling, trying not to be mad.

"Well, Susie invited me over to show her some dances, like the Mashed Potato and the Pony. Her cousin Rhonda is really nice."

You sulk all the way home in your dad's car and storm into the house and go upstairs, and you flop on your bed and start reading *Anne of Green Gables*, which you've read a thousand times. Suddenly, as you read one of your favorite chapters about Anne ruining a cake she'd made for a special dinner guest, you look up from your book and realize that you no longer feel angry at Molly for going to Susie's house without telling you. In fact, you're happy that Molly and Susie have gotten together. Molly is your best friend, and if Susie wants to be friends with her, you figure that it won't be long before she wants to be friends with you as well.

It turns out that your instincts are correct. In gym class the next day, Susie walks up to you and says, "Doesn't Miss Bushnell's nose look like a tomato?" You look at Miss Bushnell and laugh, but not hysterically, just enough to let Susie know her observation is appreciated. The next day, Susie comes into your alcove in the locker room and says, "Joanna, look at the sky tonight. The moon will be fuller than it's been in twenty years. It's called a harvest moon." That night you look at the moon and it is indeed an amazing sight. The next day, you remark on the moon to Susie in the locker room, and during class she yells "Jo!" and bounces the basketball to you, across the paths of two other girls.

A few days later, Susie walks up to you in the hall and says, "Hey stupid."

Yeah? you say, taking "stupid" as an endearment.

"You wanna come over tomorrow after school? You can read some of my crazy poems."

Sure! you say. Did you check with your cousin?

"She said it's fine. You know where it is, right?"

Yeah, you say, on Franklin Drive.

"Fifty-seven-forty-one. See you then."

Susie walks away. In gym class she's her usual snooty self and makes no reference to her invitation, but you assume that it still stands.

Your mom doesn't sound all that thrilled about your going over to Susie's. She and your dad have never been crazy about Susie's parents. They're not crazy about any Orthodox people, who they believe are all racist and dumb for believing in God. It doesn't seem to matter that Susie now lives with her cousin Rhonda, who isn't Orthodox. "What kind of supper is she serving?" your mother asks, as though some cousin isn't capable of serving a normal meal.

I don't know! You say. Just some food! I'm going!

Your mom says your dad will pick you up at eight o'clock, and you leave the house and walk to Susie's. You feel that you look pretty good. You're wearing some new red jeans, nice new sneakers, and a shiny black jacket that you pretend is a black leather jacket like the hoods wear. Most of your zits are gone, and the couple of strays are light and concealed with stuff.

Susie opens the door, wearing a crazy-looking skirt made of patches, a white tee shirt, and some goofy ballet-looking shoes. Instead of being carefully teased the way it usually is at school, her hair looks wild and messy. "Come on in, dopey," she says, and you smile and walk in. The small living room is disorderly but not chaotic like Steven's house. The carpet has a big cigarette burn in the middle and the furniture looks worn but the tables are covered with pretty pieces of embroidery. Worn copies of *Redbook* and *Ladies Home Journal* cover the coffee table. Susie takes you into the kitchen to introduce you to her cousin Rhonda, who is sitting at the table smoking a cigarette. She's probably in her thirties, maybe ten years younger than your mom. "Hi, Joanna!" she says brightly. "So nice to meet you!"

"Come on," Susie says. "Let's go upstairs."

Susie's room is really nice. Rhonda, who's single with no kids, has generously given her young cousin the larger of the two bedrooms. It has a double bed with a white spread, pink curtains with white polka dots, and a rocking chair with stuffed animals on it. There are stuffed animals on the bed, too. You assume that Susie has gotten over her fear of dogs, since her pink rug is a fluffy dog with a little round tail. Susie goes to her record player and puts on some Beatles records. She plays "Love Me Do," "Mr. Postman," and a crazy song called "Roll Over Beethoven." You flop on the bed and watch Susie dance by herself. She's a good dancer, and you feel bad that you can't dance. The only time you ever tried to dance, Molly laughed at you and you never tried it again.

After dancing a wild Mashed Potato to "Roll Over Beethoven," Susie tosses the needle from the record. She goes over to her dresser, takes out a pink notebook with a poodle on it, walks over, and dumps it on your lap. "Here are some of my poems," she says.

Oh, neat, you say, and open the notebook. Susie sits down on her rocking chair, clutches one of the stuffed animals, and starts to rock, looking at the ceiling.

You hope that at least some of the poems are about Fairview, about being locked in isolation rooms, or running away, or revolting against the counselors. The poems aren't about Fairview, but they are very disturbing. One is about bloody body parts flying through the air—"Legs and schwanzes, ears and eyes, flying all around, in a land of disembodied parts, where the beasts are silent, they make no sound." (You have to ask what a "schwanze" is and laugh yourself silly when Susie tells you the answer.) There's a poem about a rat and a snake attempting to eat each other until only half of each one is left and they merge into *one appalling creature . . . whose most distinctive feature . . . is its gooey eyes . . . crawling with black flies.* There's a poem about a boy who shoves his mother into an ice-box, and another one about the sun turning black and leaving the earth to "shrivel like a pea."

You love how weird and crazy the poems are, and besides, they're really good. When you read about the murderous son doing an Irish jig while his frozen mother "shrieks like a banshee" you become hysterical and Susie gets up and snatches the book away from you.

Whaddaya doing? you yell.

"Let's go downstairs," Susie says. "You're getting too much enjoyment from those demented poems. Come on, Bunky." She ruffles your hair and starts walking towards the door. You don't know where she got the name "Bunky," but you feel a little thrill when she ruffles your hair. You realize it's the first time Susie has ever touched you.

Down in the living room, Rhonda is sitting on the couch, smoking. "Staying for supper, Joanna?" she asks. Although you assumed that you were, you like that Rhonda has left the decision up to you. Rhonda is more like a babysitter than a real adult. She's one of the gang.

Rhonda serves Swanson's macaroni and cheese on tray tables in the living room, and the three of you sit on the couch and watch a program about Jack Ruby. Of course you're all mainly interested in seeing the replay of the most shocking moment after President Kennedy's assassination, when Jack Ruby bursts onto everyone's TV screen and kills Lee Harvey Oswald. As many times as you've seen it, there's always something terribly exciting about watching Jack Ruby kill Lee Harvey Oswald. It's the moment that the adults lost control of the country. When he bursts onto the screen clutching his gun, you glance over at Susie, who's watching with a look of eager expectation, her cheese-slathered fork frozen in front of her mouth. At that moment you understand Susie totally and completely, and all the bad blood between you is gone.

Rainy Afternoon in Mid-October

This is so fucked up because now I miss that evil wench Susan after writing about her dramatic reappearance in our lives when we were kids. I know she feels bad that I won't talk to her. She wrote me a letter after my mom died. She's called several times. But I can't have anything to do with her because she's ruined everything. We used to have so much fun. I'll never forget my excitement when she reappeared in my life, that day at school, looking like a little witch, and I was so enthralled by her transformation from goody-two-shoes to Jewish badass. After that we had a ball running around together—the three of us, Susan (she stopped being "Susie" after high school), Molly and I. We couldn't stay apart so we all ended up in New York together. For almost fifty years we were as thick as thieves. And then Susan destroyed a beautiful friendship by doing the worst thing anyone can do to a friend.

We have such an amazing history together. We had incredible adventures as kids, and even more incredible adventures as grown-ups. When we all first moved to New York this place was a mess. The Bronx was burning, you had to look down when you walked to avoid stepping in dog shit, the subways and signposts and buildings were slathered with graffiti. The city was broke and dangerous and absolutely wonderful. We were three little roommates running around New York, trying to make it. At home we would cook spaghetti and smoke endless bongs and try to fight off the cockroaches. Eventually we did achieve success—Susan in the fashion world, me in the literary world, and Molly in the nonprofit world. When that happened our lives diverged, but we got to know one another's friends and associates and we would get together in all our favorite places— Cuban-Chinese uptown, hamburgers midtown, Indian and Ukrainian and Italian etc., etc., downtown—and we would eat and drink and laugh, laugh, laugh. About Doreen Periwinkle, a middle-aged spokesperson for one of the Upper West Side neighborhoods when Molly worked at an organization called

Take Back the Night, who would run on and on at meetings about the need to put an end to the "GRAF-itti" in the city, putting the emphasis on the first syllable—"First we let them get away with the GRAF-itti, then we let them get away with murder!" And Susan's competitor in the fashion industry, Lorena Lupo, who wrote a review for the *Voice* under a false name in which she referred to one of Susan's winter shows as "a lurid display of excess." And Jane Fink, a local writer who was our friend until she got drunk at a party we all attended and announced to a room full of people that "We all know that Joanna's novel is overrated but we still love her because of her fuzzy-wuzzy hair!" (After Jane said that, Susan got up and dumped a bunch of ice on her head and walked out of the room.)

My life now isn't anything like it was when Susan was in it. There's a big hole in it now. I think one reason Molly's been irritated with me is because what happened between me and Susan fucked up her friendship with Susan But is that *my* fault? The bitch ran off with the only woman I've ever loved. My God. How *could* she? Susan used to yell at Tanya for not wanting to be my girlfriend. She would say, "Why would you even think about fucking other women when you have the sexiest, most beautiful, most loving and funny and fantastic woman right here who would love you and devote herself to you until death do you part? You're such a creep, Tanya." And Tanya would say, "Because I don't deserve her." Which was the right answer, but I knew she didn't mean it. Tanya thinks she deserves the world on a platter.

And now she has Susan. At some point early last year they decided they were in love with each other. What was even more horrible about their little relationship is that everybody knew about it except for me. Molly didn't tell me because she was trying to stop it. When I did find out I literally wanted to die (although I would never actually commit suicide unless I had a terminal illness). I still don't understand it. Why would Susan be with Tanya when she knows I love her? Susan can have anyone she wants because she's a famous personage and people are always falling at her feet. She was one of Andy Warhol's favorites. Why would she *do* this to me? And my friends keep telling me to talk to poor, poor Susan because she's so upset that I won't return her calls, and telling me the latest news about her and the other wench, like they adopted three rabbits that hop around their loft. How do my friends think *I* feel, picturing the two of them snuggling up naked in bed with their rabbits ("Tell me about the rabbits, Tanya!") while I sit here all alone writing with a dead mother and nobody buying my 9/11 book and these damn kids banging on my door at all hours. Just a couple of minutes ago they did it again—BANG BANG BANG! and one of them yelled "Open the door, old lady!" I stay in control by reminding myself that my friends and I were just as obnoxious when we were that age. We weren't tough city kids, but we were rough little customers in our own way. Especially little Susie. That girl was hell on wheels.

SUMMER OF 1964

The window of Susie's bedroom is wide open and the radio is churning out hits: "Under the boardwalk, out of the sun, under the boardwalk, we'll be having fun . . ." "It's the little old lady from Pasadena . . . go granny go granny go granny go!" "It's been a hard day's night and I've been working like a dog . . ." Rhonda is downstairs making out with Rick Fiegler, her boyfriend, who has long, greasy hair and works in a place that sells construction equipment even though he's Jewish.

"Stop it!" Susie grabs your leg to stop it from jiggling. You're sprawled out on her bed, and she's lying at your feet with her back against the wall. You've been jiggling your leg deliberately to get her to grab it. You keep jiggling it in her hand for a few seconds, and then stop. "You're a nervous wreck," Susie says, and you smile and say, I know. I need tranquilizers.

"I'm going to need tranquilizers if I have to go back to Cleveland Heights," Susie says. "I would rather get hit by a train than go back to live with my crazy parents."

That stupid social worker can't make you go back! you yell. Just tell her to go jump in the lake! You start jiggling your leg again and Susie says "Stop" and clutches it harder.

"Of course she can make her go back," Molly says. "She can send the police over here to take her back if she refuses."

Why don't you tell her your parents are crazy, or tell them some lie, like your father beat you with a stick? you suggest.

"He didn't beat me with a stick but he is so mean!" Susie says. "He never wanted me to have any fun. All he did was give me orders. My mother doesn't even like him. She sleeps on the couch to get away from him. Furthermore that house is haunted. I'm not kidding, you guys."

What do you mean, haunted? you ask, wrinkling your nose for the millionth time. You always have some twitchy thing going on with your face.

"I'm talking literally haunted!" Susie says, grabbing your leg and giving you an emphatic look. "I would wake up in the middle of the night and *smell smoke!* There was a *distinct smell of smoke* in that house. I thought I was going to suffocate. And when I told my mother about it she got real mad and told me to stop imagining things."

"Are you sure you weren't imagining it?" Molly asks.

"No, Molly, I wasn't imagining it."

Eew, that's scary, you say. I wouldn't even want to be in there during the day. You're picturing Susie running away from her parents' terrible haunted house at the age of eleven and walking with her little suitcase in the middle of the night all the way to her cousin Rhonda's house across Mayfield Road. After she was sent to Fairview for defying her teacher and school authorities at Brush Elementary (she told the principal to go to hell in front of the whole class when he told her to crouch down in the hall during a security drill), she kept running away to Rhonda's new house here on Franklin Drive, and finally they gave up and let her live with Rhonda "on a trial basis." Your whole life has changed for the better since Susie reentered it. You've been doing all kinds of fun things together, like climbing on garage roofs and spying on people, hopping rides on the backs of trucks, sneaking into the movies, and lying on the sidewalk playing dead on busy Cedar Road until drivers stop to offer help (and then speed away in irritation when they see you cracking up). When you're with Molly you all do more normal things like listen to the radio, go shopping or to the movies at Cedar Center, or hang around the pool, but it's still fun.

"People who need people are the luckiest people in the world!" Barbra Streisand sings.

"Oh God!" Susie yells. "Why are they *playing* this?"

This song should be banned from the universe! you yell.

Molly gets up, walks over to the radio, and turns it off. "There," she says. "Now you don't have to hear it."

"Let's get outa here," Susie says. "Let's do something." She jumps off the bed.

"You wanna go to Saul's?" Molly suggests.

Yeah! you say, jumping off the bed. Saul's! Saul's! Saul's! you chant. You're always ready to eat something. Yesterday at dinner you put away two steaks and three bowls of ice cream.

"I desperately need a Cel-Ray Tonic," Susie says.

"That stuff is so weird," Molly says.

"Cel-Ray Tonic is sublime."

"You just drink it to be different."

"I drink it because I love celery pop! Celery pop! Celery pop! Celery pop! Pop! Pop!" Susie bops you on the head with each *pop*! and you cover your head against the blows. Even though Molly was the one who made fun of the Cel-Ray Tonic, Susie wouldn't bop her on the head.

The three of you go downstairs. In the living room, Rhonda is smoothing her blouse and her hair, pretending that she wasn't just making out like crazy with Rick. "We're going to Saul's," Susie says.

"Sounds like a terrific idea," Rick says. "Here's five bucks. Knock yourselves out." He hands Susie a fiver.

"Rick, that's not really necessary," Rhonda says.

"Sure it is! Growing girls need their calories!"

You all bound out to the sidewalk, you in a striped tee shirt and jeans (you don't like wearing shorts), Molly in yellow shorts and a print summer top, and Susie in a black tee shirt and a pair of paint-spattered pants that she begged off of your *zadie* who retired as a house painter a couple years ago. As you head toward Warrensville Road toward Cedar Center, you pass little kids dashing through sprinklers in swimsuits and older kids strolling down the street in pairs, coming back from Beemis Pool in their clogs and still-damp swimsuits, their towels draped around their necks. A couple of young mothers stroll by, pushing strollers with little bare feet sticking out of them.

You pass the corner house, which has a strange-looking yard containing clumps of flowers all over the place, instead of just grass and hedges like all the other yards. Two women are gardening in one of the clumps of flowers. They keep to themselves and don't even answer when spoken to, and you and Susie have made it your business to engage with them.

"Hi, strange women!" Susie yells. The women ignore her and continue working. One of them, a tall woman with curly brown hair, is standing there with a hoe watching her dumpy-looking blond companion, who is on her knees planting something. "Hey!" Susie yells, cupping her hands to her mouth. "Didn't you hear me? I said hello to you!"

The brown-haired woman just waves Susie away.

Hey ladies! you yell through cupped hands. Can we pick some of your flowers to give to our mothers? They will thank you for it!

"I don't know why you insist on bothering those women," Molly says.

We're trying to make friends with them, you say. Hey ladies! you call again. Listen to this important news! You start singing through your cupped hands. 'You'll wonder where the yellow went! When you brush your teeth with Pepsodent!' While you sing the popular commercial, Susie walks along the edge of the grass with her hands out, as though she's on a balance beam.

"Get off the grass, Moscowitz," the brown-haired woman orders, and you and Susie howl with laughter. Susie has a reputation in the neighborhood, and even these reclusive women know who she is.

She was trying to push down the weeds! you say.

The woman who's been on her knees jumps up and points at you. "If you don't get away from our property we're calling the police!" she yells.

129

"You heard her," says the brown-haired woman, clutching the hoe.

"Go ahead and do it," Susie says.

"Come on, let's go," Molly says. "I'm hungry." But then as the three of you start off down the street, she turns around and glares at the women with her mad bunny face, and you and Susie screech with laughter.

You stroll into Saul's Deli and are seated at a table in the middle of the restaurant. A waitress hurries up, all business, since it's the start of the dinner hour. You all order corned beef sandwiches on rye, and you ask for Russian dressing on both sides of the sandwich. "That is so gross," Molly says. You all know that proper Jews eat their corned beef sandwiches with mustard.

I like Russian dressing, you tell her. When the sandwiches arrive you want to ask for some mayo to slather on the sandwich as well, but you decide you'd better not. The waitress gives you a chocolate phosphate, Molly a coke, and Susie her Cel-Ray Tonic. You all tear into your sandwiches.

You're about done eating when you see the hostess seat two women in a nearby booth. "Oh my God," Susie says. "Look what just walked in." You look closer and see it's the mean neighbor ladies.

I don't believe it, you say.

"I guess they're done with their gardening," Molly says. "They're wearing different clothes." The dumpy blond woman is wearing cleaner dumpy trousers and a polo shirt and the one with the curly, brown hair has on a long flowered dress.

They are so dorky-looking, you say. Why don't they wear any lipstick at least? You can see why they have to live with each other. Nobody would ever want to marry them.

"Maybe they're married to each other," Molly says solemnly.

You and Susie look at each other and then you both shriek, "Eew!"

A different waitress from the one serving you takes the women's orders and hurries away to take care of other tables. You feel a little irritated that these mean women have had the nerve to come into Saul's, where you and your friends are trying to have a nice meal.

"You wanna stare at them?" Susie says.

What do you mean? you ask.

"We used to do it at Fairview to people we didn't like. We called it 'oogling.' Like this." She folds her hands on the table and starts staring at the women.

You start laughing. What a riot! you say. You fold your hands on the table like Susie is doing and fix your gaze on the women, who are sitting glumly, not talking to each other, waiting for their food. While you stare at the women, you and Susie are snickering but manage to keep from bursting into laughter. Come on, Mu, you say. We all have to do it for it to work.

"You guys are crazy," Molly says, but then she leans forward and stares at the women with her mad bunny face, wrinkling her nose and popping out her eyes.

The brown-haired woman looks over at you and says something to the blond woman, who also looks over. You keep staring. The brown-haired woman gets up and strides over to you in her unfashionable flowered dress. When she reaches your table she puts her two hands on it and leans over you. "Excuse me," she says. "Didn't your mothers ever teach you not to stare?"

No, you say, and you all burst into giggles.

"Well, they should have," the woman says. "It's terribly rude."

"I think you should go home and comb your hair," Susie says. "It's very messy-looking." Molly smirks and you crack up into your empty plate.

"I think it's a shame that your cousin is allowing you to run unsupervised all over town," the woman says to Susie. "You should be back at Fairview where you belong."

Oh go fry an egg, you say.

"My life is none of your business," Susie says.

"It will be if I make it my business," the woman says. She walks away, calling over her shoulder, "If you don't cut out the staring I'm going to have you removed from this restaurant."

Ha! you scoff. Go ahead and try it!

"What a jerk," Susie says as the woman sits back down at her table. At that moment the waitress returns with the women's orders. As soon as they start eating their sandwiches, you and Susie start staring at them again. "She's going to complain," Molly says.

Sure enough, the brown-haired woman calls the waitress over. When she hurries over to their table, you and Susie start talking to each other as though nothing is wrong. "So how are your parents?" Susie says.

Quite well, thank you, you say. And how is Shirley, your lovely mother? you say to Molly.

"Shirley my lovely mother is driving me crazy," Molly says, looking furtively at the booth, where the brown-haired woman is talking to the waitress, and the waitress keeps glancing over at you, looking totally confused. Finally she walks over to your table.

"Excuse me, girls," the waitress says. "Were you bothering those people over there?"

"What people?" Molly asks.

"Those, um, women said you were staring at them or something," she says. She sounds exasperated. She glances over at a large table of eight, which she clearly has more interest in attending to than two strange-looking women with a vague complaint about staring children.

You look at one another with bewildered expressions. "We were looking at the mural if that's what she was talking about," Molly says. There's a big mural of Bialystok, Russia, on the wall behind the women. "We weren't looking at them."

"Oh, for Christ sake," the waitress snaps. She goes back over to the women, and you all go crazy with laughter when you see the waitress point at the mural.

As soon as the waitress walks away you all start staring at the women again. They try to ignore you, but finally they ask for the check, half-eaten sandwiches on their plates, and get up to leave. The blond woman stalks out of the restaurant, but the brown-haired woman gives you one last look, waving the check at you. "You are three sorry excuses for teenagers," she says. Then she pays the check and follows her companion out the door.

As you leave the restaurant and head down the street, you're ecstatic. There was something wonderfully strange and weird about what you did. It was as though you and your friends had made your own little movie in the restaurant. Staring at the women had made you feel powerful. You fling your arms around Susie's neck, hugging her from behind as she walks. We are the greatest! you yell.

"No, Cassius Clay is the greatest," Susie says, referring to the new heavyweight champion of the world.

"You mean Muhammed Ali," Molly says. "That's his new name."

A couple days later, you and Susie are walking down the street and see the women in their garden. There's something about them that brings out the meanness in you. Let's oogle them! you say to Susie.

"Okay." The two of you plant yourselves on old Mrs. Jensen's tree lawn across the street and start staring. "Don't pop your eyes out," Susie says. "Just stare at them normally. It's creepier that way." You adjust your staring. At first the women ignore you but then the brown-haired one stops shoveling dirt and yells, "Don't you have anything better to do?" and Susie yells, "No," and the woman goes back to her gardening.

Renee and Hilda Greenberg walk by. "What on earth are you guys doing?" Renee says.

We're oogling those weirdos, you say. Come on and do it with us! The more the merrier!

Hilda, who has her hair all teased up and is wearing green lipstick, which doesn't look as cool on her as it does on Susie, glances over at the women. "Oh, them," she says. "The circus freaks."

"The one looks like a man," Renee says, referring to the stocky blond with the shorter hair. The girls flop down and join in the staring. In a couple of minutes Ricky and Steven walk by and ask what you're doing, and Steven says you're all being kind of mean and keeps walking, but Ricky flops down and gets into the spirit of the game. Then Timmy and Tommy Shane, the ten-year-old twins, join in, and a few other younger kids, and eventually about a dozen kids are oogling the women from Mrs. Jensen's tree lawn. Finally the brown-haired woman walks halfway across the street and yells, "This stopped being funny a long time ago!" and you all roll around on the grass laughing.

Oogling "the Blobs"—which is what you and Susie have named them—becomes the main source of neighborhood entertainment. You and Susie always organize staring sessions when you see the women outside doing their gardening, summoning all the kids who are around to participate, but sometimes you'll be walking around and you'll be delighted to see a group of younger kids on Mrs. Jensen's lawn, oogling the Blobs all on their own. (Mrs. Jensen is about a hundred years old and attended by nurses and has no idea what's going on.) The idea of oogling the Blobs is to get them to react, and eventually they do either by yelling or threatening to call the cops. Once while you're oogling them with a half-dozen other kids (you're all pretending to be the kids with radioactive eyes in *Village of the Damned*) two cops do show up, and they talk to the Blobs and keep looking at you while you all pretend to be searching for four-leaf clovers, and then you hear them arguing with the Blobs, and finally they just shrug their shoulders and return to their car, giving you all a friendly little wave before they drive away. You all roll on the ground laughing as the Blobs storm into their house and slam the door. You're delighted that the Blobs called the cops on you, not only because the cops blew them off, but because now you have even more reason to hate them.

In the middle of the summer you spend two weeks at Camp Shalom, where you live in a cabin with seven other girls your age, including a couple of kids from your school. You used to go to "day camp" as a little kid, but this is your first time at overnight camp and you love it. You love running around outside, and roasting hot dogs and marshmallows over a campfire, and singing songs and playing hand-clapping games and eating in a mess hall, and teasing Laurie, your dark-haired cabin counselor, who teases you back, calling you a bunch of "turnips." Even when your new friends chatter about hair styles and crushes on boys you don't feel lonely or left out; you just feel like one of the girls. You gravitate toward a pretty, buxom girl in the cabin next door, Diane Feinstein, who possesses that irresistible combination of popularity and kindness. When you're around Diane, talking to her about life in Shaker Heights, about her parents who travel to India every year to meet with government officials, about her starring role in *Annie Get Your Gun* at school, it's like being sucked into a whirlpool of warm sudsy water. You like to touch her, bumping against her or smelling her hair, saying you love the smell of her shampoo, and she's cheerfully tolerant of your silliness.

After you get home you spend a few days sulking around the house, and then you get up the courage to call Diane, hoping she'll invite you to swim in her backyard pool in Shaker Heights. You get the little piece of paper with her number written on it, and you go into your parents' bedroom and call the number, and she answers the phone.

Hi, Diney, you say. It's Joanna. You're annoyed that your heart is thumping.

Diane misses a beat before answering. "Joanna!" she says. "How the heck are ya?"

I'm okay, you say. Just hangin' out.

"Yeah, me too," Diane says.

So whaddaya doin'?

"I'm lying by the pool, getting brown as a berry," Diane says.

Wow, you say. Sounds great. Are you having any pool parties this summer?

"I'm having one on Saturday," Diane says. "You know the boy I told you about, David Mars?"

Uh-huh.

"He's bringing some of his friends who go to University School."

Great! you say. Sounds like a riot.

"Oh, it will be," Diane says. "He told me his one friend, Freddie Canyon, can multiply any numbers in an instant, in his head."

That's amazing! you say, trying to work up some enthusiasm for this revelation. I don't believe it.

"Neither do I but David swears it's true," Diane says. There's a pause. "So what are you doing this weekend?" Diana says. "Playing ball?"

Nah, you say. That's just a camp thing. I'm just, you know, hanging out. With my friends and stuff.

"Great!" Diane says. "Listen, I gotta go. My mom wants me to help her make egg salad."

Okay, well, nice talking to you, you say. After you hang up you detach from your humiliation so your body becomes mechanical, without emotion. You sit on the couch and stare. You put *Zorba the Greek* on your parents' record console and listen to the whole album, but it doesn't make you feel any better. A feeling of icy terror creeps into you, like a little black venomous snake, a baby snake trying to wiggle into your gut.

You jump up and leave the house and ride your bike to Susie's. Before going up her driveway you look down the street and see the Blobs driving out of their yard. You ride to their house and up their driveway to the garage. You jump off your bike and walk through the side door of the garage, which is full of gardening stuff. You storm through the garage, kicking stuff around. You kick over a bag of dirt and you kick a couple plastic containers across the floor and you kick a little bag of seeds as though it's a football, and you pick up a rake and hurl it against the wall. You kick a shovel and stub your toe, which stops your rampage. You walk back through the side door, get back on your bike, and leave the Blobs' yard. As you ride over to Susie's, you feel a million times better, as though you did something good rather than bad.

Rhonda tells you that Susie has gone to the movies with Steven to see *The Unsinkable Molly Brown*. You ride over to Steven's to wait for them to come back. His mom puts down her paperback and asks you about camp and what you've been doing since you got home, and you're happy to answer her questions because, unlike your parents, Joan is just curious about your life and doesn't act all nervous about it. Of course you don't mention kicking stuff around in the Blobs' garage but when Susie and Steven come back you surprise yourself by not even mentioning it to them either. They tell you about the movie, and then Charley and your brother Mike wander in after playing baseball, and Harold grills hamburgers for all you kids and steaks for him and Joan even though he knows he'll end up eating Joan's steak while she just nibbles on salad.

On Friday night you sleep over at Susie's, which you've done already a couple of times since school let out. You and Susie lie next to each other in her cozy double bed and chatter all night about everything that happened that day. Before you fall asleep you always do at least fifteen minutes of "feel-gooders." This is your favorite part of the night, taking turns stroking each other's back, arms, or hair, depending on which part of the body you choose. Each of you gets twenty strokes apiece. As you lie there, purring as Susie's fingers stroke your skin, you wish you could do feel-gooders forever. Susie seems to feel the same way, because it's after 3 a.m. when you both drop off to sleep.

The two of you wake up late and get dressed, and after Rhonda makes a pancake breakfast you and Susie go outside to walk around the neighborhood. As you approach the Blobs' house, two girls round the corner that you recognize as older racks from your school. Both of them wear short-shorts, teased-up hair, and heavy eye makeup.

"Hi, Susie-Q!" one of the girls says as they walk up to you.

"What's up, guys?" Susie says. She turns to you. "Do you know Marlene and Connie?"

You say hi, and they glance at you and say hi, then turn their attention back to Susie. "You know the weirdos that live in that house?" Marlene says. "The ones that you all stare at?"

It's called oogling, you say.

"It's called *what*?" Marlene says, looking at you impatiently. You've always been a little afraid of the rack girls and were envious of how charmed they were by Susie when she first showed up at school with her flamboyant ways.

Susie nudges you to shut up. "What about them?" she asks.

"Wait until you hear this," Marlene says. "You know Sandy Lucas and Mike Russo?"

"Yeah," you both say. Last year they were the most famous rack couple in the ninth grade.

"Well," Marlene says. "One night last week they were sneaking through those ladies' backyard and decided to peak into their window. And you know how tall Mike is? He's, like, over six feet. And he looked into the window and the shade was up just enough for them to see into the room . . ."

"And they were, like stuck together on the bed, naked!" Connie says with a flourish.

"Oh my God," you and Susie exclaim simultaneously.

"Swear to God," Marlene says.

"Are you sure Mike wasn't lying?" Susie asks.

"No," Marlene says. "Because then he lifted Sandy up so she could see, and she swore to me that they were wrapped around each other naked like a big icky ball of wax!"

What were they doing, stuck together like that, you ask, and the three girls look at you as though you just asked who George Washington was.

"Don't mind her," Susie says, ruffling your hair. "She's just joking."

"She wasn't joking," Connie says. "She's—" and she points to her head and makes a "dumb" face.

Well what were they doing? you yell.

Susie puts her arm around you and whispers in your ear, "They were having sex, dopey."

Oh, you say, feeling your face turn beet red.

"Don't you know about lesbians, Joey?" Connie says.

"She has to know because she is one," Marlene says.

Shut up, I am not, you say.

"Leave my friend alone," Susie says. "She's not a pervert, she's just—a little unusual."

138

Yeah, you say. I'm unusual.

"You're a perv," Connie says. Then she turns back to Susie. "Anyway, my mom is going to see if she can do something about this."

"Like what?" Susie says.

"Like maybe get them removed from their house. I mean, you know, it's not good for the kids to be around that."

"Well, they would have to prove it," Susie says.

"Yeah, but at least the cops can keep an eye on them," Marlene says.

After the racks continue up the street, you feel upset and embarrassed to have acted so ignorant about what the Blobs were doing. You've heard of *lesbians* but you never connected them with anything in your life. You hated the Blobs because they were mean and unfriendly and strange, not because you thought they were perverts. The whole idea of sex disgusts you, even sex between a man and a woman. The thought of two women doing it not only is disgusting, it also seems like a lot of nerve. The Blobs should at least have the decency to be ashamed of what they are instead of rolling around naked together like "an icky ball of wax."

What is *wrong* with those women? you say to Susie. Why would they even want to *do* that?

"Because they're sick puppies," Susie says.

Well then they need to be put away, you say.

"Like where?"

Like in one of those colonies for people who don't belong in normal society.

"I don't think they have those colonies in the United States," Susie says. "Maybe in India."

Well then maybe they should move to India, you say.

That evening you drag into your house, wishing you were anyplace else. You always feel trapped at home in the summer, in the big, closed, air-conditioned house. You can't stand being around your parents, especially your father, who always tries to joke around with you, and you have to joke back instead of telling him to go away. You wolf down three hot dogs for supper and then go upstairs and turn on the radio and lie on your bed staring at the ceiling. Dusty Springfield starts singing, "Wishin' and hopin' and thinkin' and prayin' . . . that won't get you into his arms . . . all you gotta do is hold him and kiss him and love him and show him that you care . . . show him that you care just for him . . ." and you feel yourself dissolving like a bar of soap as the song fills up your bedroom.

Rainy Sunday Morning in Late October

I cannot believe what happened today. It's three o'clock in the morning and the rain is battering my bedroom window, and usually the rain helps me sleep but I don't think I'll ever get to sleep. I took a whole Ativan and it didn't even work. I'm very upset. I'm very, very upset. Early this afternoon I had just got done writing the above chapter, about my persecution of those poor lesbians when I was a child, which was disorienting enough, thinking about what a little homophobe I was, consumed with hatred for the lesbians who embodied all my self-hatred. I was lying on my couch editing the chapter and then this ludicrous thing happened, and nobody knows about it yet because I'm afraid to tell anyone. They'll tell me to call the police and I'm not going to. I'm sure you'll think I didn't handle it right. This is what upsets me. That the whole world will judge me about the way I handled this thing that happened today, and that I don't even have the confidence not to care. I've always had confidence in the way I handle things even if I do them wrong. I do things my way and the hell with what everyone thinks. But right now I'm having a panic attack about it, and when you have a panic attack you're like a naked, helpless little person about to be disemboweled by a lion.

I'm going to write about what happened this afternoon because I can't sleep and I don't know what else to do. I was lying on the couch editing my chapter about my sick homophobic adolescence, and all of a sudden I heard a loud noise in the living-room closet, not the coat closet next to the door, but the far closet where I keep my off-season clothes. I went over to the closet and stood there listening to the noise. Right away I was terrified that it was a rat. I've never had a rat in here, although there have been a couple of mice, but I'm so jumpy lately that I always fear the worst, and this noise didn't sound like a mouse. It sounded more like a badger or a hyena, to tell the truth, although I don't know what either of those animals sounds like, but anyway I was thinking of running downstairs and getting one of the guys from the chop shop to come up here and investigate but I was too scared to even move. I just stood there frozen at the door, listening to this THUMP! THUMP! THUMP! And then the door burst open and I *screamed*! And the four teenaged hoods swarmed out of the closet and walked right past me as if I wasn't even there and went to the seating area of my living room.

Obviously I was in shock. I just stood there gaping at these lunatics invading my living room and felt as though I was in some kind of absurdist play. The good-looking tattooed leader and the crazy little Jew who told me to fry in hell plopped down on my sofa, the tall skinny one planted himself on my green chair, and the chunky one with glasses who made the obscene gesture at me in the hallway flopped down on my futon. Finally I had the presence of mind to look in the closet and *there was a huge hole in the ceiling! Those crazy kids had apparently chainsawed a hole in the floor of the Chinese people's closet in order to obtain access to my apartment!* Jesus Christ. I cannot believe they had the nerve to do this.

I just kept standing there like a dope. I heard a guy talking in Chinese through the hole in the closet. I looked over at the boys and saw them all poking on their phones except for the Jewish kid, who was sitting next to the good-looking kid banging his head against the back of the sofa. I realized I had to do something besides stand there like a statue, so I shut the closet door and walked over to the seating area and planted myself in the middle of the rug like an old maid at a beer party. "*What are you people doing in here?*" I yelled.

"We're gonna make this place our clubhouse," the chunky kid said while playing some game on his phone.

"You certainly are not," I said.

"Our phones don't work up there," said the skinny kid, looking comfy on my green chair with his feet on the ottoman.

"Well that is not my problem!" I said. My voice was shaking and I tried to control it. "You can't just barge into someone's home through a closet!" I said, trying not to cry.

"We just did," said the good-looking kid, who was sitting on my couch moving his finger up and down his screen.

"Yeah, we just did," echoed the chunky kid over the beeps and shrieks coming from his phone. Between the beeps and shrieks and the Jewish kid banging his head against the sofa, I thought I was losing my mind.

"Why is he banging his head?" I yelled, pointing at the Jewish kid. He had on baggy jeans like last time and he'd replaced his yarmulke with this goofy little porkpie hat but he still looked so Jewish. He looked like a *yeshiva bocher* on steroids.

"He's always bangin' his head," said the skinny kid.

"Well he needs to stop," I said.

They didn't even look at me. They all just started talking to one another as though I wasn't there. "Jack ain't gonna like that Chu ain't paid up in a month," the skinny kid said to the good-looking kid.

"Maybe we need to kick his ass," said the chunky kid.

"You're not kicking anyone's ass," I said. "You need to leave." My voice sounded as though it was coming from underwater.

"You couldn't kick your own ass, Mikey," the skinny kid said.

"Yeah," Mikey said. "'Cause I'm lying down."

"Jakey kicks ass," the Jewish kid said, apparently referring to himself. "Jakey's a bad motherfucker."

"Jakey's a crazy fuck," the leader said. "Jakey needs to take a pill."

"He don't like them pills," the skinny kid said. "He says they make him sleepy."

"Why can't you get a connection upstairs?" I yelled. "Isn't there a hot spot up there or something?" They ignored me.

It occurred to me that Molly could come over after one of her meetings, the way she sometimes does, and find these kids sprawled all over my living room. All of a sudden I was more scared of her showing up than I was of the kids. I started getting paranoid, not because I felt in any physical danger, but because I knew that the whole world would think I wasn't handling the situation right, that I should call the police or something, and there was no way I was going to call the police on these kids but I didn't know what else to do. As I stood there immobilized I actually pictured Molly approaching my building, clutching her briefcase, and I was frantically trying to figure out what I would say to her when she marched in here and discovered these interlopers and demanded to know how they had gotten in.

"You got any soda?" The skinny kid's voice brought me back to reality.

"No I don't," I said. "I have milk and juice."

The kid got up, went into my kitchen, and came back a couple minutes later with a carton of milk. He sat back down in the chair, opened the carton, and put it to his lips.

"Stop!" I yelled.

"That's disgusting, Eric," the good-looking kid said.

"You're disgusting, Bobby," the skinny kid said.

I ran over and pulled the carton out of Eric's hands. "I'll get you a glass for God's sake!" I ran into the kitchen, got a glass, poured the kid a glass of milk, and put the carton back in the fridge. I was very proud of myself that I had been able to override Eric's decision to drink from the carton. I went back into the living room and put the glass of milk on the end table for him and he picked it up and started drinking. "How long do you all intend to stay here?" I asked. "I have things to do."

"Don't worry about it, Mommy," said Bobby.

"It's raining, man," said Mikey.

For a moment I almost felt bad sending them out into the pouring rain. It's been raining nonstop for three days in half the country. That was another surreal thing about this whole outrageous situation. That it doesn't stop raining. There was even an article about the rain on the front page of *The New York Times* today. The experts are saying that the rain seemed to come out of nowhere; it defies all the weather patterns going on in the rest of the world. I find this whole apocalyptic atmosphere in the city almost as disconcerting as those lunatic kids breaking into my house.

Eric glugged down the last of the milk and put the glass on the end table. Then he said, "You live here by yourself?" which gave me the creeps.

"Yeah, how come you're not married?" said Mikey. "How come you're an old maid?"

"Maybe she's gay," Eric said. I felt ludicrously grateful to him for making this unconscious connection with me. It made me feel less alienated from all of them. I almost told them I was gay and then I thought, *Shut up, Joanna. Are you crazy? It's none of their business.* Then I was proud of myself that I had the good sense not to tell them I was gay.

Bobby said, "We gotta go," apparently responding to some mandate on his phone. He stood up and said, "Come on, we gotta go collect from Chu."

Bobby walked to the door, and Eric and Mikey got up and followed him. Jakey got up and started walking all the way around the room.

"Come on, Jakey," Bobby called to him. "Let's go. We're gonna go see Chu. We might have to kick his ass. You wanna kick Chu's ass?"

"I'll kick Chu's ass," Jakey said.

"I do not believe this is happening," I mumbled.

Jakey joined his friends at the door, and they all walked out the door and ran down the stairs. As soon as I heard them leave the building I shut the door and started to cry. And this is another thing. I'm not somebody who cries all the time. Since my mom died all I do is cry. Yesterday I cried because my towel fell on the floor.

I felt so bad about being a victim of a home invasion by teenaged punks. I've always prided myself on how well I get along with kids, and especially teenagers. I've never been intimidated by tough kids. I'm always nice to them when I see them on the street, and sometimes I stop and shoot the breeze with them and they're always friendly to me. Kids in general think I'm cool. My niece and nephew and Molly's daughter Zoey, who I consider a niece, love hanging out with me. Why am I suddenly some old ninny who allows her home to be taken over by four audacious punks? This is not like me at all.

You know what? It's a good thing I'm writing about this, because I'm starting to realize what really happened to me today. I wasn't even really scared of those ruffians who broke into my apartment, although I'm not saying it wasn't totally freaky. I was scared of my own helplessness with them. I was scared that I had lost my mojo. Which I have! I've lost all my confidence because I haven't sold my book. Before the kids barged in here, my agent called and told me I got two more rejections from publishers. When you've written a novel, when you've put your whole heart and soul into it, *every rejection you get diminishes you*! After I got that depressing news, and then those kids burst out of my closet, I felt so—so—insubstantial. Like people in the movies who are becoming invisible but they don't know it until they can see right through their hands. You might say, oh, yeah, what would you have done with those boys if you had a publishing contract and all your mojo? I don't know, but I'm sure I would have done something other than stand there warbling at them while they ignored me and poked on their phones and talked about kicking Chu's ass.

What am I going to do when those little schmucks come back? I'm sure they'll come bursting back out of the closet tomorrow. If I call the Russian girls at the "management office," they'll say they'll send someone to fix the closet and it will never happen. Even if it did, the kids would just saw another hole in it. This is all my fault for being mean to those poor lesbians when I was a kid, and opening Pandora's box by writing about it. I was an antagonistic teenager and now I've got teenagers being antagonistic to me. And there's nobody I can talk to about this horrible poetic justice being visited on me. Molly will just tell me to call the cops. It's not her style to call the cops on people, but what other course of action is there, except to find some adult men to threaten the kids? I could do that. The Mexican guys in the chop shop would probably do it, but I don't know how far they would go. I don't want the kids hurt or anything. Even though they were talking about hurting Chu so it would serve them right.

The only person I could really talk to about this is Susan. She would understand why I don't call the cops. In fact the next time those brats pay me a visit she would come charging over here and start bossing them around. She would probably have them washing my dishes and cleaning the piss off the toilet seat. She would be here in a minute if I called her. But I can't. Not unless she breaks up with the other Mrs. Judas.

So here I am at four o'clock in the morning still not being able to sleep. Usually listening to the rain helps me sleep but now it just sounds ominous, like the rain in a haunted house movie. I'm terrified to fall asleep because I'm afraid that I'll evaporate if I don't stay awake and keep looking at my hands. I'd better take another Ativan. There's no way a second one won't work.

FALL OF 1964

That sounds like some crazy made-up story, you say while you devour your cafeteria lunch of Salisbury steak, mashed potatoes and gravy, and blueberry pie. Some gravy spills onto your new plaid jumper with a little bow and you try to wipe it off with a napkin. You liked the jumper when you bought it, but ever since Renee made fun of the bow you've decided that you hate it. I can't believe Patty Rourke actually sat on John's lap, you say.

You're jealous enough that Molly went with her cousin Vic to the Beatles concert and stormed onto the stage with hundreds of other hysterical fans and touched Paul's hand. But if it's true that Patty Rourke sneaked onto the dumbwaiter of the Sheraton hotel before the concert and somehow got up to the Beatles' room, that would be even more upsetting, because that's the kind of adventure that you would love to have. Patty Rourke doesn't seem to be deserving of this kind of adventure.

"Don't eat too fast or nothin'," Molly says as she scoops up some mashed potatoes. Sitting next to you, she looks fashionably "mod" in her short purple and chartreuse dress. You've given up trying to look as cool as Molly or Susie, who sits across from you with her hair all sticking out like the comedian Phyllis Diller, wearing a calf-length yellow and red skirt and a blouse with big black polka dots that she picked up at the Salvation Army. It never ceases to amaze you how her clothes are kind of similar to the dorky clothes she wore as a kid, but now instead of looking dorky they look cool and outrageous, although they would still be considered dorky if any other girl at school wore them.

"The story is true, Jo," Susie says, as she pulls apart the tuna fish sandwich Rhonda prepared for her. She licks the tuna fish on one of the pieces of bread as though she's licking a lollipop. "Patty's cousin Clark works in the kitchen at the Sheraton," Susie says. "He got her into the hotel before the press conference, and nobody was allowed onto the elevators without, like, a press pass or something so he put her on the dumbwaiter and got her up to their floor! And she, like, hid up there during the press conference and then afterward John came out of the room with a bucket of ice and he invited her into the room. And she sat on his lap!"

God, that's amazing, you say. Even though you had no interest in going to the concert, for some reason, now you wish you had been there. You missed all kinds of excitement. Strangely, you're more jealous of Patty sneaking up to the Beatles' floor in a dumb-waiter than you are of her getting to sit on John's lap, or even of Molly getting to storm the stage with hundreds of other kids, although you're not exactly happy about missing out on a riot.

How big was the dumbwaiter? you ask.

"How are we supposed to know?" Susie says. "Do you think Patty measured it?"

Well I don't know how she could have fit into it.

"They are very large," Molly says, enunciating each word as though talking to a three-year-old. "It's in a hotel."

I know it's in a hotel! you say, hurt by Molly's sarcasm. Since school started almost two months ago, you've been feeling out of step with the other eighth-graders. You're not lumped in with the unpopular or "queer" kids due to your friendships with high-status classmates like Renee Siegel, class president Steven Eisner, and the notorious Susie Moscowitz, who marches around Greenvale in her crazy clothes, pulling kids into her orbit like a demented queen bee. But unlike last year, when you felt part of the crowd, now you feel as though the other girls are leaving you behind. Last weekend you went to Rozzie Cohen's party and you sat awkwardly in Rozzie's tiled basement watching your friends play "spin the bottle," and when Steven's spun bottle pointed at Susie you felt terribly annoyed when Steven kissed her, and then you sat there hating yourself for not being in the spirit of the game. And then Mike Ferris, who was Molly's "date" for the evening, spun the bottle and it pointed at you, and Mike looked at you and said, "No way," and you were both humiliated and relieved. When your father picked you up from the party and asked you all jovially if you had a good time you hated him as much as you hated everyone at the party, but you just mumbled that the party was "great."

"Vic's coming over after school today," Molly says, neatly cutting into a slice of pie. "We're going to carve his pumpkin into Ghoulardi."

You want to be invited to Molly's as well, not only because it would be fun to try to carve a pumpkin into Ghoulardi, the wild beatnik host of the Friday night *Shock Theater*, but because you're intrigued with Molly's cousin Vic, who moved to Greenvale from California at the beginning of the school year. Of course, he lives in Little Jerusalem, like all the other kids except you, who live on your boring rich street.

I like Vic, you say.

"Yeah, that figures," Susie says.

Why does it figure? you ask.

"Because he's cuckoo, like you," Susie says, tapping your head. Shut up, you say, smiling, and push her hand away, but you sensed a teeny bit of meanness in her comment, and now you don't have the nerve to ask Molly if you can come over to help her and Vic carve the pumpkin. Even though Vic was embraced by the popular crowd as soon as he arrived at school, and you haven't spent much time with him, you know he likes you. He laughed with delight when you told him about the neighborhood pastime of oogling the Blobs, and the following week he told you and your friends at lunch that he and two ninth-grade boys had sneaked into the Blobs' house over the weekend and "messed things up in there." Molly wasn't amused—like Steven, she thinks tormenting the Blobs is immature—but the rest of you demanded details, and Vic said they tipped over all the furniture in the living room and then they went into the bedroom and smeared ketchup on the bed. You started laughing, picturing the Blobs' shock when they came home and found everything in disarray, and Molly said the Blobs probably called the cops, and Vic said they probably didn't because the cops don't like perverts and everyone decided he was probably right. Even though you know it was mean, you're still happy that Vic and the other boys broke into the Blobs' house because it gave everyone something exciting to talk about for the rest of the day.

"Do you have detention after school?" Molly asks, perhaps sensing that you might be feeling left out of her plans to carve a pumpkin with Vic.

When you reply in the affirmative, Susie says, "So what else is new."

Since school started early last month, you've accumulated more detentions than any other kid in the whole school. Detentions are like a reward to you. Being in detention is like being in paradise compared to being at home with your parents, who make you feel like a terrible person because you can't stand being around them.

Pickles told me yesterday that if I get into trouble one more time she'll suspend me, you say, tearing into your blueberry pie. You can't suppress a smile as you mention Pickles, aka Miss Dilley, the tall, short-haired, strutting dean of girls. You thought up the name "Pickles" a couple weeks before, after you had already become the dean's number one problem. At least twice a week you're summoned to the office by a student aide. While your girlfriends flirt with boys, you talk and whisper and pass notes in class, refuse to stay in your seat during study hall, throw food in the cafeteria, climb through the locker-room window and walk around on the roof, and make stick drawings of unpopular teachers and tape them to the walls. Strangely, you commit all these offenses blatantly and out in the open, and are always caught. Your friends assume that you're just reckless and indifferent to punishment, but the truth is that getting caught and sent to Miss Dilley's office is the whole purpose of your misbehavior. Whenever you're in Pickles' office, you're lulled by the dean's deep voice lecturing you about "proper conduct for a young lady," and you feel as though you're melting into her nubby little sofa. The dean's office is the only place in the world where the terror oozing underneath your bouncy personality gets sucked back to whatever mysterious dimension it came from, and you feel safe and warm and cared for. But as soon as the dean dismisses you and you're back out in the hallway the terror oozes back up, thicker and more odious than before. Your desperate need for the dean's attention makes you feel like the opposite of a juvenile delinquent. It makes you feel like a "queer girl"—queer meaning dorky and unpopular. Your whole life at school is devoted to hiding your true self, the dorky queer girl that you really are.

"Well, if you're suspended you can do your homework at home," Susie says. "They let me do my homework at home last year when Pickles kicked me out for wearing sneakers outside of gym." This year Susie still occasionally wears high-top sneakers to school but for some reason the dean pays no attention to it. Maybe she just hasn't noticed because she's too busy dealing with her latest problem child.

"Hey, Susie Q!" Carla Feranacci is standing behind you and Molly, smiling over at Susie. She wears a tight black skirt, a pink rayon blouse, and black shoes with a two-inch heel. You turn around and look at her. "We're meeting in the lavatory," Carla says to Susie, making a smoking gesture with her two fingers.

"Okay, I'll be there in a few," Susie says.

Can I come? you ask.

"No," Carla says, rolling her eyes, as though this is the most ridiculous request in the world.

You know the rack girls don't like you. Whenever they pass you in the hall they make a big point of ignoring you. Once you heard Carla say to Vicky Baglione as they passed you in the hall, "There's something wrong with her," and the familiar terror slithered back inside you and bit you in the gut.

Why not? you yell at Carla, figuring that you have Susie on your side.

But then Susie says, "You don't even smoke."

"Yeah, Joanna," Carla says. "You don't even smoke. I'll see ya, Susie." Before she walks away she slaps you on the head. Although it hurts, you choose to believe it's a playful slap and not an aggressive one.

Since when do you even smoke? you say to Susie.

"Oh, I just smoke with them in the lavatory," Susie says. "I only have one cig just to be sociable."

I could have one cig to be sociable, you mumble, and Molly says, "Stop being a baby."

"What did she say?" Susie asks Molly.

I didn't say anything, you say, scowling.

Susie gets up and walks off with her tray, and you see Molly's cousin Vic talking to her as they return their trays. Then Vic walks toward your table with his bouncy walk. Vic walks as though he thinks the whole world is watching him. He comes up to Molly, leans over her, flings his arm around her neck, and nuzzles her hair. "Hi, cuzzie-wuzzie," he says. Even though he's new, Vic is already a big shot at school. He's tall and lanky with dark hair flopping over his forehead and an explosive grin flashing big white teeth. He acts cocky and superior about being from California, and his notoriety increased after he got two ninth-graders to commit a blatantly delinquent act with him. "Are we still doing this pumpkin thing?" Vic asks Molly.

"Yes," Molly says, blushing a little. Even though she doesn't approve of Vic's breaking into the Blobs' house with the ninth-grade boys, she's still proud to be the cousin of this magnetic boy.

"Hot diggety," Vic says, making the corny expression sound cute. Then he turns to you. "How 'bout you, Joey?" he asks. "You gonna help us carve the pumpkin?"

Nah, I have detention, you say. You hope Vic will keep his attention focused on you, but he just turns away and says to Molly, "So what's your mom making for dinner?"

You get up, return your tray, and walk out of the cafeteria. You feel dejected and left out of everything. You didn't go to the Beatles concert. You weren't invited to smoke a cigarette in the bathroom. And even if you didn't have detention, Molly would not have invited you to carve pumpkins with her and Vic. You feel like a cootie. During the rest of your classes you slouch in your chair, daydreaming about being in Pickles' office and listening to her deep, hypnotic voice. When the final bell rings you head for the detention room, where you've decided to write your essay for English class. You're starting to miss getting attention for your writing. You continue to get A's in English, but Miss Robbins, sensing that you're more focused on getting into trouble than on writing, doesn't ask you to read your stuff out loud, as you were often asked to do last year.

As you head down the hall, four rack girls round the corner. You start to smile, but the girls stop in front of you, blocking your way past them.

"What are you doing hanging around here after school hours?" asks Carla Ferranacci, in a not-nice voice.

I'm going to detention, you say, smiling in spite of yourself.

"What's so funny about going to detention, Joanna?" Andrea Richardson says.

"She loves going to detention," says Vicky Baglione. "She deliberately does things to get detentions."

"No, she deliberately does things so she can get sent to Dilley's office ten times a day," Carla says.

"Joanna loves Miss Dilley," says Vicky. She makes kissing noises in the air.

"No, she loves Susie," Carla says. "Susie Susie Susie." She hugs herself and looks dreamily at the ceiling.

That's stupid, you say.

"Stupid but true, Joey," Carla says.

"She's so not normal," says Bonnie Danvers. "Look how she holds her books."

"Like a boy," Carla says.

You shift your books from your waist to your chest and hold them in the "proper" way. I know I hold my books wrong, you say.

"You do a lot of things wrong," Vicky says. "Why do you act so weird, Joey?"

"I don't know how Susie can even like her," Carla says. "She's—" She makes a crazy face and touches her finger to her head.

You're trying hard not to cry. "Let's go," Carla says, and they start to walk away. "You'd better watch it," Carla says, bumping against you as she walks past.

You're afraid people will see you all upset so you run into the closest lavatory and stand there, fighting back tears. You've never had an experience like that before. The girls were acting as though they wanted to beat you up. Not that you think they ever would, but you've never been physically threatened by any kids. And they said such vicious things. They made you feel like one of the Blobs. You don't know what to do. You can't go to detention and you can't stand the thought of going home. Maybe you'll have to stay in the bathroom all night. Then you get an idea. You stop up all the sinks with paper towels, turn on the faucets, and wait until water spills over the sinks onto the floor. Feeling enormously relieved, you walk out of the bathroom and stand there and wait until water runs into the hallway. You're about to dash out of the school when you see Pickles walking towards you. Oh-oh, you say out loud.

Pickles marches up and sees the river of water running down the hall. "What on earth is going on here?" she yells.

Two ninth-grade girls walk past, cradling their books.

"Ooh, Joanna flooded the bathroom," one of them says.

"You're in big trouble, Jo," the other one chirps, and they keep walking.

"Wait right here," Pickles says to you. She hurries into the bathroom and you hear the faucets being turned off. Then Pickles comes back out and says, "Come with me."

Once you're settled in Pickles' office, waiting for the dean to get off the phone with the janitor, you start feeling agitated again. What if one of the rack girls finds out what you did and makes fun of you for trying to get Pickles' attention? You're afraid that

154

the rack girls can see through you when nobody else can, not even your closest friends.

Pickles gets off the phone, folds her hands on her desk, and fixes her gaze on you the way she always does. Her eyes remind you of blue marbles, which makes it even stranger that you find her stare relaxing rather than creepy, even though you laugh with your friends about how the dean "oogles" you. "What am I going to do with you, Joanna?" the dean says. As usual her deep hypnotic voice turns your cold slimy terror into warm sludge. "I can't understand what's happened between last year and this year," Pickles says. "Last year I had no trouble with you. You were an excellent student. You wrote that wonderful essay about President Kennedy. You were on your best behavior. And this year you seem absolutely dedicated to getting into trouble. And you show no sign of stopping." You smile. "It's not funny, Joanna," the dean says. "You are headed down a very dangerous path. Did you flood the lavatory deliberately so you would get suspended?"

I don't care if I'm suspended, you say.

"You don't care about being suspended," the dean says, and looks thoughtful for a few seconds. Then she folds her hands and looks directly at you. "Joanna, I'm very concerned about you," she says. "You don't seem to be able to control your behavior, even after repeated lectures and punishments. It's become obvious to me that you won't be able to straighten yourself out without some kind of help. And it's my job to see that you get it. I'm going to call the Child Guidance Center in Cleveland Heights and arrange for you to see a social worker there. Meanwhile, I'm sending you home for three days to think about your behavior. But I'm afraid at this point you're not going to make any significant improvements without some professional help."

You feel triumphant, as though you've swum the English Channel. For years you've dreamed of having a social worker, like a real juvenile delinquent. Even Susie has a social worker. Susie hates her, but you would rather have ugly old Miss Browning than nobody. I don't need any stupid social worker, you sneer.

"I think you do," Pickles says. "You are a very confused young

155

lady. It's not only your behavior that deeply concerns me, but your attitude about it. You're the only girl in this school who won't even promise to try to improve her behavior. When I ask you to make that effort you just shrug your shoulders. You actually seem dedicated to getting into as much trouble as you can. This is evidence that you have some serious problems, and I hope that talking to a social worker will help you to iron them out. I'm going to call the agency today and set up an appointment for you, and then I'm going to call your parents. Please wait outside in the office for someone to come and pick you up. I'll let Miss Reed know you'll be waiting out there."

After you get through the horrible obligatory "talk" with your parents that night, you enjoy being suspended. It has heightened your status as a troublemaker and makes you feel special, just like being asked to read your compositions in class made you feel special last year. And there's something cozy about being at home during the day while everyone else is at school. It's kind of like the cozy feeling of being sick, with the exception of your mother's attitude, which is sarcastic instead of indulgent. But you don't have to see your mother very much because you just hang out in your room the whole time, except when you come down for lunch, but then you gallop right back upstairs and listen to the radio and wait for your friends to come home from school and start calling you. You're in a pretty good mood, not only because you got suspended, which feels like an accomplishment, but because you're going to see a social worker, who will either be a dork that you can make fun of or someone cool that can be your friend. Whenever you think about seeing a social worker, the slimy terror oozing through you loses its chill and curls up inside you like a pet snake that's just been fed.

Dark and Rainy November Afternoon

Molly is probably smirking with self-righteousness because I have made the four little gangsters who had been tormenting me into my "little friends" just as she had predicted. They are sitting here in my living room as we speak. Everyone's calling me and admonishing me for allowing these lawless children to hang out in my home. But what else was I supposed to do? They would just keep coming in here from the closet. Every afternoon for the past week they've been marching out of my closet, and I'm very proud of myself that I overcame my panic attack and have gotten control of this whole situation. I don't care what anybody thinks. I'm befriending these disturbed children, giving them "shelter from the storm" as Bob Dylan would say. It's been raining continuously for two straight weeks in the whole eastern half of the country and everyone's all freaked out about it, and I'm just trying to do something nice for these boys instead of tossing them out into the apocalypse, or whatever it is that's taking place out there.

I think it's kind of funny that they come in here through the closet. It's so wild and wacky. I don't know. Maybe I shouldn't allow it. I mean it wasn't very respectful of them to saw a hole in my closet ceiling and just barge into my home. Am I being a wimp? Molly thinks I am. She says the boys don't have any more feelings for me than they do for the furniture in this room. I have to admit they don't really talk to me very much. And it's kind of hard to concentrate on my own work while they're here. The only one who isn't totally hyper is chubby Mikey, who lies on my futon and plays loud games on his phone. Skinny Eric goes in and out of the kitchen, eating whatever food he finds in there and leaving a mess, and Bobby Chang keeps running his mouth at me while I'm trying to write, and Jakey the Jew doesn't even sit down. He walks in and out of my apartment, banging on the door whenever he needs to get back in, and comes in dripping wet, and he climbs on the windowsill and bangs on the window at people on the street. A couple days ago he went into the bathroom and started a fire in the wastebasket. He's obviously out of his mind.

They told me that with the exception of Jakey, they've all been friends since childhood. They work as debt collectors for their neighbor, Jack, who is part of an operation that smuggles Chinese people from the Fujian Province into the U.S. Once they get here, their benefactors install them in homes that are mostly crash pads and find them jobs and basically turn them into indentured servants until they pay off their debts.

"Jack must have good connections," I said.

"Yeah he's connected," Bobby said. "He's connected way high up."

"I'd like to meet him," I said.

They all laughed. "That ain't never gonna happen," Eric said.

"He's a Tong," Mikey said.

"Shut up, Mikey," Bobby said. "He ain't no Tong." He shot Mikey a look.

"Don't you all go to school?" I asked. "You should be going to school."

They laughed even harder. "Sometimes we go to school," Bobby said.

"I go to school," Mikey said.

"Yeah, when you're not in Crossroads," Bobby said.

"Shut up," Mikey said. "You was there too."

"Yeah, but that was just for stealing," Bobby said. "I didn't break no kid's arm."

I couldn't picture placid Mikey breaking somebody's arm. "I hope you don't go around hurting people when you collect money," I said. I was both alarmed and intrigued that at least two of them had been at Crossroads Juvenile Facility over in Brownsville. Even in these punitive times, a kid has to be pretty bad to get locked up.

"Nah," Bobby said. "We don't hurt nobody. We just use persuasion."

"Well, I hope that doesn't mean using threats and intimidation," I said, although I knew that Jack would want them to use any means necessary to collect the money.

"Don't worry about it, Mama," Bobby said. "We're very nice guys."

"I'm sure you are," I said with a skeptical smile. I watched

158

Jakey walking back and forth on my windowsill. "What the hell is this crazy Jewish kid doing in your crew?" I asked.

"We use him to scare people," Bobby said.

"Yeah," Eric said. "Like an attack dog."

"I thought you said you were nice guys, but that doesn't sound very nice," I said. "How do you even know him?"

"He lives in my building," Eric said.

"What!" I said. "In Chinatown? Why isn't he living with the other Hasidic Jews, like in Williamsburg or Crown Heights?"

"His mother ran away from the Jews," Eric said. "She didn't want to be a Jew anymore."

"My mother's a whore," Jakey said from up on the windowsill. "She's a *kurveh*. *Kurveh* is a Yiddish term for prostitute."

"What are you talking about?" I said to Jakey. "That sounds ridiculous. Why are you calling your mother a whore?"

"She's got a lotta boyfriends," Bobby said.

"I'm her pimp," Jakey said.

"You ain't her pimp," Eric said. "You don't even like that bitch."

After that conversation, which took place a few days ago, I decided that these boys need an adult in their lives to set a good example for them. Maybe they're not hardened criminals, but they're obviously not good boys. In fact just a few minutes ago I was telling Bobby about that asshole John Morton, the marketing guy who sabotaged the publication of my book, and he said, "Do you want us to fuck him up?"

"What do you mean, fuck him up?" I asked.

"We'll fuck up his shit, man."

I said no thank you, I can fight my own battles. "Anyway, you should not be 'fucking up' anyone," I told him. "The most successful businessmen treat people fairly. When you go upstairs to collect your money from those immigrants, you should act like gentlemen with them. You should be courteous with people who have risked their lives to come all the way over here from China, and I'm especially talking about the women."

"We don't touch them bitches," Bobby said. "They have diseases and shit."

159

"Some of 'em make a lotta money with their bodies," Eric said through his mouthful of potato chips.

"Where do you get that, man?" Bobby said. "They work at hair places."

"Well I certainly hope they're not selling their bodies, unless they choose to," I said. "You should not work for anyone who forces girls and women into prostitution to pay their debts. You should only work for honorable men." I admit that I felt kind of ridiculous when I said that, like I was on the set of *The Godfather*. What I didn't like was when I looked over at Bobby after giving my little speech, I think I saw him flick his tongue at me. It was a little bit creepy. But it could have been just a facial tic. I had plenty of those when I was a kid.

I hope these kids leave soon because I really need to go to work. They're starting to make me nervous. Right now Jakey's sitting on top of Mikey, lighting matches and tossing them onto the floor. I can't have him burning down my house. I don't even know what he's doing here now. It's Friday evening and he's supposed to be at *shul*. Even though he lives with this supposedly degenerate mother his Hasidic father makes him go to *shul* with him every week. When I asked him why he's not there now all he had to say was "Shut up, bitch." He's probably decided to hide out here instead of going to synagogue with his father. I can picture a posse of Hasidic men barging in here and dragging him away while screaming invectives at me in Yiddish for harboring a fugitive.

Well, I would rather deal with some crazy Hasidim than think about packing boxes in my dead parents' house. This morning on the phone (after making a crack about my playing "gang leader") Molly asked me when I'm going to get back to Cleveland to do it, and I just can't think about that right now because it's causing too much anxiety. Anyway, *why do I always have to do everything in my family?* Why doesn't my little brother get up off his ass and go there and start packing stuff up? I'm six hundred miles away and he's four miles away. He can't deal with her being dead so he escapes by playing fantasy football and watching *Green Acres* reruns. Meanwhile Michael, the older and supposedly more responsible brother, called me yesterday from the Amazon jungle and did he even mention the house? *No!* He just wanted to tell me that he's going to a ceremony next weekend hosted by a witch doctor who discovered an indigenous plant that you ingest with coconut milk and then you fly around the universe. After I hung up with him I called Rosie in Bolivia to tell her about this crazy ceremony and she said that she and my brother-in-law are thinking of going to it. None of my siblings live in the real world. Their lives do not contain even a semblance of normality.

Now Jakey is trying to set Mikey on fire. This is unacceptable. I really need to start setting some limits around here.

STILL 1964

Your appointment with the social worker is the Friday after you return to school, and your mom drives you to the Child Guidance Center in Cleveland Heights. You're wearing jeans, loafers, and a long-sleeved yellow shirt with flowers on it. The clinical director, a tall biddy with frizzy gray hair, takes you into her office and tells you that your social worker will be in to meet you momentarily. You wonder if she will be another old biddy. If so, you look forward to making her nervous with just one insolent look.

A few seconds later a Negro woman walks into the room. More specifically she strides into the room on red heels, her red-and-orange skirt crackling like a low fire. She's almost six feet tall, with bushy hair, loamy skin, and dangling earrings. You take one look at her and know this isn't going to go as you'd planned.

"Joanna, this is Miss Adams," the clinical director says.

The woman greets you with the understated smile of a worthy opponent in a sporting match before the opening whistle. "Hi, Joanna," she says in a rich, creamy voice poured from up high.

Hi, you say. You stand up and shake the woman's hand, wanting to show that you have a little class. Are you related to John Adams? you ask.

The social worker laughs. "Maybe distantly," she says. "You can call me Junie if you'd like." You see the clinical director wince. "How about coming along with me to my office," the social worker says. "We can talk there."

She ushers you into a small office with blue-and-gray carpeting, a desk with a leather swivel chair, two cushioned swivel chairs, and a couple of nondescript prints on the wall. You flop down on one of the cushioned chairs and stretch your legs out, and the social worker sits on the leather chair opposite you. "I understand you're here because you've had some problems at school," she says. "Do you want to tell me what's going on?"

Nothing's going on, you say. You slouch farther down in the chair and look around on the big wooden desk. You pick up a big rubber band and stretch it between your thumbs, looking at it.

"Your dean of girls, Miss Dilley, spoke to me about you," Junie says. "She told me you are constantly getting into trouble. Do you have any thoughts about why this is?"

Not really, you say. You smile and look at the ceiling and start twirling the rubber band around your finger.

"Well, sometimes kids get into trouble because they're worried about themselves and they act up to get attention," Junie says.

Ha, you say, slouching further down in the chair. If you say so. You look at the ceiling and keep twirling the rubber band. You're pretending to be bored and contemptuous, which isn't at all how you feel. You fell in love with Junie Adams the second you laid eyes on her. Not only was she nice to look at, but she also radiated confidence instead of acting scared or nervous to meet a crackpot teenager. You wish you could stay here forever. You feel even more safe and protected with this person you just met than you do with Pickles. The problem is that you know that as you leave the terror will start oozing through you again, and it will be even more intense than before. Junie Adams will make you feel even more creepy than Pickles does. Juvenile delinquents don't fall in love with their social workers. They're indifferent to them and to all adults. Their love and devotion is to their gangs. All of a sudden you think about an old *Twilight Zone* episode you recently watched, about an attractive police officer who uses his gentle charm to win the trust of a scared old woman, but he turns out to be Mr. Death. You wanted to go with Mr. Death too, when you watched the old woman walking out the door, smilingly clutching his arm.

"Do you want to tell me what you're thinking?" Junie asks.

Nothing, you say. You're certainly not going to start talking to her about Mr. Death.

"We're always thinking about something," Junie says. "Even when we're sleeping."

You notice something about the social worker's speech. She's dropping the *r* in her words. She sounds like the Dead End kids in *Angels with Dirty Faces*. You look at her curiously. Where are you from? you ask her. I'll bet you're not from stupid Cleveland.

She laughs. "No I'm not from stupid Cleveland," she says. "I'm from Brooklyn."

You bolt up in your chair, toss the rubber band on the desk, and stare at her. Brooklyn? you say. In New York?

"That's right. We lived in a neighborhood called Bedford-Stuyvesant. It's a very poor neighborhood but we lived in one of the nicer parts."

Really! you yell. You're wildly excited. Based on what you've heard and read, there are more juvenile delinquents in Brooklyn than anywhere else in the world. You picture Brooklyn being one giant slum with hordes of switchblade-wielding toughs marauding through the streets. Wow! you say. I can't believe you're from Brooklyn! Have you ever heard of the Cobras?

Junie sits very still, with her hands folded in her lap. "How do you know about the Cobras?" she asks.

I know about all the street gangs in New York, you tell her. I'm an expert on New York gangs. I know about all the Brooklyn gangs—the Cobras, the Robbins, the Green Avenue Stompers, the Red Hook Tigers, the Kane Street Midgets. The Cobras' territory was Bedford-Stuyvesant. So did you know anyone in the Cobras? You see the look on Junie's face. You did, didn't you? you say, grinning.

"I believe my brother was running around with them for awhile."

Your brother was in the Cobras? Was your brother a bad boy?

"He wasn't really such a bad boy. Today he's a doctor."

Oh. This doesn't really interest you. What kind of doctor? you say, just to be polite.

164

"He's a pathologist at Bellevue Hospital," Junie says, reaching for a pack of Larks on her desk.

That's nice. Was he ever in reform school?

The social worker laughs. "No, thankfully, it never got that far." She leans forward in her leather chair with her cigarette between her fingers. "Why are you so interested to know if my brother was a bad boy and if he was in reform school?" she asks.

I don't know.

"Do bad boys fascinate you?"

Yeah.

"Do you know any bad boys?"

You start getting depressed, realizing that you don't know any *real* bad boys. Ricky comes the closest of your buddies to being a bad boy, but he's just mischievous, not an actual delinquent. Not really, you say. I wish I knew some bad boys.

Junie lights the cigarette with a fancy lighter and blows out smoke. "So what would you do with these bad boys if you knew them?" she asks. "Would you want them to take you out? Ride with them on their motorcycles?"

What do you mean, take me out? You mean like on dates?

"Well, not necessarily." She looks more closely at you. "You don't have any interest in going on dates with boys?"

I don't like boys that way.

Junie laughs. "Well, you're still very young. You have plenty of time to like boys that way. Then I assume what you meant was that you would like to have bad boys as buddies."

Yeah.

"What about bad girls?" Junie asks. "Do you know any bad girls?"

You smile. My friend Susie is pretty bad, you say.

"Mm-hm." Junie takes a drag on her cigarette and blows out smoke. "So what kinds of things do you do with Susie?"

Oh, we do a lot of bad stuff, you say. But it's not like being bad with a whole delinquent gang, playing hooky and running wild in the streets and being chased by the cops and jumping across rooftops and fighting in rumbles!

165

Junie's looking at you now in a different way. Two little furrows have appeared between her brows. "Well!" she says finally, stubbing out her cigarette. She settles herself back in her chair, folds her arms, and smiles at you. "This is going to be interesting," she says.

What's going to be interesting?

"Getting to know more of what's inside that head of yours."

You slouch further down in the chair, fold your arms, and look up at the ceiling. Just a bunch of loose screws, you say. You feel calmer now. You're in a state of quiet ecstasy, which will last as long as you're in this office. Like the woman in *Twilight Zone* who's so happy to trust a stranger, before she's swallowed up by darkness.

Mid-November Evening, Still Raining

Junie Adams, who is now my friend, lives in Crown Heights, and I went to see her today. I am very close to her. I bonded with her right away as a kid, and then she moved back to New York and I moved to New York and I went back to see her as a young adult, when I was falling apart, and she pulled me back together. She helped me figure out why I had been nuts my whole life, and eventually I quit therapy and after awhile we became friends. And now it's thirty years later and she's old and not getting around very well and I've been neglecting her because I haven't wanted to argue with her anymore about what she refers to as my "idiotic phone call" that got the attention of the FBI, and also I don't want to argue about her horrible daughter Tanya, the woman I'm in love with, and her turncoat lover Susan. Also I haven't wanted to tell her about my little gangster friends who have taken over my apartment. But I can only neglect her for so long, so finally yesterday I drove to her house in the pouring rain. She lives in a pretty Caribbean neighborhood off of Eastern Parkway in Crown Heights, which is where the Chabad Jews have their headquarters.

166

Junie answered the door in a red-and-orange kimono. She's getting so fucking old. She's still beautiful, with that shock of bushy hair and rich creamy skin ("black don't crack" she likes to say) and big earrings and manicured hands, but she's shrunk. She's probably three inches shorter than she used to be, and she walks with a cane when she goes out. Even though we've been squabbling over the phone lately I fell into her arms and she gave me one of her hugs that makes me feel like I'm home. I folded my sopping umbrella and stuck it under the coat rack.

"This is crazy, this rain," Junie said.

"It sure is," I said. I walked through the living room and into the kitchen.

"What are you doing?" Junie yelled. "If you want something in there let me know and I'll get it. Don't start rooting around in my refrigerator!" I didn't want her to have to hobble into the kitchen so I ignored her and poured myself a glass of Lactaid and went back into the living room. "I don't know why you drink my Lactaid when you don't even have lactose intolerance," she said.

"I like it," I said, plopping onto the couch.

"When are you going to grow up," she sighed. She leaned her cane against her favorite chair and sat down. We talked for a few minutes about the rain. It's been pouring continuously east of the Mississippi River and there's a drought on the western side. It's very weird. The weather analysts are now suspecting some kind of weather "manipulation." Junie and I had a laugh about my nemesis, the newly elected Senator Sandy Shrewsbury, saying on Fox News that it was just "the atmosphere getting rid of what it doesn't need."

Junie asked me how my book was coming and I said I just finished writing about how we first met, and she laughed. "I remember that day well," she said. "You thought you were such a little toughie."

"I was a toughie," I said.

She waved at me dismissively. "You were never a toughie," she said. Then she folded her hands and gave me a pointed look and said, "So. Tell me how you're doing."

167

She wasn't just innocently asking me how I was doing. She had that look she gets when she thinks I'm going off my rocker. "What do you mean, how am I doing?" I said. "You mean you have no idea what's going on in my life?"

"How am I supposed to know what's going on in your life if you don't tell me?"

"Like if someone else tells you. Duh-uh."

"Joanna, I'm not playing games with you."

"Well, have you talked to Molly lately?" It would be just like Molly to inform Junie that I'm playing hostess to a cadre of little gangsters.

"I did speak to Molly," Junie said. "She called this morning. We had a very nice conversation. She told me about her efforts to get this legislation passed that would give tenants in rent-controlled apartments the same rights as the tenants paying market prices."

"I know," I said. "I helped her make some phone calls about that. Did she say anything about me?"

"What do you think she may have said about you?"

"I don't know! Just tell me for God's sake. All your conversations don't have to be such a big fucking secret." She still brings out the petulant teenager in me. Although when I was a teenager I never cursed around her. In fact, as bad as I was, I didn't start cursing until I was in college.

"What she told me," Junie said, "is that a gang of teenagers have taken over your apartment and you're apparently doing nothing to stop it." She folded her arms and looked at me, waiting for my inane response.

"They're just some kids from the neighborhood. I don't know why Molly had to go and blab to you about it and get you all upset."

"Of course I'm upset! You're apparently being held hostage in your own home! How did these boys get into your apartment? Molly told me some crazy story."

"Well, the crazy story is true. They cut a hole in the Chinese people's floor and came in through the closet." I started laughing hysterically.

168

"It's not funny, Joanna!" Junie yelled in her new, old voice that has a tremor in it. "You're putting yourself in a very dangerous situation!"

"Don't worry about it," I said. "I know how to take care of myself." Which is generally true. People sometimes think I don't know how to take care of myself because I'm always living on the edge, like a junkyard dog, but that's a choice that I've made. It's a writer's job to live on the edge.

But Junie had to be contentious, the way she always is lately. "Obviously you don't know how to take care of yourself," she said. "If you did you wouldn't allow this situation to occur. Molly is beside herself. She said she can't even come over anymore because you're being held captive by these teenagers. Are you aware of Stockholm syndrome?"

"Oh, for God's sake!" I yelled. "I don't have Stockholm syndrome! That is absurd! Where are you getting this? Is this some theory that you and Molly concocted? That I have Stockholm syndrome?" I gulped down the rest of my milk and put the glass down on the end table. "Look," I said. "There's nothing I can do about these kids. They come down from the Chinese people's apartment and walk out of the closet. I don't have a lock on my closet door, so what am I supposed to do, for God's sake?"

"What you're telling me doesn't make sense, Joanna," Junie said. "Of course you can do something. Any normal person would call the police under these circumstances."

"Oh, that's a wonderful idea," I said. "You call the cops on kids like this, and two days later you come home and you find your whole apartment wrecked, or spray-painted all up. Doesn't anybody understand this?"

"Well, at least you should have informed your landlord that these teenagers are running amok in your building and sawing holes through the floor!"

"Junie, in case you've forgotten, my landlord is a Russian mafia guy. He turned the upstairs apartment into a dormitory for undocumented Fujian immigrants. He runs the building as a *money-laundering operation*! All he cares about is that he gets his

169

rent. I've never even met him. The fact that some bad boys are marauding through my building would be of very little concern to him!"

"Well there must be something you can do other than sit around and wait for a gang of delinquents to walk out of your closet and take over your apartment."

"I'm dealing with it in my own way. I'm establishing a rapport with them."

"You're trying to establish a rapport with teenaged criminals who barge into your apartment through a hole they've sawed in your closet?"

"Yes." She was starting to drive me crazy. Everyone thinks I'm being so hapless and incompetent with the delinquents but nobody offers any better solutions than the ones I've chosen. "If I want to befriend a group of troubled children it's entirely my business," I said. "Anyway I feel kind of bad sending them out in the rain every day."

"Oh Joanna don't be ridiculous," Junie said. "Teenagers don't give a hoot about rain. I can understand your desire to offer sanctuary to a group of troubled children, but this is probably not the best time to do it. You're not in the most stable frame of mind at the moment."

"Oh, really."

"Yes, really. Have you considered the possibility that these boys are just a distraction for you so you don't have to think about going back to Cleveland and closing up your mother's house?"

"I don't want to talk about that!" I screamed.

"Well we're going to have to talk about it at some point," Junie said. She thinks she's still my therapist sometimes.

"If you say so," I said.

"Have you spoken at all to Susan and Tanya?" Junie asked. She probably said that because she was mad at me and wanted to upset me, although she would never admit it. It still seems kind of incestuous, that the only woman I've ever loved happens to be my ex-therapist's daughter, but that's the way things play out sometimes. But now the mere mention of Tanya's name makes my blood boil, even when it's spoken by her own mother. In fact, hearing Junie ask about Tanya upsets me even more than when other people do it.

"No, I have not spoken to them," I said to Junie. "Why? Have you?"

"Of course I've spoken to them."

"What do you mean, of course you've spoken to them? How do I know you've spoken to them? Tanya sometimes goes for months without even talking to you."

"That's when she's angry at me. We're getting along fine now."

For some reason this enraged me. "That's just fucking wonderful that you're getting along fine!" I screamed. "I'm so happy for you! Goddammit." I picked up the glass and stormed into the kitchen and put it in the sink and ran water in it. Then I went back into the living room and sat back down on the couch. "Well what did they say?" I said. "Did they talk about me when you saw them?"

"If you continue to scream and yell like that I'm not going to talk about it anymore."

"I just asked you what they said! Did they come over here?"

"Yes, they were over last week."

"Did they talk about me?"

"Everything doesn't have to be about you."

"What did they say about me?"

"They're very upset that you're not talking to them. I know they called you several times and wrote you a letter after your mom died. Obviously they were very upset about your mother. You know that Susan loved your mother."

And blah blah blah. God I hate her sometimes.

"Well I don't know why you couldn't have done something to stop them from ruining my life."

"Joanna, it's been over a year. And obviously I have no control over my daughter's choices. She and Susan are both adults. You're sounding very foolish."

"I hate them."

"All right, Joanna. Would you like another glass of milk? I have some butter cookies." She got up and went into the kitchen and came out with two glasses of Lactaid and a plate of butter cookies, and she started telling me about this doctor's appointment and an MRI she had so I couldn't keep carrying on about Tanya and Susan. After a while I got up and went home. I wanted to get home before the boys came barreling in through the closet. I instructed them never to come into my home when I'm not there, and I stick a Post-it on my door whenever I leave to let them know I'm out. I'm sure everyone thinks they ignore the Post-its and just enter my place whenever they feel like it, but I'm pretty sure they don't. I never see any signs that they've been there, when I come home.

It's raining harder now, and the wind is rattling the window, and I think of little Junie all alone in her house and I want to go back there and say something to reassure her, to brighten up her day. I hope she didn't get depressed by my visit. She probably thinks she did an awful job with me. She abandoned me when I was an upset teenager to go back to New York, and after I moved here I hunted her down when my life was falling apart and she stuck me back together, and now she thinks I've gone crazy again and have Stockholm syndrome and she's too old to rescue me again. Ha ha. Stockholm syndrome. That's kind of funny. I kind of feel bad for getting her all worried. She annoys the shit out of me but still, I love her as much as I've ever loved anyone. I really did fall in love with her the moment I met her, when I was a thirteen-year-old nutcase. I didn't bond with my mom because she was sick when I was a baby. So I attached to Junie. And I never stopped loving her. As I said, once I love someone, I always love them. I even still love Tanya and Susan, who are subhuman lesbian vermin. But I don't allow myself to feel the love. I love them like a queen loves her lowly subjects who dwell in the gutter. I bestow my love on them, like a gift. Anyway I can't keep talking about this because I can hear my little gangster friends making a ruckus in the closet. I have to go into the kitchen and see what I have to feed them. They're eating me out of house and home.

SPRING 1965

When you're in Junie's office you're home, the place that's the center of your life. Junie dresses in reds and oranges and golds and sapphires, and she sits with her legs crossed, smoking her Larks, and she throws her head back and laughs a loud, hearty laugh when you tell her about your latest pranks at school, such as sewing *me* instead of your name on your apron, or bringing a kazoo to vocal music and playing it instead of singing to "Hey Look Me Over." But then she'll get serious and ask you questions, and you slouch and look at the ceiling and grunt answers. Often you ask Junie questions about herself, and you learn that she's thirty-eight years old, that her parents were from Jamaica where they had an outdoor market and sold something called "jerk pork," and that she has an eighteen-year-old daughter who lives in New York with her father (which is better than if the daughter lived with Junie and got all her attention). When you ask silly intimate questions like, What did you eat for lunch? often she'll say, "That is not nearly as important as other things we should be discussing," but at other times she indulges you and replies, "I had a corned beef sandwich from that terrible deli down the street and I think it made me sick," or, "I had a plate of rice and beans; does that satisfy your curiosity?"

The worst moments of your life are every Tuesday and Friday when you have to leave the social worker's office. You wander the streets, the life draining out of you, avoiding going home as long as possible. You linger in the drugstore in front of the bus stop reading the latest sensational stories in the *Weekly World News*. You read obsessively the articles about horribly abused children, kids whose parents beat and torture and starve them or lock them in closets until they're discovered by authorities months later, all shriveled up like frogs. Eventually you force yourself to put the paper back and take the bus home with the images of the bruised and emaciated children floating in your mind through your dinner. As soon as you're done eating you escape from the table and go upstairs and lie on your bed and stare into space.

You now think of yourself as an "emotionally disturbed child," an identity you inhabit more comfortably than you do that of a juvenile delinquent. You pour over books and articles about mental illness and mental hospitals, and are especially fascinated with tools of restraint, like straitjackets and "hydrotherapy." You also read clinical texts about the diagnosis and treatment of mentally ill children, especially those who have been "put away" in institutions. In order to balance out the craziness you engage in normal activities, like joining the school newspaper and the volleyball team, writing amusing essays and reading them aloud in class, and attending student council meetings (even though you're not a member your presence is tolerated because of your friendship with Steven, the class president). But whenever you're by yourself, not engaged with people or activities, the same old dread seeps into you, and if you're at home you lie on your bed without moving, which doesn't make it go away but keeps you in contact with yourself. The only time you feel totally safe is when you're with Junie, but that's just an illusion. Junie's office is like a tub of warm water that feels nice except that there are baby piranhas swimming around in it.

One day about a month after your depressing fourteenth birthday party during which Susie and Steven announced that they were "going together," which made you want to puke but you pretended to be all excited for them, you're in Junie's office complaining that your life is boring and that you wish you were in a street gang in New York instead of in "stupid, boring Greenvale."

"What's really going on with you?" Junie asks. "Are you still upset about Susie and Steven going steady?"

It's so icky, you say. They walk down the street holding hands. I'll bet when it gets warm Steven is going to talk Susie out of staring at the Blobs like we did last summer.

"Well good for Steven," Junie says. "You shouldn't be tormenting those poor women anyway. They can't help being the way they are. For you and your friends to sit there gawking at them is simply cruel."

Oh big deal, you say. We're not hurting them. We only *look* at them. Molly's cousin Vic and a couple other kids broke into their house and moved the furniture around and smeared ketchup on their bed. That's way worse than staring at them. Anyway oogling the Blobs is fun. It's a lot more fun than hanging around in my stupid house.

"What's wrong with being in your house? You have a family that loves you."

I hate living there. It's so boring. I want to live with you.

"Joanna, you know you can't live with me."

You're getting depressed with the whole conversation. Let me have a cigarette, you say to Junie.

"You're too young." Junie snaps her lighter shut and blows out smoke.

Junie looks at you as you sit there and sulk. "Why don't you think about doing something constructive with your life?" she asks.

Like what.

"You might consider volunteering for a worthy cause."

I could volunteer for civil rights, you say. You believe in civil rights and Martin Luther King and all that stuff that your parents are passionate about.

"Well, there's an organization called CORE," Junie says. "The Congress of Racial Equality. They do good work. They have chapters all over the country."

Do you volunteer for them?

"No, but I've been seriously considering it, ever since I watched

175

my people get the hell beaten out of them during the march in Selma."

You watched some of the footage of the attempted march from Selma to Montgomery led by Martin Luther King. Seeing dozens of Negroes being beaten and hosed by police seems kind of normal considering it happened in Alabama where Negroes have their testicles cut off and are strung up on trees and set on fire and burned to a crisp. Your parents have always led you to believe that the American South is an evil place full of white people who wish that slavery was still legal.

I would volunteer for CORE, you tell Junie. Do they take kids?

"I believe they do," Junie says. "I have a phone number for them somewhere." She flips through her rolodex. "Ah, here it is," she says, and pulls out a card. She writes a number down on a piece of paper and gives it to you. "There you are," she says. "When you help others, you help yourself."

The next day you call CORE and find out that the next meeting of the Cleveland chapter will be taking place in a community center in Hough, which is an added incentive for you to attend since it's the worst neighborhood in Cleveland and you have always wanted to go there. (Once you asked your dad to drive you through Hough, and he asked you why you wanted to see people who are suffering and just kept driving right up Chester Avenue.) The next day at school you walk up to Steven and Susie in the hall and tell them you want them to go with you to the CORE meeting, and they say okay. (Even though they're "going together" when you're with them they act as playful and affectionate as ever and don't act at all gushy with each other, which is all the more reason you feel like a very bad person for begrudging them their little relationship.)

The CORE meeting is on a beautiful Saturday afternoon in May, and your dad drives you, Susie, and Steven to the Harriet Tubman Center in Hough so that you can attend. Your mom didn't like the idea of her daughter hanging around in dangerous Hough, even for a CORE meeting, but your father prevailed, as he always does during the rare occasions that he disagrees with your mom. When you pull up in front of the shabby storefront center on Superior Avenue your dad accompanies you and your friends into the center. About a dozen Negro teenagers are in the gymnasium-sized room, playing ping-pong or lounging on sofas and chairs. Up front, folding chairs have been set up for the meeting, and an interracial mixture of adults is milling around, socializing. A white woman with red hair catches sight of your father and calls out, "Hello, Sam!" and your father calls back, "Hi there, Doris!" The woman comes over and she and your father start chatting and you learn that Doris was with your parents in "the movement," which was what your parents always called their commie days. She asks your father if he's going to stay for the meeting and he says no, but his daughter and her friends are going to volunteer, and she smiles and says, "That's swell!" and your father tells you he'll pick you up at four o'clock and leaves. Doris tells you she remembers your grandmother's delicious *kreplach*, and you say she still makes it, and then another woman starts talking to Doris and you and your friends walk to the front of the room, and Steven, always assertive in situations like this, goes directly to the front row. The three of you sit down and you start pulling Susie's fingers back one by one with your forefinger and she lets you until you pull one of her fingers too hard and she says "Ow!" and pulls her hand away and hits you on the back.

A young woman comes out of the office and sits down next to you. She's wearing a bigger version of Junie's hairstyle, which is called an *Afro*. She's dark-skinned with a heart-shaped face and red lipstick and warm, penetrating eyes. She wears tight jeans and a crisp white blouse and sharp-looking red tie shoes.

"Hi," she says to you.

Hi, you say.

She looks at you for a moment, then she reaches over and adjusts the collar of your ivy league shirt. "There you go," she says.

My collar's always sticking up, you say. Her touch has sent a mild electric current through you.

"You need someone to dress you in the morning," the young woman says.

I guess.

"So what's a little white girl like you doing in scary Hough?" she asks.

My friends and I are here to volunteer for CORE.

"That's great," the young woman says. "What's your name?" You tell her. "Joanna," she says. "That's a pretty name. My name's Louise. I'm the assistant director of this place. Some people call me the assistant hell-raiser."

You love this young woman already. Anyone who describes herself as "assistant hell-raiser" is okay in your book. You ask her who's going to be addressing the meeting, and she says, "the assistant hell-raiser," and laughs. A man wearing one of those colorful African shirts comes out of the office and gestures at your new friend. She pats you on the shoulder, and once again the electric current rolls through you. She raises a finger at you and says, "I'll be back," and as you watch her get up and face the audience, every nerve in your body feels alive.

"I'm Louise Banks, but everyone calls me Lou," she says. "I'm nineteen years old, a graduate of East High School, and the assistant director here at the Harriet Tubman Center. I want to talk to you today about the need for resistance in the struggle against racism, intolerance, and injustice." People start applauding, and a man calls out, "Keep talkin', sister!"

Lou launches into a discussion of oppression of Negroes in northern cities like Cleveland. "We all know what occurred during the Selma march," she says. "Our people got beat with hoses and attacked by dogs. But we also know that the oppression of black people isn't confined to the Jim Crow South. There's plenty of it taking place right here at home."

"Yes, ma'am," an older woman says.

"She's right on," a younger man says, and you wonder why he didn't finish his sentence. *Right on what?*

"How many of you live here in Hough?" Lou asks, and about half the hands go up. "Then you know how badly our housing stock has deteriorated," she says.

"Oh, yes!" a woman says.

"It's gotten very bad," another woman says.

"Yes it has," Lou concurs. "It's a disgrace. Our plumbing doesn't work, our doors are off their hinges, our windows are broken, and our roofs are leaking! We've got roaches and rats running around in our living rooms!"

"Saw a big old fella in my kitchen the other day," an older man grunts.

"It's completely disgusting," Lou says. "One of my friends told me that her kids chase the rats around the house like they're puppies. My friend is a good housekeeper. She just happens to have a terrible landlord!"

"They take the money and run," a man says.

"And what about our schools?" Lou says. "Can we talk about them for a moment?"

The whole audience bursts into laughter. "Those are pathetic excuses for schools," a woman says.

"Yes they are," Lou says. "The kids have to go in shifts because of overcrowding. The buildings are completely deteriorated. The ceilings leak. There are no stalls in the bathrooms. This is unacceptable, people! Our children deserve better!"

"The kids don't have enough books to go around!" a woman says. "Tell me they don't have enough books in Beachwood and Parma!"

"They sure do, sister," a man agrees. "They got plenty of books for them white kids!"

"Well what I want to know is . . . what are we going to do about all this misery?" Lou says, raising clenched fists.

"We fight it," says another man.

"That's right," Lou says. "We fight it! By any means necessary!" There are cheers and applause. You notice that Susie has turned around and is waving at someone. Then she gets up and leaves the meeting. You watch her walk up to a tall Negro girl, and they look excited to see each other. You're dying to know who on earth this girl is, but you don't want to miss the rest of Lou's speech. Steven also remains in his seat after noting Susie's exit from the meeting.

Lou starts talking about the legacy of Malcolm X who's

recently been assassinated, and union leaders like Joe Hill, Samuel Gompers, and A. Philip Randolph, who fought for the rights of working people. "These people stood up for the rights of the common man, just like Dr. King," she says. "They resisted injustice and oppression. They used all nonviolent means that were available to them. But they also knew that sometimes you have to answer a brick with a brick!"

People start applauding again.

"They knew that you can't sit down and let them bulldoze you into the ground!" she says.

People applaud and cheer, and you know she's referring to Reverend Bruce Klunder, who was killed in Cleveland last year while lying in front of a bulldozer during a demonstration to stop the construction of a "white only" school.

"That's right!" Lou says amid the applause and cheers. "It's a new day and a new way. And *we shall not be moved!*"

You're electrified, not because of the content of the young woman's speech, but because of her energy, her passion, and the lingering sensation of her hand adjusting your collar and touching your shoulder. She asks if there are any questions or comments, and Steven, always the inquisitive reporter, asks a question about the history and the long-term goals of CORE. A few other people ask questions, and then a lot of the attendees seat themselves at a long table that's been set up for addressing postcards to remind people about a national meeting. Steven goes to see what happened to Susie, but you remain in your chair as though magnetized to it. Lou walks up to you and says, "So, Joanna. How did you like my presentation?"

I thought it was great, you tell her.

"So now it's time to get to work," she says. "Come on, girl." She takes your hand and pulls you out of the chair. "That's right, come-come-come," she says, leading you to a long table containing stacks of postcards. "Here we are," Lou says to you. "Have a seat there next to Doris." When she lets go of your hand it's as though part of you is suddenly missing.

Doris moves her chair to make more room for you. "I knew this girl when she was a baby," she says to Lou. You're embarrassed, but you're also glad that Doris knows your parents because it makes you feel less like an outsider. You sit down next to Doris and start addressing postcards. Lou goes back into the office and the whole time you work you keep looking at the office, hoping she'll come back out. When she does another jolt of electricity runs through you even though she hasn't touched you, and in fact doesn't even look at you, but instead walks across the room and starts talking to a bunch of rough-looking kids, in the center of which is Susie. You're always impressed with Susie's poise around older, badder kids. Steven is at the end of the table, addressing postcards. Apparently he has little interest in interacting with Susie's new friends.

Doris starts chattering to you and you like her. She's friendly and open, like so many of your parents' friends from "the movement." After addressing a few postcards you start getting into the spirit of being a volunteer. It makes you feel like a good person instead of like a teenaged weirdo. After a few minutes you see Susie walking up to the table with Lou and a girl of around sixteen. "Hey Joey," Susie says to you. "This is Kendra. She was at Fairview with me. She tore that place apart!" Susie looks at the girl with pride and you feel a stab of jealousy.

"What's up, Joey," Kendra says to you. She's tall and cocky-looking with a mass of tangled hair.

"I wanna come back here," Susie says. "They have a sewing circle every Saturday afternoon. Next week they're gonna learn how to make moccasins." Susie has been designing her own clothes for years using various techniques, including just ripping fabric with a razor, but she also knows how to sew the way your grandmother does, with a needle and thread.

Wow, cool, you say to Susie.

"They have ping-pong tournaments too, Jo," Susie says, knowing that you have a ping-pong table in your basement and are a really good player.

You don't need any convincing to come back here. Can anyone hang out here? you ask Lou.

Lou grins. "If your parents say it's okay you can come here as often as you want," she says. "But I thought you came down here to volunteer for CORE." She turns to Doris. "Aren't you meeting at Fred's house next week?" she asks.

"That's right," Doris says.

Are you gonna be there? you ask Lou.

Lou laughs. "No, Joanna, I won't be there. I have a job right here, keeping these crazy kids under control." Right away you know where you're going to be next Saturday, and it won't be at the CORE meeting.

Your father picks you all up and drops Steven back home, and he agrees to drop you off with Susie so you can hang out in Little Jerusalem until suppertime. You and Susie get out of the car and start walking around, and when you see the Blobs working in their garden, you have a sudden charitable feeling toward them. "Hi Penny and Geraldine!" you call out, and to your astonishment, Penny, the dark-haired one, looks up and gives you a little wave.

I think she likes me, you say to Susie.

"Yeah, right," Susie says. "She's probably thinking about how to slice you up with that hoe." You laugh. You're thinking about the enchanting young woman at the Harriet Tubman Center, and seeing her again next Saturday, and you can't summon up any ill feeling toward anyone, not even the Blobs.

Evening in Late November, Still Raining

I would love to check myself into a booby hatch right now but these days they won't admit you unless you're suicidal or homicidal so maybe I should just go out and run around the streets with a meat cleaver so I can be taken away from this crazy place for a week or two and calm myself down. I can't take this anymore! I'm losing it. I'm seriously losing it. First of all, it doesn't stop raining. It rains and rains and rains in the eastern part of the country, and in the western part the rivers are drying up. The evidence that the weather has been "manipulated" makes the whole situation more interesting, but it still doesn't compensate for the dreariness of this constant downpour. I always thought the apocalypse might be fun but it turns out that it's not fun at all.

And now I'm all agitated about this *thing* that happened yesterday. It's a little alarming when the most stable moments of your life consist of entertaining a crew of little gangsters in your home. I was actually starting to enjoy the bizarre drama of these nutty kids walking out of my closet every afternoon (except on weekends, for some reason, when they never come) and letting them eat my food and play games on their phones and discuss their "business activities" while I write this book and ask them if they want any more ice cream or whatever. I even taught them to play charades the other day, although that lasted for about thirty seconds before they blew it off. But they've really been on their best behavior, for the most part. Yesterday I told them about my mom dying, and Eric said "That sucks, man," and Mikey got up from the futon and came up and gave me a hug. Today I lured Jakey out of the bathroom before he could set fire to the wastebasket and I sat him on the couch and gave him some bubble solution, and he actually sat there merrily blowing bubbles and I felt as though I was making progress with him. After they all galloped out of here I was about to make some coffee and there was a knock on the door, and when I opened it who did I find standing there but Agent Deborah Neufeld and Agent Charles Buford.

I have to admit that when I saw Deborah I got so excited that I almost fainted. I was kind of hurt and upset when she told me the last time she was here that she was afraid that I would come to "a very sad end" and when I saw her I wondered if she had decided that maybe there was some hope for me after all. I said, "Well look who's here!" and let them right in, figuring that if they hadn't carted me off to some interrogation room by now they weren't going to do anything to me. They left their umbrellas in the hall and came in and planted themselves on my couch, as usual, and I sat on the green chair where Eric always sits. "So what's the good word, guys?" I said. "What the hell is going on with the rain? You guys have any inside dope on that?"

Buford looked annoyed, but Deborah said, "We didn't come here to discuss the rain, Joanna."

And then Buford got to the reason for their visit. "Who are those boys that you've been entertaining in your home the last couple of weeks?" he said.

I couldn't have been more surprised. I actually thought they might have been there to tell me they were closing my case, especially since Deborah had told me she was washing her hands of me. "So now you've been spying on me?" I asked. I could deal with the FBI hassling me about my imprudent phone call but their interest in my teenaged houseguests made me uneasy.

"Please answer Agent Buford's question," Deborah said.

"They're just some kids from the neighborhood," I said. "They like hanging out in my place. Is there something wrong with that?"

"This doesn't sound kosher to me," Buford said.

I glared at him. "*What are you implying*?" I said.

Deborah gave him a look, shushing him. "Look, Joanna," she said. "It's obvious that these teenagers who have been visiting your apartment are engaged in various illegal activities in your building and around your neighborhood. We would like to know the nature of your relationship with these young men."

"We also need to know your connection to the criminal enterprise that employs these people," Buford said.

"Are you kidding?" I yelled. "I'm not involved in any criminal enterprise! Who do I look like, Ma Barker?"

"If the shoe fits," Buford said.

"Why did you have to bring him?" I asked Deborah. I saw the look on her face and I realized that her solo visit to me the last time was probably unauthorized, since they always travel in pairs, at least on TV. "He's so boring," I said, trying to cover up for her. "Anyway," I said, "how do you even know that these kids are hanging out in my apartment? Why are you spying on me?"

"Remember, we never closed the file on you," Deborah said. "You're still a person of interest to us. Obviously we're going to want to know why you're being visited by a crew of teenagers that are involved with a human smuggling operation. We have eyes and ears, Joanna. We can see what's going on here in your building, and as Agent Buford says, it doesn't look kosher to us."

"Oh, for God's sake, Deborah," I said. "I have nothing to do with any of that. Why aren't you upstairs talking to the people they came to see in the first place, before they even knew me? Why are you bothering *me* with all this?"

"We're not after the illegals that live in your building," Buford said. "We're after the people that brought them over to this country with false promises in order to *extort and enslave them!* And if you have any involvement in these despicable activities we're through playing patty-cake with you!"

"You've got to be kidding!" I said. "I'm a law-abiding citizen! I'm just giving these kids a place to hang out instead of shoving them out into the pouring rain. I have nothing to do with their business activities. I'm a good influence on them, not some kind of . . . some kind of Fagan! Anyway, all they're doing is collecting debts. They're not murdering anyone. And you really need to stop barking at me, Buford!" I mean for God's sake. If I've committed a crime, go ahead and arrest me and bark at me all you want. Otherwise talk to me like a human being. I put up with Jakey saying "fuck you bitch" but he's crazy. I cut crazy people a lot of slack because I have them in my family.

"Joanna, you need to settle down right now," Deborah said.

"Well, he's way too belligerent with me," I said.

"That's just too bad," Deborah said. "You still haven't told us why these teenagers have been visiting you every day. You have to know how this looks to us. First you make an incendiary phone call to a television station, and then we find out that you're entertaining street gang members in your home. I'm not suggesting that you're involved with their illegal activities. But we do need to know why they've been spending time in your apartment. Did you just invite them in for milk and cookies one day?"

"I didn't invite them in," I said. "They came in through the closet."

Buford looked at Deborah. "What's she talking about?" he asked.

"I have no idea," Deborah said. Then she turned back to me and said, "What do you mean, they came in through the closet?"

"They sawed a hole through the floor of the Chinese people's closet, and they came down here through the hole into my closet, and walked out the door," I said. When I saw the looks on their faces I started laughing and couldn't stop. In a way I can't blame Buford for thinking I'm dangerously unhinged.

Buford got up and walked toward my coat closet. "No, that closet back there," I said, pointing. He walked across the room, opened the closet door, looked inside, and said, "There's a hole up there the size of a barrel."

Deborah walked over there and looked. Then they both walked back and sat back down on the couch.

"See?" I said. "I told you."

"This doesn't make any sense," Deborah said. "Do you mean that these boys have been coming in here against your will? Why haven't you reported this?"

"They're not here against my will," I said. "I like them." Then I started laughing again.

"Oh good lord," Buford said.

"Joanna!" Deborah yelled, and I stopped laughing and looked into her mesmerizing sapphire eyes. Then she said softly, "When are you going to grow up?"

I had no time at that moment to process that I was in love with Deborah Neufeld because someone was banging on the door. I got up and opened it and there stood Susan and Tanya. They didn't even wait for me to invite them in. Tanya snapped her umbrella shut and tossed it outside the doorway, and then they both barged in here like the Gestapo while I stood there in shock. Susan had some crazy haircut, it looked like about five curly Mohawks sticking up, and she wore jeans and boots and a

186

flak jacket and looked like a scruffy kid but of course the bitch gets away with it; she happens to be one of the most talented clothes designers in the world. And Tanya looked like Tanya, in this wavy skirt and woolen jacket and stack heels. The older she gets the more she looks like her mother, Junie. They have the same eyes, those brown eyes that want to roll you up in them like dough.

"What the fuck are you doing here?" I yelled. "Go away!"

And then Tanya saw Deborah and stopped in her tracks and said, "Well, bless my buttons."

And Deborah said, "Well, bless mine!"

And both of them started to laugh, and it was obvious that the two of them had slept together. "Oh, God," I said. "Gag me with a spoon."

Susan stood there gaping at them, and I wanted to laugh, because Tanya has been doing that kind of shit to me since I was thirty years old. "Are these the FBI people?" she demanded, pointing. Of course she knows all of my business through the grapevine.

"Yeah," I said. "That's Agent Buford, he's kind of a pain in the ass, and that's Agent Deborah Neufeld. She's my friend."

"Well, la-di-dah," Susan said.

Tanya turned away from Deborah and gave me one of her concerned looks that zapped out everyone else in the room, it was just me and her standing there, and I was wrapped up in her, like filling in a jelly roll, even though she was five feet away.

"I hate you," I said.

"You don't hate me," Tanya said. "Don't be ridiculous."

Then Deborah starts talking to Tanya as though we're at a ladies' tea. "So!" she says. "How's your latest book of poetry coming along? I haven't seen it on the shelves."

"It's due out in January," Tanya said. "Except this rain seems to be holding everything up, for some reason."

"Yeah, isn't this weather crazy?" Deborah said.

If I had had to endure this absurd situation for one more second I would have spontaneously combusted. "Everyone get the hell out of here!" I screamed. "I'm serious! All of you get out! I need to be alone!"

Then I looked at Susan and she gave me that mischievous look of hers, and I knew she was about to mock me by saying, "I vant to be alone," quoting from that movie with Greta Garbo. "Shut up," I said to her, annoyed that she almost made me laugh. Then I turned to the room at large and said, "Everyone get out of here! I mean it!" I pointed at Deborah and Buford and said, "You two don't have a warrant!" Then I glared at Tanya and Susan and said, "And you two have ruined my life! I want all of you out! I need to write my book! I don't have time to deal with all this—all this *mishegas!*"

They actually all listened to me. Buford got up and said, "This isn't over," but he started heading for the door.

"Blah blah blah," I said to him.

"We still need to talk," Deborah said, pointing at me, and instead of being annoyed I was as happy as a puppy with a bouncy little ball.

And then Tanya passed me and smoothed my hair and kissed me softly on the neck. Then, while I melted like the Wicked Witch of the West, Tanya walked out the fucking door with Deborah, who said, "I have some questions about section two of your last book of poetry."

The last person to say anything to me was Susan, who was bringing up the rear of the departing group. "I'm seriously going to throw up," she whispered in my ear, and of course then I wanted her back too. My problem is that I'm too soft. I can never throw anyone out of my life forever. As soon as those wenches marched in here all full of the devil I wanted them back. But that was just a fleeting moment of insanity. They can go back home to their three rabbits and never speak to me again. Unless I decree it.

God, I am a nervous wreck. Maybe instead of taking another pill I should do something else to relax. But you know how sometimes certain—um—*activities* work best when you're really nervous and agitated? I know, TMI. In case you're reading this a hundred years after it's written, like if you can still read, TMI means "TOO MUCH INFORMATION." I hope it's stopped raining in a hundred years. Because if it hasn't, there's no chance in hell anyone will be around to read this or anybody else's book that's ever been written. That's a rather sobering thought, isn't it?

SPRING AND SUMMER 1965

One week after the CORE meeting, Rick, Rhonda's boyfriend, drives you and Susie back to the Harriet Tubman Center. Susie wants to see Kendra again, and you're going there mainly to see Lou, although you don't tell Susie that. Since no CORE meeting is taking place there today, Steven doesn't have any interest in going.

When you walk into the center there's a commotion going on. Lou is standing behind the ping-pong table, surrounded by teenagers, and most of them are yelling. She's wearing tight jeans, a tan polo shirt, and red high-top sneakers and looks more like one of the kids than she did last week.

"They try to kick us out of the park what we suppose to do?" says Kendra, Susie's friend from Fairview. "Just run away like a bunch of pussies?"

"I didn't say you should just run away," Lou says. "I said there are other solutions besides engaging them in violence."

"Like what," says a boy of about sixteen in a striped tee shirt. "What we supposed to do, call the cops? They just tell us to leave the park and let whitey stay." He sees you and Susie approach and says, "What these marshmallows doin' here?"

"Hush up, Curtis," Lou says, looking over the kids' heads at you and Susie. "You know I don't like that kind of talk. Those white girls are on our side."

"That's right, Curtis, shut up about them white girls," says Kendra. "Susie's my friend."

"I'm gonna kill that cracker that hit me in my eye," says a young kid of around thirteen, who's wearing a bandage over one eye. "I'm gonna stab him with my knife."

"You'll do nothing of the kind, Pooh," Lou says.

"He coulda blinded him," Kendra says.

"Look, if they try messin' with you again you just stand firm," Lou says. "Don't start brandishing weapons. You remember what we talked about at our last meeting? What's your best weapon?" Nobody says anything. Then one of the boys finally says, "Your fists."

"Wrong," Lou says. "That's second best." Then she calls out to you, "Joanna! What's your best weapon?"

You're thrilled that Lou remembers your name. Your mouth, you say. Talking.

"Why she gotta be in on this?" Curtis says.

"Because she's smarter than y'all," Lou says. "Joanna is right. Talking is your best weapon. You fight only when attacked. We are not the white devil trampling over the earth, killing and enslaving. We are proud black people, setting an example for how to conduct yourself with honor and dignity. Come on over here, Joanna."

You walk over to Lou and she puts her arm around your shoulders. "Now she and her friend Susie came to the CORE meeting last week because they are committed to our cause. They're as much against racism and injustice as we are. We need white allies to help us fight the fight." She turns to you. "Joanna, if you're confronted with racist white thugs, what do you do?"

Kill them, you say and everyone laughs.

"All right, all of you," Lou says, pushing you away but still laughing. "Get outa my face and let me get some work done. Maybe after what happened yesterday those kids over on St. Clair got the message that they don't own that park."

A half-dozen girls have gathered in a corner of the room, which you assume to be the sewing circle, and Susie goes over to join them. You wander over to the ping-pong table and start watching two boys play. You hope someone invites you to play so you don't feel like a dope, standing around by yourself. After a couple minutes Lou comes over to you and your heart starts thumping. "Do you play ping-pong, Joanna?" Lou asks.

Yeah, you say.

"Henry!" Lou calls to one of the boys. "I'm gonna play Joanna next game!" The game is almost over, and while you wait for it to finish Lou rests her hand lightly on your back. When the game is over she takes the paddle from Henry and the other boy gives you his paddle. "I was the ping-pong champion of Addison Junior High," Lou says. She slaps her paddle and bounces over to her end of the table. "Let's go," she says. "Show me your stuff, Joey."

You grin at Lou's use of your nickname and serve. You start slow to make Lou think that you're not that good and then heat up after she wins a couple of points, and get a charge out of the look on her face. "Dag, woman!" she exclaims. "You're makin' this serious!" The kids at the center gather round to watch the two of you exchange points. Lou plays farther from the table than most people you know, which gives her returns a lot of spin and velocity. But she gets a little wild at the end of the game and you stay focused and manage to beat her, 21 to 19.

"She good," one of the boys says.

"Joey's practically unbeatable at ping-pong," Susie calls out from the sewing circle.

"Another game!" Lou orders, and this time she stays on task and beats you, 21 to 19. She slaps the paddle on the table and throws her arms in the air, and you laugh.

That's so neat, how you stand away from the table, you say as the kids drift away.

"That's how the Chinese play," Lou says. "I'll show you how to do it." She comes around to your side of the table and gets hold of you from behind and pulls you back a couple of steps. "That's it, right there," she says. "Now I'm gonna bounce the ball on the table and you hit it like this." She grabs hold of your wrist and directs your arm. "See?" she says. "That way you give it a topspin." Lou returns to her side of the table and serves a few balls and you practice hitting from your new position a few feet behind the table.

"All right, let's play another game and you can practice your new technique," Lou says. Her eyes are sparkling and she looks like a kid. You play, and lose 16-21, because you don't have total control with the new technique, but you love the power of standing farther away from the table, which is how you play the game from that time on.

When Rick comes to pick you up, Lou says, "Don't forget to come back and see us. Both of you," she adds, wanting to include Susie. As you ride back to Greenvale, admiring two beautiful, beaded moccasins that Susie made in just a couple of hours, you're feeling more exuberant than you've ever felt in your life. You feel as though you could sail over fences or fly over houses like a winged horse. Underneath this new ecstatic mood lurks the same terror with its creepy little fangs, but you pay no attention to it. Right now it has no power over you.

You and Susie start going to the center every Saturday. When nobody's available to drive you, you take the bus. (Your parents don't approve of you going down to Hough every week, but after your father has a talk with Rhonda over the phone they decide they don't want to be the mean guys so they stop making an issue about it.) While you're at the center Susie participates in the sewing circle and you play ping-pong with whoever is around. One tall, dark-skinned seventeen-year-old named Benson was the ping-pong champion of the center (excluding Lou) before you came along and whenever the two of you play the kids gather round to watch. Usually Lou plays one game with you, and she usually wins. Whenever you're standing around, waiting for next game, you're constantly keeping an eye out for her. When she emerges from the office and starts making her rounds you always pretend not to notice her while you eagerly wait for her to come over to you. When she does she always touches you. She walks by, ruffling your hair, or she'll say, "Don't give this next guy any mercy, baby girl," and touch your back. Once she tells you to "stand still," and pulls a long thread off of your tee shirt. When she's not touching you, you're imagining her touching you, and even though your hunger for her is starting to scare the hell out of you it also makes you feel bouncy and alive.

After school lets out for the summer you continue to go to the Tubman Center every Saturday, which is the only day Lou is there, since she has a job with the phone company during the week. (Susie attends the sewing circle on Saturdays and also goes to the center sometimes during the week, to hang around with Kendra.) When you're not at the center you're thinking about Lou and entertaining fantasies about her. When you're lying on your bed listening to hit songs on the radio ("Hey mister tambourine man play a song for me" . . . "Help me Rhonda help-help me Rhonda!" . . . "Sugar pie honey bunch you know that I love you" . . . "I—can't get—no—sa—tis—fac—tion!") you're picturing Lou grabbing you and dancing with you in the old-fashioned way, with your bodies linked together. When you go to Beemis pool with your friends you picture Lou in the pool with her arm around you as she teaches you a proper swimming stroke, even though you already know how to swim. When you watch the Indians on TV with your father and brothers, you think of yourself watching the game with Lou, cuddled up with her in the house where she lives with her mom, listening to Jimmy Dudley's soothing voice ("Sah-wing! And a miss!") and singing along with the Carling Black Label beer commercial. One thing you haven't done all summer is oogle the Blobs, who have abandoned their garden, which is now overgrown with weeds, and who now stay in the house all the time. (The only time you've seen them outside is when they were hosing off the words "CUNT PUSSIES" that someone had chalked all across their walk, which actually made you feel sad for the women, the brown-haired one standing there spraying the offending letters while the blond one smeared them around with her foot.)

At the end of July your dad takes the family on a car trip to Omaha, Nebraska, to visit chatty, big-nosed Auntie Bee and big, silent Uncle Truck, even though your dad hates Uncle Truck and hates his sister for marrying him. At least once during every road trip your dad blows up at some waitress for a perceived rudeness and storms out of the restaurant with his humiliated family trailing after him, and this year it happens the day before you return home, when he storms out of a diner in Indiana after the waitress keeps forgetting his coffee. You all pile back in the car, and when you say something about not having a chance to finish your waffles your father turns around in the seat and starts attacking you. "Joanna, you've been sullen and sour throughout this whole trip," he says. "It's obvious that you didn't want to come with us in the first place because you're stuck on this idea of running to Hough every week. You seem to have some peculiar obsession with that place that I suspect has nothing to do with a commitment to civil rights or integration. I've heard you talk about this young woman who works there as though she just can't wait to see you but I have news for you. She's barely tolerating you. Don't kid yourself that she thinks it's cool that you're hanging around with a bunch of Negro kids. There's a word for what you're doing and it's called slumming. And there's nothing admirable about it at all. In fact, it's insulting to all those people who have to live in Hough."

"All right Sam, please," your mother says. "Let's just go." Your father flashes his eyes and bares his teeth at you. Then he turns the ignition on and starts driving, leaving you feeling as small as a crumb.

After you get home you have no further interest in returning to the center. As buoyant as you felt before the vacation, that's how deflated you feel now. You tried your best to act pleasant on the car trip, but your dad had seen through your act. What he said to you made you stare the truth in the face. You don't go to the Harriet Tubman Center to get to know black people. You go there to see Lou, which is a very creepy reason. The phrase your father used—"peculiar obsession"—makes all your insides curdle. For the next two weeks you don't even feel like seeing your friends, although a couple of times you go to the pool with Molly and Susie and watch the girls flirt with the boys and feel a million miles away from everyone there.

You continue to see Junie twice a week. Junie's office is still your sanctuary. You never talk to her about anything that's really bothering you, like your dad saying what he did in the car, and withering with shame and not wanting to go back to the center. You just tell her about bad things you've done, so she won't think she can stop seeing you. You even force yourself to do some bad things, such as pouring grape pop down a mailbox and hopping a ride on a truck and sneaking into the movies by yourself, so you have something to report to her. After your appointment you do your usual thing of wandering the streets around the agency and reading about child abuse and torture in the drugstore tabloids, which makes you feel slimy and sick. You can't stand the thought of going home where you have to be nice to everyone. When you're home you escape from your family by playing "Downtown" over and over on your parents' record console—"Downtown! Where all the lights are bright! Downtown! Waiting for you tonight! Downtown! You're gonna be all right now ..." and while you listen you fantasize about wandering around downtown Cleveland in the middle of the night and seeing Petula Clark, who takes you to her hotel and orders you a hot meal and puts you to bed.

As the end of summer approaches you become more and more depressed, although you never think of yourself as "depressed" because you associate that word with sad old house-wives. You prefer to think of yourself as "disturbed," which you know you are. Your family and friends seem far away, in another world, and you just go through the motions of interacting with them. The truth is that you've never felt so alone in your life. One of your new favorite songs is "The Lonely Bull." When you listen to Herb Alpert's trumpet wail its sympathetic tribute you can feel every ounce of the anguish of the lonely, doomed beast that's surrounded by people who only see his body but not his soul. One day you wander into the den where your parents are watching the news and see a riot going on in a Los Angeles neighborhood called "Watts," and you envy the kids you see on TV who are running around breaking windows and setting fires

196

and being part of the world, even as they're busting it all up. And then you feel ashamed of not feeling grateful for your privileged suburban life where children have no need to riot in the streets.

A couple of weeks after the fateful family vacation Susie calls and asks you if you want to take a bus with her to the Harriet Tubman center. You agree to go, against your better judgment because you don't want to say no to Susie, although you're afraid that you'll act like a boring dope and Lou won't want to bother with you anymore. You and Susie take the bus, and the hot wind blowing through the window doesn't even make you feel good, the way summer wind usually does. Instead it makes you feel nervous. It's about a fifteen-minute walk to the center, and as you round Superior Avenue and approach the building you see about a dozen teenagers milling around out front, and in the middle of the group is Lou. One of the boys says, "You don't have to go with us, Lou. It might be dangerous."

"I'm going with you to enjoy an evening at the park," Lou says, standing there with her hands on her hips.

"If them white boys show up you know there's gonna be another fight," says a stringy, buck-toothed kid of around sixteen. Then he says, "Hey, here's Susie and the ping-pong girl!"

"Hi, Susie-Q!" Kendra says. One of the boys calls out, "Hi Joey Ping-Pong."

"Well hello there, ladies," Lou says, smiling. "We're just getting ready for a nice evening in the park." One look at Lou, standing there smiling in her tight jeans and red tee shirt, and your fear changes from heavy and dark to bright and crackly. In an instant you've rejoined the world.

"We gonna fight the white boys," says Pooh, whose eye bandage has been replaced with a patch. "I brought my blade just in case."

"If you have a knife you'd better give it to me," Lou says. Lou holds her hand out. "Come on, Pooh," she says, and Pooh produces a small knife from his pocket and gives it to her, and she takes it and puts it in her own jeans pocket. "Let's just hope there aren't

197

any fights," she says. "We have enough violence going on in Watts. We don't need any more in Hough."

"This is gon' turn into Watts if them crackers keep messin' with us!" Kendra says. She wears tight jeans with rolled-up cuffs, like many of the boys, and looks capable of holding her own in a fight.

"I think those idiots may have gotten the message the last time," Lou says.

"Yeah, we ran them white boys right out of the park," says Curtis, the boy who referred to you and Susie as "marshmallows" when he first saw you at the center.

"Well we goin' or not?" says one of the boys. He starts walking across Superior Avenue, and the other kids follow. Susie walks across the street with Kendra and you start following them. Lou looks back at you and says, "Joanna, go on home. There's been too much trouble in this park lately. I don't want you getting hurt."

I want to go, you say.

"I can't stop you then," Lou says, and turns and keeps walking. You keep walking behind her, not for a moment considering staying behind, but still feeling very nervous. You hope the white boys don't show up. Even though you fantasize about being a switchblade-carrying gang member, the truth is that you've never been in a fight in your whole life. When you were a kid, a "fight" consisted of wrestling someone to the ground and sitting on him. You look ahead and see Susie walking with the same aggressive strut as the other kids.

You all walk up a side street for a couple of blocks, and you get to a park that has a playground in it. Lou walks into the play-ground, and you follow her and she sits on one of the swings. You come over and push her and she says, "I can swing myself, Joanna." The boys swarm into the park and start running around, whooping and mock-fighting, and Susie runs around after them, showing them that she's not scared to fight. Kendra walks to the edge of the park and looks across St. Clair Avenue. "I don't see none of them!" she calls. You start swaggering around the play-ground, pretending to be a gang girl. Your hair is in your eyes and you picture yourself looking like Elvis in a prison movie you recently saw on TV. Then you hear Kendra scream, "Go home, punks! This park don't have your names on it!"

A bunch of white boys are walking into the park. A couple of them are holding sticks. One of them yells, "You niggers get the fuck out of our park!"

"Get your pink asses back home to your pink mamas!" one of the black boys yells.

"Shit," Lou says. She gets off the swing and runs onto the grassy area of the park and you follow her. The black kids have gathered in a bunch, facing off with the white kids. They start yelling back and forth.

"White retards!"

"Black monkeys!"

"Saw your mama in hot pants yesterday! Lookin' for action at the dog pound!"

"Your black mama was one of the dogs!"

One of the black boys throws a rock that hits a white boy on the arm. The two groups rush at each other and start brawling. Several of the boys are fighting on the ground, punching and kicking and pulling hair. Pooh smashes an empty coke bottle on the playground pavement and starts running after one of the white boys with it. Kendra trips the white boy and Pooh falls on him. Lou manages to yank Pooh off the boy and kick the smashed bottle out of his hand and Pooh jumps back on the kid and starts punching him in the face. You're the only one who's not fighting. Even Susie is swinging a stick at one of the white boys, who is trying to get it away from her. Curtis and another boy are wrestling, trying to get each other down, and before you can jump out of the way they plow into you and you fall flat on your back. Terrified of getting trampled you scramble up and run behind a bush. You're standing there panicking, more scared of not joining in the fight than joining it. You frantically search the ground and pick up a stone, but before you can throw it at some-one sirens sound, and the two groups break apart as fast as they came together and start running in opposite directions. Lou runs up to you with a bloody gash on her face. She grabs you and drags you along with her to the street and yells, "Go on home, Joanna! Go on home and don't come back here!" She lets go of you, and you stand in the middle of the sidewalk, stunned. "You heard me!" Lou yells, looking back at you. "Go back to your suburbs before you get hurt! You don't belong in Hough. Go on, now!"

You walk in a daze to the bus stop. You don't know where Susie is and you don't care. You don't want to see anyone, including her. You take the bus home and walk in the house and sneak up the stairs before your mother can ask you how your day was. You lie on your bed and stare at the ceiling. You wish you were anyone in the world besides yourself. You would even rather be an animal than yourself. You picture being a dog. It would be so nice to be a dog. That evening Susie calls and says that everyone on "our side" got away before the cops could catch them, and that she spent the rest of the afternoon walking around the neighborhood with Kendra. You barely hear what she's telling you. All you can think about right now is seeing Junie on Tuesday. You have the vague hope that Junie can make everything go away.

But on Tuesday, when you tell Junie about the fight in the park, she doesn't say anything to make you feel better. In fact she admonishes you for going in the first place. "It was very dangerous for you to get involved in this kind of wild melee," she says. "You could have gotten seriously hurt."

Well I didn't, you say. You're furious with her for saying something so stupid. You would much rather have gotten seriously hurt than not to have participated in the fight at all. You don't care that you exposed yourself to danger. All you care about is that Lou told you to "go back to your suburbs" and not come back to Hough. You've never felt such excruciating shame as you did at that moment, except the times when your father cut you up with his tongue during one of his rages, like when he made that remark about your "peculiar obsession" with going to Hough.

"Joanna."

What.

Junie rolls her chair over to you. "What's wrong?" she says, taking your hand. It's the first time she's ever touched you. "You look very sad," she says.

You blink back tears. I'm not, you say.

"Your expression tells me otherwise," Junie says.

So what if I'm sad, you say.

"I have to tell you something that's going to make you even sadder."

You start drifting into a fog, the way you do when you're afraid of being ambushed by reality.

"I'm leaving the agency," Junie says. She lets go of your hand but doesn't roll her chair away from you. She tells you she's moving back to New York to be closer to her daughter, that she's taken a job with an agency in New York. "You're going to be assigned a new social worker," Junie says. "I'm not sure who it is, but all the workers here are very nice." Her voice sounds as though it's coming through a long tunnel.

You don't even remember taking the bus home. That evening, while you pick at your food, your mother says, "What's wrong with you tonight?" Usually nobody in your family notices your moods, because you hide them.

Nothing! you say. I hate baked fish. This is true. You can't stand your mother's baked fish. It's not awful, it's just boring. I'm going over to Susie's, you say, and get up and leave the table.

"Susie *heint*, Susie *morgan*," her mother says, using a Yiddish expression that means something like, "Susie today, Susie tomorrow." Your mother still occasionally tosses Yiddish around, although she always speaks to her own parents in English. (Your *bobie* and *zadie* speak to younger people in English and to each other and relatives their own age in Yiddish.)

I'm going, you say. See ya. You know that your mother isn't going to stop you from leaving the house. It's summer and still a couple of hours before dark. Instead of walking to Susie's, you blindly walk around your own neighborhood. You walk all over the place, across Cedar, down some streets where you've never been, and then down some other streets. You don't know what to do. You think of hitchhiking to New York City and joining a gang. Then you think of going downtown and hopping a freight train and riding it across the country, like the hobos your father would see when he was growing up during the Depression. You realize that it's getting dark and you start to panic.

You wander into the gas station at the corner of Cedar and Green and stare at the cigarette machine. You notice the man looking at you, and you put thirty-five cents in the slot and buy a pack of Larks. You walk through the passageway between the gas station and the shopping strip next to it, and you enter the alley. You walk down the alley and stop behind Connie's Pizza Parlor and light one of the cigarettes. You've never smoked a cigarette before. You lean against the building smoking it, and it makes you very dizzy and you start to cry, and you toss the cigarette in a metal trash can full of newspaper. Then you reach into the trash can and try to light the newspapers on fire with the cigarette butt but it goes out. You light a match and stick it under some of the newspaper, and this time the flame slithers through the paper, and then it starts to leap out of the container. You stare at the fire as it dances in the dark, performing for you. When it dies out, leaving only tiny embers, you walk home, relieved that you've figured out something risky and dangerous to do to get your pride back.

Rainy Night in Early December

I'm writing, writing, writing because it's keeping me alive, just like setting fires kept me alive when I was a kid. The rain continues to lash against the windows, and it's getting really depressing. It doesn't stop, and it's giving everyone a grim, apocalyptic feeling. Buildings all over the city are collapsing and it's depressing to drive around Brooklyn and the Lower East Side and see piles of rubble where people used to live. Meanwhile my delinquent boys' club won't be meeting today or probably ever again because of two things that happened, which are even more depressing to me than the apocalypse.

The first thing that happened was Bobby Chang tried to rape me early this morning. I'm not even that upset with Bobby for trying to rape me. I'm upset with myself. I'm like that frog in the fable, who allows the scorpion to ride across the river on his back and then gets stung. It's not that I ever really trusted Bobby not to do something like this. I'm just so spaced out, grieving my mom, that I didn't set any limits. I mean he's an aggressive sixteen-year-old street kid. How did I expect him to behave?

I'm not saying there was any excuse for him to sneak into my bedroom at three this morning and stick his dick in my face while I was sleeping. It was one of the worst experiences of my life. I was jolted awake by this sensation, and I saw that it was a dick hitting my nose, and I shrieked and bolted up, and then I saw that the dick was attached to Bobby, who was standing there in his unzipped jeans, with that sleepy look males get when they're exposing themselves. When you're being sexually assaulted by someone you know, they turn into a stranger, like a whole different person. It's a very creepy experience.

At least I reacted in an appropriate way, instead of in my usual spacey, passive, permissive way. I yelled, "What the fuck are you doing?" and I pushed him as hard as I could. He stepped back a few paces and said, "You know you want this, mama." And I said, "I don't want anyone's dick in my face, and anyway you're a fucking kid! How dare you come into my bedroom in the middle of the night and scare the shit out of me like this!" But instead of getting the message and leaving my room he jumped on top of me and started grinding away. It's a good thing I had the covers over me and was wearing my pj's instead of one of my mom's nightgowns, because I was able to repel him long enough to frustrate him, and finally he jumped off of me and acted all mad, as though he was the wronged party. He said, "I thought I be doin' you a favor, offering an old woman some fresh young dick. I offer you the best sex you will ever have again in your old, sad life and you act like it's garbage? Fuck you, bitch." And he stormed out of my bedroom and a second later I heard the front door slam.

I lay in bed shaking and trying to calm myself. Finally I got up and went into the living room and re-locked the front door and went to the closet door and pushed my rolltop desk that I never use in front of it. Then I took an Ativan and lay in bed freaking out until I finally fell asleep about three hours later. I woke up around noon and sat on the couch and sulked. I wasn't even that upset that Bobby sexually assaulted me. I mean he never got very far. I was far more upset to realize that, after I gave him and his friends a safe space to hang out, he never had an inkling of respect for me. The fucking kid didn't assault my body as much as he assaulted my ego.

As if Bobby's early morning madness wasn't enough of a message that I need to cut these kids loose, another one of my darling delinquents drove the message home. While I was reading *The New York Times* to try to focus on the world instead of myself, I heard fire engines coming down the street, and they stopped in front of my building. I went to the door and opened it and I smelled smoke and saw firemen and cops rushing up the stairs. A few seconds later two cops dragged Jakey down the steps and I heard one of the Chinese men yell, "Don't let him come back here! He crazy! He try to set whole place on fire!" Obviously the fire wasn't very large because nobody was evacuated. But what tore me up was Jakey pointing at me and screaming, "I didn't do it on purpose! Ask her! Ask her!" I wanted to follow them down the stairs to talk to the cops, to tell them that I knew Jakey, that he was just a nice boy with problems, but he's not a nice boy at all, he's a sociopathic maniac, and after the incident with Bobby I just couldn't do anything but stand there with my heart breaking. My heart was breaking not for Jakey but for myself.

Oh, God, I feel so bad. I wanted to give those kids something—I don't know, some kind of nurturing. Anyway, what else was I supposed to do? They kept coming in here through the closet so I just decided to go with the flow. But eventually I kind of liked having them here. Of course nobody would understand something as strange as that. Even Molly told me to get rid of them when she found out that they've all been busted and adjudicated, except for Jakey, whose Hasidic community protects him. During that same conversation Molly demanded to know why these Chinese kids aren't studying all the time like the other Chinese kids, which even she knew was a ridiculous generalization. Anyway, I didn't care that much that they were bad boys. Having them in my home, feeding them and giving them shelter from the storm, reminded me that I'm a grown woman, that I care for other people's children, that those insane days of my youth are long gone.

But those days never really left me. I still feel a pang of shame when I think of Lou yelling at me to "go back to your suburbs." When Jakey set that fire today it freaked me out almost as much as Bobby trying to rape me. I was a firebug too. Was I as crazy as he is? If I was, it was all because I was a homo and couldn't let anyone know, including myself. Back in those days if you were "that way" the real you became invisible. After feeling invisible all those years, I like to be seen, which is why when I was fifty I got a tattoo on my neck. I didn't want to become one of those older women that people ignore on the street. Now when people pass me on the street they look right at me, and often they come up and ask me about it. In New York an older woman with a tattoo on her neck is considered normal. You would have to be walking around naked to shock the people of New York. (Actually you would have to be walking around naked in the financial district in the middle of the day. If you walked around naked in the Village in the middle of the night people would just laugh at you.)

Yesterday I got another rejection from a major publisher, which upset me terribly because I thought I could do a better job of marketing my book after I fired Myra, who was treating my book as though it had cooties. After I got the rejection I immediately sent it to several more places, and I know eventually somebody is going to want it. But still, I'm feeling lost and forlorn and kind of like I'm falling apart. Truthfully I don't feel any more intact than when I was a fourteen-year-old firebug. I was a really messed-up kid and now I'm a messed-up adult.

I wish I felt like doing something. There's no way I want to see any of my friends and tell them what happened this morning. It's just too embarrassing after I kept defending my decision to befriend those dopey kids. My friends are all wanting to go out lately, it's the holiday season, and they're tired of being cooped up from the rain, and I keep making up excuses not to get together when they call. I had several invitations to Thanksgiving dinners and I just stayed here by myself. I always had Thanksgiving in Cleveland with my mom and Danny and Sharon and my niece and nephew, and any of the other sibs who happened to be in town, and Steven and his wife, Bella, and his mom, Joan, and various other friends and strays. Everyone always loved to go to Isabel's. This year I was perfectly contented to do nothing. I didn't even feel that sad. I just sat here and watched TV and felt my mom close to me. If I told her I missed my delinquent boys, that they made me feel like a normal, grown-up woman, she would understand. She raised four delinquents herself. Of course they were her real kids. But she loved everybody's kids. She really didn't care how bad they were.

I wish it would stop raining.

FALL AND WINTER 1965

You're out of gas. You go to school, come home, eat. Go upstairs and lie on your bed and stare at the ceiling. You hardly have any homework because you get it done in study hall. You listen to records in the living room with your ear pressed to the speaker and the music rips through you like a million shards of glass. The exquisite agony of listening to music is better than feeling dead.

What keeps you going more than listening to music is setting fires. You set at least two fires a week. Even if you don't feel like it, if it's cold or snowing or you feel lazy, you make yourself do it anyway. After supper you say you're going to Tessie's, who lives a couple of houses from the corner of Cedar, and you go to the alley on the corner and set a fire in "your" trash can behind the pizza joint. As you stare at the flames leaping in the dark and breathe in their acrid perfume you come back to life. After the flames die down you trot over to Tessie's and tell her about the fire. Setting fires is not only exciting, it makes you feel good about yourself. You feel like a tough kid engaged in a dangerous activity instead of a creepy girl with sick and twisted thoughts. But a couple of hours after you set a fire your energy sputters out and you feel as sad and sluggish as ever.

It's bad enough that Lou and Junie have abandoned you, but now Susie is back in Fairview. Right before school started her social worker dragged her back to live with her parents, urging her to "try to get along with them," and instead of trying to get along with them she broke every plate and glass in her parents' kitchen, and her father called the police and her social worker put her back in Fairview. You talk to her on the phone a few times a week, and she tells you about what's going on in her cottage and you tell her about your fires. One day she tells you she found out that a boy in the next cottage burned down his elementary school in Detroit, and after you hang up you're so depressed about your wimpy little trash fires that you contemplate blowing up a gas station, but it all seems like too much trouble so you just forget about it.

Before Junie went back to New York she referred you to a worthless new social worker, a dry woman with curly hair and glasses named Marcia Pinsky. She has a thin, soft voice and shows no emotion when she's talking to you. The only reason you bother to keep your appointments with her is you're hoping that if she gets worried enough about your fires she'll send you to Fairview. But so far she just asks you why you "feel the need to do this," and when you tell her that you're thinking of blowing up a gas station or setting fire to a school she just says "mm-hm" and writes it down in her notebook.

Of course the day you told Marcia Pinsky you were setting fires she told your parents, and they had a talk with you and asked you to promise never to do it again, but you didn't say anything because you don't make promises you can't keep. But your parents don't make a big deal out of it. They pretty much let you do as you please, as long as you get good grades. If you want to go to Little Jerusalem and see your friends, fine. If you want to stay up until 3 a.m. on weekends and sleep till noon, fine. If you want to be driven with your friends to the movies or to Manners for Big Boy hamburgers, fine. When you leave the house with matches in your pocket and tell your parents you're going over to Tessie's, they don't try to stop you. They pretend that the phone call from Marcia Pinsky about your fire-setting never happened. Your parents are kind of annoyed with school authorities and social workers who call them and tell them about your alarming activities. It's not that they think people are lying about you, they just figure that you're getting revenge against adults who are too stupid to see what a perfect child you are.

Even with the fire-setting, nobody thinks there's anything very wrong with you in the fall and winter of 1965. You're grumpy in the mornings and pretty cheerful when you get home. In school you get decent grades and excel in English. You tease and goof around with your brothers and hang out with Rosie in your room, listening to the hit songs on the radio ..."Hang on Sloopy! Sloopy hang on!" ... "Do you believe in magic, in a young girl's heart" ... "Hey! Hey! You! You! Get off of my cloud!" ... "Let's hang on! To what we've got!" ... "We can work it out, we can work it ou-out!" ... "Everybody loves a clown, so why don't you" ..."Hello darkness my old friend, I've come to talk with you again" ... "AND YOU TELL ME! OVER AND OVER AND OVER AGAIN MY FRIEND! THAT YOU DON'T BELIEVE WE'RE ON THE EVE OF DESTRUCK— SHEE-ON!" The songs pour into you and stick to you like glittery paint.

On weekends you go on wholesome excursions with your friends. You go to plays and movies and to Saul's Deli for corned beef sandwiches. You join the JCC teen newspaper staff and spend your Sunday afternoons in a cozy tiled room typing breezy articles about Jewish teen life on a black Underwood typewriter exactly like your dad's. At school you compose brilliant stories for English class and are often asked to read them out loud, even though the subjects usually focus on crazy, murderous people. You're still not in the popular crowd but you're well-liked and dress appropriately in modish skirts and dresses, and your wavy hair is neatly brushed with a hair band keeping it out of your eyes. (Susie was the only one of your classmates to be a fashion nonconformist. You and your classmates dress in what you call "collegiate" style, except for the handful of "racky" girls who wear tighter skirts, ratted hair, and shoes with blocky heels instead of flats, and their male counterparts who prefer Elvis-style to Beatles-style hair, although any boy who wears his hair over his collar or ears risks getting hassled by school authorities.)

But while you manage to live an outwardly normal life your tension is building. It's building faster than you can release it through setting fires. You keep trying to think of something to do to get sent away to Fairview or even a reformatory. You can no longer stand being at home where you have to try to act cheerful. School no longer has any attraction for you, like it did last year when you were the dean's number one problem. One day Pickles walks by in the hall and says, "Hello, Judy," and then she says, "Oh, I mean Joanna!!," making it clear that you are no longer of any concern to her. That evening, still smarting from the dean's forgetting your name, you're watching the news with your parents, waiting for *Wagon Train* to come on, and a group of kids from the Harriet Tubman Center are interviewed by the local newscaster, saying that they're starting a youth club to fight discrimination. Among them are Kendra and Curtis. Kendra is just standing there, but Curtis rants about being treated unfairly by the police and "pushed around" by the white community, which you assume includes you, since your cowardly performance in the park. That night you lie in bed recalling Lou commanding you to "go back to your suburbs," and you think about sneaking out of the house and going downtown and becoming a bum, like the derelicts sleeping off their rotgut in the hallways of the Terminal Tower, but instead you just lie awake dreading the morning sun.

A couple of days later when you get home from school you find a letter from Junie and you fall back into your funk as you read all about Junie's wonderful life back in her hometown, where she's working "primarily with teenagers" at an agency in Brooklyn, spending a lot of time with her eighteen-year-old daughter who's moved in with her, and even doing some "crafts" in her spare time. When you're done reading the letter you feel like tearing it up, but instead you toss it in your dresser drawer. It's starting to get dark even though it's only four o'clock. You need to get out of the house before you go crazy. You call Molly, who tells you cousin Vic is visiting. "I'm coming over," you say, and you hang up and put on your jacket and boots and tell your mom you're walking over to Molly's. Since it's Friday your mother doesn't make any kind of fuss. When you get to Molly's they both have their jackets on and are waiting for you to accompany them on a walk around the neighborhood. Shirley is working her evening shift at the department store, so you're all free to do as you please.

"You wanna go over to Rhonda's?" Molly asks. That sounds like a good idea. You haven't seen Rhonda since Susie got dragged away to her parents' house. But when you get there nobody answers the door, so the three of you continue down the street. When you reach the corner you see the Blobs coming down the driveway, all bundled up in their winter jackets.

Hi, Penny and Geraldine! you yell, waving at them. But instead of returning your greeting, the way Penny did the last time you yelled hello, they both glare at you and walk to their car. Hey! you yell. Can't you say hello? I was trying to be friendly!

"I don't think you were trying to be friendly," says Penny. And the blond one says, "Just go away and leave us alone," and makes her "shooing" motion that you find unspeakably insulting, and they get in their car.

Stupid jerks! you yell. As the car backs down the driveway you punch the hood as hard as you can. Vic laughs and says, "I think you dented it," but you don't think it's funny. You had expected Penny to return your friendly overture, but instead she and the other Blob made you feel like a fool.

Vic starts trotting up the driveway, and glances back at you and Molly with a mischievous look. You follow him, but Molly stays put. "I really need to get home, you guys," she calls.

"Hey!" Vic yells. "Get a load of this!"

You walk over to see where he's pointing. Oh my God, you say. The entire side of the house is covered with red-painted insults. PERVERT SCUM. WEIRDOS. LESBO LADIES CLUB. CREEPY HOMOS. GET OUT OF THE NEIGHBORHOOD. CUNT PUSSIES. GET OUT OF TOWN. The house is covered from top to bottom with offensive words and phrases.

Molly comes over and looks. "I wonder who did it," she says.

"Probably Danny and them," Vic says. Danny Amato is one of the ninth-grade racks that sneaked into the Blobs' house with him in the fall and moved furniture around and smeared ketchup on the bed.

Why are they driving away and just leaving it there? you say.

"They probably went to get more paint to cover it up," Vic says.

"Well, whoever did it should jump in the lake," Molly says. "Those women can't help being like that. My mom says there's not even any cure for it."

You agree with Molly that this was taking things too far. The sight of the red-painted obscenities covering the side of the house is shocking to you.

Molly says she has to get home. "I'm supposed to help Sarah make supper before my mom gets back from work," she says. You've always been impressed that Molly can actually cook. All you can do is make toast.

You don't have any plans for the weekend so you hang around the house. For some reason the sight of the red-painted obscenities has made you hyper and jittery. On Saturday evening you go out and set a fire, and you come home feeling calmer. But on Sunday you wake up feeling jumpy and agitated again. After supper you're listening to the radio upstairs, waiting for *The Ed Sullivan Show* to come on, and the phone rings. You rush into your parents' room and pick up the phone and it's Steven.

"Guess what I heard today," Steven says.

What did you hear, Stevie? You plop down on your dad's desk chair.

"You know those women you guys call the Blobs?"

Yeah, you say. What about those old witches?

"You know the blond one, Geraldine Madorsky?"

Yeah, you say. You never knew Geraldine's last name.

"She's dead."

What! you yell. We just saw her on Friday!

"She hanged herself last night."

Oh my God! you scream. How do you know?

"Esther Fein just called my mom and told her. She was driving to work this morning and saw the police cars. Apparently Penny got up this morning and found Geraldine hanging in the living room."

That's crazy! you yell. You feel no sympathy for Geraldine. Instead you're furious with her. Hanging yourself seems like such a childish thing to do. Like a giant tantrum. It seems stupid for a grown woman to kill herself because the neighborhood kids were mean to her. What a dope, you say. She goes and kills herself.

"I guess she was depressed," Steven says.

Does Molly know about it? you ask.

"I only told Susie so far. I called her at Fairview." You hear Joan say something to Steven. "I gotta go," Steven says. "My mom needs to use the phone." Joan is probably going to call everyone she knows to chatter about the suicide.

As soon as you hang up with Steven the phone rings. You answer it and it's Molly. She's crying. "Susie just called me," she sobs. "Did you hear what happened?"

I know, you say. The Blob killed herself. But we didn't even like her, Mu! It's not like we killed her! You don't know why Molly is crying, but hearing her cry makes you feel terrible. You feel like the worst person in the world because you don't feel sorry for Geraldine and in fact you hate her even more now than you did before. You ask Molly if she wants you to come over and she says no. After you hang up you go downstairs to watch *Ed Sullivan* and don't tell anyone about Geraldine's suicide because for one thing, you don't think your parents will care since they didn't know her. You've never talked about the Blobs with them.

As soon as you wake up the next morning Geraldine's suicide is in your head and you feel even more agitated than you did all weekend. On the school bus you keep popping up and down in your seat, talking a mile a minute, and in homeroom you walk around the room instead of staying in your chair and Mrs. Abrams asks you if you have "schpilkes." This tragic event that should be making you sad has given you a strange feeling of excitement. When the bell rings you walk out into the hall wondering how you're going to get through the day because you don't feel at all normal.

As you walk to your first-period class you get a glimpse of a fire alarm on the wall. Your arm reaches up and your hand grabs it and pulls it. You're actually shocked to hear the *BEEP! BEEP! BEEP!* sounding through the hall. A few minutes later you're standing in the winter cold with the whole rest of the school while the fire engines roar in, the firemen go into the building, and finally come out and the announcement is made that everyone can return to class. By now the whole ninth grade knows who pulled the alarm—not that you told anyone, but some of the kids guessed that you did it and you didn't deny it. There are still a few minutes of first period remaining so you go into your social studies class but after about a minute a student aide walks in, summoning you to Pickles' office.

Pickles is in her office with the assistant principal, Mr. Richardson, a nice guy who never gets angry, and he's not even angry when you admit that you pulled the alarm, but Pickles is pretty steamed up, and goes on and on about how the fire engines have real fires to go to and that you wasted their time. She says they're suspending you for ten days and you're lucky they're not expelling you and pressing charges against you and blah blah blah, and then she sends you into the office to wait for your mother to pick you up. But instead of waiting for your mother like you did the last time you were suspended, you leave the office and get your jacket from your locker and leave the building.

It's a dark, overcast day but not too cold for December. You walk toward Mayfield Road, ignoring the discomfort of being in school clothes instead of jeans. When you reach Mayfield you cross the street to the corner shopping center. You go around to the back parking lot and stand behind a car and scan the alley behind the stores, which drops down on the other side of the narrow road where the cars drive in. In the alley is a giant dumpster behind Mike's Discount Store. You look around and see no activity in the parking lot, even though several cars are parked there. You trot across the narrow road down to the alley and over to the dumpster, which is loaded with paper and cardboard. You fish a book of

214

matches from your jacket pocket and start lighting matches and sticking them under the paper and finally a flame leaps up and you move the paper around and the flame starts spreading through the container. You run back to the parking lot and hide behind a car and watch the fire rage and roar. Then you hear the sirens, and they get louder and louder and a fire engine pulls up, and you watch the firemen hosing out the flames, and when the fire is out you look down at your skirt and your penny loafers and knee socks and for a moment you can't remember who's wearing them.

Mid-December Afternoon, Still Pouring Rain

I'm all fucked up. I can't believe I'm the same person who set that big fire, but I did. But are you the same person you were when you were fourteen, a half-century later? Does that child still live inside of you, or is the child gone? Writing this book is so disorienting. I can't tell if I'm just having vivid memories of my childhood while I'm writing this or if that child is still inside of me and I *become* her as I'm writing. I feel so bad about Geraldine now. What little shits we were, hating those women for being gay. Geraldine personified the icky, creepy part of me that I was desperately trying to hide from myself and everyone else. But I still tell Molly that if they were only nice to us instead of acting all stuck-up and unfriendly, I wouldn't have disliked them at all. And Molly says it doesn't matter, they had a right not to be friendly, and I still take everything personally, like if the cashier doesn't smile at me at CVS. And she's right. I'm still so touchy and neurotic. I don't feel good about myself right now. I'm trying to write this book, to get my career back on track, and I feel like a big loser because so far nobody wants my other book. All my professional accomplishments have become meaningless because I haven't been able to sell this one novel. I've written dozens of articles for major publications, and a well-received novel that's still in circulation, but none of that matters to me right now. Who cares what you wrote two years ago? Nobody remembers it. Two years is a long time in this day and age, when a million things happen to a person in an hour. I'm a big nobody now. I hate myself. I didn't even feel sorry for Geraldine when she killed herself. I was an evil child and I'm a big loser adult.

I'm going crazy. I need to stop this. If I talked to Junie right now she would remind me that I've had a very rich and accomplished adulthood. I've done many cool, interesting things. I wrote two books, almost three if you count this one. I've written hundreds of articles and commentaries for major publications. I've traveled all over the place. I was on a kibbutz for six months, picking oranges from trees and working in a kitchen. Well, I got kicked out of the kitchen but I picked a lot of oranges. And I went to Russia and saw the village where my *bobie* grew up and went to Minsk where both of my grandfathers grew up and I took a tour of death camps, and I heard the grandson of the commandant of Auschwitz deliver an apology to survivors, and one survivor went up and hugged him. I wandered around Havana by myself (the minder stopped to talk to someone and I walked away from him) and I made friends with a dog. I was in India where I got violently ill and almost died although my friends say I didn't almost die but I'm the one who should be believed. I've traveled in most states of America and of course I've been all over New York City.

I have dozens of friends; I'm not talking about these bullshit "friends" that people have now; I'm talking about real friends that I know. I'm part of the Jewish secular community in New York and I attend their discussions and social events, and I'm part of a monthly potluck group of ten women from that community, although I missed the last couple because I've been too distracted. I have a loving family and extended family and many gay friends and many non-white friends of all persuasions although no transgender friends because most of them are younger than I am or else those queeny guys of my generation that sometimes annoy me. I have retained my friends from childhood. I have a great relationship with my two nieces (I count Zoey, Molly's daughter) and my crazy little nephew.

I've been in love. That experience doesn't feel vague and distant, or like it never happened. In fact, my memory of falling in love, which happened more than thirty years ago, is more vivid than my recollection of writing the last paragraph. Susan and Molly and I walked into one of those wild loft parties they used to have back in Soho's bad old days, and there was Tanya reciting poetry in her red dress. (The funky little band that was accompanying her recitation was led by Billy, who became Molly's boyfriend.) I had met Tanya a couple of times. She was Junie's daughter, and when I was still a nutty little teenager in Cleveland, she was already a famous revolutionary poet in New York, a known associate of the Black Panthers even though she's half white. The night of the loft party I had come out a couple of months before in a single, explosive moment—it was the clichéd experience of your life going from black-and-white to Technicolor—and the moment I saw Tanya standing in front of the mike that night I fell madly in love with her. She isn't even that good-looking, like Junie, her black mother, who's still beautiful in her late eighties. She looks like an average soft butch lesbian with a nice short, neat 'fro, oaky skin, and average features. But she has charisma. She has perfect white teeth and lights up the world when she smiles, but even when she's not smiling she gives off powerful, crackly energy. After I had sex with her I thought, this is wonderful, I'll have a girlfriend and I will be ecstatic for the rest of my life, and when she kept having sex with other women, at first I thought maybe she didn't get it, that she could have *me*. I would get mad and stop speaking to her, and then she would drop her woman of the moment and we would have sex again, and this went on and on for decades if you can believe it. She was my exasperating lover, but mainly she was my friend. We hung around with my friends and her friends, drinking and smoking and going to movies by Fellini and Bergman and to off-off Broadway plays in which people were naked or threw buckets of paint around, and we went to CBGB's and listened to punk rock, and I went to her poetry readings and she went to my book readings.

You might say, well, Susan did you a favor taking her away, she wasn't any good for you, but even though she never committed herself to me I never wanted Tanya out of my life. My life after I met her was so much better than before. Even when she was breaking my heart at least people understood what I was going through, unlike when I was a teenager and I was all alone in my bleak, twisted little world.

But even though I was lonely and tormented and scared to death all the time when I was a teenager, I had so much energy! I can feel it pulsing through me, or maybe I'm just feeling the memory of it, as I write. Maybe that's why the past seems so much more alive than the present. Even when I masturbate lately the reason I have such incredible orgasms is that in my sexual fantasies I'm a younger version of myself. And then when it's all over I feel old and stale again.

It's all Tanya and Susan's fault that I'm feeling old and stale. It's because of them that I haven't had sex in more than two years. I'm not about to go and have sex with some woman I'm not interested in just to make Tanya jealous, like I used to do, which was terribly amoral and I'm ashamed of it now. But the fact is that women aren't really made to spend their entire lives single and childless unless they've got a partner or companion or someone to spend the night with every so often. Or else if they have some kids to take care of, like the grandmothers whose daughters are in jail, or like me before that brat tried to rape me in the middle of the night. If you're an older single woman, not a divorcee or widow but just single during your whole life, unless you have someone to care for (at least a cat, which I can't have anymore becauseof my allergies), eventually you're going to get "bats in the belfry." I know it's very politically incorrect to say this right now. You're not supposed to suggest that single, childless older women might have any kind of issues, but they do. In fact most of them are mentally deranged. You can even ask them. Only the nuttiest ones will deny it, but they all have these forced smiles on their faces while they sit around at their luncheons and book clubs, after being brainwashed by self-help gurus on daytime TV.

This is a very depressing, one-sided conversation. Here I am lying on this sofa feeling sorry for myself, with my whole apartment a mess and the rain lashing against the window and my mother gone, and the lights keep flickering in the living room and I'm afraid of a power outage. I really need to get myself together. Maybe I should call someone and get a writing assignment. OH MY GOD! WHAT WAS THAT? Jesus Christ. I think the roof just caved in. The Chinese people are running down the steps. I'd better get the fuck out of here. Should I take my computer? I could just take my flash drive that has my book saved on it. But I also have to take my computer because I didn't save what I'm writing now so it could all be lost. Why am I still writing? I can't stop writing. I'm writing, writing, writing and this whole building could collapse at any second. I could be buried alive, which is the worst way to die.

I just saw a rat run into the kitchen. I am out of here.

EARLY 1966

The day after you report to your social worker that you pulled the fire alarm and set fire to the dumpster behind Mike's Discount Store, your stunned parents drive you to the psychiatric unit of University Hospitals, where a balding, pipe-smoking shrink admits you as an emergency case. Even though you made a fuss with the social worker about being sent to a "nuthouse" instead of Fairview where you could be with Susie, as soon as you set foot onto the locked ward with its heavy wooden doors, the outside world with its falling snow fades away. It takes you about five minutes to relax into the L-shaped unit with its institutional look, the tile floors and walls painted a sullen green, the carpeted "day room" on one end of the unit and the recreation room on the other, and the lobby, dining room, and nurses station at the intersection.

When you first arrive at "Blossom Pavilion 4" the only other teenager on the unit is a tall, silent girl with greasy hair, but a couple days later she's sent back to the state hospital and you become the only teenager on a ward full of adults. You feel crazier than you've ever felt in your life, not because you're here but because you want to be here. Your parents and relatives and friends certainly would not want to tuck themselves away in a loony bin with locked doors and people muttering and shrieking through the halls.

It's the nurses swishing through the halls in their white uniforms who make you feel exuberant rather than upset and scared, the way you assume most people would feel in your situation. Most of the nurses are in their early twenties, and they smell like White Shoulders and Chanel Number 5 and Noxzema and cigarette smoke. There are "the blondies"—smart, handsome, down-to-earth Judy Rockland; sweet, simple, creamy-voiced Mary Beavers; and tall, willowy, cool Nancy Steele. And short, freckled Gail Rickey who bounces around the unit like a super-charged bunny. And an inseparable pair of pert, wiry, fun-loving Negro nurses, Ronnie Willard and Lucy Clarke. And the commanding day and evening supervisors, Jen Gianfrido and Barbara Crenshaw. You follow them around, joking with them, calling them by nicknames, touching them whenever you can get away with it, even though unnecessary physical contact between nurses and patients is not permitted. Your excitement around the nurses has eradicated your depression, but underneath the excitement is still that unsettling knowledge that you are now officially crazy.

Ironically, you feel more normal around the crazy patients than you do around the normal nurses. You always enjoy making new friends, and you find these nutty people far more interesting than the adults in the outside world. Your roommate, Lucy Capriato, is a chain-smoking, jokey woman who calls you "Shortcake" and whose husband is a big shot in the Cleveland mafia and visits every Wednesday with a pizza from Mama Santa's. Jacqueline Perry invites you into her room to listen to Billie Holiday records and hear about her life as a local jazz singer in the inner city, where she witnessed shootings and heroin overdoses. Shy Betty Yoder tells you that she was banished from her Amish community after she ran away one day and got drunk in a bar, and afterward she was discovered wandering around downtown Cleveland half-dressed and not remembering who she was. Danny Jacovich, a red-haired livewire, calls you "Popcorn" and entertains you with detailed accounts of his juvenile crimes in the rough Slavic Village neighborhood, which include successfully robbing a bank wearing a Yogi Bear costume. Most of the patients are just depressed or acting-out neurotics, but the unit has its share of crazies as well, like Martha Stone, who has bald spots in her head and clomps around in her saddle shoes muttering to herself, and squat, dark-skinned Winnie Jackson, who occasionally tears down the hall naked, and one day tells you about the men hiding in the closets of her house, "wanting to drink my pee."

The worst part of every day is when your parents visit. It makes you feel terrible to see them dragging up the hall, your father with his blank mask and your mother looking stunned, as though someone's just slapped her in the face. Your parents sit on chairs in your room, your mother making polite conversation with Lucy although you know your mother hates Lucy for reminding her that her daughter is a mental patient and not a normal girl skipping off to school every morning. You hate your mother for hating Lucy, although your mother puts on a good act. "What pretty flowers!" she says about the roses Lucy's gangster husband brought her.

"My husband brought them," Lucy says, smiling, and you see your father wince. He's already made some nasty comments about Lucy's husband, whom he knew from his days as a newspaper reporter. (He knew all the local gangsters.) You hate your father for hating Lucy's husband, just as you hate your mother for hating Lucy. You wish they would leave already. They remind you of the outside world, a world in which you will never become a normal woman who gets married and has children, like your mother or your teachers. Even though your body will get older you'll always be a monstrous child inside. But you don't allow yourself to think about these things. You try to concentrate on positive things, on how cool it is to be in a loony bin and be having this colorful adventure. But seeing your parents always busts the enchanted bubble of BP4 and brings you face to face with your own bleak future and, even worse, with the people whose lives you have ruined.

One evening in January, when you've been on BP4 for about six weeks, you storm out of the recreation room before the end of your session with your idiotic shrink, furious that you've just wasted a half-hour of your precious time with this wooden man who refuses to disclose any personal information about himself, even his stupid age. You round the corner and catch sight of a new patient sitting in the dumpy little lobby across from the nurse's station. You walk right by her, then turn and walk back and stare at her. The woman looks the same as she always has, tall and pale with a sharp nose and curly brown hair, but she's outside of her usual environment, which was why you didn't recognize her immediately.

"Hello, Joanna," she says. The new patient is Penny Weinberg, the Blob.

What are *you* doing here? you ask.

"I suppose the same thing you're doing here."

You can't believe that your old nemesis from the neighborhood is sitting right there in a mental hospital ward, even though it's exactly where you and your friends always said she belonged. How long are you gonna stay here? you say, feeling instantly pugnacious. Even though Geraldine, the other Blob, seemed like the angrier of the two of them, Penny was always the snootier one.

"I'll be staying as long as I need to," Penny says.

Well this is weird, you say.

"It certainly is," Penny says.

You dart off down the hall, dying to talk to someone about what just happened. You hunt down the evening supervisor, Miss Crenshaw, and pull her into your room.

"What's gotten you all in a tizzy?" Miss Crenshaw asks, sitting on the edge of Lucy's bed while you jump up and down.

You know that new patient, Penny Weinberg? you say.

"What about her? Stop jumping and talk to me like a normal person."

You stop jumping and say, I know her. She lives in our neighborhood. My friends and I used to stare at them.

"What do you mean, stare at them?"

We sat on the lawn across the street in a long, creepy row and stared at them with electric eyes and they would go nuts. Once they called the cops, and the cops came and told them they couldn't do anything about some children looking at them. You laugh.

"Well, that was a very mean thing for you and your friends to do," Miss Crenshaw says.

Well they were mean too, you say. And they were, like, perverted. And then her lover hanged herself.

"Yes, we know all about that. And it's not nice to call Miss Weinberg names. She has an illness, just like everyone here, and she's here to get help. Her problems are not your business, unless she chooses to discuss them with you. You need to focus on yourself, Joanna."

Everyone here does not have an illness, you say. I don't have any illness. You hate when people call you "sick."

"Yes you do," Miss Crenshaw says. "Any child who sets fires and acts out the way you do is emotionally sick."

Well, I'm not sick the way she is, you insist. Anyway, I thought what she had was incurable.

"Well, that shows how little you know about mental illness," Miss Crenshaw says. "You can always get better with the proper treatment. But you have to work at it. Why don't you give Dr. Shriner a chance to help you?"

That guy's an idiot, you say. He has no personality.

"Well refusing to go downstairs for your appointments and calling him all kinds of names isn't going to help you get better," Miss Crenshaw says. "Don't you want to leave here one day?"

No. I like it here.

"I know you do." Miss Crenshaw gives you a sad, thoughtful smile, probably thinking that your parents are totally incompetent for allowing their daughter to become crazy. Unlike on the outside, where you want people to adore your parents, here in BP4 you want everyone to think your parents are incompetent, because you don't want to be sent home.

Miss Crenshaw leaves to go on her rounds, and you rush off to the phone booth at the end of the hall and call Susie's cottage. Someone picks up the phone and says, "Yeah." It's Susie.

It's me! you yell.

"Well, hello, my little mental patient," Susie says.

Guess what! You're not gonna believe this!

"What?"

The Blob is here!

"The live one or the dead one?"

You start laughing and say, The live one, stupid. Penny. I just saw her sitting in the lobby! She said 'Hello, Joanna,' and I almost died!

"You *have* to be kidding!" Susie says. "Do you know why she's there? Is it because the other pervert killed herself?"

I don't know. I haven't talked to her. But when I saw her I suddenly didn't hate her as much, because she's finally, like, where she belongs instead of out in public.

"I know!" Susie says. "That makes perfect sense."

This means you have to come to my birthday party so you can see her, you say to Susie. Your birthday is in a couple of weeks and there will be a little party for you in the dining room after supper is served.

"I will definitely come to your party so I can see this with my own eyes," Susie says. "I'm planning to run away from this dump with my friend Judy, but it probably won't be until the spring."

After you hang up with Susie you call Molly and tell her the news, and all Molly has to say is, "How weird." Ever since Geraldine hanged herself Molly has shown no interest in talking about either of the Blobs, the live one or the dead one. You ask her if she's coming to your birthday party and she says, "We'll see." But you have a feeling that she won't come, and it hurts your feelings.

For the next couple of weeks, whenever you see Penny in the halls or the dining room, you greet her in a provocative way that isn't necessarily rude or disrespectful but could be interpreted as rude and disrespectful by someone who doesn't like you.

Hi there, Fruit Cup! you say to her as you pass her walking down the hall with her shrink.

Henny Penny! Henny Penny! you call when you see her talking to Miss Crenshaw in the lobby.

Hey! Get dressed! you wisecrack as you pass her walking down the hall in her robe.

But Penny the Blob surprises you every time you see her. Instead of acting nasty and irritated, the way she always did out in the neighborhood, she responds to your bratty greetings with a pleasant wave, or else she says, "Hello there, Joanna!" You're completely disarmed, because you can never summon up any dislike for anyone who doesn't dislike you. It's not in your nature.

The day before your birthday party, you call Susie's cottage at Fairview to find out if she's coming. The cottage house mother answers the phone and says, "Susie is not available at the moment."

What exactly does that mean, Linda? you ask.

"We're still looking for her," Linda says. "She disappeared a couple days ago, after she found out she wouldn't be permitted to attend your birthday party."

What! you yell. You're more excited that your friend has made good on her promise to run away than you're disappointed that she won't be coming to your party. You don't even have any idea where she is? you ask Linda.

"Not at the moment," Linda says. "I'm sure she'll get in touch with you as soon as she turns up."

You can't get anything more out of Linda, so as soon as you hang up you call Steven. Steven tells you that he has no idea where Susie ran off to. When he went to visit her at Fairview a couple of days ago she had already absconded with her friend, Judy Rothstein, but nobody knows where they went.

Maybe they hopped a freight train! you yell. You and Susie have talked about hopping freight trains a number of times. But you would feel kind of bad if Susie had hopped a freight train without you.

"I doubt it," Steven says, which makes you feel a little better. If Steven says that Susie probably hasn't hopped a freight train she probably didn't.

¤ ¤ ¤

226

At first your birthday party is a sad affair. None of your friends come (Steven has a big report to do for school) and your siblings are too young, which leaves your parents, who sit in the dining room with their traumatized expressions that make the patients attending the party, including the new patient, a catatonic schizophrenic, look ecstatic by comparison. You blow out your fifteen candles plus the one for good luck, and play the piano for everyone. After you finish your Schubert waltz, everyone applauds and you get up and give a little bow, and then you see Penny sitting at a table all by herself with a small wrapped box. You're absolutely stunned, because the majority of the patients did not attend your party. You walk past your parents, who are actually deigning to converse with Lucy, and go up to Penny.

"Happy birthday," Penny says.

Thanks!

"I got you a little something." You sit down at the table and start unwrapping the box. You're touched that this woman you've spent the last year tormenting has gone out of her way to get you a gift. Inside the box is a beautiful metal carousel. You've loved carousels your whole life. Oh wow, you say. You pull it out and put it on the table.

"Press the button," Penny says, and you do, and the music starts up and the horses go around and around. Thanks, Penny! you say to her.

"You're welcome. Now you'd better go back to your parents. They're glancing over this way. They look a little frightened." You actually share a laugh with Penny Weinberg, the Blob.

You show Lucy and your parents the carousel, and they tell you how lovely it is, and your dad asks you if you want them to take your carousel home and you surprise yourself by saying you do. (It will be one of your most cherished possessions for the rest of your life.) After they leave the party breaks up and you're in a much better mood than you were when it started. You wander past Penny's room and see her lying on her bed with her arms behind her head, and she sees you and waves you inside. You go in and sit on the chair and she starts talking to you. She asks you why you're in here and you tell her you're a pyro and she laughs. Then she surprises you.

"You know my friend Geraldine?" she asks.

Yeah. I'm sorry she died, you say.

"She was a very sick woman," Penny says.

You're astonished that Penny would just start talking about her pervert friend out of the blue like this, but you seem to have this effect on people. The adults on the unit tell you things they don't even tell the doctors and nurses. And now even your former enemy is doing it. You look at Penny curiously. You mean she's sick, like, physically or mentally? you ask.

"Mentally," Penny says.

Oh, you say, waiting for her to say more, and then she does.

"She was in love with me," Penny says.

You almost fall off the chair. You can't believe "the Blob" is telling you this. Really? you say. Oh my God.

"I had no idea about it when we were roommates at Western Reserve," Penny says. "I mean we were really close friends. But it wasn't until after we bought that house together that her real feelings became obvious."

So you, like, didn't feel the same way? you ask, wondering about the gossip regarding the two women "stuck together naked."

"I'm not a lesbian, Joanna," Penny says. The word *lesbian* buzzes unpleasantly through you, like an electric shock. "I just let poor Geraldine get too close," Penny says. "I feel really bad about it now. But she probably would have done what she did eventually. She wasn't ever going to get any better and she knew it." Penny heaves a long sigh. "It was so sad," she says, gazing up at the ceiling.

I always knew that you were normal and she wasn't, you say. It's only a partial lie, but Penny looks at you and smiles. "Well, I'm not exactly normal being in a loony bin," she says.

You laugh at her use of the colloquial term. Well why are you here? you ask.

"Because after what happened to her I went into a severe

depression. I'm learning that it wasn't my fault. But it's been very hard. Let my experience be a lesson to you, Joanna. Don't let the wrong people suck you into their lives. I'm telling you this because I can see that you're a kid with lots of potential, but that also includes a potential for getting yourself in trouble."

You laugh and say, I know, I could end up burning in hell.

Penny smiles and says, "That's doubtful. You're basically a good kid."

You're very happy that Penny is normal, especially after she gave you such a lovely birthday gift. After you leave her room you hunt down Miss Crenshaw and give her the news that Penny isn't "a pervert," and you're surprised when she says, "Well . . ." as though she doesn't believe you. But you don't think too much about it. After that day you feel easy and comfortable with Penny. You don't even think of her as the same person that you did on the outside. You no longer think of her as "the Blob" at all.

You keep waiting for a call from Susie, and just as you're starting to feel hurt that your runaway friend hasn't called to let you know her whereabouts, you're distracted by a flood of teenagers pouring into the unit. Until then, the only other teenager on BP4 was seventeen-year-old Robbie Heller, a quiet, intelligent boy who was admitted on Christmas Day after swallowing a bottle of his mother's Valium. But in early March the weather mellows and the teenagers roll in—tough little Frannie Kohn who occupies herself either by cutting her wrists or dancing to Motown records; Marie Masterson, a smart, defiant sixteen-year-old with exciting stories about the sadism of the nuns at her west side orphanage; Bonnie Rosen from Beachwood, who weighs sixty-eight pounds and hysterically refuses to eat fried chicken and milkshakes made specially for her; and Donnie Marcus, a sweet, funny, blue-eyed boy from Oberlin, who talks and walks like a girl and screams bloody murder when he's taken away for electroshock treatments. You and your new friends storm the halls, upsetting, annoying, and sometimes amusing the adult patients. You walk across the furniture, ride the laundry carts up and down the hall like scooters, pop paper cups under your feet, and go on rampages and break things or tear curtains from the walls and get dragged into seclusion. You laugh and scream and jump around to the music from your radios that fills the hallways . . . "Sugar pie, honey bunch" . . . "Let me tell you 'bout the birds and the bees and the flowers and the trees" . . . "Hang on Sloopy! Sloopy hang on!" . . . "Ain't too proud to beg, sweet darlin'" . . . Your explosive adolescent energy turns the formerly sedate hospital ward into bedlam.

But as excited as you are with your new friends, it's still the adults on the ward that captivate you the most. You've been hanging around with packs of kids your whole life, but you've never lived among alluring nurses or certifiably crazy adults before. (Your parents are crazy, but they pretend they're not, which makes them boring to you.) You follow the nurses around, trying to be charming, and sometimes they'll violate the no-touch rule and muss your hair or put an arm around you, and you relive those intimate moments for hours on end. Your physical longing for the nurses makes you feel creepy and infantile, and you compensate by acting as a mature confidant to the adult patients. Everyone on the unit enjoys talking to you when you're not acting like a lunatic. (Decades later, Ida Durst will see your mom at the supermarket and tell her that her daughter, and not "any of those dumb psychiatrists," was the one who helped her out of her depression.)

But Ida Durst isn't your best adult friend on the ward. Penny Weinberg is. You often hang out in Penny's room, sitting on her bed and gossiping with her about the other patients and especially the nurses. Penny receives electroshock treatments, which she says are helping her. When you ask her why Donnie Marcus has to have them when he doesn't want them, Penny says, "You know why."

Because the doctors are pod creatures, you say, laughing. You love discussing Penny's theory that BP4 is run by a "pod" of outer space creatures. You can spend hours discussing which staff members are aliens and which ones are "real humans." Among the "real humans" Penny counts Miss Crenshaw, who seems to be her favorite nurse, and the two Negro nurses, Miss Willard and Miss Clark. When you ask about your favorite, creamy-voiced Mary Beavers, she says, "Oh my God, you're kidding, she gave birth to all the other aliens," and you fall out laughing. You say you think Dr. Rosen, who organized the new teen therapy group, might be human, and Penny says no, he's also a pod creature, and that just because he's nice doesn't mean he's human. Once you tell her that you think your parents might be aliens, and she says no, unfortunately they're not, you can't use that as an excuse to run away from them. You've never said you want to run away from your parents but Penny obviously figured it out somehow.

Once Penny gets too close for comfort. "You really need to stop pestering the nurses so much," she says.

You instantly panic. You know the nurses love you. It's not as though you act totally obnoxious around them. You make sure to temper your attention-getting behavior with lively conversation and humor. So you're not sure what Penny means. Then she says, "Instead of following around those blondies, you should be pursuing someone like Robbie Heller. You need to grow up a little, babe."

You get defensive. Why don't you tell Donnie to grow up? you say, referring to Penny's other teenage confidant, who talks and walks like a girl.

"Donnie is sick," Penny says. "He can't help acting silly. But you can."

After that conversation you try to calm down around the nurses and act more silly and flirtatious with Robbie Heller, but Robbie doesn't respond at all to the "new you" and continues to focus his attention on spunky Marie Masterson. After a couple days you just go back to "pestering" the nurses although you tone it down when Penny is around.

One day in late March you and the other kids have just returned from the basement courtyard, which has a basketball hoop and a couple of picnic tables and where you can run around and even scramble up the seven-foot brick wall and escape if you're sufficiently motivated. You thought of escaping because it's an unseasonably warm day, almost 70 degrees, but you didn't want to upset Miss Willard, the full-of-the-devil Negro nurse who's one of your favorites. After you get back to the ward you feel bouncy and excited and go into Donnie's room where he's recovering from his electroshock treatment and engage him in a game of rock, paper, scissors.

"You bitch!" Donnie yells when you beat him for the third time in a row, this time with your "paper" over his "rock." He holds out his arm and you slap it with two fingers, creating a nice big welt to go with the others.

All of a sudden someone yells out in the hall, "Go to hell! I'm not taking any of your fucking pills!"

"Well, *someone* sounds upset," Donnie says.

I'm gonna go see what's going on, you say, and you run into the hall and down to the front lobby. Two nurses, Gail Rickey and the day supervisor, Miss Gianfrido, are hovering over a teenaged girl in blue jeans with wild, disheveled hair, who stands there with her hands on her hips, glaring at them. Then she sees you standing there, your face lit up like a million suns.

"JoJo!" Susie yells, breaking away from the nurses. The two of you leap onto the torn green couch and start jumping up and down like a couple of four-year-olds.

Stormy Afternoon Mid-December

You know those old ladies that refuse to leave their decrepit, falling-apart homes that are about to be condemned? That's me! Except that I don't have a million cats like most of those women. I don't even have one cat anymore, because of my asthma. But the rest of the profile kind of fits. Remember when I had to run out of my building after I heard that crash upstairs, and the Chinese people fleeing? Well, that sound was the roof collapsing. When I tried to get back into my apartment I couldn't get the door opened, so I went back down and managed to climb up the fire escape and crawl back in through the bathroom window, and when I walked into the hallway I saw that two huge chunks of my ceiling had fallen into my living room, blocking access to the kitchen, my bedroom, and my front door. So here I am, imprisoned in my living room! I still have access to the bathroom, and thank God the plumbing still works, so I don't have to do my business in a chamber pot (although where would I get a chamber pot?) Also, and this is the best part—I can climb out of the bathroom fire escape with my backpack to get my provisions. Then I come back with my food and newspaper and my phone fully charged, and I climb back up the fire escape and through the bathroom window. "SHE CAME IN THROUGH THE BATHROOM WINDOW!"

I know all my friends and my whole family are worried about me and think I'm crazy, but I'm not. I'm proud of myself that I can do all this at my advanced age. I'm very determined. I will not leave here until Alexi, my Russian gangster landlord, returns my calls and lets me know his plans to repair my building. I love my apartment! I don't even care anymore that all these Chinese people were running around in it, ignoring me, although now obviously they're gone because the roof has become the floor up there. But the building can be salvaged if that crazy Russian gets some contractors over here to clean the place out and install a new roof. I have created such a nice environment for myself without spending too much money. My walls are painted all different colors, and I have cool furniture and beautiful rugs and bookcases full of wonderful books, and my brother's paintings are all over the walls. (Michael's a talented artist, as well as an art historian, and probably should be spending his sabbatical painting instead of wandering around the Amazon jungle looking for new ways to trip his brains out.) I will never find another apartment like this with hardwood floors and high ceilings and big, tall windows except for three times what I pay for it.

But now I'm living in this horrible mess, with soggy chunks of ceiling on the floor, and I'm sleeping on a wet futon in the same clothes, although I'm absurdly washing my underpants in the sink every day because after all I do have some pride. Rain is dripping through what's left of the ceiling but I've managed to bring two garbage containers up here (don't ask me how I got them up here) to catch the rain. My mother would *plotz* if she saw me living like this. She would call Molly and Junie and everyone else I know and beg them to come over and drag me out of here. She might even call the police.

I suppose you think my mother would be right to question my sanity. If I had any credibility with you before, whoever you are, I'm probably losing it all now. But I know once I leave this apartment Alexi will never do anything to fix it. He'll think I abandoned it and just have it torn down. I can't let that happen. Yesterday I climbed down the fire escape and went to his ridiculous "management office" on Second Avenue and begged the Russian pole dancers to call him, but they wouldn't. They just listened to me rant and rave, and then Marina interrupted me and said, "You need to leave and find new place. Get over it already. In Russia people go without bread." I don't even know what she was talking about. What does my building have to do with people in Russia going without bread? Anyway, I don't even know if that's still true. I think nowadays they can get bread.

I'm starting to miss the days when the Chinese people were roaming the halls with their dour looks, and my little gangster friends were barging in here through the closet, and Agent Deborah was coming over here with that idiot Agent Buford and ordering me to get a psychiatric evaluation. Even though my mom was dead at least I had a nice place to live. It always made me happy to come home. Once Alexi gives me a commitment to repair this place I can stay with Junie or Molly until everything's all fixed. I have renter's insurance so I can replace most of what's ruined. See? That just goes to show you how stable and practical I am. How many people have renter's insurance? I can get a fresh new start. Whoops! There's the phone.

Molly just called me for the millionth time to nag at me. I shouldn't have even answered the phone, I had to hear her tell me that my building is about to be condemned, just like all these other buildings around the city that collapsed from the rain, and that if I don't get out of here and move into her place until I can find another place to live, she's going to call "those FBI people" and tell them that I have truly lost my mind. And on and on and on and blah blah blah. Yesterday Junie called and invited me over for dinner, and I'm sure her plan was to somehow prevent me from coming back here, and I told her I'll be glad to come as soon as I speak to Alexi, and she yelled, "Alexi has no intentions of fixing your building!" But how does she even know that? She hasn't talked to him. I don't know why she's trying to discourage me from getting repairs done on my home. Even though I'm living in a building with a collapsed roof I don't think I'm being unreasonable.

I hear the rat rustling around on the other side of the fallen ceiling. The rat will stay over there because that's where the food is. Not that there's so much food over there in my kitchen. But maybe it can find some crumbs or something. It better not come over here to my territory. It should appreciate that I'm letting it live over there, while I live over here. I can't believe I'm living here with a rat. It just shows how resilient people are when they have to be. Even living in a collapsed building I am still functioning. My internet is still working and I paid all my bills this morning. I even sent Alexi a rent check, to let him know that I expect to continue living here.

So here I am, writing about my life in the loony bin as though everything's normal (which obviously it isn't). I'm so glad that Penny eventually figured out that society was sick and not her. She and Helen had a good life together before they both died. So many people have died. It was really such a long time ago that I was a mentally ill child. I can't believe I was even *alive* that long ago, even before Stonewall or Woodstock or Sgt. Pepper's Lonely Hearts Club Band or the Tet Offensive, before anyone could be "openly gay," when homosexuals were considered sick, twisted perverts and even marriages between black and white people were illegal in many states, if you can believe it.

But even as ignorant as everyone was, accepting white male

superiority, we still didn't have the collective stress that we have today. For one thing, we didn't have all this crazy business with phones. We had big black stationary phones in our houses and when they rang someone answered it. Nobody screened their calls because there wasn't any way to do it, but nobody wanted to screen their calls because getting a call was fun. We didn't have texts and emails and beeps and buzzes twenty-four hours a day to irritate us and distract us from doing things that we needed to do. In fact, when people started getting answering machines everyone laughed at them and thought they were snobby. "Oh, they have one of those *machines*. Who do they think *they* are?" When you left your house you left your phones behind and entered the physical world with all the other people in the physical world. When people started getting cell phones and walked around talking into them they looked crazy, like they were talking to themselves. Now when you go out people's whole relationship is with their stupid phones. Talking, listening to music, scrolling, and playing their stupid games on the subway. Not that I don't do those things, except for the stupid games on the subway because I can't figure out how to play them. Who has any time to think anymore? At least everyone has had the good sense to figure out that our whole country has fallen apart and if we don't do anything about it we may all end up dead. After 9/11 everyone just stood back and let the military industrial complex wreak havoc on our economy and our environment and our individual lives, and now people have started to see what a mess they've made of everything and we even have civil unrest again. Even in the pouring rain, people are storming through the streets, screaming. It's about time. Normal people can hardly even afford a glass of milk with their crappy sporadic earnings, let alone the interest on their student loans. It's about time everyone got mad.

I'm on a pretty good roll now, don't you think? Ritalin really helps. But I really need this son-of-a-bitch landlord of mine to return my calls, or else I'll have to drive over to his mansion in Mill Basin and demand to speak to him. But he might not be there. *Come to think of it, he could be anywhere!* Millionaires don't just plant their asses down in one place. They fly all over the world. If he's in Dubai or Zurich or Odessa he wouldn't even know I'm trying to reach him. I can't believe I didn't think of this before. I'm assuming whenever he returns to New York he'll call me back or maybe even come over here to make an assessment.

Now that I realize Alexi might not be ignoring me I feel much better. I wonder what I should eat. I got sick yesterday from these peanut-butter-filled pretzel things. Maybe I should go down the fire escape and get a proper meal. I hope I don't smell. I've been showering every day with the rainwater that's been pouring in here because the shower doesn't work. So I should be okay. Rainwater is good, natural rain. It's not acid rain, is it? Do we still have acid rain? I'm not even going to think about it.

SPRING AND SUMMER 1966

Tell me the story again, about the cops barging onto the roof, with those people tripping on LSD! you say to Susie. You're walking around and around your room while Susie sits cross-legged on the floor, cutting holes in one of her tee shirts.

"Will you calm down!" Susie says. "You're way too hyper." She rips a bigger hole in the shirt, which she will wear over her underwear to create an entirely new "look." All the nurses tell her how "talented" she is to create her own style. If you tried to do something like that you would look like one of the crazy ladies stumbling around the ward.

Tell! Me! The story! Again! you yell, jumping up and down in front of her.

"I'll tell it one more time if you go and lie on your bed and try to calm down." You love when Susie tries to "redirect you" like one of the nurses. Since she showed up at BP4 a couple weeks ago you're in a constant state of excitement, bouncing all over the place. Even though there's no place you'd rather be than this nut-house, especially now that Susie is here, you're still upset that you weren't with her and her friend, Judy, when they hitchhiked to New York City after running away from Fairview. They had an incredible adventure in New York, making their way to the East Village where young people are living together in "communes," smoking marijuana and taking a drug called LSD that sends them on hallucinatory "trips." You're terribly jealous of Judy for having shared this experience with Susie, but hearing your friend tell the story about the uproarious conclusion of the adventure somewhat compensates for being excluded from it.

You stop jumping and obediently go and lie on your bed. Okay I'm ready to hear the story, you say.

Susie puts her project down and folds her hands in her lap. "So," she begins, looking at you in that special way she has, enjoying her power over you, her power to delight you. "Judy and I were up on the roof of that slummy building on Avenue D with the people from the commune that had kind of adopted us. And the commune people had all dropped this acid and were tripping their brains out. Gina and Frances were lying spread-eagled on the roof staring up at the sky, and Spanish Ricky and Chuckie D. decided they were pigeons and started running around the roof flapping their wings. So Judy and I decided to be baby pigeons and were running around after them."

And what were you saying? you ask, your mouth twitching.

"We were saying, 'CAW! CAW! CAW!'"

You burst into laughter. CAW, CAW, CAW sounds like a crow, not a pigeon, you say.

"Well, as I've told you, Judy and I had smoked some marijuana, so we weren't exactly connected to reality either. So while we're running around being pigeons we could hear Gina and Frances screaming how amazing it was that they could see the whole universe through the sky. They kept going on and on about it and then all of a sudden Frances started getting really upset. She said that she just had this terrible realization, that the snow was falling down through an empty sky, that there was nobody up there making it snow. She started screaming, 'It's just an accident! Nobody is making it snow! It's all just an accident!' She sounded really upset so we stopped being pigeons and came over to talk to her. And then Frances started screaming, 'There is no God! There is no God! Lord Jesus, there is no God!' Then she screams at the top of her lungs, 'I AM SO DISAPPOINTED IN THIS!'"

You're cracking up and Susie says, "I know, it was pretty funny. And then Chuckie D. yelled at her, 'Bitch, that don't make no sense! You're calling out to Jesus that there is no God. Make up your mind!'"

You're laughing so hard tears are rolling down your face. "Frances was yelling so loud you could hear her in, like, Pittsburgh," Susie continues.

So then what happened? you screech.

"So that's when these two cops walked out on the roof. And Frances pointed at one of them, the shorter one, and she said, 'Look at that little blue man!'"

Little blue man! Oh my God, that's so funny! And what did the cop say?

"He said, 'All right, all you hippy-dippy druggies, the party's over. You're all coming with us.'" Susie listens to you rolling around in hysterics, and then she says, "Well, it turned out not to be that funny because they sent Frances to a hospital and we ended up getting shipped back to Cleveland."

But now you're here and we're having fun! you say.

"Oh for God's sake we're locked up, Joanna!" Susie says.

I *know* we're locked up, you say to her. So what if we're locked up. My stupid house in the suburbs was more of a prison than this. In the several months since you last saw her, Susie seems to have gotten older and more sophisticated, more scornful of adults, and less silly and goofy. It bothers you that she's not nearly as happy here at BP4 as you are, that she has little interest in making friends with the nurses that you adore, although of course she fit herself right in with the other kids and has even started to take over your role as the rebel leader. You know she's not doing it on purpose, it's just that her strong personality appears to have become stronger. Having been to New York and smoked pot and lived in a commune with acid-dropping hippies doesn't hurt her reputation either.

But in the month since Susie arrived you've become even more dedicated to staying on this hospital ward, at least until you're eighteen (and you can't even imagine ever being eighteen). You know that your insurance will run out in July, but you're already talking to the nurses about "saving" your room for you so you can return to it in three months. Serendipitously, Lucy was discharged the day before Susie arrived, and the nurses decided to allow your friend to move in with you and since then you've turned the room into a cozy teenage retreat. You rearranged the side-by-side beds so that your bed is now parallel to the window, and you can feel the late spring breeze through the mesh and hear the cars whoosh by on Euclid Avenue and the church bells chiming every Sunday. The wall contains posters of the Beatles, one of Van Gogh's sunflower paintings, and a pretty mountain landscape, and the other day Susie contributed a pink-and-purple rug that she wove in occupational therapy. When the two of you aren't being tutored or romping through the halls socializing, you're usually hanging around in your room listening to the radio. Susie's doctor finally gave up trying to get her to take her medication, and you love watching her spin around like a top while the hit songs swirl through the room: "MY BABY DOES THE HANKY PANKY!" . . . "WILD THING! YOU MAKE MY HEART SING! YOU MAKE EVERYTHING–GROOVY!" . . . "MY LOVE IS WARMER THAN THE WARMEST SUNSHINE SOFTER THAN A SIGH" . . . "I SEE THE GIRLS GO BY DRESSED IN THEIR SUMMER CLOTHES" . . . "THESE BOOTS ARE MADE FOR WALKIN', AND THAT'S JUST WHAT THEY'LL DO! . . . ONE OF THESE DAYS THESE BOOTS ARE GONNA WALK ALL OVER YOU!"

Occasionally your friends come in to see you, even though the hospital discourages visits by children. (Fourteen is the cut-off age.) You feel smug that Susie's rack girlfriends, who once scorned you, are now in awe of you for setting the huge fire behind Mike's Discount Store and getting sent to the loony bin. Renee came by twice, and now that Susie is here Steven visits practically every week. You finally talked Molly into visiting, telling her that she could come on a Saturday when Penny would be out on a day pass, and Molly showed up one day with Shirley, and she looked thin and pale and kept snapping at her mother, who told you and Susie, "I'm constantly walking on eggshells with her."

After they left Susie remarked that Molly looked like a "ghost."

At first Susie avoided Penny Weinberg, figuring that Penny still hated her, but one evening she wandered into the day room and found you and Donnie Marcus deep into a discussion with her about how to identify the "pod people" on the unit. Susie couldn't resist joining the whimsical conversation, and she enjoyed it so much that she became another one of Penny's adolescent admirers. Many afternoons, after the tutors are gone, Penny holds court with you, Susie and Donnie, entertaining you with her wickedly accurate observations about everyone on the ward. You have even seriously considered her theory that most of the staff are space aliens, and once you all created a chart to clarify the distinction between the "pod creatures" and the humans. Recently you told Susie that the mean, brown-haired woman who used to chastise you and your friends doesn't seem like Penny at all, that she seems like a whole different person, and Susie says, "Well, wouldn't you be cranky if you had to sleep every night with Geraldine's naked body right next to you?" and you crack up laughing; then you say it's not nice to make fun of a dead woman, and Susie says, "Well, is Penny better off with Geraldine alive or dead?" and you say that even Geraldine is probably better off dead and Susie says, "Bingo!"

One day, after the tutors leave and the four of you gather in the day room, Donnie tells you how he ended up in the bin. He got furious at his father for calling him a "little fruity fairy" and hurled a plate at him, which cut him in the head and sent him to the hospital for stitches. "He's the little fruity fairy if you ask me," Donnie says. "He can't even stand up to my bitch of a mother." You agree with Donnie about his cold, pinched mother, who never speaks to anyone on the ward when she visits and barely speaks to her son. His father actually seems much nicer, asking Donnie how "things are going" and if the food is "edible" and if anyone is giving him a "hard time."

Did you tell your dad that your shrink gave you a stack of *Playboys*? you ask. You found it rather shocking that Donnie's psychiatrist gave him a bunch of girlie magazines to look at.

"No," Donnie says. "I haven't even looked at them."

"Apparently your shrink's efforts to turn you into a ladies' man are all for naught," Penny says. "Shock treatments, *Playboy* magazines, what's next? Drugs, probably."

You can give the magazines to me, you say.

"What would you want with *Playboy* magazines?" Susie asks.

I would like to look at the pictures of the naked ladies, you say.

"You are so weird," Susie says.

"Why is that weird?" Penny asked. "It's not like they're going to turn her on or anything. Joanna is a writer. She comes by her interest in the strange and bizarre honestly."

"Well, you can have them, because those magazines aren't going to cure me," Donnie says.

"Of course they can't cure you," Penny says. "You were born that way."

"Well what am I supposed to do about it? I hate these shock treatments!"

Your heart breaks for your friend. You could run away and join a tribe of savages, you say to Donnie.

"That's a super idea!" Penny says.

"I could become a cannibal," Donnie says. "Yum, yum, eat 'em up!" he growls, quoting the wild man from Borneo in the famous *Little Rascals* episode. You laugh as Donnie bares his teeth and curls his fingers at you but the conversation is putting you in a bad mood for some reason, and you change the subject by asking Penny if Lady Bird Johnson is a pod person and Penny says she most assuredly is.

Your parents continue to visit you every day, acting a little more cheerful now that they know they're closer to liberating you from this horrible place, which you experience as paradise compared to living with them. Their new cheerful moods irritate you even more than their depressed moods. You wish they would have the courtesy to only come once a week, like Susie's mother. Susie doesn't even have to see her crabby father who, according to her mother, can't bear the thought of visiting a hospital ward full of "crazy goyim." You laughed when she said that and said,

You're funny, Mrs. Moscowitz, and she said, "Yeah, about as funny as a heart attack." You like Susie's mom and feel bad that you misjudged her when you were just a dumb little kid.

One day a visit by Susie's mother turns an ordinary day into a memorable one. It's a Sunday afternoon, and Susie is sitting in her usual spot on the rug, stringing pink laces into her sneakers, and you're lying on your bed reading *The Red Pony* by John Steinbeck. Mrs. Moscowitz walks into the room, sits down on the chair, puts her purse on the floor, and says to Susie, "Well, my dear, your father and I are getting a divorce."

Susie hurls her sneaker across the room, which you take to be a celebratory act, like tossing confetti. It's about time that Mrs. Moscowitz got rid of her mean, humorless husband. But then Susie surprises you. "What do you mean, you and Daddy are getting a divorce?" she demands. "Don't you love him?"

"Honey, I haven't loved him for a long time." It's the first time you've ever heard her call her daughter "honey." "In fact," Mrs. Moscowitz continues, "I think I just felt obligated to stay with him, after all he had suffered."

"Well, you suffered too, being poor and having to eat nothing but turnips and all of that," Susie says.

"Not like him, Susie. I wasn't in a concentration camp."

"What!" Susie screams so loud that a nursing student pops her head in and asks if everything is okay; then she sees Susie's mom and leaves. You stop even trying to read your book. "What are you talking about?" Susie screams. "Daddy was in a concentration camp? Where was he?"

"Where do you think?"

Susie doesn't answer her mother but just starts banging the other sneaker against the floor.

Was he in Auschwitz? you ask. You can't help filling in the unbearable silence.

"Yes."

"But Daddy doesn't have a number!" Susie yells, referring to the tattoos the Nazis branded on new prisoners.

"Yes he does," her mother says. "Did you ever look? He always kept it covered up, even in the summer. He's ashamed of it. He's ashamed of his whole life."

"Well where were you when he was in Auschwitz?" Susie yells.

"I was in the resistance. In the forest. Fighting the Nazis."

"Well why didn't you tell me that?" Susie has not stopped yelling since the beginning of the conversation. "You should be proud of that!"

"Because I didn't want Daddy to feel more ashamed. I was out in the woods with a rifle while he was living in barracks taking orders from Nazi pigs."

"I thought you and Daddy came here before the war!" Susie says. She's still banging the sneaker against the floor.

"That's what we told you, because we didn't want to upset you," her mother says. "And anyway, Daddy didn't want you to know what he went through!" She's sitting at the edge of her chair, waving her hands around. "Do you think he wanted you to know that he had to drink his own pee out of a bowl so he could fill it with soup, or that they made him do a dance and recite prayers while they laughed at him? They made him . . . they made him whip his best friend, Susie. The Nazis were even worse to the religious Jews like Daddy than to the other Jews. He had a terrible time there. It's a miracle that he survived."

"Why are you telling me this now?" Susie screams. "*God!*" She gets up, throws the other sneaker across the room, and runs out the door. But instead of trying to stop her, Mrs. Moscowitz just keeps sitting on the chair, staring into space.

After a couple of moments you say, I guess she's upset.

"I don't blame her for being upset," Mrs. Moscowitz says. "I should have told her a long time ago. I think this is why she has all these problems. She's a smart girl, and she always felt like something was wrong."

Why weren't you in Auschwitz? you ask.

"Because I wasn't caught. It's a miracle that we're both alive, Joanna. I had only been married to Frank for two weeks when the Nazis came to our village. They rounded up all the Jews and shot them. We weren't home at the time, we were walking in the woods, and we heard the shooting and escaped into the forest. We were the only ones in the village that survived. His whole family was killed, everyone. My family was in Warsaw and almost all of them were killed but that's another story. A wonderful Polish family hid us in their barn for two years, Joanna. I corresponded with the wife, Ewa, until she died. One day I was bathing out at the stream, and their little boy ran up and warned me that the Nazis had found Frank hiding in the barn. They put him on a truck and took him to Auschwitz. Somehow our friends managed to convince the Nazis they knew nothing about the Jew in their barn, or else they would have been killed. I escaped into the woods and after three days I found a group of resistance fighters. After the war Frank and I were reunited in a refugee camp and Joanna, he was so angry, telling me all the things the Nazis had done to him. And the anger never went away. So many of our friends managed to put that terrible period behind them, but Frank never could. His memories crawl around inside of him like worms. And I just can't take it anymore. I was in the woods, killing Nazis so that he could be free, and all the thanks I get for the last twenty years is a sour face and that I should take orders from him, and I'm not doing it anymore. I'm through paying for the Nazis' crimes."

Susie walks back in the room dragging Penny by the arm.

Penny baby! you say.

"Hi," Penny says. "So what's this all about?"

"She was a Polish resistance fighter and never told me," Susie says, pointing at her mother as though she's picking her out of a police lineup. "And my father was in Auschwitz and they never told me either. And you wonder why I'm crazy."

"Hi, Mrs. Moscowitz," Penny says. "I want you to know that I think your daughter is a terrific kid."

"I know she is, Penny," Mrs. Moscowitz says. "She's a very good kid. I feel very guilty now, not being more honest with her. I was trying to protect my husband."

You're enthralled by the drama unfolding before your eyes. Your former enemy, the woman you and Susie used to call "the

Blob," is now standing in your room in a loony bin helping Susie process the shocking revelation that her mother is divorcing her father and that they were both survivors of "The Holocaust," which is what the Jews are now calling the murder of "The Six Million." You're dying to know more details about Susie's father's experiences at Auschwitz, but you know that he'll never tell you. You're slightly disappointed that Susie's mother isn't the one who was in Auschwitz. But the fact that she was a resistance fighter is very cool. In one instant, you've gone from simply liking Mrs. Moscowitz to seeing her as a heroine.

But after Mrs. Moscowitz leaves, Susie becomes so upset, tearing curtains off the walls in the day room and hurling an ashtray against the wall, that she's dragged into seclusion. For days afterwards she's constantly angry, mouthing off to even the nicest nurses and refusing to listen to them and fighting with the attendants when they try to put her in seclusion. You're also always jumping around, acting crazy and destructive, but that's only because you hunger for contact with the nurses, but unfortunately it's usually the male attendants that drag you into seclusion when you're out of control (which gives you no gratification at all). But after Mrs. Moscowitz's shocking revelations, you become totally preoccupied with helping your agitated friend. You can't understand why Susie is not as excited as you are to learn that her mother was a resistance fighter and is getting rid of her crabby old father.

Your mother was a heroine, Susie, you say. She spent the war living in a forest killing Nazis, shooting them and blowing them up with grenades! The only reason she didn't tell you was because of your father. You can't totally blame her.

"I know, but I've spent my whole life hating him and now it turns out that he was in Auschwitz!" Susie screams. "How am I supposed to hate him when he was in Auschwitz? And now that they're getting a divorce, my father is going to want to see me and I don't want to even be alone with him! Just thinking about the things that happened to him makes me sick! It gives me the creeps! I don't know what to do, Joanna. I need to get out of here. I need to run away again. Maybe I'll go to California."

I'll go with you, you say. California wouldn't be too bad, although you would rather go to New York.

Spring turns to summer, and the fans in the front lobby and the day room barely disperse the cigarette smoke swirling around the hot unit. You're filled with trepidation about going home. Your shrink is trying to get your parents to send you to a long-term hospital, but they will never go for it, and you don't want to go to another hospital anyway. You want to return to BP4 in three months, after your insurance kicks back in. But what if your parents won't let you come back? They never believed you were crazy in the first place. They don't tell you that, but it's obvious, from the way they talk about your psychiatrist. When they talk about him it reminds you of the way they used to talk about Barry Goldwater when he was running for president.

Donnie is discharged two weeks before you are scheduled to be released. While he waits for his parents to come and get him, he sits on his bed and cries. You sit next to him and try to comfort him.

"I'll die in that house in Oberlin," he sobs. "You don't understand! I can't go back there!"

You understand his despair but try to offer some hope. It's not as though your life is over, you say. You can come back here in three months, when your insurance kicks back in.

"I can't wait three months, Joanna!" Donnie said. "I can't stand being at home for one day, let alone three months! And then I have to go back to school with those awful kids! I'm sure they're all pod creatures! I don't know what I'm going to do."

I'll come and visit you, you promise. You know your father will drive you to Oberlin if you ask him to. We'll figure something out, you say.

That very night, a maniac named Richard Speck murders eight student nurses in Chicago. You watch *Huntley-Brinkley* with several patients and Miss Crenshaw when the story comes out, and tough Miss Crenshaw looks stunned and you notice her hands trembling. You feel sick, picturing the poor young nurses being systematically stabbed and strangled by a homicidal

248

maniac. When you and Susie go to Penny's room to talk about what happened, you see her sitting on her bed crying, and Miss Crenshaw is sitting next to her, holding her hand. You don't want to disturb them so you both go away to talk about it between yourselves. The next day, after you wake up, Susie tells you that Dr. Drake, the medical director, held a staff meeting in the dining room, and Susie eavesdropped on it and she heard Amy Rollins, one of the student nurses, sobbing.

With Donnie gone, Susie still reacting to her mother's revelations, your own discharge staring you in the face, and now this depressing story about the murdered nurses, you're desperate to get out of the unit and get some air. You can't escape with Susie, as you've done a couple of times before, since your friend is in seclusion for refusing to take her medication which they're trying to force on her since her mother's visit, so you wait for one of the doctors to leave the unit without pushing the wooden door shut, and then you slip through the door, dart down the stairs to the lobby, and leave the building.

You walk blindly over to Euclid Avenue and turn west toward downtown. After walking for about ten minutes you see a blockade about fifty feet down the street, and people are milling around behind it. As you approach it you can see soldiers in green uniforms standing at attention with rifles or else pulling stuff off of military trucks, and cops are all over the place. It looks like a war zone. Then you remember that Hough exploded into riots a couple days ago. You've been so preoccupied with all the drama occurring on BP4 that you've almost forgotten about the riot that has all of Cleveland in hysterics. You walk right through the blockade and start wandering around, wanting to lose yourself in the chaos and blot out the rest of your life. You see some tough-looking black kids with bandanas on their heads, and then you see Lou walk toward them and they part for her like the Red Sea parting for Moses, and she keeps walking as though she's in charge of the riot. You want to run after her but you know you can't. You look to see where she went but she's disappeared. You desperately want her to see you and drag you out of the riot and take you home with her, to rescue you, not from the riot but from "your suburbs" where she told you to go after you wimped out during the fight in the park.

"Young lady, you can't walk around in here." It takes you a couple of moments to focus on the person speaking to you, and then you see that it's an angry-looking cop. "This area is off limits," the cop says. Then he looks closer at you. "Do you know where you are?" he says. "Do you know what's happening out here?"

Yeah, you say. A riot is going on.

"Well, I don't know what the devil you're doing out here, but you need to go on home."

I live in a hospital, you mumble. You walk back through the barricade and return to BP4. Miss Steele sees you through the nurse's station and comes out and lets you in without even saying anything, and when you enter the unit nobody pays any attention to you. You see Penny on the sofa, crying, and you feel terrible that she's still so upset about the murders of the nurses in Chicago. Then Susie runs up to you and whispers in your ear.

"Donnie committed suicide."

The next two weeks are awful. Nobody will tell the patients what happened to Donnie. Finally one of the student nurses tells you that Donnie hanged himself in his basement, but she begs you not to let anyone know she told you. You're dying to talk to Penny but you can't, not only because Penny is still upset about Donnie, but also because you now have to remember that Geraldine also had hanged herself, and that Penny was the one who found her. Susie is also useless to talk to because she's all drugged up and a few days after they find out about Donnie a social worker shows up and takes her back to Fairview. You're too depressed to attend the teen therapy group that's been organized by cool young Dr Rosen, and Robbie Heller later tells you that the kids talked about you during group, and that everyone was worried about you, about what will happen to you after you leave. Knowing how concerned your friends are about you just makes you feel worse about having to leave. And then your parents come and take you home. They're so happy to get you out of there that they don't care how you feel about it, that you're being dragged away from the best home you have ever known.

Rain Beating Against the Car 1 AM

I wrote the whole last chapter while living here in my car. I love my little blue Toyota. I'm only five foot two, and I can sleep comfortably in the back seat. I bought a port-o-potty and a foam pad from Target, and I have a blanket and a pillow and my phone charger and I'm really quite comfortable at this construction site in this beat-up area of Gowanus, right next to the sludgy canal. Obviously nobody's doing any construction work in this deluge. It's 1 a.m. and the rain is beating down on the roof of the car and even though it's kind of cozy I'm feeling very lonely. But I'm also proud of myself for having the discipline to write my chapter about that insane couple of months in the loony bin. All that stuff really happened. Susan's mom's revelation and Donnie's suicide and me stumbling into the Hough riot and seeing Lou. And then my parents taking me home, which was the worst part of it. I did not want to leave that place. Right now, lying here in the rain in the middle of the night, I'm missing that loony bin more than ever. I never stopped missing it. Is that crazy or what? I loved the hell out of that place. It was better than being an aging woman living in her car, I can tell you that.

At least it's not cold. It's a week before Christmas and it's still pouring rain but the temperature is in the sixties. If it was really cold I wouldn't be here. I might be a little off the wall but I'm not insane. If it were cold I would be staying with one of my friends, who have already offered to put me up until I can find another apartment. If I chose to I could be staying at Molly's or Junie's or with Louis and Dominic who have a beautiful spare room. I can think of at least three other friends I could be staying with.

251

What do the kids call it now? Couch surfing? And I wouldn't even have to sleep on a couch. I have friends who have extra beds for God's sake. Why am I even doing this? I don't know. It seemed like the logical transition from living in a condemned building with the ceiling caved in.

I had to leave my apartment after more pieces of the ceiling fell down. Alexi sent one of the pole dancers, Marina, over to yell at me up through the window that "Alexi sent me here to tell you he is not fixing your apartment! He is tearing down your building. It is not fixable. You need to get out! Do you hear me, Joanna Jacobs? You need to vacate this building so construction crews can come and demolish this building!" I yelled back out the window that I would leave when I was ready, but after she went away I figured I was ready. I took the paintings off the walls, gathered the books that I wanted to keep that weren't water damaged, went in the bedroom and gathered up my mother's jewelry and perfume bottles and some of my own jewelry that I wanted to keep. I climbed down the fire escape and got some trash bags from the chop shop downstairs, which is still managing to operate without much of a ceiling, and Pete dragged the back seat of a Caddy underneath my fire escape to make a soft landing for my valuables, and I climbed back upstairs and put my things in the trash bags and tossed them down onto the car seat. Pete said he would store my valuables in his private locker and assured me that they would be safe and I gave him a hundred bucks. Then I climbed back up to my apartment and stuffed some clothes and toiletries in a backpack, leaving all my other clothes and shoes and outerwear behind. I climbed back down and got in my car, went to Target and got some provisions, and then I drove around in the pouring rain, looking for a place to park. I found this construction site in the depths of Gowanus, and I drove the car through a weak spot in the chain link fence and set up "camp" in this parking lot. There are several other cars here, which appear to be wrecks, but they make me feel more inconspicuous than if I were just here alone. Most people would be scared to do this, but I'm not. I've never been afraid in any part of the city. I wear this city like a comfortable old coat.

I don't think I'll end up like the homeless people with their garbage bags, sleeping on the street or languishing in shelters. Pretty soon I can collect Social Security and go back to driving for Voom, or maybe teaching at the New School, which will probably take me back, and I'll have my 9/11 book published by someone and this book published by someone. If my book had been published by now I wouldn't be here. I would have my advance and be tucked away in another apartment. But I can't drive for Voom right now since my car is my bedroom, and I'm living off my very limited savings and occasional small retainer checks from my first book, and I'm getting some money from my mom and the house (if we ever sell it in the crummy Cleveland market), but right now I can't afford to live in an apartment even remotely as nice as my old one. I know eventually things will work out, but right now living some normal New York life seems so far away. I don't get scared living in my car, but I get scared when I think I might not be able to take care of myself. My whole life, I've always been able to take care of myself. Although I don't know if this latest situation counts.

When I get up tomorrow maybe I'll go into Manhattan with more copies of my book. One thing about me, I can get editors to read my book even without an agent. I'm pretty well connected in this town. Even the rejections I've gotten have all been respectful, personally written by the editors, and in two cases my book went all the way to the top before being nixed. I can't give up hope. I can never give up hope. You just can't do that when you write a novel. Once that happens it's the kiss of death. God, I hate that fuckhead marketing schmuck who killed my book at McNally House. I wish he were dead. Well, no. I take it back. I wish he would get fired. Hopefully he has gotten fired by now. Everyone's always getting fired these days.

Even though I'm a night owl, ever since I became homeless I feel better during the day. It's kind of nice to get up at the break of dawn, which I've never done before, and experience the city in the morning. I do a little writing when I get up, and when Whole Foods opens I walk over there and go into the nice clean bathroom and take a sponge bath and wet my hair and comb it. Then I take the train to different neighborhoods and walk around in the rain, and I don't feel lonely at all because everyone is out, talking in clusters under umbrellas, and I feel part of everything that's going on. We discuss the latest news. It appears that some kind of national defense project had something to do with screwing up the weather, and the Pentagon is saying they're investigating it and acting all innocent, and nobody believes the top officials didn't know what was going on. When I tell people my building caved in and I'm living in my car, nobody even bats an eye. Usually they ask me if I'm living in the parking lot at King's Plaza. I would die before living in my car at the King's Plaza parking lot, surrounded by all these schleppy families eating Popeye's chicken and changing diapers out in the open. Not that I have any reason to act all superior, living in my car in a muddy construction site next to a toxic canal.

I wander all over Brooklyn, which is a real mess, but every neighborhood is dealing with it in its own way. In Williamsburg so many of the old buildings have been reduced to rubble, but the streets are still full of all the bouncy kids, talking and texting on their phones and not seeming at all upset about this disaster that's befallen us. I walked past a bunch of twenty-somethings crouched in a pile of rubble, painting bricks in a helter-skelter pattern with glossy paint, and the painted bricks were shimmering in the rain and it looked kind of beautiful. That same day I made my way to Red Hook and there was a sun dance going on right in the middle of Van Brunt Street. The street was roped off and dozens of people were dancing and cavorting, some with masks or paint on their faces, and the food trucks were out. It put me in a festive mood so I decided to take the F train to Coney Island, thinking maybe there was something interesting going on down there as well, but Coney Island was very sad in the rain. Nobody was out walking around. The Wonder Wheel looked like a relic from another century. In Coney Island I got the feeling that the world had ended. Coney Island doesn't have the same personality as Red Hook. Red Hook is a neighborhood. Coney Island is a state of mind.

I went to Brownsville to visit one of my friends, Darnell, who worked with me a long time ago on a project to stop violence in the 'hood. Darnell and I walked through the projects and I saw that Brownsville hasn't changed at all since the rain started. In Brownsville the apocalypse has been going on for decades, and this rain isn't a big deal there. The ladies are traipsing around with their big purses and shopping carts, chatting about their sick relatives and the visiting hours at Rikers and that they need to re-up their phones. I did hear one lady say, "Isn't this rain ever gonna stop?" and the lady next to her said, "Honey, it's keeping the kids inside," and the first lady said, "Well, that's true, at least they ain't been shootin' each other."

Yesterday I took the N train up to Sixty-Fifth and walked down Eighth Avenue, the Brooklyn Chinatown. I wanted to visit Jakey's mom. I've been worried about Jakey ever since the cops dragged him away after he set fire to the Chinese people's apartment. I walked through a sea of Asians and umbrellas and went into a corner market and asked the young cashier if she knew a crazy little white boy and she laughed and said, "Everybody knows Jakey!" and she told me where he lives. I remembered that Eric also lives there and that Bobby and Mikey live down the block, but I didn't see any of the boys as I walked to the building. A girl told me Jakey lived in 4F, and I walked up four flights of stairs and knocked on the door, and a woman in her forties opened it. She looked like a normal Jewish woman with brown wavy hair and a distinctive nose and that charged Jewish energy. I told her that her son used to hang out in my apartment, and she invited me in. Jakey was in the living room, sitting on the couch, eating. When he saw me he said to his mother, "That's the one that lets us stay at her place but the building fell down and now she's like a dog wandering the streets." Then he said it in Yiddish—"*A hunt vandern di gasn.*" I don't know how he knew this about me but news travels fast among teenagers.

His mom, whose name is Miriam, invited me to sit down, and she told me about herself. She was born into a secular household but got involved with the Jewish *Chabad* movement, which was how she met her husband, and she lived with him in Crown Heights and they had Jakey. He was a difficult child and her husband "never liked him," according to Miriam, and was constantly berating and punishing him. Once he shoved his son in a closet and didn't let him out for hours. He was also tyrannical with Miriam, barking orders at her all day long. When she didn't get pregnant with a second child he suspected her of using birth control and found the pills and dumped them all down the toilet, and at that point she decided to leave. She got her male cousins to slap him around until he agreed to a *get*, an Orthodox divorce, and then she left with seven-year-old Jakey and got an apartment in Chinatown because it was cheap. She said her son has been out of control for years. "He's got something called unsocialized aggressive disorder," Miriam said. "I'm trying to get him some therapy but there's a long waiting list." I asked her if the special education class he attended was doing any good, and she threw her head back and laughed and laughed, and Jakey picked up a piece of brisket from his plate and flung it against the wall. Miriam got up and stormed over to the piece of meat Jakey had thrown, and she hurled it back at him and it hit him in the face, and he took it and ate it. Then she said, "Don't go throwing food around my house, mister. I don't care how many diagnoses you have. I won't put up with that shit, do you hear me?" Then Jakey took another piece of brisket and walked up to his mother and dropped it on her head, and she took it and ate it and laughed and hugged him. I decided this was a good time to leave. I left my card on the table and told them both *shalom* and walked back out into the rain.

This morning Miriam called me and invited me to go with her to a free lunch program in Crown Heights. I met her there and was amazed at the delicious food those Jewish women were serving. Fresh warm bagels and cream cheese and blinzes and borscht with sour cream and boiled potatoes. Miriam was walking around schmoozing with everyone there, talking about the rain. They were all saying it was an act of God, that this was a message from the Messiah that he was coming soon. They were all so excited about it, they even got me believing it.

It just occurred to me, I never asked Miriam what happened after the cops arrested Jakey for setting the fire. I assume nothing happened to him. He gets away with all his outrageous behavior because the Hasidic community protects him, even though he's living in Chinatown. I've always kind of looked down on the Hasidim because they're so insular and I grew up among left-wing secular Jews, but I've been to *Shabbos* dinners with Hasidic Jews and said the prayers with them and eaten their meals around tables they set with their best plates and silver because to them every Sabbath is as sacred as any holiday. I suppose setting aside one day a week for rest and reflection makes more sense than the secular ritual of spending all day Saturday buying all kinds of shit you don't need online or at some depressing store.

I can't believe I'm living in my car. I know it's not my fault. I'm trying not to be too upset about it. I'm just so sad about everything. People try so hard to make their lives better, and to make other people's lives better, and now look at the mess we're all in. I look across the water at the magnificent buildings of Manhattan and I think, "People built this city. Human beings made all this." It's so amazing. The city is really beautiful in the rain, at least from a distance. Personally I've always loved the rain. I don't like it when it's cold, but when it's warm like this, I love walking around in it. It makes my hair nice and curly and I don't even bother using an umbrella. But this is getting ridiculous.

I'll bet my mom would like the rain. She always liked terrible weather. She said when the weather was bad at least she knew where her kids were. After we got older we would be all over the place on a warm summer night, and she would be crazy with worry until the last one of us was home. She had every reason to be crazy with worry, too. If she had known half of what was going on she would have gotten in the car and hunted us down.

One thing is for sure, if she were alive now I wouldn't be living in my car. If I didn't listen to her and leave here immediately she would get on a plane and fly here and not go away until I went to stay with Molly or somebody. When I was a kid she pretty much left me to my own devices, but when she decided to stop me from doing something, forget it. It was all over.

FALL OF 1966

In September you enter tenth grade at Rockefeller High School, a monstrous brick building containing almost three thousand students. Waking up, getting dressed, and walking to catch the school bus are torture because you're homesick for BP4. You miss your nutty teenage friends and the nurses swishing around in their white uniforms and the crazy, unpredictable patients and the whole carnival atmosphere of the loony bin. You miss laughing with Penny about the "pod creatures" and bouncing around the halls with Susie and having intimate talks with Donnie who is now dead. After spending six months as "the darling of BP4," as the nurses used to call you, it's depressing to walk through the cavernous hallways of Rockefeller High among throngs of students and teachers who have no idea who you are.

After your parents dragged you home from BP4 in July, you started taking the bus there almost every day and hung around for hours at a time. You socialized with the housekeeping staff, teased "the blondies" about their dark tans from lying around their pools all day, and resumed your place in the teen therapy group, which Dr. Rosen allowed even though Shriner had forbidden it, saying that it was inappropriate for a discharged patient to participate in an inpatient group. You played ping-pong with Nurse Willard and went on floor rounds with Nurse Gianfrido, the day supervisor, who indulgently played along with your self-appointment as her "deputy." You were even given a

259

dinner tray. Except for sleeping at home, it was almost as though you were still a patient there. (Years later, after all kinds of policies and restrictions curtailed the freedoms of America's children, you will marvel at being allowed to hang around in a mental hospital just because you felt like it.)But one day you showed up at the loony bin and were denied entrance because Marcia Pinsky, who had gone back to being your therapist, had called the hospital and told them she didn't think it was healthy for you to hang around there. When that happened you never again went back to see that bitch traitor Marcia Pinsky, although you did briefly entertain the notion of returning to the child guidance center one last time to set fire to her office.

So now, without any mental health intervention, your life pretty much consists of home and school even though you're just as messed up as you were before you got sent to the bin. School, which once provided some relief from being at home, is now as intolerable as home. Instead of charging around in boisterous bunches, your friends all seem to be traveling in their separate worlds. You manage to find a few girlfriends to eat lunch with, but the cozy, intimate feeling of Greenvale Junior High doesn't exist in this huge school, and even when you're with your friends you feel lonely and far away from them. They tease you about being in "the loony bin" but they don't seem very interested in your experience there, even though it was the most important experience of your life. Compared with the seductive intensity of the psychiatric ward, "normal life" seems empty and colorless.

Molly isn't making your transition back to the world any easier. Even though she calls you and wants to hang out with you, all she wants to talk about is boys that you don't even know. She has little interest in school anymore and has been hanging around on Coventry Road, the new gathering spot of Cleveland's unwashed elements—an unsavory mix of biker guys and what the respectable people are now calling "dirty hippies." Although you were fascinated with Susie's stories about the druggie New York commune, there's something about Coventry that seems alien and distasteful to you. In spite of your attraction to people living on the fringes of society, you're still a clean-cut teenager, dressing conservatively and wanting to maintain decent grades and get attention for your writing skills. You try to act enthusiastic when Molly talks about her bad boy friends, but all you can feel is a churlish kind of envy, knowing that, as usual, her maturity and sophistication are far surpassing yours. She never stops making you feel like a baby.

When you first go back to school, you don't even allow yourself to think about Susie being in Fairview because it's too painful. But two weeks after school starts you're strolling down the hall with a lavatory pass and you see her walk out of the school office. Oh my God! you yell. When did you get out of Fairview? You didn't tell me you were getting out, you idiot! You rush toward her and then stop, noticing that she looks very odd. She's wearing a billowing yellow "over the knee" skirt, a baggy white blouse, and brown tie shoes, in contrast with the short skirts, tight sweaters, and stylish shoes worn by the other high school girls, including yourself. You point at her and say, why are you wearing those weird clothes? Are you experimenting with some dorky new style?

"No, Joanna," Susie says. "We wear this attire out of respect for *Hashem.*"

You have no idea who she's talking about but it doesn't even sound like a person's name. You wonder if Susie has become psychotic, if perhaps Donnie's suicide did something to her mind.

"I'm talking about the man upstairs, Joanna," Susie says, seeing your confusion. She points up at the ceiling.

Now you're pretty sure that your friend has gone crazy, imagining some man upstairs, the way Winnie Jackson used to imagine men in her closet. Okay, that's nice, you say carefully. Are you back living with Rhonda?

"No, I'm living with my father. My parents separated while I was in Fairview and my father moved to Little Jerusalem, and I moved in with him last weekend."

Are you kidding! Why are you living with your creepy father? Is your social worker making you do that?

"No, Joanna," Susie says, smiling. "I'm living with my father voluntarily. He suffered terribly during the war and he deserves to have a daughter who honors and respects him. I plan to attend *shul* with him every Saturday and keep *Shabbos* and try to observe all the traditions of our people."

Now you feel disoriented, as though you've just been sucked into a horrible dream. This is worse than if Susie had become psychotic like Winnie Jackson. But you hate your father! you say. Why don't you go and live with your mother, at least? Your mother is cool.

"My mother supports my decision to live with my father," Susie says. "She's absolutely thrilled that my father and I are reconciled, and that I've found some structure in my life."

You stare at your friend in horror. I think you've gone crazy, you say, and walk away from her. You are so furious you can hardly see straight. It seems as though Susie has regressed back into the hoity-toity nine-year-old on the tablecloth.

Without your two best friends to keep you sane, you seek refuge in your advanced placement English class, which includes Steven and a few other kids you're friendly with. The teacher is a gently humorous intellectual who reminds you of Mr. Toledo, the sixth-grade teacher in the "gifted" class at your elementary school. You read *The Iliad* and *The Odyssey*, and you're introduced to bawdy Chaucer, and the Romantic poets, Byron and Shelley and Keats, and just for variety Mr. Heron has you read some poems by American poets, several of which pierce your soul ("and I have miles to go before I sleep . . ." "Quoth the raven, nevermore . . ." "Because I could not stop for death, he kindly stopped for me . . .") You work hard on your writing and everyone considers you one of the top writers in your class, even among these super-smart students.

But outside of English class, the whole culture of Rockefeller High School is alien to you. Steven has become good friends with Cassie Marshall, the beautiful, sweet, blond girl who's the most popular girl in your class, and who reminds you a lot of Diane Feinstein, the voluptuous girl at camp you couldn't stay away from. Cassie is very sweet to you, and she smells like honey, and she calls you "Joey girl." You and Steven go over to her house a couple of times and play records. (For the rest of your life you associate the Sonny and Cher song "I Got You Babe" with Cassie.) You're magnetized by Cassie, but you don't allow yourself to give in to it like you gave in to your attraction to Diane or Lou or your favorite nurses in the loony bin. Cassie is like a forbidden city that you're allowed to view from its gates but never enter. When she's crowned homecoming queen, you and Steven (who hangs out mainly with girls) help her pick out a dress for the dance, and you *ooh* and *ahh* as she emerges from the dressing room wearing it, and on the way home you act all excited for her and Tim Rogers, the homecoming king, who will be the stars of the dance that you're not going to. (You know Steven would like to go to the dance with Susie, but she won't go with him because she's become religious, so he asks Marcia Bowman, a girl in your English class, who gladly accepts.)

Susie keeps trying to get you to stop being mad at her, but you can barely look at her in her frumpy outfits. "You should come with me and my father to *shul* sometime," she says to you one day in the hall, flicking you on the head. "Steven's coming with me this Friday for services and then to the *oneg*."

The *what?*

"The *oneg Shabbat*, dummy. It's the celebratory gathering after Friday services, to welcome in the *Shabbos*. There will be food there. I know how much you love food." She gives you an ingratiating smile.

Oh for God's sake! you yell at her. Why can't you just go back to being *normal?* You're acting like such a goody-goody! Instead of going to your stupid *oneg* or whatever it is on Friday, put on some jeans and we can find some trouble to get into. We can hop a freight train like you always wanted to do. Or if you don't want to do that we can do something else. Like . . . like . . .

"Like torment the Blobs?" Susie asks, with an adult smile, like a teacher who's just shocked a refractory pupil into seeing the truth.

How dare you even mention that! you yell. After we became friends with Penny I never thought of her as a Blob anymore and I'm assuming you didn't either! It's terrible of you to even mention that! (Penny is now living in Vermillion, Ohio, with a traveling salesman who she described in one of her letters as "disturbingly boring and almost definitely a pod person.")

"Well, we did think of her as a Blob before we knew her," Susie says. "And it was very wrong, so I plan to seek forgiveness for the harm I caused during Yom Kippur, which is the Day of Atonement. It's the most important holiday of the year."

Well I think Hanukkah is the most important holiday of the year because you get presents. And I have to get to study hall. You turn and walk away.

As the days and weeks go on instead of missing the loony bin less, you miss it more and more. Even though the counselors give you special treatment as an ex-mental patient, and allow you to wander the halls and show up to class whenever you feel like it, you still can't stand school. You especially hate having to wear skirts and slips and panty hose every day instead of your comfortable jeans. You walk around school feeling stiff and constricted. Everyone ignores you in the halls, unlike the football players and cheerleaders and popular kids that are always surrounded by admirers. You wish you could be like Molly, who has fun outside of school, and gets older boys to take her to underground clubs even though she's only fifteen. You don't even have fire-setting as an outlet anymore, because you haven't felt the urge to set fires ever since you burned up a mattress in the seclusion room and Miss Crenshaw got mad and told you there was nothing "cute" about arson.

You wake up one Saturday around eleven with nothing to look forward to. Your social life has dwindled down to nothing and you're more homesick than ever for BP4. Three months have gone by since you left the nuthouse and technically you can be readmitted, but you know that your parents won't let you go back there in a million years. Even if you did something really terrible, like burn down a building, your father would probably figure out a way to get you out of trouble and keep you imprisoned in your big, boring house. Just when you're thinking of staying in bed all day you get a brainstorm. You jump out of bed, put on some jeans, sneakers, and a long-sleeved polo shirt, and you go downstairs and put on your jacket. Your mother asks where you're going and you say probably to Little Jerusalem. You walk down the street into a beautiful October day, and when you get to Cedar Road you cross the street and stick out your thumb.

A car stops and a shaggy-haired, youngish man asks you where you're going.

I'm going to New York.

"Are you running away from home? Because I don't wanna get into any trouble."

No, my parents are cool. How far can you take me?

"I can take you to the turnpike. I'm going down in that direction. After that you can try to catch a ride on U.S. 80. That'll take you all the way to New York City."

The man drops you off on the turnpike and tells you where to stand. "You be careful now," he calls to you when you leave the car. "Not everyone is as nice a guy as I am." You're not really worried. People have always been pretty nice to you.

You stick your thumb out again and in about two minutes a woman picks you up and as soon as you get in her car you know she's a little nuts just by looking at her face and hair. She starts talking and doesn't stop. She's going to Pittsburgh to pick up a dog, she went on a carrot juice fast that gave her parasites, she spent two weeks in the Bahamas with a guy who turned out to be a "homo." You're relieved when she lets you off at the junction of 76 and 80.

It doesn't take long for a maroon Buick to stop. The driver is a middle-aged man who looks normal, and you get in the car. "What's a young girl doing out here hitchhiking?" the man asks.

I'm going to New York to visit my friend.

"Don't you know that hitchhiking is dangerous?" You tell him everyone does it. "That doesn't make it right," he says, shifting back into drive. Then he starts telling you about two girls he's heard of who were killed by "maniacs" that picked them up hitchhiking. You're afraid he's going to make you leave his car, but after delivering his lecture he tells you he's going to New York City for a business conference and he can take you there. He's actually a very nice guy. He asks you who you're visiting in New York and you say it's your former social worker and he says his own daughter had to get "some help" for her problems. For a while you ride along in silence, and then the driver, whose name is George, turns on the radio to a classical music station and it almost lulls you to sleep. You stop for lunch at a truck stop, and after you give your orders George insists that you call home, so you go to the phone booth and make a collect call.

"Where are you?" your mother yells.

I'm hitching to New York City, you say, shutting the door to the phone booth so the whole diner won't hear your mother scream through the phone. I'm going to visit Junie.

"You get back home immediately! I've been worried sick!" You're a little surprised that your mother was so worried, because you often go off with your friends for hours, but your mother has a sixth sense.

I told you I'm going to New York! you yell at her. I'm already in the middle of Pennsylvania!

"Sam!"

I'm not talking to him!

"Sam! Joanna's on the phone! She's hitchhiking to New York!"

I'm hanging up, you say, and you do.

George treats you to a big lunch of meatloaf, mashed potatoes and cherry pie, and back in the car you drift off to sleep. When you wake up it's getting dark and you're in New Jersey, and George tells you you're about an hour from New York City. You tell him that he can drop you off at a subway and he says that at ten o'clock at night he'll do nothing of the sort, that he'll drive you directly to your friend's house.

You enter a long tunnel and ride under the Hudson River. When you exit the tunnel you're in New York City. It's nighttime but the city is alive. You're surrounded by cars and yellow taxis, and throngs of people are on the sidewalks and stores are still open with fruits and vegetables and flowers displayed outside. Horns are honking and a siren wails in the distance. Crossing the Brooklyn Bridge you look to the right and to the left and you start pouring into the city, you no longer know where you stop and the city begins, but unlike the usual unpleasant feeling of losing your boundaries, this feels like a gain rather than a loss. The city is inside you, and you feel electrified and powerful. You're sure that this magnificent city has been inside you all along, that it's blasted you out of your doldrums and into this life-changing adventure. And the strangest thing is, even when you're experiencing these overwhelming sensations there's a feeling of comfort about this place; it feels like home, even though you've never been here in your life.

Junie's house in Crown Heights is on a pretty street of single-family homes a block away from a broad boulevard called "Eastern Parkway." You and George go to the door and you ring the bell—*DING dong DING dong—ding dong DING dong!*—and a second later the door opens and Junie stands there, looking radiant in a green-and-blue caftan.

"Hello," George says. "I picked up this young lady in Pennsylvania. She was apparently hitchhiking from Cleveland to New York to see you."

"Yes, I know," Junie says, looking at you. "Thank you so much for keeping her safe." Obviously your parents have called her. You can tell she's not mad, but it's probably because she's relieved that you're not dead.

"Well, gotta get to my hotel," George says.

So long, George! you say. Thanks a whole bunch!

"You behave yourself, young lady," George says, and walks back down the walk to his car.

"Well!" Junie says. "You made it!" She opens the door and lets you in. You walk in the house and a young woman is walking toward the door. She wears a black leather skirt and red ankle boots and she has a big Afro and a small nose ring and she looks very tough and cool.

"Joanna, this is my daughter Tanya," Junie says. "She's a famous poet. She's about to go out for the evening and heaven knows when I'll see her again."

Junie's daughter Tanya smiles, showing her teeth, and says, "Hello, you young runaway." When she walks past you she ruffles your hair, and then she walks out the door.

End of December 8 PM, Raining

That was the night I fell in love with New York. It's funny that it was also the night I met Tanya, who was my other "first love," although that wouldn't happen for another fifteen years. After Tanya left, Junie ushered me into the dining room and had the table all set for me, and served paella, which I'd never had before but it's her specialty, and I've eaten it many times since. While I ate dinner she called my parents (I refused to talk to them); then she sat down with me at the table and watched me eat. Afterward we went into the living room to talk. Her house was so cozy, full of nice old furniture and casual throw rugs and decorative stuff, African masks and wall hangings, and lots of books. It was a warm night for October, and the windows were partway open and I could hear cars going by. We sat down on her sofa and I talked and talked and she listened. I told her about setting fires and she didn't sound surprised. I later found out that the boring social worker had called and talked to her about me. I told her how much fun I had in the loony bin and that I hated being home in the "lily-white" suburbs and I hated school and Susie had gone off her rocker and become religious (that didn't last very long, as it turned out), and I said that I didn't want to go back to Cleveland ever again, that I wanted to live in New York. After listening to me ramble on and on, Junie told me that I needed to go back to Cleveland and return to school and concentrate on developing my writing talent. She said I had to work on finding my best self, the person she knew was in there, who cared about her friends and family and the world, and that I could work for a better future for the country. She told me she was always impressed at the way I ventured out of the suburbs and went down to Hough and hung around with black kids. "I think you probably do belong here in New York City, and I predict that eventually you'll make your home here, but you can't stay here now," Junie said. And she sent me home on the bus the next day.

And guess what? It's now fifty years later and I'm writing this in that very same house that I ran away to that fateful Saturday. Do you know how fast fifty years can go by? In a blink of an eye. Over the years I've spent countless hours in this house and even had sex in it, actually on this very bed. I've been sleeping in Tanya's room for the past three days, ever since Junie lured me here with her paella. She tried to get me to come for Christmas dinner, but I refused because Tanya and Susan were going to be here, but when I called her the next day from my car to see how the dinner went she told me she was making paella and that I had to come and eat it. I came over here and she fed me this delicious dinner, which included wine, and afterward she told me to take a bath (even though I've been showering at the health club and am perfectly clean) and she actually *ran* the bath and put some expensive bath oil in the water (I could tell it was expensive because it was in a dainty white bottle), and after my bath she led me into this room where she laid out some clothes for me to wear since my other clothes are in my car. She did not want me to go back to my car even though it could get towed. So now I'm lying in the bed of my ex-lover, which has traces of her rich, loamy smell like when you're driving deep in the country where there are horses and cows and the sweet smell of grass, that's how Tanya smells, and the smell is turning me on but I haven't been able to masturbate on her damn bed with Junie meandering through the house, and anyway my "device" is tucked away in a box at the chop shop.

Junie is trying to imprison me here. She was horrified that I was sleeping in my car at a muddy construction site, even though I pointed out to her that it's not as though I'm some hardcore derelict; my building fell down for God's sake! And now I'm kind of stuck here, because I've gotten much too comfortable, being tucked away in the house of the woman who's been like a second mom to me, and sleeping in the bed of my former lover. My whole life is on hold, not only because I have no home, but because writing this book about my lunatic childhood has transported me back in time and I can't function in the real world. Right now as we speak not only am I languishing in the home of my ex-therapist that I've known since I was thirteen, but I'm also listening to the voices of my two best friends, one that I've known since I was seven and the other that I've known since I was eight, blabbering in the next room.

For some reason Junie took it upon herself to invite Susan, Tanya, Molly, Molly's daughter Zoey, and my niece Ellie over for dinner. A few minutes ago she came in here and ordered me to go out there and be sociable, not seeming to care that I'm in the middle of writing and that I hate her whore daughter and her whore daughter's lover. Junie tried to lay a guilt trip on me by telling me that I'm being rude to my niece, which is very unfair because I've spent a lot of time with Ellie since she got here, including taking her out to dinner twice—well once was to McDonald's so I guess that doesn't count, but still, I've always been a very good aunt to her. I can't help it that she doesn't seem to want to go back to Cleveland. She came here for a mixology conference, but it was canceled after she got here because of the weather, and instead of going home she's been staying at Molly's and running around New York with Zoey. You'd think she might want to return to her bartending job, but these younger people just jump from one job to another; they have no sense of continuity.

Meanwhile, *it's still raining!* But the mystery is on its way to being solved. Just as people have been suspecting, the Pentagon is almost definitely responsible, which is kind of funny. The warmongers hired this idiotic private company to develop a weather manipulation system and they screwed up the formula and tested it in one of their black sites (that they refuse to disclose) and it created what they're calling a "pervasive weather pattern." Junie and I were watching CNN yesterday and Jerome Plesco, the defense secretary, was being interviewed and making up some bullshit excuse for what happened, but the president is getting ready to fire his ass, especially after Maureen Dowd wrote in yesterday's *Times* that Beltway insiders had him pegged as a "nutcase" years before he took this job.

Oh-oh. Someone's coming.

Tanya just came in here and now I have the smell of her body all over me as well as the smell of her bed. She lay down next to me and held me and now I want to have sex with her; actually I never stopped wanting to have sex with her but I detached from my desire because I hated her, but now I don't hate her anymore because she's about to leave Susan. She told me that she broke up with Susan this morning because after they both burst into my meeting with the FBI agents she realized that she has "unfinished business" with Agent Deborah. Why am I not furious with her about this, the way I was furious at her for running off with Susan? She even just told me some of the prurient details of their relationship way back in the sixties, when Deborah was a fledgling agent assigned to gather intelligence on the Black Panthers, with whom Tanya associated. Even though they were on enemy sides Tanya and Deborah couldn't stay away from each other and were having rendezvous all over the city—on the docks of the Hudson River and in Central Park and on a rooftop in the Lower East Side and—I'm not making this up—in a *bathtub* in an alley in Hell's Kitchen. Here's Tanya lying here with her arm around me waxing poetic about her sexual adventures with Agent Deborah, and instead of getting upset I was getting extremely horny picturing the two women I'm in love with having sex— especially when she told me about the bathtub in the alley.

Oh-oh. Susan is yelling at Tanya in the living room. She just called her a sociopathic whore. This is too juicy for words. How am I supposed to concentrate on my writing with all that melodrama going on out there? Now the door just slammed. Someone walked out of the house. I'm assuming it was either Susan or Tanya. Oh, for God's sake. Someone's coming again.

I thought Junie was coming in here to tell me again to go out there and be sociable but it was Susan, who has smoke coming out of her ears. She's mad as hell that Tanya broke up with her this morning after saying that she has unfinished business with Agent Deborah. I tried to act sympathetic even though obviously I'm elated. She told me that even after the unpleasant scene this morning, she was still determined to come to Junie's dinner, mainly to see me. But now she realizes that she should not have come because she can't stand the sight of Tanya for even one minute, but because Tanya's mother was in the room she kept trying to act nice until Tanya said something about Agent Deborah's "sweet little townhouse" in Astoria. That was when Susan lost it and called Tanya a "sociopathic whore" and Tanya got all huffy and walked out of the house.

"I hope she stepped in dog shit on her way to the train," Susan said. I told her she probably shouldn't have come here with Tanya tonight and she said, "I know. I should have killed her in the middle of her little speech this morning. I should have taken a fork and stabbed her through the heart. I don't know how you could ever have been in love with her."

I said, "I don't know. I still am. It's like being in love with Satan." Then I said, "So you weren't in love with her? I mean what are you even talking about?"

And Susan said, "Well, I thought I was." But Susan doesn't fall in love the way I do. She wasn't "in love" with Steven either, although they had a nice relationship that lasted into their twenties, and that was the closest she came to loving anyone.

After sounding off about Tanya, Susan announced that she and Molly have decided to go to Cleveland with me to help me get my mother's house in order. This is just wonderful. The last thing I want to do right now is go to that godforsaken city and root around in fifty years of my family's history and hold my mother's clothes and cry. But they're making an offer I can't refuse. My two best friends accompanying me to assist with this painful chore. Of course Steven will be there to help, and maybe little brother Danny will grace us with his presence. He'll probably fill two boxes and then say he's done, he has to get home to catch some *Gilligan's Island* reruns. God, this is going to be awful. At least if the weather was nice there I could get some relief from the rain, but it's pouring rain in Cleveland too.

Junie just yelled at me to come out for dinner. I feel kind of bad for her because she's probably upset about the big fight that Susan and Tanya had under her roof. Junie likes everyone to be civilized. So I need to go out there and act civil. Except I'm afraid when I go out there and start talking to them I'm going to get into an argument. I don't mind fighting with Susan, or even Junie, which is kind of like fighting with my mother, but I can't stand arguing with Molly because I never seem to say anything right. Like yesterday, we were talking on the phone about her latest project, which is to figure out how to take possession of some of those luxury apartments owned by absentee rich people to create more living space for homeless New Yorkers whose buildings have collapsed in the rain.

"I don't see why you should have to go through official channels," I said. "The communist revolutionaries didn't bother with eminent domain precedents or anything like that. They just barged into the rich people's homes and killed the fat cats or shipped them off to labor camps and moved the farmers and peasants right in! If we took possession of the luxury apartments, we wouldn't even be killing the billionaires or even displacing them. We would just be making use of all this wasted space!"

And Molly had to get all sarcastic with me. "Okay, you can lead the charge into the buildings," she said. She's so touchy lately, probably because she's allowed Billy to move in again, and while she runs the household he hangs around doing his drugs and making Zoey and Ellie laugh. It's not my fault that she's being a martyr. And I hate to say it, but Molly will get permission to take over those apartments when hell freezes over. It really pisses me off that all those urban palaces should just be sitting there with nobody living in them while thousands of displaced people are crashing with friends and relatives or living in their cars like yours truly.

This country has become so wimpy if you ask me. People say, "Well, the richest of the rich people earned their money." Which is largely true. But so did some poor old black lady shlepping to two jobs on a bus. If they just gave her one million of their billions she wouldn't have chilblains anymore, and would they miss that lousy million? No. They all make me sick. And also, why is everyone on TV telling me, a homeless person, to give money to save some African child with bones sticking out of her chest? Where are the billionaires when those damn commercials are on?

Junie is standing in the doorway waiting for me to stop writing so I can come out for dinner. ALL RIGHT JUST GIVE ME ONE SECOND! Like she can actually hear me when I'm just writing it. I have to say that it is kind of comforting to be in this house full of people who love me, because I'm really so scared. I'm scared to go to Cleveland and I'm scared that my book will never be published and I'm scared about running out of money and that I'll end up being one of those homeless women picking bottles and cans out of the trash. At least all of New York and the whole country is in a crisis, so I don't feel so lonely. It's kind of like when I was young and I knew I was crazy, but the whole country had lost its mind so it wasn't so bad. Although I didn't start to realize it until, like, my late teens. That was when it started to dawn on me that when it came to being crazy, my friends and I were light-weights compared to all the people running things. But instead of upsetting me, it was a big relief. It made me feel superior to them.

Junie's still standing in the doorway. She looks like she's about to physically stop me from writing so I'd better go.

SPRING 1968

"You're not a man—you're a mouse!" Mr. Rugby yells. "Little skinny baby boy, standing up for the creeps and faggots and traitors and retards that are trying to destroy this good country!"

"I have a right to my opinion," Steven says. He's sitting at his desk in social studies class with his hands folded, and you can see his body shaking but he's trying to remain calm.

"Oh, yeah, of course!" Mr. Rugby snarls. He's a beefy man with a butch haircut, a red face, and a huge, bumpy nose. "You're the big intellectual! The A student! The student council *president!*" He pronounces "president" with vicious sarcasm. "Well let me tell you something, Eisner!" He stabs a meaty finger toward Steven. "Your four-point grade average won't amount to diddly-squat when this country's security is at stake! You know where the really valuable men of this country are? They're fighting over there in Vietnam, protecting the freedom of you and your fellow—*intellectuals*—when you go sneaking off to college to avoid serving your country! Like a bunch of pussies! God, I hate you and your ilk!"

You're enraged at the teacher's unprovoked attack on your friend. What does this have to do with Martin Luther King getting killed? you yell. Steven wasn't even talking about Vietnam! He was talking about the reaction in this country to Dr. King's death!

"Oh, here's another member of the liberal brigade putting in her two cents!" the teacher yells. "Dr. King, Dr. King—give me a

275

break, lady! He wasn't a real doctor! He was a troublemaking preacher that got a whole bunch of people all worked up, and now half of them are running up and down the streets of our cities, tearing down everything respectable people have built!"

"You mean respectable white people," Steven says.

"I mean respectable people, and you get that tone out of your voice, Eisner," the teacher says. "You show some respect! Obviously you didn't learn respect for your elders at home!"

He respects people who deserve respect! you yell.

"Both of you, get the hell out of my classroom before I throw you out," Mr. Rugby says. You and Steven get up and hurry out of the class. You slam the door, and then you hear the teacher's loud footsteps and you look at Steven with alarm. The teacher flings open the door and yells, "Which one of you slammed my door?"

I did, you say.

"Well, you're gonna shut it quietly, Missy, or you're gonna be very sorry."

Shut it yourself.

"Excuse me?" The teacher sticks his hand to his ear. "Can you repeat that?"

I said SHUT IT YOURSELF!

Mr. Rugby grabs your arm. "We're going to the office," he says, and starts trying to drag you off.

"Get your hands off her," Steven says.

Get your hands off me, you say, trying to pull out of his grasp.

Susie walks up with a hall pass. She's wearing a short black skirt, a green rayon blouse, and red sneakers. "Get your hands off her!" she yells.

"Get the hell out of my way," the teacher says.

Susie takes her loose leaf notebook and slams Mr. Rugby in the shoulder with it, and he lets go of your arm. The three of you run off down the hall. You run up the stairs, and when you're sure the teacher hasn't followed you, you all stand there trying to catch your breath.

Oh my God, you say. What a jerk.

"He's a real pig," Susie says.

He's gonna go fink on us to the office, you say.

"Yes, but he won't get anywhere," Steven says.

Why not? you ask.

"Because we're going to get our parents involved."

You usually don't like to get your parents involved in anything, but you trust Steven so completely that you don't even think twice about it. Yeah, we need to do that, you say. Then you say to Susie, Thank God you live with your mother now and not your cranky old father. Susie looks away sullenly, but you don't care that you said it.

The Monday after the confrontation with Mr. Rugby, you, Steven, Susie, Susie's mom, Steven's dad, and both of your parents seat yourselves in the conference room of the school office. (Steven's mom, Joan, is at an adult education retreat.) On the other side of the long table are the vice principal and two guidance counselors.

"We're here to discuss a serious complaint brought to us by one of our teachers that these three students demonstrated overt acts of defiance toward him, and that one of these students, Miss Moscowitz, struck him with a notebook," says Mr. Evans, the vice principal. He's a thin, harried man with glasses that are always falling down to his nose and an unruly mass of curly dark hair.

"Susie, you do know that physically assaulting a teacher is strictly forbidden," says Mrs. Link. Both Susie and Steven have her as a guidance counselor, and you're jealous. Mrs. Link is gorgeous, with thick, curly red hair and perfect features. Being beautiful also makes her popular among the students.

"That lunatic was dragging Joanna down the hall," Susie says.

"What do you mean, dragging?" Mrs. Link looks to Steven for confirmation. "Did you see Mr. Rugby drag Joanna down the hall?" she asks.

"Yeah, he grabbed her arm and tried to drag her down the hall," Steven says. "He was obviously hurting her."

"I'm not sure that gave Susan an excuse to strike him with a loose-leaf notebook," says your guidance counselor, Mr. Pelligrini, a tall, kind man with gray hair. "The story we got was that Joanna and Steven were causing a scene in class and Mr. Rugby asked them to leave and when they did, Joanna slammed the door. Now, we've always given Joanna plenty of leeway here at Rockefeller, and she's responded by turning in all her assignments on time and achieving good grades. But if she slammed the door and disrupted his class Mr. Rugby may have been justified in trying to escort her to the office."

"Listen, I don't care what happened before," Susie's mother says. "This man was abusing her friend here. I've always taught my daughter to fight back when someone is doing wrong." Mrs. Moscowitz is sitting next to you and she puts her manicured hand over your hand, and you feel a surge of warmth. Since separating from her husband, Susie's mother has become as beautiful and vibrant as your own mom. She's wearing slacks and a stylish yellow blouse and her brown hair is nicely styled and her angular face is bright and expressive.

"I'm not sure taking hold of a student's arm constitutes abuse," the vice principal says slowly, as though trying to work it out in his own mind.

"Let's get something clear," says Harold Eisner, Steven's dad. "This man is a fascist. We know that he's a card-carrying member of the John Birch Society. He knows that Steven and Joanna come from liberal families. He abused and humiliated my son in class simply for that reason. Steven did nothing to provoke this verbal attack."

"The man isn't fit to teach children," Susie's mother says.

"That sums it up!" your mom says. "He's not fit to teach children. That . . . that . . . idiot!" Your mother has been fuming ever since the evening of the "incident," when Steven's parents came over and told your parents the whole story, including that Mr. Rugby was a member of the racist John Birch Society. When the parents were summoned to this meeting with the school administrators, they came without any intention of listening to the "other side."

"Let me make something clear," your father says, and of course everyone shuts up and acts as though the president of the United States is about to speak. "These kids were reacting appropriately to a vicious attack. If you're being mauled by a vicious animal you try to fend off the attack. Now we all know what kind of guy this Rugby is. I don't have to elaborate because we're all intelligent people here. What specifically was he saying to Steven during the class? If I recall, it was the worst kind of vitriol."

"Tell Sam what he said to you," Harold says to Steven.

"He said I wasn't a man, that I was a mouse, and that I was trying to stick up for all the creeps and faggots and retards that are destroying the country."

"Well . . ." says Mr. Pelligrini, your guidance counselor. "That's Mr. Rugby."

He also said, like, I hate you to Steven, you add.

"Wait a minute," Mr. Pelligrini says. "He said what?"

"He said, 'I hate you and your ilk,'" Steven says.

"That's uncalled for," Mrs. Link says, shaking her gorgeous head in a brief, involuntary motion. She looks down and flicks imaginary lint off her cashmere sweater.

He said all kinds of things, you say. He was screaming at Steven. All Steven said was that the people rioting in the streets of all the cities were provoked by Martin Luther King's assassination, and Mr. Rugby just went crazy. He said he knew all about Steven and the other intellectuals in the country, that they were cowards who were going to sneak off to college while the real men fight in Vietnam.

"Disgusting," your mom says. "Absolutely disgusting."

"It's worse than disgusting," your father says. "It's unconscionable. Clearly Mrs. Moscowitz is right. The man isn't fit to teach children."

"He is an abomination," Mrs. Moscowitz says, patting your hand, and once again, you feel the warmth slide through you from her comforting touch. You're almost sad when the vice principal ends the meeting, saying something about some teachers being incompatible with some students, and the parents all leave. You and Steven are not reassigned to another class, but

279

when you return to Mr. Rugby's class it's clear that he knows who "won" at the meeting because he pretends nothing at all ever happened.

A week after the meeting you're lounging around in Susie's small bedroom at her mom's house in Cleveland Heights. You and Susie are curled up on the bed and Mrs. Moscowitz is sitting on an antique rocking chair. Even though Susie had once said this house was "haunted," you've never detected any supernatural presence, probably because scary Mr. Moscowitz isn't living here anymore. Susie's room is small, and the chest and lamp and bed look like they're from the forties. The bed even has posts, like your parents' bed. The wood floor is uncovered but shiny and clean. The blue-and-green wallpaper, the yellow-patterned sheets, and the stuffed animals scattered around make the room seem cozy rather than depressing.

"They should have fired that teacher of yours," Mrs. Moscowitz says. "If it were my daughter that he put his hands on he would be without a job today."

You wonder if your parents were a little wimpy not insisting that Mr. Rugby be fired. Yeah, you're right, Mrs. Moscowitz, you say. He's not fit to teach. He's an abomination, you add, using her own word.

"Oh, don't listen to her," Susie says. "She thinks everyone in America is stupid."

"I never said that," her mother says.

"But that's what you think. You think because you came from Europe and fought the Nazis you're the only one that knows how to deal with bad people."

"I don't know why you're always complaining about me," Mrs. Moscowitz says. "You never say a bad word about your father. You even decided to become an Orthodox Jew." She turns to you and says, "What did you think about that crazy business, Joanna?" The disapproval in her voice makes you like Mrs. Moscowitz even more than you ever did.

Well, she did it to please her father because he went through so much during the war, you say diplomatically.

"I always thought it was ridiculous," Mrs. Moscowitz snorts. "How could her father still believe in God after Auschwitz? I never understood it. I put up with it for all those years because he had suffered so much, but I'm not the kind of person who allows people to boss me and finally I couldn't take it anymore." She sighs and looks at the ceiling. "I still can't believe that I put up with it all those years," she says.

Ever since that day in the hospital when Mrs. Moscowitz announced to Susie that she was divorcing her husband, she always speaks to you as though you're a grown-up person who can understand grown-up issues. It reminds you of how many of the adult patients used to confide in you in the loony bin. You love conversations like this. Your parents never confide in you about anything. All they talk about is what you should be doing at the moment, or else they goof around with you. You find your parents excruciatingly boring.

But Susie obviously doesn't share your point of view. "Joanna's parents never put her in the middle of their disagreements, like you do to me," she says. Then, to your astonishment, she starts to cry. You don't know what to do. You just stare straight ahead uncomfortably.

"She feels bad for Frank about what he went through in Auschwitz," Mrs. Moscowitz says. "She can't stop talking about how they made him dance and that he had to drink his own pee. She wishes I had never told her that. I think it traumatized her."

"Well it did!" Susie screams. "I can't stand thinking about it!"

"Darling, you made the decision to come back to live with me. I had nothing to do with it. You were angry at Daddy because he didn't even have the decency to approve of your going to take care of your sick cousin, and then he refused to go to her funeral."

A year ago, in the spring of tenth grade, Rhonda became very sick, and the doctor gave her the terrible news that she had advanced ovarian cancer. Since Susie's father had moved near Rhonda in Little Jerusalem, Susie started going to Rhonda's several times a week. She tucked the covers around her, mopped her sweaty brow, brought her her pain pills, and cooked soup and other comfort foods without caring that they weren't kosher. Her father, who never liked Rhonda, tried to stop her from going there, saying she had doctors to take care of her and that Susie had responsibilities at home, and that's when the fighting started. When Rhonda died Mr. Moscowitz didn't go to the funeral, and the next day Susie called her mother and told her she wanted to come "home," and her mother was happy to oblige. (In order for Susie to continue her schooling at Rockefeller High, Mrs. Moscowitz had to persuade the authorities that she was likely to have another "breakdown" if she had to change schools in the middle of the year.)

"I didn't blame you for being angry with your father, trying to keep you from taking care of Rhonda after she was so kind to you," Mrs. Moscowitz says. "I thought it was very appropriate for you to want to come back to live with me."

"But he begged me not to leave!" Susie screams. "He apologized for being so mean about Rhonda. He said he always thought my love for Rhonda meant that I hated him. He said he couldn't stand to think that his beautiful daughter hated him. He sat on a chair and cried when I was about to walk out with my suitcase! And now we're leaving him forever!"

Well, you can still see him whenever you want, you say. You assume Susie is just being dramatic. But then she gives you a strange look, and Mrs. Moscowitz says, "Didn't you tell Joanna our big news?"

Susie looks at you with her tear-streaked face. "We're moving to New York City," she says.

What? you yell.

"I got a wonderful job in New York, Joanna," Mrs. Moscowitz says. "I'm going to be working with Holocaust survivors at a foundation that's just been established for them. We try to get them compensation from the countries and the people who stole from them while they were being enslaved and persecuted by the Nazis. It's a wonderful job opportunity for me in Manhattan, New York. So! Your friend Susie is going to become a New Yorker."

Your feelings are all mixed up. Ever since you hitchhiked to New York last year, you've never doubted that you're going to end up living there. Now you can be assured of having Susie there with you. This is very exciting. But you're also sad, and you know this has nothing to do with Susie moving to New York. You're used to her being taken away from you, but you always end up back together.

While you're riding home with your dad, who has picked you up, you realize what the sadness is all about. It's not about Susie leaving. It's about Mrs. Moscowitz leaving. You don't know when you developed a crush on Susie's mom, but now that she's going to New York you realize that you have one.

When you get home you go upstairs and play "Mrs. Robinson" by Simon and Garfunkel on your new record player. When you saw *The Graduate*, you had a crush on her, too. Although she was played by Anne Bancroft. But you didn't have a crush on Anne Bancroft. You had a crush on Mrs. Robinson.

That night you dream that Mrs. Moscowitz is slicing off your hand with a machete. You don't even know exactly what a machete is, but you know it's a machete. The strange thing is, she's not slicing off your hand to hurt you. She's doing it to help you. The dream sticks with you throughout the next day, like part of a meal that you can't digest.

January Afternoon, Raining in Cleveland

I'm sitting on the floor in my parents' bedroom writing in a notebook while Molly, Susan, and Steven pack up boxes in my old bedroom which I turned into a den. My parents' bed is gone because Danny wanted it for his basement. The rest of the furniture, the dresser and nightstand and my mom's vanity table, are now mine. Until I find another apartment they have to go into storage. My friends and I are meandering around in this ghost town of my family home. Right after my mom died I could feel her energy rippling through the house, but now her energy is gone. The house is dead. When somebody buys it they will fill it with life again. But the life that was here is gone.

My heart is breaking right now. It's breaking for my parents. There are boxes and boxes here of my father's fiction writing that was never sold. I never knew he was writing all this stuff. There are detective stories and a strange book about an eccentric woman who lives alone and helps the cops solve mysteries, and a five-act play about some roughneck newsmen, and many copies of his historical novel, which I did know about, that never got published. There are many, many rejection letters among the manuscripts. The whole time we were growing up I thought the *tap-tap-tap* of my father's typewriter was the sound of him doing his newspaper work. Now that I think about it, that made no sense because in those days a newspaperman worked at his office. But I was just a kid; I never thought too much about what he was doing. He was writing books and short stories and screen-plays and sending them out and getting rejection letters back, and each rejection letter was another bleeding wound, and he stiffened his upper lip and came out for dinner, read books to us, went to work the next day, and sometimes he blew up and the volcanic rock spewed all over the place, hitting his kids at ran-dom, leaving permanent bruises. But this is so strange because I didn't really *know*! That he was a writer like me. I thought he was just a journalist, and then a PR guy. I didn't know that he was writing fiction that whole time. Except I did know about that last book, that he poured his heart and soul into writing for more than ten years, and he couldn't get it published, and it embittered him. Maybe that's why he got that weird aphasia that started his long decline.

When I told him and my mom I was gay, my mom was kind of freaked out, but my dad actually seemed relieved. He said all he cared about was that I was happy, which is a cliché but he meant it. But if they had found out I was a "lesbian," or whatever term they used back in my loony bin days, it would have been horrible for him and my mom, as bad as if they were told I had cancer. In those days even the most open-minded Americans took offense at the arrests and persecution of homosexuals not because they thought they were normal, but because they "couldn't help it." They never saw homosexuals as people who would eventually live among them, having backyard barbecues and going to their kids' soccer games. I used to try to get my mom to admit that she and my dad would have been devastated back then if they had found out I was a lesbian, but she kept saying they would have understood and defended my right to be that way, which is ridiculous. I guess it irritates me how straight people today have such short memories about their real feelings toward homos before it was truly okay to be one. Even *I* acknowledge my own homophobia back in those days, but these straight people pretend they were always as enlightened back in the dark ages as they are now. It's such poppycock.

But right now I can't feel annoyed with my mother because I'm sitting here with Joe's Purple Heart in my hands. I'm picturing her getting that telegram at the age of twenty-three. She was just a kid, really, when her first husband, Joe Shatsky, was killed while serving in a tank unit in France. Two months after Joe was killed her coworkers encouraged her to remove his photograph from her desk. "It's time to move on, Isabel," they told her, and she did. Time was speeded up during the war. A few months later the war ended and an old flame of hers, Sam Jacobs, came home. The war had also taken its toll on him. He'd gotten malaria in North Africa, his best buddy was killed by a sniper and bled to death in his arms, and the older of his two younger brothers had been killed in the Pacific. They got married only a year after Joe was killed, hoping to put all the grief and tragedy behind them, but the bad news kept coming. Dad's beloved father died of lung cancer. President Roosevelt died. The news pouring in about the destruction of the European Jews became more and more horrific. They found out that Joseph Stalin, the communist leader they had foolishly supported, was a butcher almost as bad as the Nazis. My mom had three miscarriages. My dad couldn't find a job at a daily newspaper because the McCarthy pigs had blacklisted him after he had served his country honorably for four years.

Finally, six years after the end of the war, my mother carried a baby to term. The whole family was ecstatic, but the celebrating was short-lived because my mom wasn't well. She tried to nurse me but the milk wouldn't come out. She tried to hold me but she shook like a jackhammer. She lost thirty pounds and looked gaunt and exhausted. Everyone told her she needed a vacation, that she was a nervous wreck. But she couldn't relax. My dad still couldn't find work. And then my dad's remaining brother, Uncle Bill, was killed in a car accident. During all of this turmoil my *bobie* came over as often as she could to help out, but she would leave in the evenings and I screamed and fussed all night. It wasn't until eight months after I was born that a doctor finally figured out that my mother had severe hyperthyroidism. She waited three more months to have surgery and then there was a long recovery time, and by the time she was pink and healthy, and my father had landed a job at the *News*, I was a year and a half old and had no attachment to my parents at all. In fact they terrified me with their desperate grasping and needy, haunted looks. (Once, I ran after the mailman.) After Michael was born I remember sitting on the daybed in our apartment watching my parents hovering over the new baby, and I will never forget that feeling of exclusion, of being utterly alone, and I was only two and a half years old.

Naturally I grew up with behavior problems, but my parents never connected my dramatic acting-out with my train wreck of an infancy. They were part of a generation that just kept marching forward. It may have worked for them but it wasn't really fair to me, because when I was growing up I assumed that I was uncomfortable around my parents because I was inherently evil, like little Patty McCormack in *The Bad Seed*, instead of just wounded by circumstances. And then when I became an adolescent I was once again deprived of normal physical intimacy because I was gay. I was starving for love, but because I came from a loving family nobody knew it. As an adult I was jealous of my mother because she had everything I didn't—the happy marriage, the four kids—of course mom had cancer three times and her kids were all crazy and out of control, but still, she had the marriage, the kids, the life women are supposed to have. I loved her, but I also resented her nice, normal life.

But right now I'm sitting here in her bedroom, surrounded by boxes and my father's manuscripts and my mother's clothes, her pretty dresses and scarves and shoes, her vintage perfume bottles that were new when she got them. And the old furniture from the forties. And that young woman is here with me, scared to death, trying to calm a screaming baby, the baby that she's wanted so badly. She's wanted her for so many years but instead of feeling joyful she's miserable. She can't hold her baby without shaking. She can't make her stop screaming. She wants it all to go away. She still sometimes aches for her first husband but she can't ever talk about him because it would upset Sam, who lost his father and best friend and two brothers and is breaking his neck to find a job. Right now she feels all alone in the world, sitting there clutching her screaming baby. She's been through so much, and she's not even thirty years old. And I want to hold her and comfort her, even if she couldn't do it for me.

I feel so sad for both of us right now. My mom wanted to be the person I ran to when I was scared or upset, but I spent my early life running away from her, looking for mother figures who were calm and authoritative and in control, the opposite of her. I was a scared kid wandering through life alone. It took me so long to come out because I confused my sexuality with my need for nurturing. Of course I had erotic feelings for Lou, and at least a half-dozen nurses in the loony bin, and that busty girl at camp, and Cassie, that sweet little homecoming queen. I suppose I even had erotic feelings for Susie. But I think that my tumultuous early years screwed up my sexual wiring. I'm the only person I know who's never had a real girlfriend or a boyfriend. I've been single my whole life.

But I have plenty of love. Right now my very best friends—Molly and Susan and Steven—the same friends who are the costars of my story, are right here in this house with me, helping me pack it up. They're nostalgic for the good times they had in this house, for my mom's welcoming warmth and my dad's jolly tolerance for adolescent mayhem. I'm so lucky to be with these wonderful friends who have grown up and grown old with me. But it's raining, I haven't seen the sun in weeks, I have no home to go back to, and I have no more home here, and I'm sitting here looking at this Purple Heart and feeling so alone. Instead of feeling connected to the living people in the next room, I'm connected to dead people. But I *am* those dead people. So I've always been connected to them. The funny thing is, I spent my childhood feeling disconnected from them. I thought I didn't need them.

But I did need them. I just didn't want them. We never had anything to talk about when I was a kid. But now we could talk and talk. If they were here.

FALL 1969

For a lot of kids in middle America, "the sixties" don't really start until the very end of that decade or the beginning of the next. For you "the sixties" in the spiritual rather than the numeric sense begin in October of 1969, in your freshman year at Ohio State University, while you're lounging on the green space in the center of the campus known as "the oval." Next spring, after President Nixon invades Cambodia, you'll be running around this green space yelling at the National Guard through a wet washcloth, "hell, no, we won't go!" and "one two three four we don't want your fucking war," and "pigs off campus!" But right now you're sitting peacefully on this beautiful fall day, smoking marijuana. You've smoked a few times before but only got stoned the last time, and it was what's called a "bummer" because you felt disoriented and panicky. But now you're feeling pretty good, even though you don't feel high. You're lounging on the lawn with Ricky and his roommate and one of your roommates, Janet Millstein, a big, loud girl from Beachwood who you adore. Ricky has grown a beard and a mustache and his hair is as long as yours. Lester, his roommate, looks like a biker, with dark curly hair down to his shoulders and a great big beard, but he's really a charming Jewish kid from Cleveland Heights. You're all wearing bell-bottoms and tee shirts and sandals on this unseasonably warm day. Lester has brought a large transistor radio with great sound, which is playing an FM station while you smoke.

I'm not feeling anything, you say.

"Shut up," Janet says. "You will. Remember last time?"

You look at her and smile. You think of flopping down into her lap but you don't. You and Janet live in a suite of sixteen girls in "the Towers," two monstrous buildings in a remote part of campus where they stick a lot of incoming freshmen. At first you tried to get transferred to an older part of campus, but now you love Lincoln Tower with its concentrated madness. You're looking forward to Molly visiting next weekend. She's attending Cuyahoga Community College with very little enthusiasm. Susie, on the other hand, is writing you ecstatic letters from Barnard College in New York City.

You take another hit on the joint and pass it to Lester. Maybe this shit isn't that good, you say to your friends.

"It's Colombian, Joey," Ricky says. "It's some of the best weed around."

Lester moves over to you and puts his arm around you. "Hi, Joanna," he says playfully. You say, Hi Lester, but stiffen slightly and he withdraws his arm.

A song comes on the radio that you've never heard before. The frenetic guitar intro obliterates all your boundaries. You've never heard music like this before. No song has ever had this effect on you. You look around at your friends and the frolicking kids around you, and the sky and the grass and the collegiate brick buildings, and there's no separation between them and you. Last time you got stoned the feeling of losing yourself was terrifying. Now it's rapturous. You're exploding with energy and feel as though you could lift a car or fly through the air. You look at Janet and her face bursts with joy and she points at the radio. I can't believe this song, you say, which turns out to be "Whole Lotta Love" by Led Zeppelin. She says, "This is so amazing." And Ricky says, "This is a fucking great song." And Lester, a musician, makes a comment about the "conversation" between Jimmy Page's guitar and Robert Plant's voice.

Ricky looks at you with his sparkling blue eyes. "Now are you stoned?" he asks.

"Look at her," Janet says dryly.

You fall into Janet's lap and laugh and laugh and laugh. Then you sit back up and once again look around. Your rapture swallows up all your loneliness. Everyone is right here with you. Ricky and Lester and Janet. The hippie girl gamboling past you yelling, "I'm tripping my brains out!" The cluster of stoned kids rolling around on the grass. The two boys playing Frisbee a few feet away. The boys and girls chasing one another around on the grass like five-year-olds. All of you are wearing jeans and funky shirts and sandals or sneakers and big leather belts, and some of you wear headbands. "Whole Lotta Love" has been playing for what seems like an hour. It's such a relief, not to feel lonely anymore. To feel part of this youth nation. The best part of it is that it's a nation of children who have decided to be bad, to walk away from the black and white world of their parents and create their own society of forbidden pleasures. You got a taste of this joy years ago, when Molly announced her intention to "get the teacher's goat," and it dawned on you that if well-behaved Molly was going to be bad, that it must be *good* to be bad. But now hundreds, thousands, maybe *millions* of kids have joined you in being bad. You feel vindicated. You feel like you've just come home to a hero's welcome, even though nobody's even looking at you.

There will be one other moment in your life when you will experience this kind of joy and relief. But it will be a solitary moment, while you're standing in your friend's kitchen, pouring yourself a drink. Then, too, you will suddenly realize that there's nothing at all wrong with you, that you've been fine all along, and your loneliness will vanish and you will look around in amazement and see everything differently. But that will be a moment in which you enter the world. This is a moment in which the world enters you.

Springtime

Everything is a big mess, and I'm still a homeless bum, but I'm happy because I finally found a home for my 9/11 novel. After running around in the rain with my manuscript to publishing offices all over Manhattan, I sold my book to Harry Holloway and Company. Harry's "company" consists of his wife, Margaret, and their dog, who licks their stamps even though stamps no longer have to be licked. Don't ask me to explain. Small publishing houses all have their eccentricities. But even though it's a small business, it's not as though Harry is some old guy having a midlife crisis who decided to try his hand at publishing. He's a respected editor who was a *macher* (big shot in Yiddish) at Randall House for decades, and last year they promoted this twenty-seven-year-old kid to be his boss, and Harry said no way is this going to work, and he left and opened up his own operation, which is kind of a dump on the edge of Chinatown. But he's getting plenty of queries from major authors and he accepted my book which will come with a $50,000 advance.

Until that money comes through I will continue to be homeless. I'm living in a trailer in Red Hook on the edge of Brooklyn, in this camp set up for New Yorkers whose buildings have collapsed in the rain. (Molly actually did manage to get some people housed in the absentee owners' apartments but then the billionaires got some mandate to have them kicked out.) So here I am living in this trailer, which has been divided into four units. There's a lovely, sweet old African-American lady here, and a Hispanic couple, and a young Albanian couple from Queens. Every day I get up and take a shower in one of the detached showers they've provided. (I'm trying to still look good because once you neglect your physical appearance everything else starts going to hell.) After showering and getting dressed I sit on my cot and write this book; then I eat some junk from my refrigerator and then I go out and walk around Red Hook.

I can't drive around Red Hook or anywhere else because my car is gone. Now that I'm getting my book published nothing bothers me anymore but I was pretty upset about my car disappearing. It was such a faithful little car. I drove it all the way to Cleveland in the rain, and then I drove it back to New York in the rain and parked it back at that muddy construction site and went back to sleeping in it. And then one day I went out to do my daily ablutions and when I went back it was gone. I was so upset. I really loved that car. And then I had to come here and move into this trailer. But after a couple days I got used to it. Nothing is normal in New York right now, so it's not that hard to fit yourself into the abnormality. Anyway, by now I would have had to leave the construction site because it's springtime and I'm sure whatever project was going on there has resumed.

The rains finally stopped and we had an unseasonably warm winter and now it's springtime both literally and metaphorically. The divided country actually had to come together in order to get the infrastructure rebuilt. We're fixing the damaged roads and bridges and the buildings that collapsed, and we're even upgrading some of the rail lines so we can have newer, faster trains. We have to concentrate on domestic programs now, and nobody's arguing with that. I think the rain might have been a blessing in disguise because it brought people together, although a lot of the right-wingers are still complaining that we're spending too much money. They're especially upset about the upgrading of the rail system. They think if we start riding trains we'll turn into Europe.

One of the right-wing nuts who's been carrying on about all the money being "squandered" on public projects is Sandy Shrewsbury, who got herself elected as a U.S. Senator. The other day she made a speech at this place called the Economic Forum in Manhattan, and I went to it. But it was for kind of an immature reason. I didn't go to her speech to learn more about her point of view. I went there with the intention of getting kicked out. I was going to ask some kind of confrontational question, hoping that Shrewsbury would identify me as the caller who railed against her on the Mike Stevens show, and then they would escort me out and inform the FBI that the woman who said someone should plant a bomb under Shrewsbury's ass was stalking her. And then I hoped that Agent Deborah, who is totally ignoring me these days, would find out and hunt me down in Red Hook, and she would drag me to her apartment in Astoria, and she and Tanya would lecture me about my foolhardy adventure, and I won't go into the grand finale of this fantasy because it's my own private business.

But as it turned out, my admittedly absurd plan went up in smoke. I did get into the speech by locating one of my press passes at Pete's chop shop where my stuff is being stored, and I listened to Shrewsbury blather about our federal funds being poured into "unnecessary urban projects that our representatives have been conned into supporting." After the speech she called on me and I stood up and clearly stated my name, and then I said, "I'm going to ask you a personal question. Do you have any concern about anyone outside of the wilds of Montana where you have your ranch or whatever it is? The impression I get from all your complaints about federal spending is that you're only concerned about what happens in your little neck of the woods and the hell with everyone else. Would you be happy if cars started tumbling off the Brooklyn Bridge? Would you say, well, that's what they get for living in this morally depraved metropolis?" But instead of recognizing my name and calling security to haul my ass out of there, Sandy answered my question very diplomatically, saying that she certainly did care about each and every person in our country but that she was afraid that we're going to use up all our resources and then when the next weather event happens we'll pretty much be wiped out. And then she took the next question, and there went my plan to get kicked out of her speech and kidnapped by Agent Deborah and dear old Tanya.

Obviously since I've been homeless I've been going kind of bonkers. I can't even imagine returning to normal life, like, going back to being a writer and living in a nice apartment and maybe meeting some women on some goofy website. It feels more normal to be living in this trailer than going back to normal life. One thing is that the people I'm living with here are all very nice and considerate. I've made friends with Mildred, the black lady, and we smoke pot every night and walk around the neighborhood. I love Red Hook. It's cut off from the rest of Brooklyn by the expressway, and it juts into the water, and it's full of abandoned factories and stuff, and there are feral cats roaming around that people feed and shelter. And it's got a lot of vacant lots, and more community gardens are being cultivated here than anywhere else in Brooklyn.

And guess who I saw working in one of those gardens in Coffey Park yesterday? Eric and Mikey and Bobby. They were there with a bunch of other kids from various schools around town. I walked right up to Bobby and stood there with my hands on my hips, and he gave me this weird smile. Then he said, "I'm sorry." And I said, "You're such a little asshole." And that was the end of it.

They said they're not just working in the garden as a school requirement. "It's optional," Mikey said. "We're here because everyone's got to do their part to rebuild New York. This is fresh, organic food here. None of that poison stuff. Here. Have a cucumber." He snapped off a little cucumber and gave it to me. Eric, who I always considered a ruffian, nodded his head and said, "Mikey's right, we need to be part of this rebuilding effort." Bobby had this smarmy look on his face and is obviously still up to no good, but I wasn't going to worry about it. America will always have its outlaws.

Speaking of outlaws they told me that they kicked Jakey out of their crew after he set fire to the Chinese people's apartment. "He was too crazy," Bobby said. "He was gonna get us arrested." My first thought was that I should pay a visit to Jakey's apartment, which I still intend to do. I'm worried about him. His mom loves him but she has no idea how to handle him. I asked the kids what happened to my Chinese neighbors, and they told me that Jack found them new living quarters off of Eighth Avenue. "It's a lot smaller than the other place," Mikey said. "The beds are all right next to each other."

"They're never there anyway," Eric said. "They're working all the time."

Well, with any luck and a lot of perseverance my former neighbors will pay off their debts to the snakeheads and establish themselves in American society. This is the only country in the world where an immigrant can achieve all the status of a native-born person. You can come here from any country and become an American. But you don't become an American just by working your ass off; you have to feel a connection with all other Americans. You have to *feel* like an American. We're a very self-centered country. We think everyone should want to be like us. When I was a kid I rebelled against my country but I never would have wanted to be from somewhere else. And even with the mean-spiritedness that's infected us over the years, I still think this is the greatest country on earth. We never accept defeat. When something terrible happens, we might adopt a cynical attitude like the Europeans, but underneath we're outraged and indignant that such a terrible thing should happen to us, and we're determined to rise up out of the mud and make everything even better than it was before. Our can-do spirit is why people from other countries still want to come here, even when we don't welcome them with open arms. They still see America as the city on the hill. They might not see the floodwaters running through the streets. But we're building bigger and better sewer systems and dams and barrier walls so that we don't all drown. I think maybe we will stay alive for a long time, and hopefully get nicer to one another because more people are working.

Don't I sound like Pollyanna playing the "glad game"? I'm just feeling rhapsodic about getting my book published. Maybe tomorrow I'll go back to yelling about how stupid everyone is acting. But what I really need to do right now is look for an apartment. I've decided I want to live in Red Hook because there's something about this neighborhood that feels like home. It's still kind of old and rough, like my old neighborhood on Third Avenue. And miraculously the rain didn't even cause that much damage here. The only thing is, I don't want to live here without a car because the subway is way the hell across the expressway. So where the hell is my car? I'm assuming it was towed, not stolen, because when I asked Pete at the chop shop if it might have been stolen he laughed and said nobody would want that piece of shit, which hurt my feelings a little. But I'm sure he's right and it was towed and who knows what god-forsaken junkyard has it now.

Tomorrow Molly and Susan are going to drive me around to try to find it. We're going to borrow a minivan from Stretch, a bass player Billy used to work with. He's sick with MS now and his van is just sitting idle in his carport in Queens, actually just a couple of miles from where Agent Deborah and Tanya are cohabitating. After we pick up Stretch's van, instead of looking for my car right away we're going to sneak over to Deborah's and do something to annoy her and Tanya. Susan and I have already thought of some good ideas. Molly said we're crazy and she wishes we were still not speaking to each other, but I'm sure she'll go along with whatever we do because Billy's still driving her nuts and she's drinking a lot of wine every night.

Well, I think this is a good place to end my story. I can't believe I wrote this whole book after my mom died. She would be proud of me. Now I just have to worry about getting it published. I hope Harry Holloway will like it. It's not iconoclastic like the 9/11 novel. It doesn't have any sociopathic rogue CIA agents in it. But there's still some pretty crazy stuff in it, like those lunatic kids walking out of my closet. And that really happened! I didn't make it up, like I made up the CIA agent. It's the absolute truth. You should only write the truth, or at least what you believe to be the truth. Even if you're writing some bullshit advertisement, like saying your oil-spilling corporate client is leading the green energy movement, you should at least believe it's true while you're writing it. Otherwise you're just full of shit.

My mom wouldn't like that ending. She wouldn't want me to end my book with a profanity. So I'll end it like this: Otherwise you should be ashamed of yourself.

And I really believe that. It's the truth.

About the Author

Lisa Gitlin is a novelist living in Brooklyn, NY. Her debut novel, *I Came Out for This?* was awarded the Independent Publisher Book Award (IPPY) Gold Medal in both the Humor and LGBT Fiction categories. She is currently working on her third novel.

Acknowledgments

First of all, thanks to all my people at Bywater Books—Kelly Smith, Marianne K. Martin, Salem West, Ann McMan, Elizabeth Anderson and Nancy Squires, and all their dedicated workers and colleagues—I am so grateful to be able to entrust my precious manuscript(s) to women whose experience and expertise are unrivalled in the hardscrabble world of publishing. Also, you are all such nice people! This is no small thing.

Thank you, all my patient readers, in order of their readings: (I will eliminate all the affectionate nicknames to maintain the dignity of this exercise). My sister, Nina Dworkin—what would I do without your editing skills and your loving support? My brother Robert (Bobby to us) Gitlin—another great editor (and most eloquent writer)—your enthusiasm for my work inspires me to keep going! My friend from birth, Larry B. Elsner (I couldn't resist the "B"!)—thanks for the astute observations about key details, and also for just being you. My sister-friend (not in blood but in bond) Shaz Wagner—I'm always terrified to show you my manuscripts—but what would this book be without you kicking my butt all over the pages? My darling cousin Barbara Kent—you instilled me with confidence in the final work—I love you! Finally, my wonderful friend Kati Gimes—when you said you liked my book I knew I could like it too—your vote of approval meant everything to me, because you are an unsparing critic and you never hesitate to tell me the truth.

Thanks also to the rest of my family—siblings, nieces, aunt and uncle and cousins—and all my friends in Cleveland and D.C. and Maryland and New York City and Florida and various other places, who put up with me year after year while I'm being the exasperating person that I am. Without my family and my family of friends I would be swirling around in a vortex with nothing to hold me in place.

I CAME OUT FOR THIS?

}This, her first novel, demonstrates that Gitlin is a writer to contend with—both plot and character development are detailed and convincing, and even though the protagonist's circular logic might serve to drive a roommate or best friend mad, Gitlin's pacing is such that she holds the reader's interest in confident hands." —*Foreword Reviews*

I Came Out for This?
Paperback 978-1-93285-973-7
eBook 978-1-61294-019-9

www.bywaterbooks.com

Bywater
BOOKS

At Bywater Books we love good books about lesbians just like you do, and we're committed to bringing the best of contemporary lesbian writing to our avid readers. Our editorial team is dedicated to finding and developing outstanding writers who create books you won't want to put down.

We sponsor the Bywater Prize for Fiction to help with this quest. Each prize winner receives $1,000 and publication of their novel. We have already discovered amazing writers like Jill Malone, Sally Bellerose, and Hilary Sloin through the Bywater Prize. Which exciting new writer will we find next?

For more information about Bywater Books and the annual Bywater Prize for Fiction, please visit our website.

www.bywaterbooks.com